THE BEST SHORT STORIES OF FYODOR DOSTOEVSKY

THE BEST SHORT STORIES OF FYODOR DOSTOEVSKY

Translated, with an Introduction, by David Magarshack

THE MODERN LIBRARY

NEW YORK

2001 Modern Library Paperback Edition

 Published in the United States by Modern Library, an imprint of The Random House Publishing Group, a division of Random House, Inc., New York, and simultaneously in Canada by Random House of Canada Limited, Toronto.

The excerpt from "Dostoeffsky" from *Master Builders, An Attempt at the Typology of the Spirit: The Three Masters: Balzac, Dickens, Dostoeffsky,* vol. 1, by Stefan Zweig, was originally published in the German language by Williams Verlag AG, Switzerland, and in the English language by Viking Penguin, a division of Penguin Putnam, Inc.

Grateful acknowledgment is made to New Directions Publishing Corporation for permission to reprint an excerpt from *Dostoevsky,* by André Gide, translated by Arnold Bennett.

LIBRARY OF CONGRESS CATALOGING-IN-PUBLICATION DATA
Dostoevsky, Fyodor, 1821–1881.
[Short stories. English. Selections]
The best short stories of Fyodor Dostoevsky / translated, with a translator's introduction by David Magarshack.
p. cm.
Contents: White nights—The honest thief—The Christmas tree and a wedding—The peasant Marey—Notes from the underground—A gentle creature—The dream of a ridiculous man.
ISBN 0-375-75688-4
1. Dostoevsky, Fyodor, 1821–1881—Translations into English. 2. Russia—Social life and customs—Fiction. I. Magarshack, David. II. Title.
PG3326.A2 2001 00-048951
891.73'3—dc21

Modern Library website address: www.modernlibrary.com

Printed in the United States of America

15 14 13 12 11 10

Fyodor Dostoevsky

Great thinkers of the modern age from Nietzsche to Freud and Sartre have recognized Dostoevsky as a preeminent analyst of the human condition in the post-Enlightenment age. His pathbreaking novels, such as *Crime and Punishment* (1866) and *The Brothers Karamazov* (1879–80)—his last and crowning achievement—depicted the often devastating personal consequences of new political and social ideas by exploring his characters' internal struggles with the rapidly changing moral, social, economic, and religious order of the time. The remarkable depth of his analysis with respect both to individual psychology and to the complex fabric of human interaction has secured Dostoevsky his place as one of the greatest and most widely read masters of the novel.

Dostoevsky was born in Moscow on October 30, 1821. His father, an army surgeon, was granted noble status in 1828 and purchased a small estate. In 1837, he sent his son to be educated at the Military Engineering Academy in St. Petersburg, where the latter remained even after his father's death to finish his education and receive his officer's rank. However, after just a year in government service, Dostoevsky retired to devote himself full-time to literature. His first work of fiction, *Poor Folk*, was published in 1846 to great acclaim and praised by one critic as the first "social novel" in Russia. Dostoevsky's early commitment to social problems was not limited to his fiction. He was a participant in several politically subversive groups that called for radical changes such as the emancipation of the serfs and reform of the judicial system. In 1849, he was arrested along with other members of the so-called Petrashevsky circle and condemned to death. Though the sentence was commuted, the prisoners were not informed of this until after they had been led in front of the firing squad. The anticipation of certain death left an indelible impression on Dostoevsky and he wrote about the experience at length in later works, such as *The Idiot* (1868–69).

Dostoevsky served four years of hard labor in Omsk followed by six years as a soldier in another Siberian town before being allowed to return to St. Petersburg, where he revived his literary reputation with the publication of his fictionalized prison memoir, *Notes from the Dead House* (1861–62). Two years later he published *Notes from Underground,* a work that proved seminal in its use of an alienated anti-hero who anticipates Raskolnikov and Ivan Karamazov. Although he enjoyed literary success, Dostoevsky was continually plagued by a variety of personal troubles—worsening epilepsy, an unhappy marriage, a failed affair abroad, and the deaths of his wife and brother in the mid-sixties. In addition, there were great financial difficulties (compounded by gambling), at one point forcing him to complete his novel *The Gambler* (1866) in a mere twenty-six days. To flee his creditors, he went abroad again, where he remained with his second wife until 1871, writing *The Idiot* and much of *Demons* (1871–72).

Upon his return to Russia, Dostoevsky lived a largely retiring life in a small town with his wife and young children. His growing conservatism, religious focus, and scathing repudiation of the new generation of radicals had estranged some of his former associates. However, he was reconciled to his critics in June of 1880, when he delivered a rousing speech at the commemoration ceremonies of Russia's national poet, Alexandr Pushkin. The speech declared the Russian character to have a unique genius for universality and affirmed Russia as the unifying force of Western civilization. In the wake of his electrifying proclamation of Russia's world mission, Dostoevsky was hailed as a prophet. When he died the following year, just two months after the completion of *The Brothers Karamazov,* his funeral was attended by fifty thousand mourners.

Contents

Introduction

David Magarshack

With a writer of such great genius and such vast output as Fyodor Dostoevsky it is perhaps natural that criticism should be concerned mainly with his larger works. And yet it is in Dostoevsky's smaller works that we find the highest expression of his creative power and profundity of thought. In these smaller works we find reflected as in a convex mirror the whole immensity of Dostoevsky's world, concentrated with gem-like brilliance and startling clarity. Here and there in Dostoevsky's great novels passages occur which reveal an inability to take a detached view of life and overcome political and racial prejudices, and it is in these works in particular that those "streaks of cruelty" appear that did not escape the notice of the Russian critics of his own day. In his smaller works, however, Dostoevsky was singularly free from partizanship. In the greatest of them, such as in *Notes from the Underground* and *The Dream of a Ridiculous Man,* Dostoevsky showed that he was capable of withdrawing from the conflict of human passions and of surveying the human scene with complete detachment. It is in these works, therefore, that the reader will obtain a clearer, if not deeper, insight into his genius and will be able to judge him more fairly than those who form their judgments about him mainly from his great novels.

The stories in this volume are (with one exception) published in their chronological order so as to afford the reader an idea of the growth of Dostoevsky's genius through the different phases of its development. The exception is the short story, *The Peasant Marey,* which is placed after the three stories belonging to Dostoevsky's first period, ending with his arrest and imprisonment in Siberia in 1849. As it deals with Dostoevsky's life in prison, it forms a convenient connecting link between the young and the mature Dostoevsky.

Fyodor (Theodor) Dostoevsky was born in Moscow on October 30, 1821. His father was an army doctor, and Fyodor was the second of his six children. His childhood was spent in Moscow and on his father's small estate in the Tula province. Already, as a child, Dostoevsky was distinguished by his highly excitable, "fiery" temperament, and from his early years he showed a great interest in literature. His father, however, decided that he should be an engineer, and accordingly in 1837, soon after the death of his mother, he and his elder brother Mikhail were sent to Petersburg to be placed in the Army Engineering College. Here Dostoevsky spent over five years, devoting most of his time, however, to reading and writing, having made up his mind to become a writer as soon as he could conveniently give up the career which had been forced upon him. An interesting light on Dostoevsky's reading as a boy is shed in a letter he wrote to his brother on August 9, 1838. In that year he read through the whole of Shakespeare and Pascal, almost the whole of Balzac, Goethe's *Faust* and his shorter poems, most of the works of Victor Hugo, and all the works (both in the original and translation) of the German romantic novelist Hoffmann. Curiously enough, his first literary efforts were two historical dramas, *Mary Stuart* and *Boris Godunov,* which he wrote in 1841, the extracts from which he read to his brother in the same year. These two plays have not been preserved. In 1841 Dostoevsky obtained his commission, and in 1842 he became a lieutenant. A year later he finished his course at the Engineering College and was attached to the Army Engineering Corps in Petersburg, in the drawing department. In the same year appeared his first published work, a translation of Balzac's novel *Eugénie Grandet.*

Already during his student years Dostoevsky revealed the characteristic trait which was to cause him so much trouble during his life, namely, his utter inability to manage his own personal affairs and his uncanny gift for getting into debt. In spite of his more than adequate allowance of five thousand roubles a year, he seemed incapable of living within his means. He spent his money almost as soon as he got it and during the rest of the year he literally starved. An illustration of his unpractical turn of mind is provided by the fact that he rented an expensive flat while still at college. He paid 1,200 roubles a year for it, although he only lived in one small room in which he froze during the winter as he never had enough money to keep even that one room warm. In 1844 Dostoevsky resigned his commission and devoted himself entirely to literary work.

From October, 1844, when Dostoevsky gave up his army career, to April, 1849, when he was arrested and imprisoned in the Petropavlovsk Fortress in Petersburg, Dostoevsky published ten novels and short stories. His first novel, *Poor Folk,* written in 1846, brought him fame literally overnight. He was hailed by the poet and editor Nekrassov, to whom he had sent the novel, and the great Russian critic Belinsky, as a successor to Gogol. At the age of twenty-four he became a celebrity, and it is perhaps not surprising that his success went to his head and that some of his subsequent stories did not come up to the expectations of his admirers, two of them, *The Landlady* and *Prokharchin,* being sharply criticised by Belinsky.

In his first appreciation of Dostoevsky, Belinsky at once singled out those characteristic features of his art which were later to make him (in spite of his exasperatingly careless style) one of the giants of Russian and, indeed, of world literature. What were these characteristic features? First of all, his amazing truthfulness in the description of life. Secondly, his masterly delineation of character and the social conditions of his heroes. Thirdly, his profound understanding and his wonderful artistic re-creation of the tragic side of life. Belinsky, too, from the very outset put his finger on the weakest spot of Dostoevsky's genius: his diffuseness and his tendency to tire the reader by unnecessary repetitions and digressions.

As for Gogol's influence on Dostoevsky, Belinsky was also the first to point out that in the case of so outstandingly original a writer as Dostoevsky this influence was merely superficial. "Dostoevsky as a writer of great talent," Belinsky wrote, "cannot be called an imitator of Gogol, though he certainly owes a great deal to him. Gogol's influence can even be seen in the structure of his sentences,* but there is so much originality in Dostoevsky's talent that this obvious influence of Gogol will most probably disappear with his other shortcomings as a writer, though Gogol will always remain, as it were, the fount from which he drew his inspiration."

Dostoevsky himself, in the often quoted phrase, "We have all emerged from under Gogol's *Overcoat,*" acknowledged his indebtedness to Gogol, and, specifically, to Gogol's faith in "the divine spark in man," however degraded socially or however poor in spirit he might be. It was this deeply humane attitude to the lowly and the downtrodden that made Dostoevsky such a great admirer of Charles Dickens, to whom he had paid what is surely the finest compliment one great writer can pay to another by writing his own version of *The Old Curiosity Shop* in *The Insulted and Injured* (published in 1861).

The Honest Thief, the second story in this volume, written in 1848, is perhaps the best example of this early tendency in Dostoevsky's works. Yemelyan is the first of Dostoevsky's characters whose tragedy consists of their helplessness to resist evil in spite of, and perhaps even because of, the fact that they recognise it as evil. He is, as it were, the embryo from which the Yezhevikins, Marmeladovs, and Lebedevs later emerged. As with many another of Dostoevsky's characters, he is merely the original theme of the different variations which Dostoevsky wrote as his own perception of life and his sensibility deepened and broadened.

The Honest Thief as well as *White Nights* is also remarkable for the fact that in them we find the first statement of the central idea of one of Dostoevsky's greatest novels, *Crime and Punishment,* published in 1866. In *White Nights* the sentence expressing this idea,

*Belinsky was writing about Dostoevsky's first novel, *Poor Folk.*

which Dostoevsky eliminated from subsequent editions of the story, ran: "I am told that the proximity of punishment arouses real repentance in the criminal and sometimes awakens a feeling of genuine remorse in the most hardened heart; I am told this is due to fear." A more elaborate statement of the same idea (also omitted in the subsequent editions of the story) is found in *The Honest Thief.*

White Nights (i.e., the twilight summer nights in Petersburg), also published in 1848, is perhaps one of the most characteristic works of the young Dostoevsky. It is to a large extent autobiographical, the sentimental theme being developed against the background of his own personal impressions during his nocturnal wanderings in Petersburg. The story is remarkable for the way Dostoevsky avoids the more obvious pitfalls of such a romantic theme, for its gentle humour, and for its delicate touches of genuine feeling. Dostoevsky was to re-write this story in his true manner of creative artist and thinker seventeen years later under the title *Notes from the Underground.*

The Christmas Tree and a Wedding is perhaps the most artistically perfect short story Dostoevsky wrote during his first period as a fiction writer. Satiric in character, it drives home its main point in the last sentence with shattering force: the contrast between the young helpless victim of a stupid social order and the ruthless pursuit of wealth by a middle-aged careerist who calculates the amount of money he is to get by marrying the young girl with almost inspired correctness five years before the actual event. It is one of Dostoevsky's most savage judgments on "success" under the acquisitive system of society.

In 1849 Dostoevsky was arrested and sent to prison in Siberia. His imprisonment at Omsk marks a break with the rather mild liberalism of his youth, a break that was much more complete than it would have been if he had not been involved in the so-called Petrashevsky case. Petrashevsky was a young and very rich political dilettante who dabbled in the utopian socialism of the French school. He was an enthusiastic admirer of Fourier, and his Friday at homes were frequented by the liberal-minded intellectuals of the day, of whom Dostoevsky was one. Politics was only one of the topics discussed at those social gatherings, and on one occasion Dostoevsky read Belinsky's famous letter to Gogol, in which the Russian liberal critic attacked the reactionary opinions expressed by Gogol in his *Correspondence with Friends.*

Dostoevsky was arrested with the other members of the Petrashevsky "group" on April 23, 1849, imprisoned for eight months in the Petropavlovsk Fortress in Petersburg, and then sentenced to death, a sentence which was immediately commuted to eight years of imprisonment in Siberia. But this commuted sentence was only read out to Dostoevsky and his associates after the gruesome ceremony on Semyonovsky Square where they had been brought to face a firing squad. In a letter to his elder brother, Dostoevsky gives this description of his mock execution:

"Today, December 22nd, we were all taken to Semyonovsky Square. There the sentence of death was read out to us, we were all made to kiss the cross, a sword was broken over our heads, and we were told to put on our white execution shirts. Then three of us were tied to the posts to be executed. I was the sixth, and therefore in the second group of those to be executed. I had only one more minute to live. I thought of you, dear brother, and all of yours; during the last minute it was only you I was thinking of, my dear, dear brother. I had time to embrace Plescheyev and Durov who were standing beside me and to take leave of them. Then the retreat was sounded on the drums, those tied to the posts were taken back, and an order from His Imperial Majesty was read to us granting us our lives. Afterwards our sentences were read out to us."

The sentence against Dostoevsky ran: "For taking part in criminal plots, for circulating the letter of the writer Belinsky, full of insolent attacks against the Orthodox Church and the Government, and for attempting, with others, to circulate articles directed against the Government by means of a home-printing press, to be sentenced to eight years penal servitude."

The sentence was reduced to four years by the Emperor Nicholas I. Dostoevsky finally broke with his liberal past during his imprisonment in Siberia, though signs of the coming change can already be discerned in *A Little Hero,* the "children's story" Dostoevsky wrote while under arrest in the Petropavlovsk Fortress. In that story Dostoevsky draws a scathingly frank picture of Petrashevsky in the guise of the husband of the story's heroine, M-me M., as a man with "a lump of fat instead of a heart."

The Peasant Marey is a biographical account of Dostoevsky's life in prison, containing a vivid flash-back to his early childhood on his father's small country estate. It was published in February, 1876, in *A Writer's Diary,* a monthly periodical "without contributors or programme" which Dostoevsky published between 1876 and 1878. The theme of the story was provided by Konstantin Aksakov, son of Sergey Aksakov, the famous author of *A Family Chronicle,* and leader of the so-called Slavophiles, who, in an article published posthumously, argued that the common people in Russia had always shown a high degree of culture. After discussing this statement at length and acknowledging the close ties that bound the best Russian writers to the common people, Dostoevsky begins his story of the peasant Marey in these words: "But all these professions of faith are, I think, extremely boring to read and, therefore, I will tell you an anecdote, or perhaps not even an anecdote but just an old reminiscence of mine which for some reason I want very much to tell you here at the conclusion of my treatise on the common people. I was only nine years old at the time . . . but no—perhaps I'd better start with my twenty-ninth year."

The episode of the peasant Marey probably took place in 1831, shortly after Dostoevsky's father had bought the small estate in the Tula province. The prison episode occurred during Easter of 1850 (April 24th), and is described at much greater length in *The House of the Dead* (published in 1861). Dostoevsky also made use of this childhood incident in *The Adolescent,* the novel he wrote in 1874.

Dostoevsky was released from prison in March, 1854. At that time his political views had completely changed and he became a passionate adherent of the most reactionary forces in Russia. Before his release from prison he wrote a number of "Odes" to members of the Czar's family, couched in the most fulsomely servile language (Dostoevsky's rather poor poetic efforts were usually connected with some political event, such as the Crimean War). After his release from prison he was forced to join the army as a private, being promoted to non-commissioned rank in January, 1856, and in October of the same year to the commissioned rank of lieutenant. He was still forbidden to return to Russia. In February, 1857, he married a twenty-nine-year-old widow, Maria Dmitriyevna Issayeva. Two years later he resigned from the army. In the same year he was granted permission to return to Russia, but not to Petersburg or Moscow. He spent some months in Tver (Kalinin of today) and only at the end of 1859 was he allowed to return to Petersburg. Between 1859 and 1861 he published three novels, including his comic masterpiece *The Village of Stepanchikovo.* In March, 1861, Dostoevsky embarked on his journalistic career with the publication of the monthly periodical *Vremya* ("Time"), under the editorship of his brother Mikhail (being still under police supervision, Dostoevsky himself could not appear as the editor of the journal). *Vremya* was a great financial success. In June, 1862, Dostoevsky left for his first journey abroad, mainly for reasons of health. In July of that year he was in London, where he visited the famous Russian political exile and writer, Alexander Herzen.

In London Dostoevsky came face to face for the first time with the industrial society which he regarded as "the triumph of Baal." The thing that struck him most was the contrast between the "colossal façade" of riches, luxury, and general prosperity of the few and the abject poverty of the many and their "coolie-like" acquiescence in their fate. "In the face of such enormous riches, such immense pride of the spirit of domination, and such triumphant perfection of the creations of the spirit," Dostoevsky wrote in the April, 1863, issue of *Vremya,* in which he described his impressions of his first visit abroad, "the starving soul is humbled and driven to submission, seeking salvation in gin and dissipation and beginning to believe that this is the way things ought to be. Facts oppress the spirit, and if scepticism is born, it is a gloomy, accursed sort of scepticism which seeks salvation in religious fanaticism."

This is the glimpse of London in the early sixties of the last century that Dostoevsky gives in the same issue of *Vremya:*

"In London you can see crowds so vast, and in such an environment, as you will not see anywhere else in the world. For instance, I was told that every Saturday night half a million workers, men and women, with their children, spill into the streets like a flood, flocking to certain parts of the town, and all through the night, till five o'clock in the morning, they are taking part in a bacchanalian revel, eating and drinking like beasts, to last, one would think, the whole week. All this, of course, means going short for the rest of the week, saving up their meagre earnings gained with toil, sweat, and curses. In the butchers' and grocers' shops flaring gas jets are burning, lighting up the streets brightly. It is as though a ball had been prepared for these white negroes. The people swarm round the open taverns and in the streets, eating and drinking everywhere. The public houses are as gay as palaces. All are drunk, but not cheerfully; everything is sombre, dull, and somehow ominously quiet. Only from time to time is this brooding silence, which weighs so heavily upon everything, broken by loud curses and bloody fights. All seem to be set on getting dead drunk as quickly as possible. Wives are no better than their men and get drunk with them; the children run about and crawl among them.

"On such a night, at two o'clock in the morning, I lost my way and wandered about for hours in the streets among the countless multitudes of this gloomy city, driven to ask the way almost by signs as I don't know a word of English. I found my way at last, but the impression of what I had seen weighed on my mind for three days and would not let me rest. The common people are the same everywhere, but here everything is so overwhelming and so startling that what existed before only in my imagination, now confronts me as a solid reality. Here you are no longer aware even of people, but of an insensible human mass, a general loss of consciousness, systematic, resigned, encouraged. When you look on these outcasts of society, you feel that for a long time to come the prophecy will not be fulfilled for them; that for a long time there will be no palm branches for them, nor white robes; that for a long time they will call in vain to the throne of the Almighty, 'How long, O Lord!'

"But they know this themselves, and so far they have been protesting against the wrongs society has inflicted on them by forming all kinds of dark religious sects. We are surprised at the folly of people embracing such superstitions, but we fail to realise that what we see here is a rejection of our social formula, an obstinate, unconscious, instinctive separation, a separation at all costs, for the sake of salvation, a separation accompanied by a feeling of disgust with us, and fear, too. These millions, abandoned and driven away from the rich man's table, jostling and crushing each other in the outer darkness in which they have been flung by their more fortunate brothers, are groping blindly to knock at the gates—any gates, looking desperately for a way of escape from the suffocating dark cellar. Here we are witnessing a last desperate attempt to hold together in a community among themselves, prepared to abandon even the semblance of human beings, so long as they can have a life of their own, so long as they can keep out of our way.

"Anyone who has ever visited London has probably been to the Haymarket, if only once. This is the quarter which is at night crowded with women of the street. In the Haymarket I saw mothers who had brought their young daughters, girls who were still in their teens, to be sold to men. Little girls of about twelve seize you by the hand and ask you to go with them. Once I remember seeing among the crowd of people in the street a little girl who could not have been more than six years old. Her clothes were in tatters. She was dirty, barefoot, and beaten black and blue. Her body, which could be seen through the holes in her clothes, was all bruised. She was walking along aimlessly, hardly knowing where she was, and without apparently being in any hurry to get anywhere. Goodness knows why she was roaming about in the crowd; perhaps she was hungry. No one paid any attention to her. But what struck me most about her was that she looked so wretched and unhappy. Such hopeless despair was written all over her face that to see that little creature already experiencing so much damnation and despair was to the highest degree unnatural and terribly painful. She kept shaking her dishevelled head from side to side, as though debating some highly important question with herself, waving her little hands about and gesticulating wildly, and then, suddenly, clapping them together and pressing them to her bosom. I went back and gave her sixpence. She seized the small silver coin, gave me a wild look of startled surprise, and suddenly began running in the opposite direction as fast as her little legs would carry her, as though terrified that I should take the money away from her . . ."

Dostoevsky never forgot the little girl in the Haymarket. Fourteen years later he was to use her as a symbol of the pitiful and as an object of mercy in one of the most imaginative of his "philosophic tales," *The Dream of a Ridiculous Man.*

Dostoevsky returned to Petersburg from his first trip abroad in August, 1862. His periodical *Vremya* was still flourishing, but its success was beginning to worry the authorities who finally suppressed it in May, 1863.* In August of the same year Dostoevsky went abroad again (he was beginning to be drawn there by the gaming tables, his passion for gambling becoming more and more irresistible). On his return in January, 1864, he and his elder brother Mikhail embarked on their second journalistic venture which was to end in disaster. They were planning to publish another monthly, but met with disappointment at the very start. Dostoevsky wanted it to be called *Pravda* ("Truth"), but the authorities thought the title too provocative. After a few more suggestions, it was at last agreed to call it *Epokha* ("Epoch"), and the first number appeared on March 21, 1864. It lasted only one year. One disaster after another overwhelmed Dostoevsky. His wife died in Moscow on April 15, 1864, and, worst blow of all, his brother Mikhail, the business manager of the paper, died in July of the same year. The death of his brother brought about the closing of the journal, involving Dostoevsky in a debt of over 15,000 roubles, which he was repaying almost to the end of his life. This was the beginning of the financial disasters which drove Dostoevsky to seek refuge from his creditors

*The special reason for the banning of the journal was an article on the Polish uprising by Strakhov, a regular contributor.

abroad, where the fascination of the roulette table only involved him more deeply.*

It was in the first and the second issues of *Epokha* that Dostoevsky published the most concentrated and profound of his reflections on the destiny of man—*Notes from the Underground.* Dostoevsky himself used to say that as a philosopher he was "weak."† And, no doubt, it was only as a creative artist, that is, through the mind and heart of the characters he created, that he could reach out beyond the borderlines of conscious thought into the darkest recesses of the human personality and, at the same time, provide the deepest analysis of human nature and human destiny that any creative writer before or after him was ever able to achieve. In these *Notes* Dostoevsky discusses the workings of the intellect and inevitably meets the challenge of the scientific determinism of his day. No one saw more clearly and from the very outset the limitations of the scientific approach to the ethical problems of mankind. He understood the lure of material prosperity which the developing powers of science were beginning to present to mankind, and the unlimited resources open to exploitation. The whole of this splendid vision he sums up under the symbol of a *Crystal Palace,* which recurs again and again in his writings. The use of this symbol by Dostoevsky is interesting as showing his immediate recognition of the significance of the Exhibition of 1851 in London, housed in Paxton's Palace, the fame of which had spread to the farthest corners of Europe. He saw in this the sign of an advent of a new epoch which threatened by a new temptation to un-

*Dostoevsky went abroad in July, 1865, while writing *Crime and Punishment,* which was published in 1866. In the same year he met his second wife, Anna Grigoryevna Snitkina, whom he engaged as a stenographer for his novel *The Gambler,* and whom he married in 1867. She was nineteen at the time. On April 14 of the same year he went abroad again, where he started work on *The Idiot,* which was published in 1868. This time he spent four years abroad, during which he wrote *The Eternal Husband* and *The Possessed.* He returned to Russia in July, 1871, leaving for his next trip abroad in June, 1874, when he began to work on *The Adolescent.* He went abroad again in May, 1875, July, 1876, and finally, in July, 1879, when he was working on *The Brothers Karamazov,* published in 1879 and 1880.

†"I am weak in philosophy, (but not in my love for it;) in my love for it I am strong." (Letter from Dresden to the Russian journalist Strakhov, June 6, 1870.)

dermine all the cultural values of European life, and which he later expounded so explicitly in the story of "The Grand Inquisitor" in *The Brothers Karamazov.* Within the compass of a few short chapters, the bewilderment of the self-conscious intellect grappling with the ultimate problems is portrayed with brutal frankness in the first part of the *Notes from the Underground.* No regard for self-respect, charity, or pride is allowed to impede the deliberate dissection until the inescapable truth has been stated. Dostoevsky rejects one after another the palliatives so dear to the romantic humanitarian and forces on him the acknowledgment of his own guilt and ineffectiveness. This, indeed, appears very clearly from the way Dostoevsky dismisses Nekrassov's poem with which he introduces the second part of the *Notes;* for his two etceteras are in themselves sufficient to dispose of Nekrassov's plea for the "fallen woman" with utter contempt; he then proceeds to elucidate his thesis by an appeal to uncompromising realism.

The parallelism between *White Nights* and *Notes from the Underground* has been noted earlier. In both the hero is a dreamer of dreams; but while the story in *White Nights* moves along smoothly and pleasantly on the surface of human thought and emotion, in the *Notes from the Underground* it penetrates deep into the human heart and mind, so deep indeed that the main subject of the story transcends the personal fortunes of the anonymous hero and assumes a universal significance; it is all mankind and not individual man that is the real subject of the discourse.

The two last stories in this volume belong to Dostoevsky's last years. He died on February 9, 1881, from a burst artery in his lungs, aggravated by an attack of epilepsy, an illness from which he had suffered all his life. *A Gentle Creature* was published in 1876, in the November number of *A Writer's Diary,* and *The Dream of a Ridiculous Man* in the April number of the next year.

A Gentle Creature filled the whole of the November issue of Dostoevsky's monthly. It is clear from his short preface that he was busy on this story for the better part of a month. The first page of the original draft of the story bears the date of November 19, 1876. In the previous number of *A Writer's Diary* Dostoevsky tells of the incident which led him to write the story. "About a month ago," he writes, "all the Petersburg papers carried a small news item in a few lines of small print about a suicide in Petersburg. A poor girl, a sempstress, threw herself out of a fourth floor window 'because she could find no work to keep herself alive.' It was added that she had thrown herself out of the window *clasping an icon in her hands.* This icon in the hands of the young girl is a strange and unheard-of feature in a suicide case! This indeed is a gentle, meek sort of suicide."

In this story, one of the most powerful he ever wrote, Dostoevsky analyses one more reason leading to disaster in human relationships. It is the insensibility of one human being towards another, the failure to realise what is passing in another human being's heart, the lack of sympathy which is the cause of so much cruelty of man towards man.

Dostoevsky was very fond of sub-titles to his stories, and one cannot help feeling that the sub-title *A Fantastic Story* to *A Gentle Creature* is due to this fondness rather than to the reasons he adduces for it in his preface. But the same sub-title to *The Dream of a Ridiculous Man* is fully justified, since it is essentially a tale of the imagination. The subject of the Golden Age occupied Dostoevsky for many years. He refers to it in *Notes from the Underground,* and he again refers to it in 1865 in his first draft of *Crime and Punishment,* where he puts the following stray reflections into the mouth of Raskolnikov: "Oh, why isn't everything a matter of happiness? The picture of the Golden Age. It is implanted in men's hearts and minds. How is it that it doesn't come?" Among Raskolnikov's other reflections are these anticipatory echoes of *The Dream:* "I never saw Venice or the Golden Horn, but I expect life must be long extinct there. . . . Flew to another planet." But Dostoevsky made no use of any of these fragmentary notes in the final draft of the novel. The picture of the Golden Age was first outlined by him in a finished form in the so-called "Stavrogin's Confession," a chapter of *The Possessed* not included in the novel, where the episode of the Golden Age was connected with Claude Lorrain's picture *Acis and Galatea* which Dostoevsky had seen in the Dresden Museum. The whole episode was later incorporated by Dostoevsky in his novel

The Adolescent, where it is given as part of Versilov's speech. For the last time Dostoevsky dealt with this theme in *The Dream of a Ridiculous Man.*

Taken together with the first part of the *Notes from the Underground, The Dream* gives us Dostoevsky's final judgment on man. And negative though this judgment is on the whole, Dostoevsky never despaired of man. The vision of the Golden Age may be a dream, but it is a dream that makes life worth while even if it can never be realised; indeed, it makes life worth while just because it can never be realised. In this paradox Dostoevsky the creative artist seemed to glimpse some meaning in man's tragic story. But he did not stop there. He was appalled by the arrogance of the intellect, and in *The Dream* he again stresses the fact that reason without feeling, mind without heart, is *evil,* is a *dark cellar;* for reason bears within itself the seeds of destruction. Only through pity, love and mercy can man be saved. This message, as Dostoevsky himself put it in *The Dream,* is "an old truth"; but, like the hero in *The Dream,* he went on preaching it all his life.

—

DAVID MAGARSHACK's translations include works by Dostoevsky, Turgenev, Chekhov, Gorky, and Pushkin. He has also written biographies of Dostoevsky and Gogol.

The Best Short Stories of Fyodor Dostoevsky

White Nights

A SENTIMENTAL LOVE STORY

From the Memoirs of a Dreamer

And was it his destined part
Only one moment in his life
To be close to your heart? . . .
—IVAN TURGENEV

FIRST NIGHT

It was a lovely night, one of those nights, dear reader, which can only happen when you are young. The sky was so bright and starry that when you looked at it the first question that came into your mind was whether it was really possible that all sorts of bad-tempered and unstable people could live under such a glorious sky. It is a question, dear reader, that would occur only to a young man, but may the good Lord put it into your head as often as possible! . . . The mention of bad-tempered and unstable people reminds me that during the whole of this day my behaviour has been above reproach. When I woke up in the morning I felt strangely depressed, a feeling I could not shake off for the better part of the day. All of a sudden it seemed to me as though I, the solitary one, had been forsaken by the whole world, and that the whole world would have nothing to do with me. You may ask who "the whole world" is. For, I am afraid, I have not been lucky in acquiring a single acquaintance in Petersburg during the eight years I have been living there. But what do I want acquaintances for? I know the whole of Petersburg without them, and that, indeed, was the reason why it seemed to me that the whole world had forsaken me when the whole town suddenly arose and left for the country. I was terrified to be left alone, and for three days I wandered about the town plunged into gloom and absolutely at a loss to understand what was the matter with me. Neither on Nevsky Avenue, nor in the park, nor on the embankment did I meet the old familiar faces that I used to meet in the same place and at the same time all through the year. It is true I am a complete stranger to these people, but they are not strangers to me. I know them rather intimately, in fact; I have made a very thorough study of their faces; I am happy when they are happy, and I am sad when they are overcast with care. Why, there is an old gentleman I see every day on the Fontanka Embankment with whom I have practically struck up a friendship. He looks so thoughtful and dignified, and he always mutters under his breath, waving his left hand and holding a big knotty walking-stick with a gold top in his right. I have, I believe, attracted his attention, and I should not be surprised if he took a most friendly interest in me. In fact, I am sure that if he did not meet me at a certain hour on the Fontanka Embankment he would be terribly upset. That is why we sometimes almost bow to one another, especially when we are both in a good humour. Recently we had not seen each other for two days, and on the third day, when we met, we were just about to raise our hats in salute, but fortunately we recollected ourselves in time and, dropping our hands, passed one another in complete understanding and amity. The houses, too, are familiar to me. When I walk along the street, each of them seems to run before me, gazing at me out of all its windows, and practically saying to me, "Good morning, sir! How are you? I'm very well, thank you. They're going to add another storey to me in May"; or, "How do you do, sir? I'm going to be repaired tomorrow"; or, "Dear me, I nearly got burnt down, and, goodness, how I was scared!" and so on and so on. Some of them are great favourites of mine, while others are my good friends. One of them is thinking of undergoing a cure with an architect this summer. I shall certainly make a point of coming to see it every day to make sure that its cure does not prove fatal (which God forbid!). And I shall never forget the incident with a pretty little house of a pale pink hue. It was such a dear little house; it always welcomed me with such a friendly smile, and it looked on its clumsy neighbours with such an air of condescension, that my heart leapt with joy every time I passed it. But when I happened to walk along the street only a week ago and looked up at my friend, I was welcomed with a most plaintive cry, "They are going to paint me yellow!" Fiends! Savages! They spared nothing, neither cornices, nor columns, and my poor friend turned as yellow as a canary. I nearly had an attack of jaundice myself, and even to this day I have not been able to screw up my courage to go and see my mutilated friend, painted in the national colour of the Celestial Empire!

So now you see, dear reader, how it is that I know the whole of Petersburg.

I have already said that until I realised what was the trouble with me, I had been very worried and upset for three whole days. In the street I felt out of sorts (this one had gone, that one had gone, and where on earth had the other one got to?), and at home I was not my old self, either. For two evenings I had been racking my brains trying hard to discover what was wrong with my room. What was it made me so peevish when I stayed there? And, greatly perplexed, I began examining my grimy green walls and the ceiling covered with cobwebs which Matryona was such a genius at cultivating. I went over my furniture and looked at each chair in turn, wondering whether the trouble lay there (for it upsets me to see even one chair not in its usual place); I looked at the window—but all to no purpose: it did not make me feel a bit better! I even went so far as to call in Matryona and rebuke her in a fatherly sort of way about the cobwebs and her untidiness in general. But she just gave me a surprised look and stalked out of the room without saying a word, so that the cobwebs still remain cheerfully in their old places. It was only this morning that at last I discovered the real cause of my unhappiness. Oh, so they are all running away from me to the country, are they? I'm afraid I must apologise for the use of this rather homely word, but I'm not in the mood now for the more exquisite refinements of style, for everybody in Petersburg has either left or is about to leave for the country; for every worthy gentleman of a solidly-prosperous and dignified position who hails a cab in the street is at once transformed in my mind into a worthy parent of a family who, after his usual office duties, immediately leaves town and, unencumbered by luggage, hastens to the bosom of his family—to the country; for every passer-by now wears quite a different look, a look which almost seems to say to every person he meets, "As a matter of fact, sir, I'm here by sheer chance, just passing through, you understand, and in a few hours I shall be on the way to the country." If a window is thrown open and a most ravishing young girl, who a moment ago had been drumming on it with her lovely white fingers, pokes out her pretty head and calls to the man selling pots of plants in the street, I immediately jump to the conclusion that the flowers are bought not for the purpose of enjoying the spring and the flowers in a stuffy old flat in town, for very soon everybody will anyway be leaving for the country and will take even the flowers with them. Why, I've got so far in my new discovery (quite a unique discovery, you must admit) that I can tell at once, just by looking at a man, in what sort of a cottage he lives in the country. The residents of the Stone and Apothecary Islands can be recognised by their studied exquisiteness of manners, their smart summer clothes, and their wonderful carriages in which they come to town. The inhabitants of Pargolov and places beyond "inspire" your confidence at the first glance by their solidly prosperous position and their general air of sobriety and common sense; while the householder of Krestovsky Island is distinguished by his imperturbably cheerful look. Whether I happen to come across a long procession of carters, each walking leisurely, reins in hand, beside his cart, laden with whole mountains of furniture of every description—tables, chairs, Turkish and non-Turkish divans, and other household chattels—and, moreover, often presided over by a frail-looking cook who, perched on the very top of the cart, guards the property of her master as though it were the apple of her eye; or whether I look at the barges, heavily laden with all sorts of domestic junk, sailing on the Neva or the Fontanka, as far as the Black River or the Islands—both carts and barges multiply tenfold, nay, a hundredfold in my eyes. It really seems as though everything had arisen and set off on a journey, as though everything were moving off in caravan after caravan into the country; it seems as though the whole of Petersburg were about to turn into a desert, and it is hardly surprising that in the end I am overwhelmed with shame, humiliation, and sadness. For I have no possible excuse for going to the country; neither have I any country cottage I can go to. I am willing to leave with every cart or every gentleman of respectable appearance who hails a cab; but no one, absolutely no one, invites me to go with him, as though they had all forgotten me, as though I were no more than a stranger to them!

I walked for hours and hours, and, as usual, had for some time been completely oblivious of my surroundings, when I suddenly found myself near the toll-gate. I felt cheerful at once, and, stepping beyond the bar, walked along the road between fields of corn and meadows of lush grass, unconscious of any fatigue, and feeling with every breath I drew that a heavy weight was being lifted from my heart. All the travellers I met looked so genially at me that it seemed that in another moment they would most assuredly bow to me. All of them seemed to be happy about something, and every one of them without exception smoked a cigar. And I, too, was happy as never before in my life. As though I had suddenly found myself in Italy—so strong was the impact of nature upon me, a semi-invalid townsman who had all but been stifled within the walls of the city.

There is something indescribably moving in the way nature in Petersburg, suddenly with the coming of spring, reveals herself in all her might and glory, in all the splendour with which heaven has endowed her, in the way she blossoms out, dresses up, decks herself out with flowers. . . . She reminds me somehow rather forcibly of that girl, ailing and faded, upon whom you sometimes look with pity or with a certain compassionate affection, or whom you simply do not notice at all, but who in the twinkling of an eye and only for one fleeting moment becomes by some magic freak of chance indescribably fair and beautiful; and, stunned and fascinated, you ask yourself what power it was that made those sad and wistful eyes blaze forth with such a fire? What caused the rush of blood to her pale and hollow cheeks? What brought passion to that sweet face? Why did her bosom heave so wildly? What was it that so instantaneously suffused the face of the poor girl with life, vigour, and beauty? What forced it to light up with so brilliant a smile? What animated it with so warm, so infectious a laugh? You look round; you wonder who it could have been; you begin to suspect the truth. But the brief moment passes, and tomorrow perhaps you will again encounter the same wistful and forlorn gaze, the same wan face, the same resignation and diffidence in her movements, and, yes, even remorse, even traces of some benumbing vexation and despondency for that brief outburst of passion. And you feel sorry that the beauty, so momentarily evoked, should have faded so quickly and so irrevocably, that she should have burst upon your sight so deceptively and to so little purpose—that she should not have given you time even to fall in love with her. . . .

But all the same my night was much better than the day! This is how it happened:

I came back to town very late, and, as I was approaching the street where I lived, it struck ten. My way lay along a canal embankment where not a single living soul could be seen at that hour. It is true, I live in a very remote part of the town. I was walking along and singing, for when I am happy I always hum some tune to myself like every happy man who has neither friends nor good acquaintances, and who has no one to share his joy with in a moment of happiness. Suddenly I became involved in a most unexpected adventure.

A little distance away, leaning against the railing of the canal, a woman was standing with her elbows on the rail; she seemed to be engrossed in looking at the muddy water of the canal. She wore a most enchanting yellow hat and a very charming black cloak. "She's young," I thought, "and I'm sure she is dark." She did not seem to hear my footsteps, for she did not stir when I walked past her with bated breath and a thumping heart. "Funny!" I thought, "she must be thinking about something very important." Suddenly I stopped dead, rooted to the spot. The sound of suppressed weeping reached me. No, I was not mistaken. The girl was crying, for a minute later

I distinctly heard her sobbing again. Good gracious! My heart contracted with pity. And timid though I am with women, this was too good a chance to be missed! . . . I retraced my steps, walked up to her, and in another moment would have certainly said "Madam!" if I had not known that that exclamation had been made a thousand times before in all Russian novels of high life. It was that alone that stopped me. But while I was searching for the right word with which to address the girl, she had recovered her composure, recollected herself, lowered her eyes, and darted past me along the embankment. I immediately set off in pursuit of her, but she must have guessed my intention, for she left the embankment and, crossing the road, walked along the pavement. I did not dare to cross the road. My heart was fluttering like the heart of a captured bird. But quite an unexpected incident came to my assistance.

A gentleman in evening dress suddenly appeared a few yards away from the girl on the other side of the street. He had reached the age of discretion, but there was no discretion in his unsteady gait. He was walking along, swaying from side to side, and leaning cautiously against a wall. The girl, on the other hand, walked as straight as an arrow, quickly and apprehensively, as girls usually walk at night when they do not want any man to offer to accompany them home. And the reeling gentleman would most certainly not have caught up with her, if my good luck had not prompted him to resort to a stratagem. Without uttering a word, he suddenly set off in pursuit of the girl at an amazing speed. She was running away from him as fast as her legs would carry her, but the staggering gentleman was getting nearer and nearer, and then caught up with her. The girl uttered a shriek and—I have to thank my good genius for the excellent knobbly walking-stick which, as it happened, I was at the time clutching in my right hand. In less than no time I found myself on the other side of the street, and in less than no time the unwelcome gentleman took in the situation, took into account the undeniable fact of my superior weapons, grew quiet, dropped behind, and it was only when we were far away that he bethought himself of protesting against my action in rather forceful terms. But his words hardly reached us.

"Give me your arm," I said to the girl, "and he won't dare to molest you any more."

She silently gave me her arm, which was still trembling with excitement and terror. Oh, unwelcome stranger! How I blessed you at that moment! I stole a glance at her—I was right! She was a most charming girl and dark, too. On her black eyelashes there still glistened the tears of her recent fright or her recent unhappiness—I did not know which. But there was already a gleam of a smile on her lips. She, too, stole a glance at me, blushed a little, and dropped her eyes.

"Well, you see, you shouldn't have driven me away before, should you? If I'd been here, nothing would have happened."

"But I didn't know you. I thought that you too . . ."

"But what makes you think you know me now?"

"Well, I know you a little. Now why, for instance, are you trembling?"

"So you've guessed at once the sort of man I am," I replied, overjoyed that the girl was so intelligent (this is never a fault in a beautiful girl). "Yes, you've guessed at once the sort of man I am. It's quite true, I'm afraid, I'm awfully shy with women, and I don't want to deny that I'm a little excited now, no less than you were a moment ago when that fellow scared you. Yes, I seem to be scared now. It's as though it were all happening to me in a dream, except that even in a dream I did not expect ever to be talking to any woman."

"How do you mean? Not really?"

"Yes, really. You see, if my arm is trembling now, it's because it has never before been clasped by such a pretty little hand as yours. I've entirely lost the habit of talking to women. I mean, I never really was in the habit of talking to them. You see, I'm such a lonely creature. Come to think of it, I don't believe I know how to talk to women. Even now I haven't the faintest idea whether I've said anything to you that I shouldn't. Please, tell me frankly if I ever do. I promise you I shan't take offence."

"No, I don't think you've said anything you shouldn't. And if you really want me to be frank with you, I don't mind telling you that women rather like shy men like you. And if you want me to speak more frankly, I like it too, and I promise not to send you away till we reach my home."

"I'm afraid," I began, breathless with excitement, "you'll make me lose my shyness at once, and then goodbye to all my schemes!"

"Devices? What schemes, and what for? I must say that isn't nice at all."

"I beg your pardon. I'm awfully sorry. It was a slip of the tongue. But how can you expect me at this moment not to wish. . . ."

"To make a good impression, you mean?"

"Well, yes. And do, for goodness sake, be fair. Just think—who am I? At twenty-six—yes, I'm twenty-six—I've never really known anyone. So how can you expect me to speak well, cleverly, and to the point? You, too, I think, would prefer us to be straightforward and honest with each other, wouldn't you? I just can't be silent when my heart is moved to speak. Well, anyway . . . I know you'll hardly believe me, but I've never spoken to any woman, never! Never known one, either! I only dream that some day I shall meet someone at last. Oh, if only you knew how many times I've fallen in love like that!"

"But how? Who with?"

"With no one, of course. Just with my ideal, with the woman I see in my dreams. I make up all sorts of romantic love stories in my dreams. Oh, you don't know the sort of man I am! It's true I have known two or three women—you can't help that, can you?—but what sort of women were they? They were all so mercenary that . . . But let me tell you something really funny, let me tell you how several times I longed to talk to a society lady in the street, I mean, talk to her when she was alone, and without any formality. Very humbly, of course, very respectfully, very passionately. Tell her how horribly depressed I am by my lonely life; ask her not to send me away; explain to her that I have no other way of knowing what a woman is like; suggest to her that it is really her duty as a woman not to reject the humble entreaty of an unhappy man like me; finally, explain to her that all I want of her is that she should say a few friendly words to me, say them with sympathy and understanding, that she should not send me away at once, that she should believe my protestations, that she should listen to what I had to tell her, laugh at me by all means, if she wanted to, but also hold out some hope to me, just say two words to me, and then we need not see each other again! But you're laughing. . . . Well, as a matter of fact, I only said that to make you laugh. . . ."

"Don't be cross with me. I'm laughing because you are your own enemy, and if you had tried you would, I'm sure, have perhaps succeeded, even though it all happened in the street. The simpler, the better. Not one kind-hearted woman, provided, of course, she was not a fool, or angry at something at the time, would have the heart to send you away without saying the two words you were so humbly asking for. But I may be wrong. She would most likely have taken you for a madman. I'm afraid I was judging by myself. I know very well, I assure you, how people live in the world!"

"Thank you," I cried, "thank you a thousand times! You don't know how much I appreciate what you've just done for me!"

"All right, all right! Only tell me how did you guess I'm one of those women with whom . . . well, whom you thought worthy . . . of your attention and friendship. I mean, not a mercenary one, as you call it. What made you decide to come up to me?"

"What made me do that? Why, you were alone, and that fellow was much too insolent. It all happened at night, too, and you must admit it was my duty. . . ."

"No, no! I mean before. On the other side of the street. You wanted to come up to me, didn't you?"

"On the other side of the street? Well, I really don't know what to say. I'm afraid I . . . You see, I was so happy today. I was walking along and singing. I had spent the day in the country. I don't remember ever having experienced such happy moments before. You were . . . However, I may have been mistaken. Please, forgive me, if I remind you of it, but I thought you were crying, and I—I couldn't bear to hear it—I felt miserable about it. But, goodness, had I no right to feel anxious about you? Was it wrong of me to feel a brotherly compassion for you? I'm sorry, I said compassion . . . Well, what I meant was that I couldn't possibly have offended you because I had an impulse to go up to you, could I?"

"Don't say anything more, please," said the girl pressing my hand and lowering her head. "I'm to blame for having started talking about it. But I'm glad I was not mistaken in you. Well, I'm home now. I live in that lane, only two steps from here. Goodbye and thank you."

"But shall we never see each other again? Surely, surely, you can't mean it. Surely, this can't be our last meeting?"

"Well, you see," the girl said, laughing, "at first you only asked for two words, and now. . . . However, I don't think I'd better make any promises. Perhaps we'll meet again."

"I'll be here tomorrow," I said. "Oh, I'm sorry, I seem to be already making demands. . . ."

"Yes, you are rather impatient, aren't you? You're almost making demands. . . ."

"Listen to me, please, listen to me!" I interrupted. "You won't mind if I say something to you again, something of the same kind, will you? It's this: I can't help coming here tomorrow. I am a dreamer. I know so little of real life that I just can't help re-living such moments as these in my dreams, for such moments are something I have very rarely experienced. I am going to dream about you the whole night, the whole week, the whole year. I'll most certainly come here tomorrow. Yes, here, at this place and at this hour. And I shall be happy to remember what happened to me today. Already this place is dear to me. I've two or three places like this in Petersburg. Once I even wept because I remembered something, just as you—I mean, I don't know of course, but perhaps you too were crying ten minutes ago because of some memory. I'm awfully sorry, I seem to have forgotten myself again. Perhaps you were particularly happy here once. . . ."

"Very well," said the girl, "I think I will come here tomorrow, also at ten o'clock. And I can see that I can't possibly forbid you to come, can I? You see, I have to be here. Please don't imagine that I am making an appointment with you. I hope you'll believe me when I say that I have got to be here on some business of my own. Oh, very well, I'll be frank with you: I shan't mind at all if you come here too. To begin with, something unpleasant may happen again as it did today, but never mind that . . . I mean, I'd really like to see you again to—to say two words to you. But, mind, don't think ill of me now, will you? Don't imagine I'm making appointments with men so easily. I wouldn't have made it with you, if . . . But let that be my secret. Only first you must promise. . . ."

"I promise anything you like!" I cried, delighted. "Only say it. Tell me anything beforehand. I agree to everything. I'll do anything you like. I can answer for myself. I'll be obedient, respectful. . . . You know me, don't you?"

"Well, it's because I know you that I'm asking you to come tomorrow," said the girl, laughing. "I know you awfully well. But, mind, if you come it's on condition that, first (only you will do what I ask you, won't you?—You see, I'm speaking frankly to you), don't fall in love with me. That's impossible, I assure you. I'm quite ready to be your friend. I am, indeed. But you mustn't fall in love with me. So please, don't."

"I swear to you . . ." I cried, seizing her hand.

"No, no. I don't want any solemn promises. I know you're quite capable of flaring up like gunpowder. Don't be angry with me for speaking to you like this. If you knew . . . You see, I haven't got anyone, either, to whom to say a word, or whom to ask for advice. Of course, it's silly to expect advice from people one meets in the street, but you are different. I feel I know you so well that I couldn't have known you better if we'd been friends for twenty years. You won't fail me, will you?"

"You can depend on me! The only thing is I don't know how I shall be able to survive for the next twenty-four hours."

"Have a good sleep. Good night, and remember I've already confided in you. But, as you expressed it so well a few minutes ago, one hasn't really to account for every feeling, even for brotherly sympathy, has one? You put it so nicely that I felt at once that you're the sort of person I could confide in."

"For goodness sake, tell me what it is. Please do."

"No, I think you'd better wait till tomorrow. Let it remain a secret for the time being. So much the better for you: at least from a distance it will seem more like a romance. Perhaps I'll tell you tomorrow, perhaps I won't. I'd like to have a good talk to you first, get to know you better. . . ."

"All right, I'll tell you all about myself tomorrow. But, good Lord, the whole thing is just like a miracle! Where am I? Tell me, aren't you glad you weren't angry with me, as some other women might well have been? Only two minutes, and you've made me happy for ever. Yes, happy. Who knows, perhaps you've reconciled me with myself, resolved all my doubts. Perhaps there are moments when I . . . But I'll tell you all about it tomorrow. You shall know everything, everything. . . ."

"All right, I agree. I think you'd better start first."

"Very well."

"Goodbye!"

"Goodbye!"

And we parted. I walked about all night. I couldn't bring myself to go home. I was so happy! Till tomorrow!

SECOND NIGHT

"Well, so you have survived, haven't you?" she said to me, laughing and pressing both my hands.

"I've been here for the last two hours. You don't know what I've been through today!"

"I know, I know—but to business. Do you know why I've come? Not to talk a lot of nonsense as we did yesterday. You see, we must be more sensible in future. I thought about it a lot yesterday."

"But how? How are we to be more sensible? Not that I have anything against it. But, really, I don't believe anything more sensible has ever happened to me than what's happening to me at this moment."

"Oh? Well, first of all, please don't squeeze my hands like that. Secondly, let me tell you I've given a lot of thought to you today."

"Have you? Well, and what decision have you come to?"

"What decision? Why, that we ought to start all over again. For today I've come to the conclusion that I don't know you at all, that I've behaved like a child, like a silly girl, and of course in the end I blamed my own good heart for everything. I mean, I finished up, as everybody always does when they start examining their own motives, by passing a vote of thanks to myself. And so, to correct my mistake, I've made up my mind to find out all about you to the last detail. But as there's no one I can ask about you, you'll have to tell me everything yourself. Everything, absolutely everything! To begin with, what sort of man are you? Come on, start, please! Tell me the story of your life."

"The story of my life?" I cried, thoroughly alarmed. "But who told you there was such a story? I'm afraid there isn't any."

"But how did you manage to live, if there is no story?" she interrupted me, laughing.

"Without any stories whatsoever! I have lived, as they say, entirely independently. I mean by myself. Do you know what it means to live by oneself?"

"How do you mean by yourself? Do you never see anyone at all?"

"Why, no. I see all sorts of people, but I'm alone all the same."

"Don't you ever talk to anyone?"

"Strictly speaking, never."

"But who are you? Please explain. But wait: I think I can guess. You've probably got a grandmother like me. She's blind, my granny is, and she never lets me go out anywhere, so that I've almost forgotten how to talk to people. And when I behaved badly about two years ago and she saw that there was no holding me, she called me in and pinned my dress to hers—and since then we've sat pinned to one another like that for days and days. She knits a stocking, blind though she is, and I have to sit beside her sewing or reading a book to her. It's a funny sort of situation to be in—pinned to a person for two years or more."

"Good gracious, what bad luck! No, I haven't got such a grandmother."

"If you haven't, why do you sit at home all the time?"

"Look here, do you want to know who I am?"

"Yes, of course!"

"In the strict meaning of the word?"

"Yes, in the strictest meaning of the word!"

"Very well, I'm a character."

"A character? What kind of a character?" the girl cried, laughing merrily, as though she had not laughed for a whole year. "I must say, you're certainly great fun! Look, here's a seat. Let's sit down. No one ever comes this way, so no one will overhear us. Well, start your story, please! For you'll never convince me that you haven't got one. You're just trying to conceal it. Now, first of all, what is a character?"

"A character? Well, it's an original, a queer chap," I said, and, infected by her childish laughter, I burst out laughing myself. "It's a kind of freak. Listen, do you know what a dreamer is?"

"A dreamer? Of course I know. I'm a dreamer myself! Sometimes when I'm sitting by Granny I get all sorts of queer ideas into my head. I mean, once you start dreaming, you let your imagination run away with you, so that in the end I even marry a prince of royal blood! I don't know, it's very nice sometimes—dreaming, I mean. But, on the whole, perhaps it isn't. Especially if you have lots of other things to think of," the girl added, this time rather seriously.

"Fine! Once you're married to an emperor, you will, I think, understand me perfectly. Well, listen—but don't you think I ought to know your name before starting on the story of my life?"

"At last! It took you a long time to think of it, didn't it?"

"Good lord! I never thought of it. You see, I was so happy anyway."

"My name's Nastenka."

"Nastenka! Is that all?"

"Yes, that's all. Isn't it enough for you, you insatiable person?"

"Not enough? Why, not at all. It's more than I expected, much more than I expected, Nastenka, my dear, dear girl, if I may call you by your pet name, if from the very first you—you become Nastenka to me!"

"I'm glad you're satisfied at last! Well?"

"Well, Nastenka, just listen what an absurd story it all is."

I sat down beside her, assumed a pedantically serious pose, and began as though reading from a book:

"There are, if you don't happen to know it already, Nastenka, some very strange places in Petersburg. It is not the same sun which shines upon all the other people of the city that looks in there, but quite a different sun, a new sun, one specially ordered for those places, and the light it sheds on everything is also a different, peculiar sort of light. In those places, dear Nastenka, the people also seem to live quite a different life, unlike that which surges all round us, a life which could only be imagined to exist in some faraway foreign country beyond the seven seas, and not at all in our country and in these much too serious times. Well, it is that life which is a mixture of something purely fantastic, something fervently ideal, and, at the same time (alas, Nastenka!), something frightfully prosaic and ordinary, not to say incredibly vulgar."

"My goodness, what an awful introduction! What shall I be hearing next, I wonder?"

"What will you be hearing next, Nastenka (I don't think I shall ever get tired of calling you Nastenka), is that these places are inhabited by strange people—by dreamers. A dreamer—if you must know its exact definition—is not a man, but a sort of creature of the neuter gender. He settles mostly in some inaccessible place, as though anxious to hide in it even from the light of day; and once he gets inside his room, he'll stick to it like a snail, or, at all events, he is in this respect very like that amusing animal which is an animal and a house both at one and the same time and bears the name of tortoise. Why, do you think, is he so fond of his four walls, invariably painted green, grimy, dismal and reeking unpardonably of tobacco smoke? Why does this funny fellow, when one of his new friends comes to visit him (he usually ends up by losing all his friends one by one), why does this absurd person meet him with such an embarrassed look? Why is he so put out of countenance? Why is he thrown into such confusion, as though he had just committed some terrible crime within his four walls? As though he had been forging paper money? Or writing some atrocious poetry to be sent to a journal with an anonymous letter, in which he will explain that, the poet having recently died, he, his friend, deems it his sacred duty to publish his verses? Can you tell me, Nastenka, why the conversation between the two friends never really gets going? Why doesn't laughter or some witty remark escape the lips of the perplexed caller, who had so inopportunely dropped out of the blue, and who at other times is so fond of laughter and all sorts of quips and cranks? And conversations about the fair sex. And other cheerful subjects. And why does the visitor, who is most probably a recent acquaintance and on his first visit—for in this case there will never be a second, and his visitor will never call again—why, I say, does this visitor feel so embarrassed himself? Why, in spite of his wit (if, that is, he has any), is he so tongue-tied as he looks at the disconcerted face of his host, who is, in turn, utterly at a loss and bewildered after his herculean efforts to smooth things over, and fumbles desperately for a subject to enliven the conversation, to convince his host that he, too, is a man of the world, that he too can talk of the fair sex? The host does everything in fact to please the poor man, who seems to have come to the wrong place and called on him by mistake, by at least showing how anxious he is to entertain him. And why does the visitor, having most conveniently remembered a most urgent business appointment which never existed, all of a sudden grab his hat and take his leave, snatching away his hand from the clammy grasp of his host, who, in a vain attempt to recover what is irretrievably lost, is doing his best to show how sorry he is? Why does his friend burst out laughing the moment he finds himself on the other side of the door? Why does he vow never to call on this queer fellow again, excellent fellow though he undoubtedly is? Why at the same time can't he resist the temptation of indulging in the amusing, if rather farfetched, fancy of comparing the face of his friend during his visit with the expression of an unhappy kitten, roughly handled, frightened, and subjected to all sorts of indignities, by children who had treacherously captured and humiliated it? A kitten that hides itself away from its tormentors under a chair, in the dark, where, left in peace at last, it cannot help bristling up, spitting, and washing its insulted face with both paws for a whole hour, and long afterwards looking coldly at life and nature and even the bits saved up for it from the master's table by a sympathetic housekeeper?"

"Now, look," interrupted Nastenka, who had listened to me all the time in amazement, opening her eyes and pretty mouth, "look, I haven't the faintest idea why it all happened and why you should ask me such absurd questions. All I know is that all these adventures have most certainly happened to you, and exactly as you told me."

"Indubitably," I replied, keeping a very straight face.

"Well," said Nastenka, "if it's indubitably, then please go on, for I'm dying to hear how it will all end."

"You want to know, Nastenka, what our hero did in his room, or rather what I did in my room, since the hero of this story is none other than my own humble self? You want to know why I was so alarmed and upset for a whole day by the unexpected visit of a friend? You want to know why I was in such a flurry of excitement, why I blushed to the roots of my hair, when the door of my room opened? Why I was not able to entertain my visitor, and why I perished so ignominiously, crushed by the weight of my own hospitality?"

"Yes, yes, of course I do," answered Nastenka. "That's the whole point. And, please, I do appreciate the beautiful way in which you're telling your story, but don't you think perhaps you ought to tell it a little less beautifully? You see, you talk as if you were reading from a book."

"Nastenka," I said in a very grave and solemn voice, scarcely able to keep myself from laughing, "dear Nastenka, I know I'm telling my story very beautifully, but I'm afraid I can't tell it any other way. For at this moment, Nastenka, at this moment, I am like the spirit of King Solomon when, after being imprisoned for a thousand years in a jar under seven seals, all the seven seals have at last been removed. At this moment, dear Nastenka, when we've met again after so long a separation—for I've known you for ages, dear Nastenka, for I've been looking for someone for ages and that's a sure sign that it was you I was looking for and, moreover, that it was ordained that we two should meet now—just at this very moment, Nastenka, a thousand floodgates have opened up in my head and I must overflow in a cataract of words, or I shall burst. So I beg you to listen to me like a good and obedient girl and not to interrupt me, Nastenka, or I shan't say another word."

"No, no, no! Please, go on. You mustn't stop. I shan't say another word, I promise."

"Well, to continue. There is, Nastenka, my dear, dear friend, one hour in my day which I love exceedingly. It is the hour when practically all business, office hours and duties are at an end, and everyone is hurrying home to dinner, to lie down, to have a rest, and as they walk along they think of other pleasant ways of spending the evening, the night, and the rest of their leisure time. At that hour our hero—for I must ask your permission, Nastenka, to tell my story in the third person, for one feels awfully ashamed to tell it in the first—and so at that hour our hero, who has not been wasting his time, either, is walking along with the others. But a strange expression of pleasure plays on his pale and slightly crumpled-looking face. It is not with indifference that he looks at the sunset which is slowly fading on the cold Petersburg sky. When I say he looks, I'm telling a lie: he does not look at it, but is contemplating it without, as it were, being aware of it himself, as though he were tired or preoccupied at the same time with some other more interesting subject, being able to spare only a passing and almost unintentional glance at what is taking place around him. He is glad to have finished till next day with all tiresome *business*. He is happy as a schoolboy who has been let out of the classroom and is free to devote all his time to his favourite games and forbidden pastimes. Take a good look at him, Nastenka: you will at once perceive that his feeling of joy has had a pleasant effect on his weak nerves and his morbidly excited imagination. Look! he is thinking of something. Of dinner perhaps? Or how he's going to spend the evening? What is he looking at like that? At the gentleman of the solidly prosperous exterior who is bowing so picturesquely to the lady who drives past in a splendid carriage drawn by a pair of mettlesome horses? No, Nastenka, what do all those trivial things matter to him now? He is rich beyond compare with his *own individual* life; he has become rich in the twinkling of an eye, as it were, and it was not for nothing that the farewell ray of the setting sun flashed so gaily across his vision and called forth a whole swarm of impressions from his glowing heart. Now he hardly notices the road on which at any other time every trivial detail would have attracted his attention. Now 'the Goddess of Fancy' (if you have read your Zhukovsky, dear Nastenka) has already spun the golden warp with her wanton hand and is at this very moment weaving patterns of a wondrous, fantastic life before his mind's eye—and, who knows, maybe has transported him with her wanton hand to the seventh crystalline sphere from the excellent granite pavement on which he is now wending his way home. Try stopping him now, ask him suddenly where he is standing now, through what streets he has been walking, and it is certain he will not be able to remember anything, neither where he has been, nor where he is standing now, and, flushing with vexation, he will most certainly tell some lie to save appearances. That is why he starts violently, almost crying out, and looks round in horror when a dear old lady stops him in the middle of the pavement and politely asks him the way. Frowning with vexation, he walks on, scarcely aware of the passers-by who smile as they look at him and turn round to follow him with their eyes. He does not notice the little girl who, after timidly making way for him, bursts out laughing as she gazes at his broad, contemplative smile and wild gesticulations. And still the same fancy in her frolicsome flight catches up the old lady, the passers-by, the laughing little girl, and the bargees who have settled down to their evening meal on the barges which dam up the Fontanka (our hero, let us suppose, is walking along the Fontanka Embankment at that moment), and playfully weaves everybody and everything into her canvas, like a fly in a spider's web. And so, with fresh food for his fancy to feed on, the queer fellow at last comes home to his comfortable little den and sits down to his dinner. It is long after he has finished his meal, however, when, after clearing the table, Matryona, the preoccupied and everlastingly melancholy old woman who waits on him, gives him his pipe, that he recovers from his reverie and is shocked to find that he has had his dinner, although he has no recollection whatever how it has all happened. It has grown dark in the little room; he feels empty and forlorn; his castle in the air comes crumbling noiselessly around him, without a sound, and it vanishes like a dream, without leaving a trace behind, and he cannot remember himself what he was dreaming of. But a vague sensation faintly stirs his blood and a perturbation such as he has known many times before agitates his breast. A new longing temptingly tickles and excites his fancy, and imperceptibly conjures up a whole swarm of fresh phantoms. Silence reigns in the little room; solitude and a feeling of indolence enfold his imagination in a sweet embrace; it catches fire, burning gently at first, simmering like the water in the coffee-pot of old Matryona, who is moving placidly about her kitchen, making her execrable coffee. Very soon it begins flaring up fitfully, and the book, picked up aimlessly and at random, drops out of the hand of my dreamer, before he has reached the third page. His imagination is once more ready for action, excited, and in a flash a new world, a new fascinating life, once more opens up enchanting vistas before him. A new dream—new happiness! A new dose of subtle, voluptuous poison! Oh, what is there in our humdrum existence to interest him? To his corrupted mind, our life, Nastenka, yours and mine, is so dull, so slow, so insipid! To his mind we are all so dissatisfied with our fate, so tired of our life! And, to be sure, Nastenka, how cold, gloomy, and, as it were, out of humour everything about us is at the first glance! 'Poor things!' my dreamer thinks. And it is not surprising that he should think so! Look at those magical phantoms which so enchantingly, so capriciously, so vastly, and so boundlessly, are conjured up before his mind's eye in so magical and thrilling a picture, a picture in which, needless to say, he himself, our dreamer, in his own precious person, occupies the most prominent place! Look what an amazing sea of adventures, what a never-ending paradise of ecstatic dreams! You will perhaps ask me what is he dreaming of? But why ask? He is dreaming of everything—of the mission of the poet, first unrecognised, then crowned with laurels, of St. Bartholomew's Night, of Diana Vernon, the heroine of 'Rob Roy,' of what a heroic role he would have played at the taking of Kazan by Ivan Vassilyevich, of Walter Scott's other heroines—Clara Mowbray and Effie Deans, of the Council of the Prelates and Huss before them, of the rising of the dead in 'Robert the Devil' (remember the music? It smells of the churchyard!), of the Battle of Berezina, of the poetry reading at Countess Vorontsova-Dashkova's, of Danton, of Cleopatra *i suoi amanti,* of Pushkin's 'Little House in Kolomna,' of his own little home and a sweet creature beside him, who is listening to him, with her pretty mouth and eyes open, as you are listening to me now, my dear little angel.... No, Nastenka, what can he, voluptuous sluggard that he is, what can he find so attractive in the life which you and I desire so much? He thinks it a poor, miserable sort of life, and little does he know that some day perhaps the unhappy hour will strike for him too, when he will gladly give up all his fantastical years for one day of that miserable life, and give them up not in exchange for joy or happiness, but without caring what befalls him in that hour of affliction, remorse, and unconstrained grief. But so long as that perilous time is not yet—he desires nothing, for he is above all desire, for he is sated, for he is the artist of his own life, which he recreates in himself to suit whatever new fancy he pleases. And how easily, how naturally, is this imaginary, fantastic world created! As though it were not a dream at all! Indeed, he is sometimes ready to believe that all this life is not a vision conjured up by his overwrought mind, not a mirage, nor a figment of the imagination, but something real, something that actually exists! Why, Nastenka, why, tell me, does one feel so out of breath at such moments? Why—through what magic? through what strange whim?—is the pulse quickened, do tears gush out of the eyes of the dreamer? Why do his pale, moist cheeks burn? Why is all his being filled with such indescribable delight? Why is it that long, sleepless nights pass, as though they were an infinitesimal fraction of time, in unending joy and happiness? And why, when the rising sun casts a rosy gleam through the window and fills the gloomy room with its uncertain, fantastic light, as it so often does in Petersburg, does our dreamer, worn out and exhausted, fling himself on the bed and fall asleep, faint with the raptures of his morbidly overwrought spirit, and with such a weary, languorously sweet ache in his heart? No, Nastenka, you can't help deceiving yourself, you can't help persuading yourself that his soul is stirred by some true, some genuine passion, you can't help believing that there is something alive and palpable in his vain and empty dreams! And what a delusion it all is! Now, for instance, love pierces his heart with all its boundless rapture, with all its pains and agonies. Only look at him and you will be convinced. Can you, looking at him, Nastenka, believe that he really never knew her whom he loved so dearly in his frenzied dream? Can it be that he has only seen her in ravishing visions, and that his passion has been nothing but an illusion? Can it be that they have never really spent so many years of their lives together, hand in hand, alone, just the two of them, renouncing the rest of the world, and each of them entirely preoccupied with their own world, their own life? Surely it is she who at the hour of their parting, late at night, lies grieving and sobbing on his bosom, unmindful of the raging storm beneath the relentless sky, unmindful of the wind that snatches and carries away the tears from her dark eyelashes! Surely all this is not a dream—this garden, gloomy, deserted, run wild, with its paths overgrown with weeds, dark and secluded, where they used to walk so often together, where they used to hope, grieve, love, love each other so well, so tenderly and so well! And this queer ancestral mansion, where she has spent so many years in solitude and sadness with her morose old husband, always silent and ill-tempered, who frightened them, who were as timid as children, and who in their fear and anguish hid their love from each other. What misery they suffered, what pangs of terror! How innocent, how pure their love was, and (I need hardly tell you, Nastenka) how malicious people were! And why, of course, he meets her afterwards, far from his native shores, beneath the scorching southern sky of an alien land, in the wonderful Eternal City, amid the dazzling splendours of a ball, to the thunder of music, in a *palazzo* (yes, most certainly in a *palazzo*) flooded with light, on the balcony wreathed in myrtle and roses, where, recognising him, she hastily removes her mask, and whispering, 'I'm free!' breaks into sobs and flings herself trembling in his arms. And with a cry of rapture, clinging to each other, they at once forget their unhappiness, their parting, all their sufferings, the dismal house, the old man, the gloomy garden in their far-away country, and the seat on which, with a last passionate kiss, she tore herself away from his arms, numbed with anguish and despair. . . . Oh, you must agree, Nastenka, that anyone would start, feel embarrassed, and blush like a schoolboy who has just stuffed in his pocket an apple stolen from a neighbour's garden, if some stalwart, lanky fellow, a fellow fond of a joke and merry company, opened your door and shouted, 'Hullo, old chap, I've just come from Pavlovsk!' Good Lord! The old count is dying, ineffable bliss is close at hand—and here people come from Pavlovsk!"

Having finished my pathetic speech, I lapsed into no less pathetic a silence. I remember I wished terribly that I could, somehow, in spite of myself, burst out laughing, for I was already feeling that a wicked little devil was stirring within me, that my throat was beginning to tighten, my chin to twitch, and my eyes to fill with tears. I expected Nastenka, who listened to me with wide-open, intelligent eyes, to break into her childish and irresistibly gay laughter. I was already regretting that I had gone too far, that I had been wasting my time in telling her what had been accumulating for so long a time in my heart, and about which I could speak as though I had it all written down—because I had long ago passed judgment on myself, and could not resist the temptation to read it out loud, though I admit I never expected to be understood. But to my surprise she said nothing, and, after a pause, pressed my hand gently and asked with timid sympathy:

"Surely you haven't lived like that all your life, have you?"

"Yes, Nastenka, all my life," I replied, "all my life, and I'm afraid I shall go on like that to the very end."

"No, you mustn't do that," she said, "that must not be, for if it were so, I too might spend all my life beside my granny. Don't you think it's just too awful to live like that?"

"I know, Nastenka, I know," I cried, unable to restrain my feelings any longer. "More than ever do I realise now that I've been wasting the best years of my life. I know that, and the realisation of it is all the more painful to me now that God has sent me you, my good angel, to tell me that and to prove it to me. Sitting beside you and talking to you now, I feel terrified to think of the future, for in my future I can discern nothing but more loneliness, more of this stale and unprofitable life. And what is there left for me to dream of now that I've been so happy beside you in real life and not in a dream? Oh, bless you, bless you a thousand times, my dear, for not having turned away from me at first, for making it possible for me to say that for at least two evenings in my life I have really lived!"

"Oh, no, no," Nastenka cried, and tears glistened in her eyes, "it can't go on like that! We shan't part like that! What are two evenings in a man's life?"

"Oh, Nastenka, Nastenka, do you realise that you've reconciled me to myself for a long, long time? Do you know that I shall never again think so ill of myself as I have sometimes done in the past? Do you know that I shall never again accuse myself of committing a crime and a sin in the way I live, for such a life is a crime and a sin? And for goodness sake don't imagine I've exaggerated anything. Please, don't imagine that, Nastenka, for there are moments when I'm plunged into such gloom, such a black gloom! Because at such moments I'm almost ready to believe that I shall never be able to start living in earnest; because the thought has already occurred to me often that I have lost all touch with life, all understanding of what is real and actual; because, finally, I have cursed myself; because already after my fantastic nights I have moments of returning sanity, moments which fill me with horror and dismay! You see, I can't help being aware of the crowd being whirled with a roaring noise in the vortex of life, I can't help hearing and seeing people living real lives. I realise that their life is not made to order, that their life will not vanish like a dream, like a vision; that their life is eternally renewing itself, that it is eternally young, that not one hour of it is like another! No! Timid fancy is dreary and monotonous to the point of drabness. It is the slave of every shadow, of every idea. The slave of the first cloud that of a sudden drifts across the sun and reduces every Petersburg heart, which values the sun so highly, to a state of morbid melancholy—and what is the use of fancy when one is plunged into melancholy! You feel that this *inexhaustible* fancy grows weary at last and exhausts itself from the never-ending strain. For, after all, you do grow up, you do outgrow your ideals, which turn to dust and ashes, which are shattered into fragments; and if you have no other life, you just have to build one up out of these fragments. And meanwhile your soul is all the time craving and longing for something else. And in vain does the dreamer rummage about in his old dreams, raking them over as though they were a heap of cinders, looking in these cinders for some spark, however tiny, to fan it into a flame so as to warm his chilled blood by it and revive in it all that he held so dear before, all that touched his heart, that made his blood course through his veins, that drew tears from his eyes, and that so splendidly deceived him! Do you realise, Nastenka, how far things have gone with me? Do you know that I'm forced now to celebrate the anniversary of my own sensations, the anniversary of that which was once so dear to me, but which never really existed? For I keep this anniversary in memory of those empty, foolish dreams! I keep it because even those foolish dreams are no longer there, because I have nothing left with which to replace them, for even dreams, Nastenka, have to be replaced by something! Do you know that I love to call to mind and revisit at certain dates the places where in my own fashion I was once so happy? I love to build up my present in harmony with my irrevocably lost past; and I often wander about like a shadow, aimlessly and without purpose, sad and dejected, through the alleys and streets of Petersburg. What memories they conjure up! For instance, I remember that exactly a year ago, at exactly this hour, on this very pavement, I wandered about cheerlessly and alone just as I did today. And I can't help remembering that at the time, too, my dreams were sad and dreary, and though I did not feel better then I somehow can't help feeling that it was better, that life was more peaceful, that at least I was not then obsessed by the black thoughts that haunt me now, that I did not suffer from these gloomy and miserable qualms of conscience which now give me no rest either by day or by night. And you ask yourself—where are your dreams? And you shake your head and murmur: how quickly time flies! And you ask yourself again—what have you done with your time, where have you buried the best years of your life? Have you lived or not? Look, you say to yourself, look how everything in the world is growing cold. Some more years will pass, and they will be followed by cheerless solitude, and then will come tottering old age, with its crutch, and after it despair and desolation. Your fantastic world will fade away, your dreams will wilt and die, scattering like yellow leaves from the trees. Oh, Nastenka, what can be more heartbreaking than to be left alone, all alone, and not have anything to regret even—nothing, absolutely nothing, because all you've lost was nothing, nothing but a silly round zero, nothing but an empty dream!"

"Don't," said Nastenka, wiping a tear which rolled down her cheek, "please don't! You'll make me cry if you go on like that. All that is finished! From now on we shall be together. We'll never part, whatever happens to me now. You know, I'm quite an ordinary girl, I'm not well educated, though Granny did engage a teacher for me, but I do understand you, for I went through all that you've described when Granny pinned me to her dress. Of course, I could never have described it as well as you," she added diffidently, for she was still feeling a sort of respect for my pathetic speech and my high-flown style, "because I'm not educated; but I'm very glad you've told me everything about yourself. Now I know you properly. And—do you know what? I'd like to tell you the story of my life too, all of it, without concealing anything, and after that you must give me some good advice. You're so clever, and I'd like to ask your advice. Do you promise to give it me?"

"Oh, Nastenka," I replied, "though I've never given any advice to anyone before, and though I'm certainly not clever enough to give good advice, I can see now that if we always lived like this, it would be very clever of us, and we should give each other a lot of good advice! Well, my sweet Nastenka, what sort of advice do you want? I'm now so gay, happy, bold, and clever that I'm sure I shan't have any difficulty in giving you the best advice in the world!"

"No, no," Nastenka interrupted, laughing, "it isn't only good advice that I want. I also want warm, brotherly advice, just as though you'd been fond of me for ages!"

"Agreed, Nastenka, agreed!" I cried with enthusiasm. "And if I'd been fond of you for twenty years, I couldn't have been fonder of you than I am now!"

"Your hand!" said Nastenka.

"Here it is!" I replied, giving her my hand.

"Very well, let's begin my story!"

NASTENKA'S STORY

"Half my story you know already, I mean, you know that I have an old grandmother."

"If the other half is as short as this one—" I interrupted, laughing.

"Be quiet and listen. First of all you must promise not to interrupt me, or I shall get confused. Well, please listen quietly.

"I have an old grandmother. I've lived with her ever since I was a little girl, for my mother and father are dead. I suppose my grandmother must have been rich once, for she likes to talk of the good old days. It was she who taught me French and afterwards engaged a teacher for me. When I was fifteen (I'm seventeen now) my lessons stopped. It was at that time that I misbehaved rather badly. I shan't tell you what I did. It's sufficient to say that my offence was not very great. Only Granny called me in one morning and saying that she couldn't look after me properly because she was blind, she took a safety-pin and pinned my dress to hers. She told me that if I didn't mend my ways, we should remain pinned to each other for the rest of our lives. In short, at first, I found it quite impossible to get away from her: my work, my reading, and my lessons had all to be done beside my grandmother. I did try to trick her once by persuading Fyokla to sit in my place. Fyokla is our maid. She is very deaf. Well, so Fyokla took my place. Granny happened to fall asleep in her armchair at the time, and I ran off to see a friend of mine who lives close by. But, I'm afraid, it all ended most disastrously. Granny woke up while I was out and asked for something, thinking that I was still sitting quietly in my place. Fyokla saw of course that Granny wanted something, but could not tell what it was. She wondered and wondered what to do and in the end undid the pin and ran out of the room. . . ."

Here Nastenka stopped and began laughing. I, too, burst out laughing with her, which made her stop at once.

"Look, you mustn't laugh at Granny. I'm laughing because it was so funny. . . . Well, anyway. I'm afraid it can't be helped. Granny is like that, but I do love the poor old dear a little for all that. Well, I did catch it properly that time. I was at once told to sit down in my old place, and after that I couldn't make a move without her noticing it.

"Oh, I forgot to tell you that we live in our own house, I mean, of course, in Granny's house. It's a little wooden house, with only three windows, and it's as old as Granny herself. It has an attic, and one day a new lodger came to live in the attic. . . ."

"There was an old lodger then?" I remarked, by the way.

"Yes, of course, there was an old lodger," replied Nastenka, "and let me tell you, he knew how to hold his tongue better than you. As a matter of fact, he hardly ever used it at all. He was a very dried up old man, dumb, blind and lame, so that in the end he just could not go on living and died. Well, of course, we had to get a new lodger, for we can't live without one: the rent we get from our attic together with Granny's pension is almost all the income we have. Our new lodger, as it happened, was a young man, a stranger who had some business in Petersburg. As he did not haggle over the rent, Granny let the attic to him, and then asked me, 'Tell me, Nastenka, what is our lodger like—is he young or old?' I didn't want to tell her a lie, so I said, 'He isn't very young, Granny, but he isn't very old, either.'

"'Is he good-looking?' Granny asked.

"Again I didn't want to tell her a lie. 'He isn't bad-looking, Granny,' I said. Well, so Granny said, 'Oh dear, that's bad, that's very bad! I tell you this because I don't want you to make a fool of yourself over him. Oh, what terrible times we're living in! A poor lodger and he would be good-looking too! Not like the old days!'

"Granny would have liked everything to be like the old days! She was younger in the old days, the sun was much warmer in the old days, the milk didn't turn so quickly in the old days—everything was so much better in the old days! Well, I just sat there and said nothing, but all the time I was thinking, Why is Granny warning me? Why did she ask whether our lodger was young and good-looking? Well, anyway, the thought only crossed my mind, and soon

I was counting my stitches again (I was knitting a stocking at the time), and forgot all about it.

"Well, one morning our lodger came down to remind us that we had promised to paper his room for him. One thing led to another, for Granny likes talking to people and then she told me to go to her bedroom and fetch her accounts. I jumped up, blushed all over—I don't know why—and forgot that I was pinned to Granny. I never thought of undoing the pin quietly, so that our lodger shouldn't notice, but dashed off so quickly that I pulled Granny's armchair after me. When I saw that our lodger knew all about me now, I got red in the face, stopped dead as though rooted to the floor, and suddenly burst into tears. I felt so ashamed and miserable at that moment that I wished I was dead! Granny shouted at me, 'What are you standing there like that for?' But that made me cry worse than ever. When our lodger saw that I was ashamed on account of him, he took his leave and went away at once!

"Ever since that morning I've nearly fainted every time I've heard a noise in the passage. It must be the lodger, I'd think, and I'd undo the pin very quietly just in case it was he. But it never was our lodger. He never came. After a fortnight our lodger sent word with Fyokla that he had a lot of French books, and that they were all good books which he knew we would enjoy reading, and that he would be glad to know whether Granny would like me to choose a book to read to her because he was sure she must be bored. Granny accepted our lodger's kind offer gratefully, but she kept asking me whether the books were *good* books, for if the books were bad, she wouldn't let me read them because she didn't want me to get wrong ideas into my head."

"'What wrong ideas, Granny? What's wrong with those books?'

"'Oh,' she said, 'it's all about how young men seduce decent girls, and how on the excuse that they want to marry them, they elope with them and then leave them to their own fate, and how the poor creatures all come to a bad end. I've read a great many such books,' said Granny, 'and everything is described so beautifully in them that I used to keep awake all night, reading them on the quiet. So mind you don't read them, Nastenka,' she said. 'What books has he sent?'

"'They're all novels by Walter Scott, Granny.'

"'Walter Scott's novels? Are you certain, Nastenka, there isn't some trickery there? Make sure, dear, he hasn't put a love letter in one of them.'

"'No, Granny,' I said, 'there's no love letter.'

"'Oh, dear,' said Granny, 'look in the binding, there's a good girl. Sometimes they stuff it in the binding, the scoundrels.'

"'No, Granny, there's nothing in the binding.'

"'Well, that's all right then!'

"So we started reading Walter Scott, and in a month or so we had read through almost half of his novels. Then he sent us some more books. He sent us Pushkin. And in the end I didn't know what to do if I had no book to read, and I gave up dreaming of marrying a prince of royal blood.

"So it went on till one day I happened to meet our lodger on the stairs. Granny had sent me to fetch something. He stopped. I blushed and he blushed. However, he laughed, said good morning to me, asked me how Granny was, and then said, 'Well, have you read the books?' I said, 'Yes, we have.' 'Which did you like best?' I said, 'I liked *Ivanhoe* and Pushkin best of all.' That was all that happened that time.

"A week later I again happened to meet him on the stairs. That time Granny had not sent me for anything, but I had gone up to fetch something myself. It was past two in the afternoon, when our lodger usually came home. 'Good afternoon,' he said. 'Good afternoon,' I said.

"'Don't you feel awfully bored sitting with your Granny all day?' he said.

"The moment he asked me that, I blushed—I don't know why. I felt awfully ashamed, and hurt, too, because I suppose it was clear that even strangers were beginning to wonder how I could sit all day long pinned to my Granny. I wanted to go away without answering, but I just couldn't summon enough strength to do that.

"'Look here,' he said, 'you're a nice girl, and I hope you don't mind my telling you that I'm more anxious even than your Granny that you should be happy. Have you no girl friends at all whom you'd like to visit?'

"I told him I hadn't any. I had only one, Mashenka, but she had gone away to Pskov.

"'Would you like to go to the theatre with me?' he asked.

"'To the theatre? But what about Granny?'

"'Couldn't you come without her knowing anything about it?'

"'No, sir,' I said. 'I don't want to deceive my Granny. Goodbye.'

"'Goodbye,' he said, and went upstairs without another word.

"After dinner, however, he came down to see us. He sat down and had a long talk with Granny. He asked her whether she ever went out, whether she had any friends, and then suddenly he said, 'I've taken a box for the opera for this evening. They're giving *The Barber of Seville.* Some friends of mine wanted to come, but they couldn't manage it, and now the tickets are left on my hands.'

"'*The Barber of Seville!*' cried my Granny. 'Why, is it the same barber they used to act in the old days?'

"'Yes,' he replied, 'it's the same barber,' and he glanced at me.

"Of course I understood everything. I blushed and my heart began thumping in anticipation.

"'Oh,' said Granny, 'I know all about him! I used to play Rosina myself in the old days at private theatricals.'

"'Would you like to go today?' said the lodger. 'My ticket will be wasted if nobody comes.'

"'Yes, I suppose we could go,' said Granny. 'Why shouldn't we? My Nastenka has never been to a theatre before.'

"My goodness, wasn't I glad! We started getting ready at once, put on our best clothes, and went off. Granny couldn't see anything, of course, because she is blind, but she wanted to hear the music, and, besides, she's really very kind-hearted, the old dear. She wanted me to go and enjoy myself, for we would never have gone by ourselves. Well, I won't tell you what my impression of *The Barber of Seville* was. I'll merely mention that our lodger looked at me so nicely the whole evening, and he spoke so nicely to me that I guessed at once that he had only meant to try me out in the afternoon, to see whether I would have gone with him alone. Oh, I was so happy! I went to bed feeling so proud, so gay, and my heart was beating so fast that I felt a little feverish and raved all night about *The Barber of Seville.*

"I thought he'd come and see us more and more often after that, but it turned out quite differently. He almost stopped coming altogether. He'd come down once a month, perhaps, and even then only to invite us to the theatre. We went twice to the theatre with him. Only I wasn't a bit happy about it. I could see that he was simply sorry for me because I was treated so abominably by my grandmother, and that otherwise he wasn't interested in me at all. So it went on till I couldn't bear it any longer: I couldn't sit still for a minute, I couldn't read anything, I couldn't work. Sometimes I'd burst out laughing and do something just to annoy Granny, and sometimes I'd just burst into tears. In the end I got terribly thin and was nearly ill. The opera season was over, and our lodger stopped coming down to see us altogether, and when we did meet—always on the stairs, of course—he'd just bow to me silently, and look very serious as though he did not want to talk to me, and he'd be out on the front steps while I'd still be standing half way up the stairs, red as a cherry, for every time I met him all my blood rushed to my head.

"Well, I've almost finished. Just a year ago, in May, our lodger came down to our drawing-room and told Granny that he had finished his business in Petersburg and was leaving for Moscow where he would have to stay a whole year. When I heard that I went pale and sank back in my chair as though in a faint. Granny did not notice anything, and he, having told us that he was giving up his room, took his leave and went away.

"What was I to do? I thought and thought, worried and worried, and at last I made up my mind. As he was leaving tomorrow, I decided to make an end to it all after Granny had gone to bed. I tied up all my clothes in a bundle and, more dead than alive, went upstairs with my bundle to see our lodger. I suppose it must have taken me a whole hour to walk up the stairs to the attic. When I opened the door of his room, he cried out as he looked at me. He thought I was a ghost. He quickly fetched a glass of water for me, for I could hardly stand on my feet. My heart was beating very fast, my head ached terribly, and I felt all in a daze. When I recovered a little, I just put my bundle on his bed, sat down beside it, buried my face in my hands, and burst into a flood of tears. He seemed to have understood everything at once, and he stood before me looking so pale and gazing at me so sadly that my heart nearly broke.

"'Listen, Nastenka,' he said, 'I can't do anything now. I'm a poor man. I haven't got anything at present, not even a decent job. How would we live, if I were to marry you?'

"We talked for a long time, and in the end I worked myself up into a real frenzy and told him that I couldn't go on living with my grandmother any more, that I'd run away from her, that I didn't want to be fastened by a pin all my life, and that, if he liked, I'd go to Moscow with him because I couldn't live without him. Shame, love, pride seemed to speak in me all at once, and I fell on the bed almost in convulsions. I was so afraid that he might refuse to take me!

"He sat in silence for a few minutes, then he got up, went to me, and took me by the hand.

"'Listen to me, darling Nastenka,' he began, also speaking through his tears, 'I promise you solemnly that if at any time I am in a position to marry, you are the only girl in the world I would marry. I assure you that now you are the only one who could make me happy. Now, listen. I'm leaving for Moscow and I shall be away exactly one year. I hope to settle my affairs by that time. When I come back, and if you still love me, I swear to you that we shall be married. I can't possibly marry you now. It is out of the question. And I have no right to make any promises to you. But I repeat that if I can't marry you after one year, I shall certainly marry you sometime. Provided of course you still want to marry me and don't prefer someone else, for I cannot and I dare not bind you by any sort of promise.'

"That was what he told me, and the next day he left. We agreed not to say anything about it to Granny. He insisted on that. Well, that's almost the end of my story. A year has now passed, exactly one year. He is in Petersburg now, he's been here three days, and—and—"

"And what?" I cried, impatient to hear the end.

"And he hasn't turned up so far," said Nastenka, making a great effort to keep calm. "I haven't heard a word from him."

Here she stopped, paused a little, lowered her pretty head, and, burying her face in her hands, suddenly burst out sobbing so bitterly that my heart bled to hear it.

I had never expected such an ending.

"Nastenka," I began timidly, in an imploring voice, "for goodness sake, Nastenka, don't cry! How can you tell? Perhaps he hasn't arrived yet. . . ."

"He has, he has!" Nastenka exclaimed. "I know he's here. We made an arrangement the night before he left. After our talk we went for a walk here on the embankment. It was ten o'clock. We sat on this seat. I was no longer crying then. I felt so happy listening to him! He said that immediately on his return he would come to see us, and if I still wanted to marry him, we'd tell Granny everything. Well he's back now, I know he is, but he hasn't come, he hasn't come!"

And once more she burst into tears.

"Good heavens, isn't there anything we can do?" I cried, jumping up from the seat in utter despair. "Tell me, Nastenka, couldn't I go and see him?"

"You think you could?" she said, raising her head.

"No, of course not," I replied, checking myself. "But, look here, why not write him a letter?"

"No, no, that's impossible!" she replied firmly, but lowering her head and not looking at me.

"Why is it impossible? What's wrong with it?" I went on pleading with her, the idea having rather appealed to me. "It all depends what sort of a letter it is, Nastenka. There are letters and letters, and—oh, Nastenka, believe me it's true. Trust me, Nastenka, please! I wouldn't give you bad advice. It can all be arranged. It was you who took the first step, wasn't it? Well, why not now—?"

"No; it's quite impossible! It would look as if I was thrusting myself on him. . . ."

"But, darling Nastenka," I interrupted her, and I couldn't help smiling, "believe me, you're wrong, quite wrong. You're absolutely justified in writing to him, for he made a promise to you. Besides, I can see from what you've told me that he is a nice man, that he has behaved decently," I went on, carried away by the logic of my own reasoning and my own convictions. "For what did he do? He bound himself by a promise. He said that he wouldn't marry anyone but you, if, that is, he ever married at all. But he left you free to decide whether or not you want to marry him, to refuse him at any moment. This being so, there's no reason on earth why you shouldn't make the first move. You're entitled to do so, and you have an advantage over him, if, for instance, you should choose to release him from his promise. . . ."

"Look, how would you have written—?"

"What?"

"Such a letter."

"Well, I'd have started, 'Dear Sir . . .' "

"Must it begin with 'Dear Sir'?"

"Of course! I mean, not necessarily. . . . You could . . ."

"Never mind. How would you go on?"

" 'Dear Sir, you will pardon me for . . .' No, I don't think you should apologise for writing to him. The circumstances themselves fully justify your letter. Write simply: 'I am writing to you. Forgive me for my impatience, but all the year I have lived in such happy anticipation of your return that it is hardly surprising that I cannot bear the suspense even one day longer. Now that you are back, I cannot help wondering whether you have not after all changed your mind. If that is so, then my letter will tell you that I quite understand and that I am not blaming you for anything. I do not blame you that I have no power over your heart: such seems to be my fate. You are an honourable man. I know you will not be angry with me or smile at my impatience. Remember that it is a poor girl who is writing to you, that she is all alone in the world, that she has no one to tell her what to do or give her any advice, and that she herself never did know how to control her heart. But forgive me that doubt should have stolen even for one moment into my heart. I know that even in your thoughts you are quite incapable of hurting her who loved you so much and who still loves you.' "

"Yes, yes, that's exactly what I was thinking!" Nastenka cried, her eyes beaming with joy. "Oh, you've put an end to all my doubts. I'm sure God must have sent you to me. Thank you, thank you!"

"What are you thanking me for? Because God has sent me to you?" I replied, gazing delighted at her sweet, happy face.

"Yes, for that too."

"Oh, Nastenka, aren't we sometimes grateful to people only because they live with us? Well, I'm grateful to you for having met you. I'm grateful to you because I shall remember you all my life!"

"All right, all right! Now listen to me carefully: I arranged with him that he'd let me know as soon as he came back by leaving a letter for me at the house of some people I know—they are very nice, simple people who know nothing about the whole thing; and that if he couldn't write me a letter because one can't say all one wants in a letter, he'd come here, where we had arranged to meet, at exactly ten o'clock on the very first day of his arrival. Now, I know he has arrived, but for two days he hasn't turned up, nor have I had a letter from him. I can't possibly get away from Granny in the morning. So please take my letter tomorrow to the kind people I told you of, and they'll see that it reaches him. And if there is a reply, you could bring it yourself tomorrow evening at ten o'clock."

"But the letter! What about the letter? You must write the letter first, which means that I couldn't take it before the day after tomorrow."

"The letter . . . ?" said Nastenka, looking a little confused. "Oh, the letter! . . . Well—"

But she didn't finish. At first she turned her pretty face away from me, then she blushed like a rose, and then all of a sudden I felt that the letter which she must have written long before was in my hand. It was in a sealed envelope. A strangely familiar, sweet, lovely memory flashed through my mind.

"Ro-o-si-i-na-a!" I began.

"Rosina!" both of us burst out singing. I almost embraced her with delight, and she blushed as only she could blush and laughed through the tears which trembled on her dark eyelashes like pearls.

"Well, that's enough," she said, speaking rapidly. "Goodbye now. Here's the letter and here's the address where you have to take it. Goodbye! Till tomorrow!"

She pressed both my hands warmly, nodded her head, and

darted away down her side-street. I remained standing in the same place for a long time, following her with my eyes.

"Till tomorrow! Till tomorrow!" flashed through my mind as she disappeared from sight.

THIRD NIGHT

It was a sad and dismal day today, rainy, without a ray of hope, just like the long days of my old age which I know will be as sad and dismal. Strange thoughts are crowding into my head, my heart is full of gloomy forebodings, questions too vague to be grasped clearly fill my mind, and somehow I've neither the power nor the will to resolve them. No, I shall never be able to solve it all!

We are not going to meet today. Last night, when we said good-bye, the sky was beginning to be overcast, and a mist was rising. I observed that the weather did not look too promising for tomorrow, but she made no answer. She did not wish to say anything to cloud her own happy expectations. For her this day is bright and full of sunshine, and not one cloud will obscure her happiness.

"If it rains," she said, "we shan't meet! I shan't come!"

I thought she would not pay any attention to the rain today, but she never came.

Yesterday we had met for the third time. It was our third white night. . . .

But how beautiful people are when they are gay and happy! How brimful of love their hearts are! It is as though they wanted to pour their hearts into the heart of another human being, as though they wanted the whole world to be gay and laugh with them. And how infectious that gaiety is! There was so much joy in her words yesterday, so much goodness in her heart towards me. How sweet she was to me, how hard she tried to be nice to me, how she comforted and soothed my heart! Oh, how sweet a woman can be to you when she is happy! And I? Why, I was completely taken in. I thought she—

But how on earth could I have thought it? How could I have been so blind, when everything had already been taken by another, when nothing belonged to me? Why, even that tenderness of hers, that anxiety, that love—yes, that love for me was nothing more than the outward manifestation of her happiness at the thought of her meeting with someone else, her desire to force her happiness upon me too. When he did not turn up, when we waited in vain, she frowned, she lost heart, she was filled with alarm. All her movements, all her words, seemed to have lost their liveliness, their playfulness, their gaiety. And the strange thing was that she seemed doubly anxious to please me, as though out of an instinctive desire to lavish upon me what she so dearly desired for herself, but what she feared would never be hers. My Nastenka was so nervous and in such an agonising dread that at last she seemed to have realised that I loved her and took pity upon my unhappy love. It is always so: when we are unhappy we feel more strongly the unhappiness of others; our feeling is not shattered, but becomes concentrated. . . .

I came to her with a full heart; I could scarcely wait for our meeting. I had no presentiment of how I would be feeling now. I little dreamt that it would all end quite differently. She was beaming with happiness. She was expecting an answer to her letter. The answer was he himself. He was bound to come; he had to come running in answer to her call. She arrived a whole hour before me. At first she kept on laughing at everything; every word of mine provoked a peal of laughter from her. I began talking, but lapsed into silence.

"Do you know why I'm so happy?" she said. "Do you know why I'm so glad when I look at you? Do you know why I love you so today?"

"Well?" I asked, and my heart trembled.

"I love you so, because you haven't fallen in love with me. Another man in your place would, I'm sure, have begun to pester me, to worry me. He would have been sighing, he would have looked so pathetic, but you're so sweet!"

Here she clasped my hand with such force that I almost cried out. She laughed.

"Oh, what a good friend you are!" she began a minute later, speaking very seriously. "You're a real godsend to me. What would

I have done if you'd not been with me now? How unselfish you are! How truly you love me! When I am married, we shall be such good friends. You'll be more than a brother to me. I shall love you almost as I love him! . . ."

Somehow I couldn't help feeling terribly sad at that moment. However, something resembling laughter stirred in my soul.

"Your nerves are on edge," I said. "You're afraid. You don't think he'll come."

"Goodness, what nonsense you talk!" she said. "If I hadn't been so happy, I do believe I'd have burst out crying to hear you express such doubts, to hear you reproaching me like that. You've given me an idea, though. And I admit you've given me a lot to think about, but I shall think about it later. I don't mind telling you frankly that you're quite right. Yes, I'm not quite myself tonight. I'm in awful suspense, and every little thing jars on me, excites me, but please don't let us discuss my feelings! . . ."

At that moment we heard footsteps, and a man loomed out of the darkness. He was coming in our direction. She almost cried out. I released her hand and made a movement as though I were beginning to back away. But we were both wrong: it was not he.

"What are you so afraid of? Why did you let go of my hand?" she said, giving me her hand again. "What does it matter? We'll meet him together. I want him to see how we love one another."

"How we love one another?" I cried.

"Oh, Nastenka, Nastenka," I thought, "how much you've said in that word! Such love, Nastenka, at *certain* moments makes one's heart ache and plunges one's spirit into gloom. Your hand is cold, but mine burns like fire. How blind you are, Nastenka! How unbearable a happy person sometimes is! But I'm afraid I could not be angry with you, Nastenka!"

At last my heart overflowed.

"Do you know, Nastenka," I cried, "do you know what I've gone through all day?"

"Why? What is it? Tell me quickly! Why haven't you said anything about it before?"

"Well, first of all, Nastenka, after I had carried out all your commissions, taken the letter, seen your good friends, I—I went home and—and went to bed."

"Is that all?" she interrupted, laughing.

"Yes, almost all," I replied, making an effort to keep calm, for I already felt foolish tears starting to my eyes. "I woke an hour before we were due to meet. But I don't seem to have really slept at all. I don't know how to describe the curious sensation I had. I seemed to be on my way here. I was going to tell you everything. I had an odd feeling as though time had suddenly stopped, as though one feeling, one sensation, would from that moment go on and on for all eternity, as though my whole life had come to a standstill. . . . When I woke up it seemed to me that some snatch of a tune I had known for a long time, I had heard somewhere before but had forgotten, a melody of great sweetness, was coming back to me now. It seemed to me that it had been trying to emerge from my soul all my life, and only now—"

"Goodness," Nastenka interrupted, "what's all this about? I don't understand a word of it."

"Oh, Nastenka, I wanted somehow to convey that strange sensation to you," I began in a plaintive voice, in which there still lurked some hope, though I'm afraid a very faint one.

"Don't, please don't!" she said, and in a trice she guessed everything, the little rogue.

She became on a sudden somehow extraordinarily talkative, gay, playful. She took my arm, laughed, insisted that I should laugh too, and every halting word I uttered evoked a long loud peal of laughter from her. I was beginning to feel angry; she suddenly began flirting.

"Listen," she said, "I'm really beginning to be a little annoyed with you for not being in love with me. What am I to think of you after that? But, sir, if you insist on being so strong-minded, you should at least show your appreciation of me for being such a simple girl. I tell you everything, absolutely everything. Any silly old thing that comes into my head."

"Listen, I think it's striking eleven!" I said, as the clock from some distant city tower began slowly to strike the hour.

She stopped suddenly, left off laughing, and began to count.

"Yes," she said at last in a hesitating, unsteady voice, "it's eleven."

I regretted at once that I had frightened her. It was brutal of me to make her count the strokes. I cursed myself for my uncontrolled fit of malice. I felt sorry for her, and I did not know how to atone for my inexcusable behaviour. I did my best to comfort her. I tried hard to think of some excuse for his failure to come. I argued. I reasoned with her. It was the easiest thing in the world to deceive her at that moment! Indeed, who would not be glad of any word of comfort at such a moment? Who would not be overjoyed at the faintest glimmer of an excuse?

"The whole thing's absurd!" I began, feeling more and more carried away by my own enthusiasm and full of admiration for the extraordinary clarity of my own arguments. "He couldn't possibly have come today. You've got me so muddled and confused, Nastenka, that I've lost count of the time. Why, don't you see? He's scarcely had time to receive your letter. Now, suppose that for some reason he can't come today. Suppose he's going to write to you. Well, in that case you couldn't possibly get his letter till tomorrow. I'll go and fetch it for you early tomorrow morning and let you know at once. Don't you see? A thousand things may have happened: he may have been out when your letter arrived, and for all we know he may not have read it even yet. Anything may have happened."

"Yes, yes!" said Nastenka. "I never thought of that. Of course anything may have happened," she went on in a most acquiescent voice, but in which, like some jarring note, another faintly perceptible thought was hidden away. "Yes, please do that. Go there as soon as possible tomorrow morning, and if you get anything let me know at once. You know where I live, don't you?"

And she began repeating her address to me.

Then she became suddenly so sweet, so shy with me. She seemed to listen attentively to what I was saying to her; but when I asked her some question, she made no reply, grew confused, and turned her head away. I peered into her eyes. Why, of course! She was crying.

"How can you? How can you? Oh, what a child you are! What childishness! There, there, stop crying please!"

She tried to smile, to compose herself, but her chin was still trembling, and her bosom still rising and falling.

"I'm thinking of you," she said to me after a minute's silence. "You're so good that I'd have to have a heart of stone not to feel it. Do you know what has just occurred to me? I was comparing the two of you in my mind. Why isn't he you? Why isn't he like you? He's not as good as you, though I love him more than you."

I said nothing in reply. She seemed to be waiting for me to say something.

"Of course it's probably quite true that I don't know him very well. No, I don't understand him very well. You see, I seemed always a little afraid of him. He was always so serious, and I couldn't help thinking proud as well. I realise of course that he merely looked like that. I know there's more tenderness in his heart than in mine. I can't forget the way he looked at me when—you remember?—I came to him with my bundle. But all the same I seem to look up to him a little too much, and that doesn't seem as if we were quite equals, does it?"

"No, Nastenka, no," I replied. "It does not mean that you are not equals. It merely means that you love him more than anything in the world, far more than yourself even."

"Yes, I suppose that is so," said Nastenka. "But do you know what I think? Only I'm not speaking of him now, but just in general. I've been thinking for a long time, why aren't we all just like brothers to one another. Why does even the best of us seem to hide something from other people and keep something back from them? Why don't we say straight out what's in our hearts, if we know that our words will not be spoken in vain? As it is, everyone seems to look as though he were much harder than he really is. It is as though we were all afraid that our feelings would be hurt if we revealed them too soon."

"Oh, Nastenka, you're quite right, but there are many reasons for that," I interrupted, for I knew that I myself was suppressing my feelings at that moment more than ever before.

"No, no!" she replied with great feeling. "You, for instance, are not like that. I really don't know how to tell you what I feel. But it seems to me, for instance—I mean I can't help feeling that you—that just at this moment you're making some sacrifice for me," she added shyly, with a quick glance at me. "Please forgive me for telling you that. You know I am such a simple girl. I haven't had much experience of the world and I really don't know sometimes how to express myself," she added in a voice that trembled from some hidden emotion, trying to smile at the same time. "But I just wanted to tell you that I'm grateful, that I'm aware of it too. . . . Oh, may God grant you happiness for that! I feel that what you told me about your dreamer is not true, I mean it has nothing to do with you. You are recovering, you're quite different from the man you described yourself to be. If you ever fall in love, may you be happy with her. I don't need to wish her anything, for she'll be happy with you. I know because I'm a woman myself, so you must believe me when I tell you so."

She fell silent and pressed my hand warmly. I was too moved to say anything. A few minutes passed.

"Yes, it seems he won't come tonight," she said at last, raising her head. "It's late."

"He'll come tomorrow," I said in a very firm, confident voice.

"Yes," she added, looking cheerful again, "I realise myself now that he couldn't possibly come till tomorrow. Well, goodbye! Till tomorrow! I may not come, if it rains. But the day after tomorrow I shall come whatever happens. You'll be here for certain, won't you? I want to see you. I'll tell you everything."

And later, when we said goodbye to each other, she gave me her hand and said, looking serenely at me—

"Now we shall always be together, shan't we?"

Oh, Nastenka, Nastenka, if only you knew how terribly lonely I am now!

When the clock struck nine, I could remain in my room no longer. I dressed and went out in spite of the bad weather. I was there. I sat on our seat. I went to her street, but I felt ashamed and went back when I was only a few yards from her house without even looking at her windows. What a day! Damp and dreary. If it had been fine, I should have walked about all night.

But—till tomorrow, till tomorrow! Tomorrow she'll tell me everything.

There was no letter for her today, though. However, there's nothing surprising in that. They must be together by now. . . .

FOURTH NIGHT

Good Lord, how strangely the whole thing has ended! What a frightful ending!

I arrived at nine o'clock. She was already there. I noticed her a long way off. She was standing, leaning with her elbows on the railing of the embankment, just as she had been standing the first time I saw her, and she did not hear me when I came up to her.

"Nastenka!" I called her, restraining my agitation with difficulty.

She turned round to me quickly.

"Well?" she said. "Well? Tell me quickly!"

I looked at her utterly bewildered.

"Well, where's the letter? Haven't you brought the letter?" she repeated, gripping the railing with her hand.

"No, I haven't got any letter," I said at last. "Hasn't he come?"

She turned terribly pale and stared at me for a long time without moving. I had shattered her last hope.

"Well, it doesn't matter," she said at last in a strangled voice. "If he leaves me like that, then perhaps it's best to forget him!"

She dropped her eyes, then tried to look at me, but couldn't do it. For a few more minutes she tried to pull herself together, then she turned away from me suddenly, leaned on the railing with her elbows, and burst into tears.

"Come, come," I began, but as I looked at her I hadn't the heart to go on. And, besides, what could I have said to her?

"Don't try to comfort me," she said, weeping. "Don't tell me he'll come—that he hasn't deserted me so cruelly and so inhumanly as he has. Why? Why did he do it? Surely there was nothing in my letter, in that unhappy letter of mine, was there?"

Here her voice was broken by sobs. My heart bled as I looked at her.

"Oh, how horribly cruel it is!" she began again. "And not a line, not a line! If he'd just written to say that he didn't want me, that he rejected me, but not to write a single line in three days! How easy it is for him to slight and insult a poor defenceless girl whose only fault is that she loves him! Oh, what I've been through these three days! Lord, when I think that it was I who went to him the first time, when I think how I humiliated myself before him, how I cried, how I implored him for a little love! And after that! . . . But, look here," she said, turning to me, and her black eyes flashed, "there's something wrong! There must be something wrong! It's not natural! Either you are mistaken or I am. Perhaps he didn't get my letter. Perhaps he still doesn't know anything. Tell me, for heaven's sake, explain it to me—I can't understand it—how could he have behaved so atrociously to me. Not one word! Why, people show more pity to the lowest creature on earth! Perhaps he has heard something, perhaps someone has told him something about me," she cried, turning to me for an answer: "What do you think?"

"Listen, Nastenka, I'll go and see him tomorrow on your behalf."

"Well?"

"I'll try and find out from him what the position is. I'll tell him everything."

"Well? Well?"

"You write a letter. Don't refuse, Nastenka, don't refuse! I'll make him respect your action. He'll learn everything, and if—"

"No, my friend, no," she interrupted. "Enough! Not another word, not another word from me, not a line—I've had enough! I don't know him any more, I don't love him any more, I'll f-f-forget him."

She did not finish.

"Calm yourself, calm yourself, my dear! Sit here, Nastenka," I said, making her sit down on the seat.

"But I am calm. I tell you this is nothing. It's only tears—they'll soon dry. You don't really think I'm going to do away with myself, drown myself, do you?"

My heart was full: I tried to speak, but I couldn't.

"Listen," she said, taking my hand, "you wouldn't have behaved like this, would you? You wouldn't have abandoned a girl who had come to you of her own free will, you wouldn't have made a cruel mockery of her weak foolish heart, would you? You would have taken care of her. You would have reminded yourself that she had nobody in the whole world, that she was so inexperienced, that she could not prevent herself from falling in love with you, that she couldn't help it, that it wasn't her fault—no, it wasn't her fault!—that she had not done anything wrong. Oh, dear God, dear God . . ."

"Nastenka," I cried, unable to restrain myself any longer, "this is more than I can endure! It's sheer torture to me! You wound me to the heart, Nastenka! I can't be silent! I must speak! I must tell you of all the anguish in my heart!"

Saying this, I raised myself from the seat. She took my hand and looked at me in surprise.

"What's the matter?" she said at last.

"Listen to me, Nastenka," I said firmly, "listen to me, please! What I'm going to say to you now is all nonsense. It is foolish. It cannot be. I know it will never happen, but I cannot remain silent. In the name of all that you're suffering now, I beseech you beforehand to forgive me!"

"Well, what is it? What is it?" she demanded, and she stopped crying and looked intently at me, a strange gleam of curiosity in her startled eyes. "What is the matter with you?"

"It's out of the question, I know, but—I love you, Nastenka! That is what's the matter with me. Now you know everything!" I said, with a despairing wave of my hand. "Now you can judge for yourself whether you ought to go on talking to me as you did just now, and—what is perhaps even more important—whether you ought to listen to what I'm going to say to you."

"Well, what about it?" Nastenka interrupted. "Of course I knew long ago that you loved me, only I always thought that—well, that you loved me in the ordinary way, I mean that you were just fond of me. Oh dear, oh dear! . . ."

"At first it was in the ordinary way, Nastenka, but now—now I'm in the same position as you were when you went to him with your bundle that night. I'm in a worse position Nastenka, because he wasn't in love with anyone at the time, and you—you are."

"Goodness, what are you saying to me! I really can't understand you. But, look, what has made you—I mean, why did you—and so suddenly too! Oh dear, I'm talking such nonsense! But you—"

And Nastenka got completely confused. Her cheeks were flushed. She dropped her eyes.

"What's to be done, Nastenka? What can I do about it? It's entirely my fault, of course. I've taken an unfair advantage of—But no—no, Nastenka, it isn't my fault. I know it isn't. I feel it isn't because my heart tells me I'm right, because I could never do anything to hurt you, because I could do nothing that you would ever take offence at. I was your friend? Well, I still am your friend. I have not been unfaithful to anyone. You see, I'm crying, Nastenka. But never mind. What if tears do run down my cheeks? Let them. They don't hurt anyone. They'll soon dry, Nastenka."

"But sit down, do sit down, please," she said, making me sit down on the seat. "Oh dear, oh dear!"

"No, Nastenka, I shan't sit down. I can't stay here any longer. You'll never see me again. I'll say what I have to say and go away. I only want to say that you'd never have found out that I loved you. I'd never have told my secret to a living soul. I'd never have tormented you with my egoism at such a moment. Never! But I could not bear to be silent now. It was you who began talking about it. It's your fault, not mine. You just can't drive me away from you."

"But I'm not—I'm not driving you away from me!" Nastenka said, doing her best, poor child, not to show how embarrassed she was.

"You are not driving me away? No—but I meant to run away from you myself. And I will go away. I will. Only first let me tell you everything, for, you see, when you were talking to me here, I couldn't sit still; when you cried here, when you tormented yourself because—well, because (I'd better say it, Nastenka)—because you were jilted, because your love was slighted and disregarded, I felt that in my heart there was so much love for you, Nastenka, so much love! And I so bitterly resented not being able to do anything to help you with my love that—that my heart was bursting and I—I couldn't be silent any longer, Nastenka. I had to speak!"

"Yes, yes, tell me everything, do speak to me like that!" said Nastenka with a gesture that touched me deeply. "It may seem strange to you that I should be speaking to you like this, but—do say what you have to say! I will tell you afterwards. I'll tell you everything!"

"You are sorry for me, Nastenka. You're just sorry for me, my dear, dear friend! Well, what's done is done. No use crying over spilt milk, is it? Well, so you know everything now. At any rate, that's something to start with. All right. Everything's fine now. Only, please, listen. When you were sitting here, when you were crying, I thought to myself (Oh, do let me tell you what I was thinking!), I thought that (I know of course how utterly impossible it is, Nastenka)—I thought that you—that you somehow—I mean quite apart from anything else—that you no longer cared for him. If that is so, then—I already thought of that yesterday, Nastenka, and the day before yesterday—then I would—I most certainly would have done my best to make you care for me. You said yourself, Nastenka—you did say it several times, didn't you?—that you almost loved me. Well, what more is there to tell you? That's really all I wanted to say. All that remains to be said is what would happen if you fell in love with me—that's all—nothing more! Now listen to me, my friend—for you are my friend, aren't you?—I am of course an ordinary sort of fellow, poor and insignificant, but that doesn't matter (I'm afraid I don't seem to be putting it very well, Nastenka, because I'm so confused), what matters is that I'd love you so well, so well, Nastenka, that even if you still loved him and went on loving the man I don't know, my love would never be a burden to you. All you'd feel, all you'd be conscious of every minute, is that a very grateful heart was beating at your side, Nastenka, an ardent heart which for your sake—Oh, Nastenka, Nastenka, what have you done to me?"

"Don't cry, I don't want you to cry," said Nastenka, rising quickly from the seat. "Come along, get up, come with me. Don't cry, don't cry," she said, drying my tears with her handkerchief. "There, come along now. Perhaps I'll tell you something. Well, if he has really given me up, if he has forgotten me, then though I still love him (and I don't want to deceive you)—But, listen, answer me! If, for instance, I were to fall in love with you—I mean, if only I—Oh, my friend, my friend, when I think, when I only think how I must have offended you when I laughed at your love, when I praised you for not falling in love with me! Oh dear, why didn't I foresee it? Why didn't I foresee it? How could I have been so stupid? But never mind, I've made up my mind now. I'm going to tell you everything."

"Look here, Nastenka, do you know what? I'll go away. Yes, I'll go away! I can see that I'm simply tormenting you. Now you're sorry you've been making fun of me, and I hate to think—yes, I simply hate to think that in addition to your own sorrow—Of course, it's all my fault, Nastenka, it's all my fault, but—goodbye!"

"Stop! Listen to me first, please. You can wait, can't you?"

"Wait? What should I wait for? What do you mean?"

"You see, I love him, but that will pass. It must pass. It's quite impossible for it not to pass. As a matter of fact, it's already passing. I can feel it. Who knows, maybe it'll be over today, for I hate him! Yes, I hate him because he has slighted me, while you were weeping with me. I hate him because you haven't let me down as he has, because you love me, while he has never really loved me, because—well, because I love you too. Yes, I love you! I love you as you love me. I've told you so before, haven't I? You heard me say it yourself. I love you because you're better than he is, because you're more honourable than he is, because he—"

She stopped crying at last, dried her eyes, and we continued our walk. I wanted to say something, but she kept asking me to wait. We were silent. At last she plucked up courage and began to speak.

"Look," she said, in a weak and trembling voice, in which, however, there was a strange note which pierced my heart and filled it with a sweet sensation of joy, "don't think I'm so fickle, so inconstant. Don't think that I can forget him so easily and so quickly, that I can be untrue to him. I have loved him for a whole year, and I swear I have never, never for a moment, been untrue to him even in thought. He has thought little of that, he has scorned me—well, I don't mind that. But he has also hurt my feelings and wrung my heart. I don't love him because I can only love what is generous, what is understanding, what is honourable, for I'm like that myself, and he's not worthy of me. Well, let's forget about him. I'd rather he behaved to me like that now than that I was disappointed later in my expectations and found out the sort of man he really was. Anyway, it's all over now. And, besides, my dear friend," she went on, pressing my hand, "who knows, perhaps my love for him was nothing but self-deception, nothing but imagination. Perhaps it started just as a joke, just as a bit of silly nonsense because I was constantly under Granny's supervision. Perhaps I ought to love another man and not him, quite a different man, a man who'd have pity on me, and—and—anyway," Nastenka broke off, overcome with emotion, "don't let's speak of it. Don't let's speak of it. I only wanted to tell you—I wanted to tell you that even if I do love him (no, did love him), even if in spite of this you still say—or rather feel that your love is so great that it could in time replace my love for him in my heart—if you really and truly have pity on me, if you won't leave me alone to my fate, without consolation, without hope, if you promise to love me always as you love me now, then I swear that my gratitude—that my love will in time be worthy of your love. Will you take my hand now?"

"Nastenka," I cried, my voice broken with sobs, "Nastenka! Oh, Nastenka!"

"All right, all right!" she said, making a great effort to speak calmly. "All right! That's enough! Now everything's been said, hasn't it? Hasn't it? Well, you are happy now, aren't you? And I too am happy. So don't let's talk about it any more. Just wait a little—have patience—spare me! Talk of something else, for God's sake!"

"Yes, Nastenka, yes! Of course don't let's talk about it. Now I'm happy. Well, Nastenka, do let's talk of something else. Come on, let's. I don't mind."

But we did not know what to talk about. We laughed, we cried, we said a thousand things without caring whether they made sense or not. One moment we walked along the pavement, and the next we suddenly turned back and crossed the road, then we stopped and crossed over to the embankment again. We were like children. . . .

"I'm living alone, now, Nastenka," I began, "but tomorrow—You know, of course, Nastenka, that I'm poor, don't you? I've only got twelve hundred roubles, but that doesn't matter."

"Of course not, and Granny has her pension, so that she won't be a burden to us. We'll have to take Granny, of course."

"Of course we'll take Granny! Only—there's Matryona."

"Goodness, I never thought of that! And we've got Fyokla!"

"Matryona is a good soul, only she has one fault: she has no imagination, Nastenka, none whatever! But I don't suppose that matters!"

"It makes no difference. They can live together. You'll move to our house tomorrow, won't you?"

"How do you mean? To your house? Oh, very well, I don't mind."

"I mean, you'll take our attic. I told you we have an attic, didn't I? It's empty now. We had a woman lodger, an old gentlewoman, but she's left, and I know Granny would like to let it to a young man. I said to her, 'Why a young man, Granny?' But she said, 'Why not? I'm old and I like young people about. You don't think I'm trying to get a husband for you, do you?' Well, I saw at once of course that that was what she had in mind."

"Good Lord, Nastenka!"

And we both laughed.

"Oh, well, never mind. But where do you live? I've forgotten."

I told her I lived near a certain bridge in Barannikov's house.

"It's a very big house, isn't it?"

"Yes, it's a very big house."

"Oh, yes, I know it. It's a nice house, but I still think you ought to move out of it and come and live with us as soon as possible."

"I'll do so tomorrow, Nastenka, tomorrow. I'm afraid I'm a little behindhand with my rent, but that doesn't matter. I shall be getting my salary soon and—"

"And you know I could be giving lessons. Yes, why not? I'll learn everything myself first and then give lessons."

"That's an excellent idea, Nastenka, an excellent idea! And I'll be getting a bonus soon. . . ."

"So tomorrow you'll be my lodger. . . ."

"Yes, and we'll go to *The Barber of Seville,* for I believe they're going to put it on again soon."

"Oh yes, I'd love to," said Nastenka, laughing. "Perhaps not *The Barber*, though. We'd better see something else."

"Oh, all right, something else then. I don't mind. I suppose something else would be better. You see, I didn't think—"

Talking like this, we walked along in a sort of a daze, in a mist, as though we did not know ourselves what was happening to us. One moment we would stop and go on talking in one place for a long time, and the next we would be walking again till we would find ourselves goodness knows where—and more laughter, more tears. Then Nastenka would suddenly decide that she ought to be going back home, and I would not dare to detain her, but would insist on accompanying her to her house. We would start on our way back, and in about a quarter of an hour would find ourselves on the embankment by our seat. Then she would sigh, and tears would come into her eyes again, and I would be plunged into despair and a chilly premonition of disaster would steal into my heart. But she would at once press my hand and drag me off again to walk, talk, chatter. . . .

"It's time—time I went home now," Nastenka said at last. "I think it must be awfully late. We've been behaving like children long enough!"

"Yes, of course, Nastenka. Only I don't suppose I shall be able to sleep now. No, I won't go home."

"I don't think I shall sleep, either. Only see me home, will you?"

"Of course, I'll see you home. . . ."

"On your word of honour? Because, you see, I must get back home some time, mustn't I?"

"On my word of honour!" I replied, laughing.

"All right, let's go."

"Let's go. Look at the sky, Nastenka, look! It'll be a lovely day tomorrow! What a blue sky! What a moon! Look, a yellow cloud is drifting over it. Look! Look! No, it has passed by. Look, Nastenka, look!"

But Nastenka did not look. She stood speechless, motionless. A minute later she clung somewhat timidly close to me. Her hand trembled in mine. I looked at her. She clung to me more closely.

At that moment a young man passed by us. He suddenly stopped, looked at us intently for a moment, and then again took a few steps towards us. My heart missed a beat.

"Nastenka," I said in an undertone, "who is it, Nastenka?"

"It's him!" she replied in a whisper, clinging to me still more closely, still more tremulously.

I could hardly stand up.

"Nastenka! Nastenka! It's you!" we heard a voice behind us, and at the same time the young man took a few steps towards us.

Lord, how she cried out! How she started! How she tore herself out of my hands and rushed to meet him! I stood and looked at them, utterly crushed. But no sooner had she given him her hand, no sooner had she thrown herself into his arms, than she suddenly turned to me again, and was at my side in a flash, faster than lightning, faster than the wind, and before I could recover from my surprise, flung her arms round my neck and kissed me ardently. Then, without uttering a word, she rushed back to him again, clasped his hands, and drew him after her.

I stood a long time, watching them walking away. At last both of them vanished from my sight.

MORNING

My nights came to an end with a morning. The weather was dreadful. It was pouring, and the rain kept beating dismally against my windowpanes. It was dark in the room; it was dull and dreary outside. My head ached. I felt giddy. I was beginning to feel feverish.

"A letter for you, sir," said Matryona, bending over me. "Came by the city post, it did, sir. The postman brought it."

"A letter? Who from?" I cried, jumping up from my chair.

"I don't know, sir, I'm sure. I suppose whoever sent it must have signed his name."

I broke the seal: the letter was from her!

> "Oh, forgive me, forgive me!" Nastenka wrote to me. "I beg you on my knees to forgive me! I deceived you and myself. It was all a dream, a delusion. I nearly died today thinking of you. Please, please forgive me!

"Don't blame me, for I haven't changed a bit towards you. I said I would love you, and I do love you now, I more than love you. Oh, if only I could love both of you at once! Oh, if only you were he!"

"Oh, if only he were you!" it flashed through my mind. "Those were your own words, Nastenka!"

"God knows what I would do for you now. I know how sad and unhappy you must be. I've treated you abominably, but when one loves, you know, an injury is soon forgotten. And you do love me!

"Thank you, yes! thank you for that love. For it remains imprinted in my memory like a sweet dream one remembers a long time after awakening. I shall never forget the moment when you opened your heart to me like a real friend, when you accepted the gift of my broken heart to take care of it, to cherish it, to heal it. If you forgive me, I promise you that the memory of you will always remain with me, that I shall be everlastingly grateful to you, and that my feeling of gratitude will never be erased from my heart. I shall treasure this memory, I'll be true to it. I shall never be unfaithful to it, I shall never be unfaithful to my heart. It is too constant for that. It returned so quickly yesterday to him to whom it has always belonged.

"We shall meet. You will come and see us. You will not leave us, will you? You'll always be my friend, my brother. And when you see me, you'll give me your hand, won't you? You will give it to me because you've forgiven me. You have, haven't you? You love me *as before,* don't you?

"Oh, yes, do love me! Don't ever forsake me, because I love you so at this moment, because I am worthy of your love, because I promise to deserve it—oh, my dear, dear friend! Next week I'm to be married to him. He has come back as much in love with me as ever. He has never forgotten me. You will not be angry with me because I have written about him, will you? I would like to come and see you with him. You will like him, won't you?

"Forgive me, remember and love your
Nastenka."

I read this letter over and over again. There were tears in my eyes. At last it dropped out of my hands, and I buried my face.

"Look, love, look!" Matryona called me.

"What is it, Matryona?"

"Why, I've swept all the cobwebs off the ceiling. Looks so lovely and clean, you could be wed, love, and have your wedding party here. You might just as well do it now as wait till it gets dirty again!"

I looked at Matryona. She was still hale and hearty, quite a *young-looking* old woman, in fact. But I don't know why all of a sudden she looked old and decrepit to me, with a wrinkled face and lustreless eyes. I don't know why, but all of a sudden my room, too, seemed to have grown as old as Matryona. The walls and floors looked discoloured, everything was dark and grimy, and the cobwebs were thicker than ever. I don't know why, but when I looked out of the window the house opposite, too, looked dilapidated and dingy, the plaster on its columns peeling and crumbling, its cornices blackened and full of cracks, and its bright brown walls disfigured by large white and yellow patches. Either the sun, appearing suddenly from behind the dark rainclouds, had hidden itself so quickly that everything had grown dark before my eyes again, or perhaps the whole sombre and melancholy perspective of my future flashed before my mind's eye at that moment, and I saw myself just as I was now fifteen years hence, only grown older, in the same room, living the same sort of solitary life, with the same Matryona, who had not grown a bit wiser in all those years.

But that I should feel any resentment against you, Nastenka! That I should cast a dark shadow over your bright, serene happiness! That I should chill and darken your heart with bitter reproaches, wound it with secret remorse, cause it to beat anxiously at the moment of bliss! That I should crush a single one of those delicate blooms which you will wear in your dark hair when you walk up the aisle to the altar with him! Oh no—never, never! May your sky be always clear, may your dear smile be always bright and happy, and may you be for ever blessed for that moment of bliss and happiness which you gave to another lonely and grateful heart!

Good Lord, only a *moment* of bliss? Isn't such a moment sufficient for the whole of a man's life?

The Honest Thief

From the Memoirs of an Unknown

One morning as I was leaving for my office, Agrafena, my cook, washerwoman, and housekeeper, came into my room and, to my great surprise, began a conversation with me. Until that morning this simple, ordinary woman of the people had been so uncommunicative that, except for a few words about my dinner each day, she had for the last six years scarcely uttered a word to me. At least I never heard her speak of anything else.

"I'd like to have a word with you, sir," she began abruptly. "Why don't you let the little room?"

"Which little room?"

"Why, as if you didn't know, sir. The one next to the kitchen, of course!"

"What for?"

"What for, sir? Why, don't you know? Because other people let their rooms, of course!"

"But who would take it?"

"Who would take it, sir? Why, surely, sir, you know who would take it. A lodger, of course."

"But, my good woman, who'd like to live in a cubbyhole like that? Why, it's nothing but a boxroom. I doubt if you could put a bed in it, and even if you could, there wouldn't be any room left to move about in."

"Why, sir, nobody wants to live in it. All he wants is a place to sleep in. He'd live on the windowsill."

"Which windowsill?"

"Why, as if you didn't know, sir! The windowsill in the passage, of course. He could sit there and sew, or do whatever he liked. He could sit on a chair, if he liked. He's got a chair, and a table, too. He's got everything, sir."

"But who is he?"

"Oh, he's a good man, sir. He's had a lot of experience in his life, he has, sir. I'll cook for him, and I'll only charge him ten roubles a month for his board and lodging."

After the exercise of a great deal of patience, I found that an elderly man had persuaded or somehow induced Agrafena to admit him to her kitchen as a paying guest. Now, I knew very well that if Agrafena ever took it into her head to do a thing, it had better be done at once, or she would give me no peace. For whenever anything was not to her liking, Agrafena became moody and fell a prey to the blackest melancholy which lasted for a fortnight or three weeks. During that time my dinners were uneatable, my floors remained unscrubbed, and several indispensable articles were missing from my personal washing, in short, my life became one long chapter of the most unfortunate accidents. I had long ago observed that this inarticulate woman was quite incapable of making up her mind or of fixing her mind on an idea that might be said to be her own. But if her feeble brain did once in a while conceive something resembling an idea or a plan, then to prevent her from carrying it into immediate execution was tantamount to putting her for some time morally out of existence. That being so, and my peace of mind being dearer to me than anything else in the world, I at once accepted Agrafena's proposal to take in a lodger.

"Tell me, has he at least some papers? A passport or something?"

"Why yes, sir. Of course he has. He's a good man, sir, just as I was telling you. A man with experience. Promised to pay me ten roubles a month, he did."

The very next day my new lodger installed himself in my modest bachelor quarters. I can't say that I was very sorry; on the contrary, in my heart of hearts I felt rather pleased. I live, on the whole, a very secluded sort of life, the life of a regular recluse. I have no acquaintances to speak of and I scarcely ever go out. Having spent ten years of my life in complete isolation from the world, I had naturally got used to solitude. But another ten, fifteen, or even more years of the same solitude, with the same Agrafena and in the same bachelor quarters, did not strike me as a particularly inviting prospect. So that in these circumstances another man, a man, moreover, of quiet habits, was a real blessing.

Agrafena had not deceived me; my lodger was a man of great experience of the world. His passport brought to light the fact that he was an old soldier; but that I knew even before I had opened it. One look at a man is sufficient to tell you that. My lodger, Astafy Ivanovich, was the finest specimen of an old soldier that it was ever my good fortune to come across. But what I liked best about him was that now and again he would tell some really good stories, mostly incidents from his own life. In view of the habitual boredom of my sort of existence, such a story-teller was a real find to me. One of the stories he told me left a vivid impression upon my mind. It arose out of the following circumstance.

I was alone in my flat, Astafy and Agrafena having gone out on business. Suddenly I heard somebody come in, and thinking it was a stranger, I went out of my room to see who it might be. It really was a stranger, a short man, who in spite of the cold autumn day, wore no overcoat.

"What do you want?"

"Does a civil servant by the name of Alexandrov live here?"

"No, I'm afraid there's no one here of that name," I replied, and I bade him a curt goodbye.

"That's odd," the stranger said, beating a cautious retreat to the door, "the caretaker told me he lived here."

"Get out! Beat it!"

Next day after dinner, while Astafy was fitting on a coat he was altering for me, someone came into the passage. I opened the door a little, and there before my very eyes my yesterday's visitor calmly took down my short winter overcoat from the coat-rack and, putting it under his arm, dashed out of the flat. Agrafena did nothing but gape at him, struck dumb with astonishment, and did not lift a finger to protect my property. Astafy Ivanovich ran out after the thief, and he came back ten minutes later, out of breath and empty-handed. The man had just vanished into thin air!

"That's a bit of bad luck, Astafy Ivanovich," I said. "A good job I've still got my winter cloak, or the villain would have left me absolutely stranded."

But Astafy Ivanovich was so overcome by it all that, looking at him, I almost forgot the loss I had suffered. He simply couldn't get over it. Every minute he would throw down the work on which he was engaged and start recounting the whole incident, how it had all happened, how he had been standing only a few feet away from the man, how the thief had taken down the coat before his very eyes, and how it had come about that he had not been able to catch him. Then he would sit down at his work again, but only to leave it a minute later, and I saw him go down to the caretaker to tell him all about it and to remonstrate with him for allowing such things to happen in his house. Then he came back and began lecturing Agrafena. When at last he did finally sit down to his work, he went on muttering to himself a long time, how it all happened, how he stood here and I there, how before his very eyes, hardly a few feet away, the man took the coat off the rack, and so on. In short, though a good man at his trade, Astafy Ivanovich was a terrible fellow for getting himself all worked up and making no end of a fuss.

"We've been fooled, Astafy Ivanovich," I said to him in the evening, offering him a glass of tea and hoping to dispel my boredom by making him tell me again the story of the stolen coat; for from its frequent repetition and the great sincerity of the speaker, I was beginning to find the story highly amusing.

"Aye, sir, we've been fooled all right," said Astafy Ivanovich. "Mind you, it's not my business, of course, but I can't help being upset all the same. It fairly makes my blood boil, it does, sir, though it's not my coat that's been stolen. For to my thinking, sir, there's no worse villain in the world than a thief. Aye, I've known many a man who'd take your things and never dream of paying for them, but a thief, sir, steals the work of your hands, the sweat of your brow, and your time, too. A nasty piece of work, that's what he is sir. Makes my blood boil just to talk about him. But begging your pardon, sir, how is it you don't seem to care about the loss of your property?"

"Well, Astafy Ivanovich, you're quite right of course. It is a confounded nuisance. I'd much rather burn my things than let a thief have them."

"Well, sir, it's a nuisance all right. Though, mind you, there are thieves and thieves. I well remember, sir, coming across an honest thief once."

"An honest thief? Why, how can a man be honest and a thief at the same time, Astafy Ivanovich?"

"Well, sir, that's true enough. There are no honest thieves, and there never have been any. What I wanted to say, sir, was that the man I had in mind seemed honest enough, but he stole all the same. Aye, I just couldn't help being sorry for him."

"Why, how did that happen, Astafy Ivanovich?"

"Well, sir, it happened two years ago. At the time I'd been out of work for nearly a year, and just before I lost my job I struck up an acquaintance with a man I accidentally met in a pub. Down and out he was. A terrible drunkard, loafer, vagabond. Been a clerk in some government office, but got chucked out a long time ago on account of his drinking. Lord, what a disgraceful sight he was! Walked about in rags, and sometimes I wasn't sure he had a shirt under his coat. No sooner did he get something than he'd spend it on drink. Not that he was what you might call obstreperous. No, sir, he was a very quiet man, kind and gentle, and he'd never ask you for anything on account of being very shy by nature. But of course I couldn't help seeing how badly the poor fellow wanted a drink, so I'd stand him one. Well, so we became good friends. I mean to say, sir, it was he really who got himself attached to me. I didn't mind either way. And what a funny man he was, sir! Stuck to me like a dog, followed me about everywhere, and that after I'd only met him once. No character at all. A rag of a man! At first he asked me to let him stay the night. Well, I did. For you see, sir, I had a look at his passport, and there was nothing wrong with it—the man was all right! The next day he wanted to stay again, and on the following day he came and spent the whole day on my windowsill. Stayed the night, too. 'Good Lord,' I thought to myself, 'I shan't be able to get rid of him now—provide food and drink for him, and a bed as well!' Just a poor man's luck, sir. Nothing to eat myself, and here's a perfect stranger to carry about on my back! Nor was it the first time he had hung on to somebody he'd never seen before. He used to spend his days with some clerk before he ran across me in the pub. They were always out drinking together. Only the poor man seemed to have had some serious trouble, for he soon drank himself to death. Anyway, the man I'm telling you about, sir, was called Yemelyan Ilyich. I was racking my brains what to do with him. I couldn't just chuck him out. I was dreadfully sorry for the poor beggar. You can't imagine, sir, what a pitiful wreck of a man he was. Never uttered a word, never asked for anything, just sat there gazing into my eyes like a dog. That's what drink does to a man, sir! Well, so there I was wondering what to say to the man. I couldn't very well say, 'Look here, Yemelyan, you'd better go. This is no place for you. You've come to the wrong man. Soon I shall have nothing to eat myself, so how can you expect me to keep you?' I wondered, sir, what he would have done if I'd said that to him. Well, I knew very well of course that if I told him that he'd sit there looking at me a long time without at first being able to take in what I was saying, and when he at last saw what I meant he'd get up from the window, pick up his little bundle (I can see that bundle now, sir, a red check bundle full of holes that he carried about with him everywhere and that he used to stuff all sorts of rubbish into), and set his tattered old coat to rights to make it look decent and keep him warm, and so that the holes didn't show—very particular he was about his appearance! Then he'd open the door and go out on the landing with tears in his eyes. Well, sir, I couldn't let a man go to the dogs like that—I was really sorry for him! But, I thought next, what was going to happen to me when I lost my job? 'Wait a bit, Yemelyan, my dear fellow,' I says to myself, 'you won't be eating and drinking and making merry at my expense very much longer now. I'll be moving soon, and then, my lad, it's ten to one you'll never find me.'

"Well, sir, one fine day I did move. My old master, Alexander Filimonovich (he's dead now, God rest his soul!), said to me at the time, 'I'm very satisfied with you, Astafy,' he said. 'We shan't forget you, and when we come back from the country we'll take you on again.' I had been his butler, oh, for many years—a grand man he was, too, but he died a few months later. Well, so after seeing them off, I collected my belongings, what little money I had, thinking to take it easy for a bit, and went to live with an old lady I knew. Took a small room in her flat. She had only that small room to spare. She used to be in service herself, a nursemaid she was but now she lived by herself on her pension. 'Well,' I says to myself, 'it's goodbye for good, Yemelyan, old fellow. You'll never find me now!'

"Well, sir, what do you think? I came back in the evening (I had gone out to see a man I knew), and there was Yemelyan sitting quietly on my chest in his tattered old coat and with his bundle beside him, and to while away the time he had borrowed a book from my landlady (a prayer book it was), and he was holding it in his hands—upside-down! So he had found me after all! I gave up. 'It's no use,' I thought to myself. 'It can't be helped. Why didn't you get rid of him at first?' So knowing very well that he had come to stay, I just said to him, 'You haven't forgotten your passport, Yemelyan, have you?'

"Well, sir, so I sat down and began to consider what to do next. 'After all,' thought I, 'what harm can a homeless old tramp do you?' And on thinking it over, I decided that the harm he'd do me wouldn't amount to much. 'He'll have to have something to eat of course,' I thought. 'Well, I'll give him a piece of bread in the morning, and to make the meal more tasty like, buy an onion or two. At midday I'll give him another bit of bread and onion, and for supper some more onion with *kvas,* and bread, too, if he asks for it. And should some cabbage soup come our way, we'll have a real feast, the two of us.' I'm no great eater myself, and it's a well-known fact, sir, that a drinking man never eats: all he wants is vodka and a drop of brandy. 'He'll ruin me with his drinking,' thought I, and as I was thinking of that something else occurred to me, something I couldn't get out of my head. For I suddenly realised, sir, that if Yemelyan was to go, there'd be nothing left for me to live for. So I made up my mind there and then to be his only provider and benefactor. 'I must get him to give up drinking,' I thought, 'I must save him from utter ruin.' 'All right, Yemelyan, old fellow,' I says to myself, 'you can stay if you like, but, mind, behave yourself—orders is orders!'

"The first thing I decided to do, sir, was to teach Yemelyan some trade, find a job of work for him to do. Naturally, it couldn't be done all at once. 'Let him enjoy himself a little first,' I says to myself, 'and in the meantime I'll think of something, find out what special abilities you possess, Yemelyan, what kind of work you're good at.' For every job, sir, first of all requires that the man engaged in it should have the right kind of ability. Well, sir, so I starts observing him on the quiet, and it didn't take me long to find out that poor old Yemelyan was a desperate case. Aye, there was nothing at all he was good for. So I first of all gives him a piece of good advice. 'Why, Yemelyan,' I says to him, 'take a look at yourself, and do,' I says, 'try to make yourself a bit more respectable like. Look at the rags you go about in. Look at that disgraceful old coat of yours! Why, God forgive me, all it's good for is to make a sieve out of. Fie, for shame, Yemelyan,' I says. 'It's about time you turned over a new leaf and became a changed man!'

"Well, sir, poor old Yemelyan just sits listening to me with his head hanging down. There was nothing you could do with him. Why, drink had robbed him even of speech. Couldn't say a sensible word, he couldn't. Talk to him about cucumbers and he talks back to you about kidney-beans! He listened to me a long time, then he just heaved a sigh.

"'What are you sighing for, Yemelyan?'

"'Oh, nothing,' he says, 'don't take any notice of me, Astafy. Do you know,' he says, 'do you know, Astafy, I saw two women fighting in the street today. One upset the other's basket of cranberries on purpose.'

"'Well, what about it?'

"'Well, you see, Astafy, so the second woman upsets the first woman's cranberries on purpose and starts stamping on them!'

"'Well, so what about it, Yemelyan?'

"'Oh, nothing, Astafy. I just thought I'd tell you, that's all.'

"'That's all! Oh, Yemelyan, Yemelyan,' thought I, 'drink has been your undoing, and no mistake!'

"'And you know, Astafy, a gentleman dropped a note on the pavement in Gorokhovaya Street—no, not in Gorokhovaya Street, in Sadovaya Street it was—and a peasant saw it and said, My lucky day! But another peasant also saw it and said, No, sir, it's my lucky day! I saw it first! . . .'

"'Well, Yemelyan?'

"'Well, so the two peasants had a fight, and a policeman came up, picked up the note, gave it back to the gentleman, and threatened to take the two peasants to the police station!'

"'Well, so what about it, Yemelyan? I mean what is there specially instructive about it?'

"'Why, I didn't mean anything, Astafy. Only the people in the street did laugh a lot.'

"'Oh, Yemelyan, Yemelyan, what does it matter what the people in the street do? Think of yourself, Yemelyan, think of your immortal soul which you've sold for a few coppers. You know what, Yemelyan?'

"'What, Astafy?'

"'Why don't you get yourself some work? You really ought to, you know. For the hundredth time I'm telling you, Yemelyan—have pity on yourself!'

"'But what work do you want me to get, Astafy? I really don't know what work I can do, and besides, I don't think anyone will give me any work.'

"'Of course they won't give you any work, you drunkard! Why else do you think they chucked you out of the civil service?'

"'You know, Astafy, Vlas, the potboy, was summoned to the office today.'

"'And why did they summon him to the office?'

"'I really don't know, Astafy. I suppose they must have wanted him, so they sent for him.'

"'Ah well,' thought I, 'there's no hope, it seems, for either of us, Yemelyan, old fellow. The good Lord must be punishing us for our sins!' And what indeed can you do with a man like that, I ask you, sir!

"But he was devilishly cunning, Yemelyan was. He'd listen quietly to me a long time, but sooner or later he'd get bored, and the minute he noticed that I was beginning to lose my temper, he'd pick up his old coat and sheer off. He'd loaf about all day and come back dead drunk in the evening. I don't know who paid for his drinks or where he got the money to pay for them himself. I had nothing to do with it!

"'Now look here, Yemelyan,' I says to him at last, 'if you go on like this very much longer, you're sure to come to a bad end. Stop drinking, do you hear? Give it up! Next time you come home drunk,' I says, 'you'll jolly well have to spend the night on the stairs. I'm damned if I'll let you in!'

"Well, sir, he saw of course that I really meant it this time, so for the next two days he didn't go out, but on the third day he cleared off again. I sat up waiting for him, but he didn't come back. To tell you the truth, sir, I was beginning to feel a bit uneasy, and, besides, I couldn't help feeling sorry for him. 'What have I done to him?' I thought. 'I've gone and scared him away good and proper now! Where could he have got to, the poor wretch? Pray God, nothing happens to him!' Well, night came and he wasn't back. In the morning I went out on the landing and there he was, sir! Spent the night on the landing, he had. Puts his head on the top step and falls asleep like that. Chilled to the marrow he was.

"'What made you do it, Yemelyan? What a place to spend the night in!'

"'Well, you were so angry with me the other night, Astafy. You were so terribly vexed and—er—promised to make me spend the night on the landing, so I—well—I didn't dare to come in, Astafy, and went to sleep here.'

"I felt mad at him and sorry for him, too, at the same time.

"'Why, surely, Yemelyan,' I says, 'you might have got yourself a different kind of job. What's the use of guarding a flight of stairs?'

"'But what different kind of job do you mean, Astafy?'

"'Why, you good-for-nothing loafer,' I says (fair mad I was at him, sir!), 'you could at least have tried to learn the tailor's trade! Look at that coat of yours! You're not satisfied, it seems, to have it all in holes, you have to sweep the stairs with it, too! Why don't you take a needle and thread and patch it up? You would have done it long ago, if you had had any sense of decency left. Oh,' I says, 'you drunkard!'

"Well, would you believe it, sir? He did take a needle and thread! I had meant it as a joke, but he got properly scared, so he took off his coat and sat down to patch it up. I looked at him: his eyes were red and bleary, and his hands shook something terrible! He shoved and shoved, but the thread just wouldn't go through the eye of the needle. How he tried, sir! Screwed up his eyes, wetted the thread, twisted it in his fingers, but it was no use. So he gave it up and looked at me.

"'Well, Yemelyan,' I says, 'you've certainly made me proud of you! If there'd been anybody about,' I says, 'I'd have sunk through the floor for shame. Why, you poor fool, don't you realise that I was joking, that I just meant it as a reproach? Now, leave it alone,' I says, 'and don't attempt to do anything you can't, and for goodness sake don't sleep on the stairs! Don't disgrace me by doing such a disreputable thing ever again!'

"'But what am I to do, Astafy? I know very well that I'm always drunk and that I'm not good for anything. It seems to me all I am good for is to cause you, my be-ne-factor, unnecessary trouble. . . .'

"And, sir, as he said it his blue lips started quivering all of a sudden, and a tear rolled down his pale cheek and trembled on his stubby chin, and in another minute the poor fellow burst into a regular flood of tears.

"'Well, Yemelyan,' I says to myself, 'I never thought you had it in you. Who could have guessed you had such tender feelings?' No, I says to myself, 'no, it's no use deceiving myself. I ought to give up having anything to do with you. Go to the devil for all I care!'

"Well, sir, why make a long story of it? And, besides, it was such a sorry, miserable business that it is hardly worth wasting words on. I mean, sir, you wouldn't, so to speak, give a brass farthing for the whole thing, though I would gladly have given a fortune, if I had

had a fortune to give, that it should never have happened to me. You see, sir, I had a pair of riding breeches (the devil take 'em!), lovely breeches they were, too, blue ones with a check pattern. They were ordered by a country gentleman who was on a visit to town, but he wouldn't take 'em, after all: they were too narrow for him, he said. Well, so they were left on my hands. 'It's a valuable article,' I thought. 'I might get fifteen roubles or more for them in the second-hand market, and even if I didn't, I might manage to get two pairs of trousers for our Petersburg gentleman out of them, and have a piece over for a waistcoat for myself.' To poor folk like us, sir, every little counts. Well, as it happened Yemelyan was having a very poor time just then. I had noticed that he had not had a drop of liquor for some days. He lost heart and looked down in the mouth. Aye, very miserable he looked, and that's the truth. I couldn't help feeling sorry to see him in such a sad state. 'Well,' I says to myself, 'either you've got no money, my lad, or you've turned over a new leaf in good earnest, listened to reason at last, and given up drink for good.' That's how things stood just then, sir. As it happened, we had a church holiday at the time, and I went to evening service. When I came back, I found Yemelyan sitting on the windowsill blind drunk, rocking to and fro. Aha, thought I, so you've gone and done it again, my lad! And I went to fetch something from my chest. I opened it and the first thing I noticed was that my breeches were no longer there. Looked for them everywhere I could think of, but couldn't find them. Well, after I'd turned the place upside down and all to no purpose, something seemed to stab me to the heart. I rushed off to my landlady and at first accused her of the theft. Aye, acted like a real madman, I did. Hardly knew what I was doing. You see, sir, it hadn't entered my head that Yemelyan was the real culprit, though the evidence was staring me in the face, as you might say, for the man was blind drunk! 'No, sir,' says my landlady, 'I never seen your breeches, and, anyway, what would I want with your breeches? I couldn't wear them, could I? Why,' she says, 'I missed a skirt of mine myself the other day, and I shouldn't wonder,' she says, 'if it wasn't one of those nice friends of yours who took it. As for your breeches,' she says, 'I know nothing about 'em.' 'But who was here while I was out,' I asked. 'Did anyone call?' 'No, sir,' she says, 'no one called. I've been here all the time and I ought to know. Yemelyan went out and came back. There he is. Why don't you ask him?' So I asked Yemelyan. 'Tell me, Yemelyan,' I says, 'you haven't by any chance taken them breeches of mine, have you? The new riding breeches,' I says, 'I made specially for the country gentleman. You remember them, don't you?'

"'No, Astafy,' he says, 'I'm sure I—er—never took 'em.'

"Well, of all things! I started searching for them again, looked everywhere, but it was no use. And Yemelyan, sir, was sitting there all the time, rocking to and fro. I squats down over the chest on my heels in front of him, and all of a sudden I looks at him out of the corner of my eye. 'Ah well,' thought I, and fairly mad at him I was I can tell you. Got red in the face even. Then, quite unexpectedly, Yemelyan, too, looks at me.

"'No, Astafy,' he says, 'I never took your breeches. You're—er—perhaps thinking I did, but I never touched them!'

"'But where could they have got to, Yemelyan?'

"'Haven't the faintest idea, Astafy,' he says. 'I've never seen them.'

"'Well, in that case, Yemelyan,' I says, 'it seems they must have walked off by themselves, don't it?'

"'Maybe they have, Astafy,' he says. 'Maybe they have.'

"Well, sir, having heard what Yemelyan had to say for himself, I got up without another word, went over to the window, lighted my lamp, and set down to work. Altering a waistcoat for a civil servant on the floor below, I was just then. I was boiling with rage. I mean, sir, I'd have felt much happier if I'd taken all my clothes and lighted the stove with them. Well, Yemelyan must have guessed how bitter I felt. For a man given to wickedness, sir, scents trouble far off, like a bird before a storm.

"'You know, Astafy,' began Yemelyan, and his weak voice shook as he spoke, 'the male nurse Antip Prokhorovich got married this morning to the wife of the coachman who died the other day. . . .'

"Well, sir, I just gave him a look, and I suppose it must have been a very nasty look, too, for Yemelyan saw what I meant all right. So he gets up at once, goes over to the bed and starts searching for something on the floor there. I waited. He goes on rummaging a long time, muttering to himself, 'No, not here—not here. Where can the blessed thing have got to?' I waited to see what would happen. Then, believe it or not, sir, he crawled under the bed on all fours! Well, when I saw him do that, I couldn't hold out any longer.

"'What are you crawling about under the bed for, Yemelyan?' I says.

"'Why, Astafy,' he says, 'I'm looking for your breeches, of course. Maybe they've dropped down there somewhere.'

"'But why, sir,' I says (called him 'sir' out of sheer spite, I did), 'why, sir, should you go to so much trouble for a poor ignorant man like me? Why crawl on your knees for nothing?'

"'Why, Astafy,' he says, 'I don't mind. Who knows, they might turn up if we go on looking for them long enough.'

"'Indeed?' I says. 'Look here, Yemelyan. . . .'

"'Yes, Astafy?'

"'Are you sure,' I says, 'you haven't simply stolen them, like a common thief, in return for everything I done for you?'

"You see, sir, it made me mad to see him crawling on his knees before me—the last straw, that was!

"'No, I haven't . . . Astafy.'

"But he didn't come out from under the bed. No, sir. Lay there a long time on his face, and when at last he did crawl out, he was as white as a sheet. He stood up, sat down beside me on the windowsill, and stayed sitting there for ten minutes, I reckon.

"'No, Astafy,' he says all of a sudden, standing up and advancing towards me, looking (I can see him still) ghastly, 'no, Astafy,' he says, 'I've never—er—touched your breeches.'

"He was shaking all over, pointing a quivering finger at his breast, and his voice shaking so dreadfully it gave me an awful turn and I just sat there as though I was stuck to the window.

"'Well, Yemelyan,' I says, 'I'm sorry if, fool that I am, I've accused you unjustly. As for the breeches,' I says, 'I don't care if they are lost. We can get along without them. We've still got our hands, thank God, and there's no need for us to go thieving or . . . begging from some poor devil, either. We can always earn our bread. . . .'

"Yemelyan listened to me in silence, and after a while he sat down on the windowsill again. He stayed there all the evening, never stirring from his place. He was still there when I went to bed, and when I got up the next morning I found him curled up in his old coat on the bare floor. He was too humiliated, you see, to come to bed. Well, sir, since that day I conceived a violent dislike for him, and to tell you the truth, sir, during the first few days I simply hated the sight of him. It was as though my own son, so to speak, had robbed me or done me some mortal injury.

"Well, sir, for the next fortnight Yemelyan was out on the spree, drinking hard all the time. Went off the rails good and proper, that is. He'd go out in the morning and come back late at night, and for the whole of that fortnight I never heard him utter a single word. I suppose he must have felt pretty low at the time, or maybe he even wanted to do himself in, one way or another. However, at last it was all over. There was no more drinking. I reckon he must have run through his money by then. At all events, there he was sitting in the window again. Sat there, if my memory serves me right, for three whole days, without uttering a word. Then all of a sudden I saw that he was crying. You see, sir, one minute he sat there as if nothing was wrong, and the next minute he was crying. And, Lord, how that man did cry! Tears streamed in a flood out of his eyes, while he seemed to be unaware of them, just like water pouring out of a well. Well, sir, it's a terrible thing to see a man, and, particularly, an old man like Yemelyan, crying from sorrow and despair.

"'What's the matter, Yemelyan?' I says.

"He started shaking all over. Was very startled, you see, for it was the first time that evening I had spoken to him.

"'Nothing, Astafy. . . .'

"'Now, look here, Yemelyan, what does it matter? Let the whole thing go hang, so far as I'm concerned. What are you sitting like a broody hen for?'

"Felt very sorry for him, I did, sir.

"'Oh, it's nothing, Astafy. It isn't because of that at all. I've been thinking—er—I'd like to get some work, Astafy.'

"'What sort of work, Yemelyan?'

"'Oh, any sort of work. Maybe I could find a job, same as I had before. I've already been to ask Fedossey Ivanovich. . . . I don't want to be a burden to you, Astafy. Maybe when I find a job I'll pay it all back and reward you for all your trouble.'

"'Don't talk such nonsense, Yemelyan. Suppose you did something you didn't ought to—what does it matter? To hell with it! Let's go on as we used to!'

"'No, Astafy. I can see you're still—er—harping on it, but I told you I never took your breeches.'

"'Well, have it your own way. I don't mind, I'm sure.'

"'No, Astafy, I can see I can't go on living with you. I'm sorry, Astafy, but I shall have to go.'

"'But, bless my soul,' I says, 'who's been offending you, Yemelyan? Who's driving you out of the house? You don't mean to say I'm doing it, do you?'

"'No, Astafy, I can't possibly stay with you now. I'd better be going.'

"You see, sir, the man was too cut up, kept harping on the same thing. And sure enough, he gets up and starts pulling his old coat over his shoulders.

"'But where are you off to, Yemelyan? Be sensible, man. What are you doing? Where will you go?'

"'Goodbye, Astafy. Don't try to stop me (here he began whimpering again). I think it's time I got out of your way. You're no longer the same.'

"'How do you mean I'm no longer the same? Of course I am the same! Mark my words, Yemelyan, you'll perish like a helpless child by yourself.'

"'No, Astafy, you're not the same,' he says. 'Every time you go out now you lock up your chest, and I can't help crying when I see you do that. No, you'd better not try to stop me, Astafy, and forgive me if I done anything to offend you while living with you.'

"Well, sir, he did go. Left me that very day, he did. I waited the whole day for him, expecting him to be back in the evening, but no, he didn't come. There was no sign of him next day, either, nor the day after. I got really worried, so worried that I could neither eat, drink nor sleep. The fellow had quite disarmed me! On the fourth day I went out to look for him. Went round all the pubs asking for him, but he wasn't to be found anywhere: gone, vanished! 'Not dead, are you, Yemelyan?' I thought to myself. 'Yielded up the ghost under some fence in a drunken stupor maybe and now you're lying there like a piece of rotten wood.' I just dragged myself home, feeling more dead than alive. Made up my mind to go out looking for him again the next day. And all the time I was cursing myself for having let such a helpless fool of a man go off by himself. Very early on the morning of the fifth day (it was a holiday) I heard the door creak. I looked up and saw Yemelyan coming in. His face was gone a bluish colour and his hair was caked in mud, as though he'd been sleeping in the street. Thin as a lath he was. He took off his tattered old coat, sat down beside me on the chest, and looked at me. I was glad to see him, I can tell you, sir, but at the same time I was more cut up than ever. For you see, sir, it's like this: if I had ever done something wrong, I'd have died like a dog sooner than come back. Aye, it's the gospel truth I'm telling you. But Yemelyan came back. And, naturally, it fairly broke my heart to see a man in such a terrible plight. I made much of him, talked kindly to him, comforted him.

"'Well, Yemelyan, my dear old fellow,' I says to him, 'I'm certainly glad to see you back. Had you been a few minutes later, I'd have gone round the pubs again looking for you. Have you had anything to eat at all?'

"'Yes, thank you, Astafy,' he says, 'I have.'

"'Come now, are you sure? Here, my dear fellow, here's some cabbage soup left over from yesterday. It's good stuff, had some beef in it. And here's some bread and an onion. Come on, eat it,' I says. 'It'll do you good.'

"I gave it to him, and saw at once that the poor chap had not tasted food for maybe three days—he was so ravenous! Aye, it was hunger that had driven him to me. Well, I felt real sorry for the poor wretch. My heart overflowed with pity as I looked at him. 'I think,' I says to myself, 'I'd better run out to the pub and get him a drink to cheer him up a little, and let's put an end to all that sorry business. There's not a drop of bitterness left in my heart against you,

Yemelyan, old fellow!' So I ran out to the pub and brought back some vodka. 'Here, Yemelyan,' I says, 'come on, let's have a drink, seeing it's a holiday today! Like a drink? It's good for your health.'

"He held out his hand, held it out greedy-like, but stopped before taking the glass. A minute later I saw him take it, lift it to his mouth, and spill some of the drink on his sleeve. He got it as far as his lips, but put it down at once on the table.

"'Why, what's the matter, Yemelyan?'

"'No, thank you, Astafy, I—er—I don't think I—'

"'Don't you want a drink?'

"'No, thank you, Astafy, I—er—I—well—I'm not going to—er—drink any more, Astafy.'

"'But why not, Yemelyan? Have you given up drink altogether, or is it only today you don't feel like having one?'

"He made no answer. A moment later I noticed that he dropped his head wearily on his hand.

"'What's the matter, Yemelyan? Are you ill?'

"'Yes, Astafy. Afraid so.'

"I put him to bed at once. I could see he was in a bad way: his head was burning and he was shivering in a fever. I sat by him all day, and towards night his illness took a turn for the worse. I mixed some vegetable oil and *kvas,* put in some chopped-up spring onions and breadcrumbs, and gave it to him. 'Come,' I says, 'have some of this, Yemelyan. It'll make you feel better.' But he shook his head. 'No, thank you, Astafy,' he says. 'If you don't mind I'd much rather not have any dinner today.' I made some tea, tired my landlady out preparing all sorts of things for him, but he wouldn't have anything. 'Well,' I says to myself, 'it certainly looks bad!' The third morning I went to fetch a doctor. There was one living quite near, Kostopravov his name was. I'd known him when I was in service with the Bossomyagins. Had him in myself when I was ill. The doctor came and had a look at Yemelyan. 'He's in a bad way, isn't he?' he says. 'You could have spared yourself the trouble of calling me in. Still,' he says, 'I suppose I'd better give him some powders.' Well, sir, I never gave Yemelyan the powders, for I could see that the doctor himself hadn't any faith in them. In the meantime the fifth day came.

"Well, sir, there he lay dying before my eyes. I sat in the window with my work in my hands. My landlady was heating the stove. None of us spoke. My heart bled on account of that worthless drunkard, sir. I felt like I was losing my own son. I knew Yemelyan was looking at me all the time. I noticed that the poor fellow had been trying hard since morning to tell me something, but it seemed as if he couldn't screw up his courage to do it. At last I looked up at him. Oh, the agony in the poor fellow's eyes, sir! He'd never taken them off me for a moment; but when he saw me looking at him he dropped them quickly.

"'I say, Astafy. . . .'

"'What is it, Yemelyan?'

"'If you took my old coat to the second-hand market, Astafy, do you think they'd give you a lot for it?'

"'Well,' I says, 'I hardly think they'd offer me a great deal for it, Yemelyan. Three roubles, perhaps.'

"But as a matter of fact, sir, if I had taken it, they wouldn't have given me as much as a penny for it. Most likely they would have laughed in my face for trying to sell them a useless old rag like that. I said it just to comfort the old fellow, seeing what a simpleton he was.

"'And I was thinking, Astafy, that they might give you ten roubles for it. It's made of fine cloth, Astafy. They'd give you more than three roubles for a coat made of fine cloth, wouldn't they?'

"'Well, I don't really know, Yemelyan,' I says, 'but if you want me to take it, then of course I'll ask ten roubles for it to begin with.'

"Yemelyan was silent for a minute or two; then he called me again.

"'Astafy!'

"'What is it, Yemelyan?'

"'Sell my coat when I die. Don't bury me in it. I'll be all right without it. It's a valuable article, Astafy. It might come in very handy for you.'

"Well, sir, I can't tell you how dreadful I felt when he said that! I could see that the end was near. We were silent again. So a whole hour passed. Then I looked at him. He was still staring at me, but when he met my eyes he looked down again.

"'Want a drink of water, Yemelyan?'

"'Yes, thank you, Astafy.'

"I gave him some water and he drank it.

"'Thank you, Astafy,' he says again.

"'Is there anything else you'd like, Yemelyan?'

"'No, thank you, Astafy, I don't want anything. Only—'

"'Only what, Yemelyan?'

"'I—er—'

"'What is it, Yemelyan?'

"'The riding breeches, Astafy. It was me who—er—took them.'

"'Well,' I says, 'I'm sure the Lord will forgive you, you poor fellow. You can die in peace.'

"And feeling a lump coming up to my throat and tears gushing out of my eyes, I turned away for a moment.

"'Astafy—'

"I turned round and saw that Yemelyan was trying to say something to me. He was trying desperately to sit up, and his lips were moving soundlessly. All of a sudden he reddened, and looked at me. Then I saw him go pale again, paler and paler, and suddenly he seemed to shrivel up. His head fell back, he drew one last breath, and gave up his soul to his Maker."

The Christmas Tree and a Wedding

From the Memoirs of an Unknown

The other day I saw a wedding. But no! I'd better tell you about the Christmas tree. The wedding was all right; I liked it very much, but the other affair was much better. I don't know how it was that, looking at the wedding, I should have remembered the Christmas tree. It happened like this. Exactly five years ago, on New Year's Eve, I was invited to a children's party. The person who had invited me was a well-known business man, a man of good connections, a man with an influential circle of acquaintances, a man who knew all there was to know about pulling strings, so that there was good reason to believe that the children's party was merely an excuse for the parents to get together and have a talk about other interesting matters in an innocent, casual, unpremeditated sort of way. I was a stranger there; I had no interesting matters to discuss, and for that reason I spent the evening more or less as I pleased. There was another man there who, too, apparently had neither friends nor relations and who, like me, just happened to be present on that happy family occasion. He was the first to catch my eye—a tall, spare man, very serious, very decently dressed. But it was quite evident that he was in no mood for fun or happy family occasions. Indeed, whenever he found himself alone in some corner he left off smiling at once and knit his bushy, black brows. Apart from our host, he did not know a single soul at the party. One could see that he was terribly bored, but he kept up valiantly and to the bitter end the part of a perfectly happy man who was having a really good time. I found out afterwards that he was from the provinces and had come up to town on some extremely important and highly complicated business. He had brought a letter of introduction to our host who extended his patronage to him by no means *con amore*, and who invited him to his children's party out of mere courtesy. There were no card games, no one offered him a cigar, no one engaged him in conversation, having, perhaps, recognised at a distance the sort of awkward customer he was, and for that reason the poor fellow, not knowing what to do with his hands, was forced to spend the whole evening stroking his whiskers. His whiskers were indeed extremely handsome. But he stroked them with such enthusiasm that one could not help feeling that his whiskers were brought into the world first, and the gentleman himself was only afterwards attached to them in order to stroke them.

In addition to this odd character who took part in this extraordinary manner in the family celebration of our host (the proud father of five strapping boys), there was another man in the room who aroused my curiosity. But he was a person of quite a different sort. He was a man of consequence. His name was Julian Mastakovich. From the first glance it was obvious that he was on the same terms with our host as our host was with the gentleman who was stroking his whiskers. Our host and hostess overwhelmed him with compliments, danced attendance on him, offered him drinks, fawned upon him, took their visitors up to him to be introduced, but did not take him to be introduced to anybody. I noticed the glint of a tear in our host's eye when Julian Mastakovich observed apropos of the party that he did not often spend his time so pleasantly. I don't know why, but I felt overawed in the presence of so important a personage and, consequently, having admired the children, I withdrew to a small drawing-room, which was completely deserted, and sat down in the arbour of flowers arranged by our hostess which occupied almost half the room.

All the children were incredibly sweet and quite determined not to behave like *grown-ups* in spite of the admonitions of their fond mothers and governesses. They stripped the Christmas tree to the last sweetmeat in a twinkling and even found time to break half the toys before they knew what toy was meant for which. One black-eyed, curly-headed boy, who kept trying to shoot me with his wooden gun, was particularly lovely to look at. But it was his sister who attracted more attention than any other child at the party. She was a girl of eleven, pretty as a picture, very quiet, pale, dreamy, with a pair of large, pensive, prominent eyes. The children must have done something to hurt her feelings, for she went away to the same drawing-room in which I was sitting and busied herself in a corner—with her doll. The visitors respectfully pointed out a wealthy government contractor, her father, and I heard someone saying in a whisper that he had already set aside three hundred thousand roubles for her dowry. I turned round to see who was so interested in such a circumstance, and my glance fell on Julian Mastakovich, who, with his hands behind his back and his head slightly inclined to one side, seemed to listen with rapt attention to the idle talk of these people. Afterwards I could not help admiring the wisdom of our hosts in the distribution of the children's presents. The little girl who already had a portion of three hundred thousand roubles received the most expensive doll. There followed presents which decreased in value in accordance with the decrease in the social rank of the parents of all these happy children. Finally, the last child to receive a present, a small, thin, freckled, red-haired little boy of ten, got nothing but a book of stories with descriptions of the grandeur of nature, the tears shed under the influence of strong emotion, etc., without pictures or even a tail-piece. He was the son of a poor widow, the governess of our host's children, a completely cowed and scared little boy. He was dressed in a jacket of cheap material. Having received his book, he wandered round the other toys for a long time. He wanted terribly to play with the other children, but he did not dare: one could see that he already felt and understood his position. I am very fond of watching children. I find their first manifestation of independence most fascinating. I noticed that the red-haired boy was so tempted by the expensive toys of the other children, and especially by the theatre, in which he wanted very badly to take some part, that he did not hesitate to do a bit of cringing. He smiled and ingratiated himself with the other children, he gave away his apple to a pasty-faced boy who already had a large number of presents tied up in a handkerchief, and he even went so far as to give a ride on his back to another boy so as not to be driven away from the theatre. But a minute later some scamp of a boy gave him a really good thrashing. The little boy did not dare to cry. His mother, the governess, immediately intervened and told him not to interfere with the games of the other children. The child went away into the same drawing-room where the little girl was playing by herself. She made friends with him, and the two set about dressing the expensive doll, in which occupation they soon became intently absorbed.

I had been sitting there for about half an hour in the ivy arbour and had almost fallen asleep, as I listened to the brisk chatter of the red-haired boy and the beautiful little girl with the dowry of three hundred thousand, both so busy with their doll, when Julian Mastakovich suddenly walked into the room. He had taken advantage of a rather disgraceful scene caused by a quarrel among the children to escape unnoticed from the ballroom. I noticed that only a minute ago he had been talking very animatedly to the father of the future heiress, to whom he had just been introduced, about the superiority of some branch of public service over another. Now he stood absorbed in meditation and seemed to be doing a sum on his fingers.

"Three hundred . . . three hundred . . ." he was whispering. "Eleven . . . twelve . . . thirteen . . ." he went on counting "Sixteen—five years! Suppose it's at four per cent—that'll make twelve, five times twelve is sixty, and the interest on the sixty . . . well, say, in five years it'll be four hundred. Yes, that's it! . . . But, good Lord, he won't invest it at four per cent, not that blackguard! More likely at eight or ten per cent. Well, then, say, five hundred, yes, five hundred thousand at least, that's certain. Of course, there may be something over for her trousseau . . . h'm . . ."

He stopped meditating, blew his nose and was about to go out of the room when his glance suddenly fell on the little girl and he stopped dead. He did not see me behind the pots of greenery. He appeared to me to be in a state of great agitation. Whether it was the sum he had been doing that had so wrought upon his imagination, or whether it was something else, I could not tell, but he kept rubbing his hands and could not stand still for a moment. This excitement increased to *nec plus ultra* when he stopped and threw another determined glance on the future heiress. He was about to walk up to her, but first threw a furtive look round the room. Then he began approaching the child on tiptoe as though feeling guilty of something. He went up to her with a little insinuating smile and kissed her on the head. The little girl, not expecting this attack, uttered a frightened cry.

"And what are you doing here, my sweet child?" he asked in a whisper, throwing another furtive look round him and patting the little girl's cheek.

"We're playing. . . ."

"Oh? With him?" Julian Mastakovich looked askance at the little boy. "Run away to the ballroom, there's a good boy," he said to him.

The boy stared at him, but made no answer. Julian Mastakovich again looked around furtively and again bent down to the little girl.

"What have you got there, my sweet child?" he asked. "A dolly?"

"A dolly," the little girl answered, frowning and a little frightened.

"A dolly. . . . And do you know, my sweet child, what your dolly is made of?"

"No, sir," the girl replied in a whisper, hanging her head.

"Why, it's made of rags, darling," and looking sternly at the little boy, Julian Mastakovich added, "Go to your playmates in the ballroom, boy!"

The boy and girl frowned and clutched at each other. They did not want to be separated.

"And do you know why they gave you that doll?" asked Julian Mastakovich, lowering his voice more and more.

"No, sir."

"Because you've been a sweet and well-behaved child all the week."

Julian Mastakovich, now in a ferment of excitement, threw a careful glance round the room, and lowering his voice more and more, asked in a scarcely audible whisper, his voice broken with emotion and impatience—

"And do you promise to love me, my little darling, when I come and see your mummy and daddy?"

Saying this, Julian Mastakovich tried once more to kiss "the little darling," but the red-haired boy, seeing that she was on the point of bursting into tears, seized her hand and began to whimper from sympathy with her. Julian Mastakovich got angry in good earnest.

"Go away, go away from here!" he said to the boy. "Go on, go to your playmates in the ballroom!"

"No, no," cried the little girl. "You go away! Leave him alone, leave him alone, will you?" she said, almost in tears.

Someone made a noise at the door. Julian Mastakovich took fright and drew himself up majestically to his full height. But the red-haired boy, who was even more frightened than Julian Mastakovich, abandoned the girl and, keeping close to the wall, slunk out of the drawing-room into the dining-room. To avoid suspicion, Julian Mastakovich, too, went into the dining-room. He was red as a lobster, and, glancing into the looking-glass, seemed to be ashamed of himself. I expect he was sorry for his excitement and impatience. It was of course possible that he was so taken aback at the very beginning by the sum he was doing on his fingers, that he was so tempted and inspired by it, that in spite of all his importance and dignity he had decided to act like a hot-headed youth and take the object of his desires by storm, without reflecting that the object of his desires could not become a real object for at least another five years. I followed the worthy gentleman into the dining-room and there I beheld a strange sight. Julian Mastakovich, flushed with vexation and anger, was bullying the red-haired boy, who, retreating further and further from him, did not know where to run in his terror.

"Go away, you beastly little beggar, go away! What are you doing here? Stealing fruit, are you? Stealing fruit, eh? Off with you, you naughty boy! Get out, you snivelling little idiot! Away to your playmates! Go!"

The terrified little boy, in a frantic effort to escape his pursuer, tried to crawl under the table. But Julian Mastakovich, beside himself with fury, took out his large cambric handkerchief and started lashing out with it viciously in an attempt to force the child, who had grown as quiet as a mouse, to come out from under the table. It should be recorded here that Julian Mastakovich was somewhat corpulent. He was a sleek, ruddy-cheeked, solidly built, paunchy man, with fat thighs, in a word, strong as a horse, as they say, and round as a nut. He was perspiring, panting, and getting terribly red in the face. At last he got almost mad with rage, so great was his indignation and perhaps—who knows?—jealousy. I burst out laughing. Julian Mastakovich turned round and, in spite of all his self-importance, was thrown into utter confusion. At that moment our host walked in from the opposite door. The young lad crawled out from under the table and wiped his elbows and knees. Julian Mastakovich hastened to put the handkerchief, which he was holding by one end, to his nose.

Our host regarded the three of us with a somewhat puzzled expression; but as a man of experience who took a serious view of life, he immediately availed himself of the opportunity of catching his visitor by himself.

"This is the boy, sir," he said, pointing at the red-haired boy, "I spoke to you about . . ."

"I beg your pardon," said Julian Mastakovich who had not entirely recovered himself.

"The son of my children's governess, sir," our host went on in the tone of a man asking for a favour. "She's a woman in rather poor circumstances, sir, the widow of a very honest civil servant, and that's why I thought you might . . ."

"No, no, no," Julian Mastakovich cried quickly. "I'm sorry, sir, but it's quite out of the question. I've made inquiries and there is no vacancy, and even if there had been one, there are a dozen candidates waiting for it who have a better claim than he. Sorry, sir. Very sorry."

"A pity," said our host, "he's such a quiet, inoffensive little boy."

"A very mischievous boy, sir, from what I've seen of him," replied Julian Mastakovich with a convulsive twist of his lips. "Get along, boy! What are you waiting for? Go and join your playmates!" he said, addressing the boy.

Here it seemed he could not keep it up any longer and glanced at me out of the corner of one eye. I, too, was not able to keep it up and laughed straight in his face. Julian Mastakovich at once turned away and asked our host in a voice loud enough for me to hear who that strange young man was. They began to exchange whispered confidences and left the room. Afterwards I saw Julian Mastakovich shaking his head incredulously as he listened to our host.

Having laughed to my heart's content, I returned to the ballroom. There the great man, surrounded by fathers and mothers, including our host and hostess, was holding forth very warmly about something to a lady he had just been introduced to. The lady was holding by the hand the little girl with whom Julian Mastakovich had had the scene in the drawing-room about ten minutes before. Now he waxed ecstatic in his praises of the beauty, talents, grace, and good breeding of the sweet child. He quite undisguisedly grovelled before the mother, who listened to him almost with tears of rapture. The father's lips were smiling. Our host was delighted at these manifestations of universal joy. Even the guests were deeply sympathetic; even the children were told to stop playing so as not to interfere with the conversation; the air itself was charged with reverence. I heard afterwards how the dear mother of the charming little girl, touched to the bottom of her heart, begged Julian Mastakovich to be so kind as to honour her house with the presence of his inestimable person; how Julian Mastakovich accepted her invitation with unfeigned enthusiasm; and how later on the guests, going their several ways as demanded by the rules of propriety and decorum, vied with each other in paying the most touching compliments to the contractor, the contractor's wife, the little girl, and, last but not least, Julian Mastakovich.

"Is that gentleman married?" I asked in a rather loud voice of one of my acquaintances who was standing nearest to Julian Mastakovich.

Julian Mastakovich threw a vindictive and searching glance at me.

"No," replied my acquaintance, shocked by my breach of good manners, a breach which, I must say, I had committed deliberately.

—

As I was passing a certain church a few days ago, I was surprised to see a large crowd and a great number of carriages in front of it. Everyone around me was talking about a wedding. The day was cloudy; it was beginning to sleet. I followed the crowd into the church and there I saw the bridegroom. He was a small, rotund, sleek, paunchy little man, highly adorned. He never sat still, was in every part of the church at once, attending to everything and issuing orders. At last a rumour passed through the crowd that the bride had arrived. I pushed my way through the people and saw an extraordinarily beautiful girl for whom the spring-tide of life had scarcely begun. But the beautiful girl was sad and pale. She looked about her without interest; I even fancied that her eyes were red with recent tears. The classic severity of every feature of her face added a touch of solemn dignity to her beauty. And through this severity and dignity, through this sadness, a faint glimmer of the first innocent bloom of childhood could still be caught. The sensation I got was of something incredibly naïve, of something that had not yet had time to set, of something young and fresh, and—of something, too, that seemed to be mutely beseeching for mercy.

People were saying that she was only just sixteen. Looking closely at the bridegroom, I recognised in a flash Julian Mastakovich. I looked at her. Dear God! . . .

I began to make my way quickly to the door. In the crowd they were saying that the bride was an heiress, that her dowry was worth five hundred thousand, not to mention the thousands that must have been spent on her trousseau. . . .

"He got his sum right, by Jove," I thought as I elbowed my way into the street.

The Peasant Marey

It was Easter Monday. The air was warm, the sky blue, the sun high, "warm" and bright, but I was plunged in gloom. I wandered aimlessly behind the barracks in the prison yard, looked at the palings of the strong prison fence, counting them mechanically, though I did not particularly want to count them, but doing it more out of habit than anything else. It was the second day of "holidays" in prison. The convicts were not taken out to work, lots of them were drunk, cursing and quarrelling broke out every minute in different corners of the prison. Disgusting, coarse songs; groups of convicts playing cards under the bunks; several convicts who had run amok and had been dealt with summarily by their own comrades, were lying half dead on the bunks, covered with sheepskins, until they should recover consciousness; the knives that had already been drawn several times—all this had so harrowing an effect on me during the two days of holidays that it made me ill. I could never bear without disgust the wild orgies of the common people, and here in this place this was specially true. On such days even the officials never looked into the prison, carried out no searches, did not look for drinks, realising that once a year even these outcasts had to be given a chance of enjoying themselves and that otherwise things would be much worse. At last blind fury blazed up in my heart. I met the Pole, M—ski,* one of the political prisoners. He gave me a black look, with flashing eyes and trembling lips. "*Je hais ces brigands!*" he hissed at me in an undertone and walked past me. I went back to the barracks, although I had rushed out of them like a madman only a quarter of an hour before, when six strong peasants had hurled themselves on the drunken Tartar Gazin in an attempt to quieten him and had begun beating him. They beat him senselessly—a camel might have been killed by such blows. But they knew that it was not easy to kill this Hercules, and they beat him therefore without any qualms. Now, on my return, I noticed Gazin lying unconscious and without any sign of life on a bunk in a corner at the other end of the barracks; he lay covered with a sheepskin, and they all passed by him in silence, knowing very well that if the man was unlucky he might die from a beating like that. I made my way to my place opposite the window with the iron bars and lay on my back with my eyes closed and my hands behind my head. I liked to lie like that: no one would bother a sleeping man, and meanwhile one could dream and think. But I found it difficult to dream: my heart was beating uneasily and M—ski's words were still echoing in my ears: "*Je hais ces brigands!*" However, why dwell on these scenes; I sometimes even now dream of those times at night, and none of my dreams is more agonising. Perhaps it will be noticed that to this day I have hardly ever spoken in print of my life in prison; *The House of the Dead* I wrote fifteen years ago in the person of a fictitious character who was supposed to have killed his wife. I may add, incidentally, just as an interesting detail, that many people have thought and have been maintaining ever since the publication of that book of mine, that I was sent to Siberia for the murder of my wife.

By and by I did forget my surroundings and became imperceptibly lost in memories. During the four years of my imprisonment I was continually recalling my past and seemed in my memories to live my former life all over again. These memories cropped up by themselves; I seldom evoked them consciously. It would begin from

*O. Miretski, who was serving a prison sentence with Dostoevsky.

some point, some imperceptible feature, which then grew little by little into a complete picture, into some clear-cut and vivid impression. I used to analyse those impressions, adding new touches to an event that had happened long ago, and, above all, correcting it, correcting it incessantly, and that constituted my chief amusement. This time I for some reason suddenly remembered one fleeting instant in my early childhood when I was only nine years old—an instant that I seemed to have completely forgotten; but at that time I was particularly fond of memories of my early childhood. I remembered an August day in our village; a dry, bright day, though rather cold and windy; summer was drawing to a close, and we should soon have to leave for Moscow and again have to spend all winter over the boring French lessons, and I was so sorry to leave the country. I walked past the threshing floors and, going down a ravine, climbed up into the dense thicket of bushes which stretched from the other side of the ravine to the wood. I got amongst the bushes, and I could hear not very far away, about thirty yards perhaps, a peasant ploughing by himself on a clearing. I knew he was ploughing up the steep slope of a hill. The horse must have found it very hard going, for from time to time I heard the peasant's call from a distance: "Gee up! Gee up!" I knew almost all our peasants, but I did not know which of them was ploughing now, nor did it really matter to me who it was because I was occupied with my own affairs—I too was busy, breaking off a switch from a hazel-tree to strike frogs with; hazel twigs are very lovely, but they are also very brittle, much more brittle than birch twigs. I was also interested in beetles and other insects, and I was collecting them; some of them were very beautiful. I also liked the small quick red and yellow lizards with black spots, but I was afraid of snakes. However, there were many fewer snakes than lizards. There were not many mushrooms there; to get mushrooms one had to go to the birch wood, and I was about to go there. And there was nothing in the world I loved so much as the wood with its mushrooms and wild berries, its beetles and its birds, its hedgehogs and squirrels, and its damp smell of rotted leaves. And even as I write this I can smell the fragrance of our birch wood: these impressions remain with you for your whole life. Suddenly amid the dead silence I heard clearly and distinctly the shout, "Wolf! Wolf!" I uttered a shriek and, panic-stricken, screamed at the top of my voice and rushed out to the clearing straight to the ploughing peasant.

It was our peasant Marey. I do not know if there is such a name, but everybody called him Marey. He was a peasant of about fifty, thick-set and over medium height, with a large, grizzled, dark-brown beard. I knew him, but till that day I had scarcely ever spoken to him. When he heard my cry, he even stopped his old mare, and when, unable to stop myself I clutched at his wooden plough with one hand and at his sleeve with the other, he saw how terrified I was.

"There's a wolf there!" I cried, breathless.

He threw up his head and looked round involuntarily, for a moment almost believing me.

"Where's the wolf?"

"Someone shouted—shouted just now 'Wolf! Wolf!' " I stammered.

"There, there! There are no wolves hereabouts," he murmured, trying to calm me. "You've been dreaming, sonny. Who ever heard of wolves in these parts?"

But I was trembling all over and I was still clutching at his smock, and I suppose I must have been very pale. He looked at me with a worried smile, evidently anxious and troubled about me.

"Dear, dear, how frightened you are," he said, shaking his head. "Don't be frightened, sonny. Oh, you poor thing, you! There, there."

He stretched out his hand and suddenly stroked my cheek.

"There now! Christ be with you, cross yourself, there's a good lad!"

But I did not cross myself; the corners of my mouth were still twitching, and that seemed to strike him particularly. He quietly stretched out his thick finger with its black nail, smeared with earth, and gently touched my trembling lips.

"Dear, oh dear," he smiled at me with a slow motherly sort of smile, "Lord, how frightened he is, the poor lad!"

I realised at last that there was no wolf and that I had imagined the shout, "Wolf! Wolf!" The shout, though, was very clear and distinct, but such shouts (and not only about wolves) I had imagined once or twice before, and I knew it. (I grew out of these hallucinations a few years later.)

"Well, I'll go now," I said, looking up at him, questioningly and shyly.

"Run along, run along, son, I'll be awatching you," he said, adding, "Don't you worry, I shan't let the wolf get you!" and he smiled at me with the same motherly smile. "Well, Christ be with you. Run along, run along, sonny," and he made the sign of the cross over me, and then crossed himself too.

I walked away, looking back anxiously every few yards. While I was walking away, Marey stood still with his mare and looked after me, nodding his head at me every time I looked round. As a matter of fact, I was a little ashamed of myself for having let him see how frightened I was, but I was still very much afraid of the wolf as I was walking away till I climbed up the steep side of the ravine and came to the first threshing barn. There my terror left me completely, and our watchdog Volchok suddenly appeared out of nowhere and rushed at me. With Volchok at my side I completely recovered my spirits and turned round to Marey for the last time. I could no longer see his face clearly, but I felt that he was still nodding and smiling tenderly at me. I waved to him and he waved back to me and started his mare.

"Gee up!" I heard his call in the distance again, and the mare pulled at the wooden plough once more.

All this came back to me all at once, I don't know why, but with an amazing accuracy of detail. I suddenly came to and sat up on my bunk and, I remember, I could still feel the gentle smile of memory on my lips. For another minute I went on recalling that incident from my childhood.

When I returned home from Marey that day I did not tell anybody about my "adventure." It was not much of an adventure, anyway. And, besides, I soon forgot all about Marey. Whenever I happened to come across him now and then, I never spoke to him either about the wolf or anything else, and now twenty years later in Siberia I suddenly remembered this meeting so distinctly that not a single detail of it was lost, which means of course that it must have been hidden in my mind without my knowing it, of itself and without any effort on my part, and came back to me suddenly when it was wanted. I remembered the tender, motherly smile of that serf, the way he made the sign of the cross over me and crossed himself, the way he nodded at me. "Lord, how afeared he is, the poor lad!" And particularly that thick finger of his, smeared with earth, with which he touched my twitching lips so gently and with such shy tenderness. No doubt, anyone would have done his best to calm a child, but something quite different seemed to have happened during that solitary meeting; and if I had been his own son, he could not have looked at me with eyes shining with brighter love. And who compelled him to look like that? He was one of our serfs, a peasant who was our property, and after all I was the son of his master. No one would have known that he had been so good to me, and no one would have rewarded him for it. Did he really love little children as much as that? There are such people, no doubt. Our meeting took place in a secluded spot, in a deserted field, and only God perhaps saw from above with what profound and enlightened human feeling, and with what delicate, almost womanly, tenderness the heart of a coarse, savagely ignorant Russian serf was filled, a serf who at the time neither expected nor dreamt of his emancipation.

Tell me, was not this what Konstantin Aksakov perhaps meant when he spoke of the high degree of culture of our people?

And so when I got off the bunk and looked round, I suddenly felt I remember, that I could look at these unhappy creatures with quite different eyes, and that suddenly by some miracle all hatred and anger had vanished from my heart. I walked round the prison peering into the faces I came across. That rascal of a peasant with his shaven head and branded face, yelling his hoarse drunken song at the top of his voice—why, he, too, may be the same sort of peasant as Marey: I cannot possibly look into his heart, can I? That evening I again met M—ski. Poor man! He could have no memories about Marey or peasants like him and he could have no other opinion of these people except, "*Je hais ces brigands*!" Yes, it was much harder for those Poles than for us!

Notes from the Underground

PART I
UNDERGROUND*

I

I am a sick man. . . . I am a spiteful man. No, I am not a pleasant man at all. I believe there is something wrong with my liver. However, I don't know a damn thing about my liver; neither do I know whether there is anything really wrong with me. I am not under medical treatment, and never have been, though I do respect medicine and doctors. In addition, I am extremely superstitious, at least suf-

*Both the author of the Notes and the Notes themselves are, of course, fictitious. Nevertheless, such persons as the author of such memoirs not only may, but must, exist in our society, if we take into consideration the circumstances which led to the formation of our society. It was my intention to bring before our reading public, more conspicuously than is usually done, one of the characters of our recent past. He is one of the representatives of a generation that is still with us. In this extract, entitled *Underground,* this person introduces himself and his views and, as it were, tries to explain those causes which have not only led, but also were bound to lead, to his appearance in our midst. In the subsequent extract *(Apropos of the Wet Snow)* we shall reproduce this person's *Notes* proper, dealing with certain events of his life.

FYODOR DOSTOEVSKY

ficiently so to respect medicine. (I am well educated enough not to be superstitious, but I am superstitious for all that.) The truth is, I refuse medical treatment out of spite. I don't suppose you will understand that. Well, I do. I don't expect I shall be able to explain to you who it is I am actually trying to annoy in this case by my spite; I realise full well that I can't "hurt" the doctors by refusing to be treated by them; I realise better than any one that by all this I am only hurting myself and no one else. Still, the fact remains that if I refuse to be medically treated, it is only out of spite. My liver hurts me—well, let it damn well hurt—the more it hurts the better.

I have been living like this a long time—about twenty years, I should think. I am forty now. I used to be in the Civil Service, but I am no longer there now. I was a spiteful civil servant. I was rude and took pleasure in being rude. Mind you, I never accepted any bribes, so that I had at least to find something to compensate myself for that. (A silly joke, but I shan't cross it out. I wrote it thinking it would sound very witty, but now that I have seen myself that I merely wanted to indulge in a bit of contemptible bragging, I shall let it stand on purpose!)

Whenever people used to come to my office on some business, I snarled at them and felt as pleased as Punch when I succeeded in making one of them really unhappy. I nearly always did succeed. They were mostly a timid lot: what else can you expect people who come to a Government office to be? But among the fine gentlemen who used to come to me to make inquiries there was one officer in particular whom I could not bear. He would not submit with a good grace and he had a disgusting habit of rattling his sword. For sixteen months I waged a regular war with him over that sword. In the end, I got the better of him. He stopped rattling. However, all this happened a long time ago when I was still a young man. And do you know, gentlemen, what was the chief point about my spitefulness? Well, the whole point of it, I mean, the whole nasty, disgusting part of it was that all the time I was shamefully conscious—even at the moments of my greatest exasperation—that I was not at all a spiteful or even an exasperated man, but that I was merely frightening sparrows for no reason in the world, and being hugely amused by this pastime. I might foam at the mouth, but just present me with some little toy, give me a cup of tea with sugar in it, and I shouldn't be at all surprised if I calmed down completely, even be deeply touched, though afterwards I should most certainly snarl at myself and be overcome with shame and suffer from insomnia for months. That's the sort of man I am.

Incidentally, I was rather exaggerating just now when I said that I was a spiteful civil servant. All I did, as a matter of fact, was to indulge in a little innocent fun at the expense of the officer and the people who came to my office on business, for actually I never could become a spiteful man. I was always conscious of innumerable elements in me which were absolutely contrary to that. I felt them simply swarming in me all my life and asking to be allowed to come out, but I wouldn't let them. I would not let them! I would deliberately not let them. They tormented me to the point of making me ashamed of myself; they reduced me to a state of nervous exhaustion and, finally, I got fed up with them. Oh, how thoroughly I got fed up with them in the end! But doesn't it seem to you, gentlemen, that I might possibly be apologising to you for something? Asking you to forgive me for something? Yes, I'm sure it does. . . . Well, I assure you I don't care a damn whether it does seem so to you or not. . . .

Not only did I not become spiteful, I did not even know how to become anything, either spiteful or good, either a blackguard or an honest man, either a hero or an insect. And now I've been spending the last four years of my life in my funk-hole, consoling myself with the rather spiteful, though entirely useless, reflection that an intelligent man cannot possibly become anything in particular and that only a fool succeeds in becoming anything. Yes, a man of the nineteenth century must be, and is indeed morally bound to be, above all a characterless person; a man of character, on the other hand, a man of action, is mostly a fellow with a very circumscribed imagination. This is my conviction as a man of forty. I am forty now and, mind you, forty years is a whole lifetime. It is extreme old age. It is positively immoral, indecent, and vulgar to live more than forty years. Who lives longer than forty? Answer me that—

sincerely and honestly. I'll tell you who—fools and blackguards—they do! I don't mind telling that to all old men to their face—all those worthy old men, all those silver-haired and ambrosial old men! I'll tell it to the whole world, damned if I won't! I have a right to say so, for I shall live to the age of sixty myself. I'll live to be seventy! I'll live to be eighty! Wait a minute, let me take breath. . . .

I expect you must be thinking, gentlemen, that I want to amuse you. Well, you're mistaken there too. I'm not at all the jolly sort of person you think I am, or may think I am. However, if irritated with all this idle talk (and I feel that you are irritated), you were to ask me who I really am, then I should reply, I'm a retired civil servant of humble rank, a collegiate assessor. I got myself a job in the Civil Service because I had to eat (and only for that reason), and when a distant relative of mine left me six thousand roubles in his will last year, I immediately resigned from the Civil Service and settled in my little corner. I used to live in this corner before, but now I'm settled permanently here. My room is a dreadful, horrible hole, on the very outskirts of the town. My maidservant is an old country woman, bad-tempered from sheer stupidity, and there is, besides, always a bad smell about her. I'm told the Petersburg climate isn't good for me any more and that with my small means it is very expensive to live in Petersburg. I know that perfectly well, much better than all those experienced and wise mentors and counsellors. But I'm staying in Petersburg. I shall never leave Petersburg! I shan't leave it—oh, but it really makes no damned difference whether I leave it or not.

By the way, what does a decent chap talk about with the greatest possible pleasure?

Answer: about himself.

Very well, so I will talk about myself.

II

I should like to tell you now, gentlemen, whether you want to listen to me or not, why I've never been able to become even an insect. I declare to you solemnly that I've wished to become an insect many times. But even that has not been vouchsafed to me. I assure you, gentlemen, that to be too acutely conscious is a disease, a real, honest-to-goodness disease. It would have been quite sufficient for the business of everyday life to possess the ordinary human consciousness, that is to say, half or even a quarter of the share which falls to the lot of an intelligent man of our unhappy nineteenth century who, besides, has the double misfortune of living in Petersburg, the most abstract and premeditated city in the whole world. (There are premeditated and unpremeditated cities.) It would have been quite sufficient, for instance, to possess the sort of consciousness with which all the so-called plain men and men of action are endowed. I bet you think I'm writing all this just out of a desire to show off or to crack a joke at the expense of our men of action, and that if I'm rattling my sword like my army officer it is merely because I want to show off, and in rather bad taste, too. But, gentlemen, who wants to show off his own infirmities, let alone boast about them?

However, what am I talking about? Everyone does it; everyone does show off his infirmities, and I more than anyone else perhaps. But don't let us quibble about it; the point I raised was absurd. Still, I firmly believe that not only too much consciousness, but any sort of consciousness is a disease. I insist upon that. But let us leave that, too, for a moment. Tell me this: why did it invariably happen that just at those moments—yes, at those very moments—when I was acutely conscious of "the sublime and beautiful," as we used to call it in those days, I was not only conscious but also guilty of the most contemptible actions which—well, which, in fact, everybody is guilty of, but which, as though on purpose, I only happened to commit when I was most conscious that they ought not to be committed? The more conscious I became of goodness and all that was "sublime and beautiful," the more deeply did I sink into the mire and the more ready I was to sink into it altogether. And the trouble was that all this did not seem to happen to me by accident, but as though it couldn't possibly have happened otherwise. As though it were my normal condition, and not in the least a disease or a vice, so that at last I no longer even attempted to fight against this vice. It ended by my almost believing (and perhaps I did actually believe) that this was probably my normal condition. At first, at the very outset, I mean, what horrible agonies I used to suffer in that struggle! I did not think others had the same experience, and afterwards I kept it to myself as though it were a secret. I was ashamed (and quite possibly I still am ashamed); it got so far that I felt a sort of secret, abnormal, contemptible delight when, on coming home on one of the foulest nights in Petersburg, I used to realise intensely that again I had been guilty of some particularly dastardly action that day, and that once more it was no earthly use crying over spilt milk; and inwardly, secretly, I used to go on nagging myself, worrying myself, accusing myself, till at last the bitterness I felt turned into a sort of shameful, damnable sweetness, and finally, into real, positive delight! Yes, into delight. Into delight! I'm certain of it. As a matter of fact, I've mentioned this because I should like to know for certain whether other people feel the same sort of delight. Let me explain it to you. The feeling of delight was there just because I was so intensely aware of my own degradation; because I felt myself that I had come up against a blank wall; that no doubt, it was bad, but that it couldn't be helped; that there was no escape, and that I should never become a different man; that even if there still was any time or faith left to make myself into something different, I should most likely have refused to do so; and even if I wanted to I should still have done nothing, because as a matter of fact there was nothing I could change into. And above all—and this is the final point I want to make—whatever happened, happened in accordance with the normal and fundamental laws of intensified consciousness and by a sort of inertia which is a direct consequence of those laws, and that therefore you not only could not change yourself, but you simply couldn't make any attempt to. Hence it follows that as a result of that intensified consciousness you are quite right in being a blackguard, as though it were any consolation to the blackguard that he actually is a blackguard. But enough. . . . Good Lord, I have talked a lot, haven't I? But have I explained anything? How is one to explain this feeling of delight? But I shall explain myself. I shall pursue the matter to the bitter end! That is why I've taken up my pen. . . .

Now, for instance, I'm very vain. I'm as suspicious and as quick to take offence as a hunchback or a dwarf, but as a matter of fact there were moments in my life when, if someone had slapped my face, I should perhaps have been glad even of that. I'm saying this seriously: I should quite certainly have found even there a sort of pleasure, the pleasure of despair, no doubt, but despair too has its moments of intense pleasure, intense delight, especially if you happen to be acutely conscious of the hopelessness of your position. And there, too, I mean, after you'd had your face slapped, you'd be overwhelmed by the consciousness of having been utterly humiliated and snubbed. The trouble is, of course, that however much I tried to find some excuse for what had happened, the conclusion I'd come to would always be that it was my own fault to begin with, and what hurt most of all was that though innocent I was guilty and, as it were, guilty according to the laws of nature. I was guilty, first of all, because I was cleverer than all the people round me. (I have always considered myself cleverer than any one else in the world, and sometimes, I assure you, I've been even ashamed of it. At least, all my life I looked away and I could never look people straight in the face.) I was, finally, guilty because even if I had had a grain of magnanimity in me, I should have suffered a thousand times more from the consciousness of its uselessness. For I should most certainly not have known what to do with my magnanimity—neither to forgive, since the man who would have slapped my face, would most probably have done it in obedience to the laws of nature; nor to forget, since though even if it is the law of nature, it hurts all the same. Finally, even if I had wanted to be utterly ungenerous and, on the contrary, had desired to avenge myself on the man who had offended me, I couldn't have avenged myself on anyone for anything because I should never have had the courage to do anything even if I could. Why shouldn't I have had the courage? Well, I'd like to say a few words about that by itself.

III

You see, people who know how to avenge themselves and, generally, how to stand up for themselves—how do they, do you think, do it? They are, let us assume, so seized by the feeling of revenge that while that feeling lasts there is nothing but that feeling left in them. Such a man goes straight to his goal, like a mad bull, with lowered horns, and only a stone wall perhaps will stop him. (Incidentally, before such a stone wall such people, that is to say, plain men and men of action, as a rule capitulate at once. To them a stone wall is not a challenge as it is, for instance, to us thinking men who, because we are thinking men, do nothing; it is not an excuse for turning aside, an excuse in which one of our sort does not believe himself, but of which he is always very glad. No, they capitulate in all sincerity. A stone wall exerts a sort of calming influence upon them, a sort of final and morally decisive influence, and perhaps even a mystic one. . . . But of the stone wall later.) Well, that sort of plain man I consider to be the real, normal man, such as his tender mother nature herself wanted to see him when she so lovingly brought him forth upon the earth. I envy such a man with all the forces of my embittered heart. He is stupid—I am not disputing that. But perhaps the normal man should be stupid. How are you to know? Why, perhaps this is even beautiful. And I'm all the more convinced of that—shall we say?—suspicion, since if we take, for instance, the antithesis of the normal man, that is to say, the man of great sensibility, who of course has sprung not out of the lap of nature, but out of a test tube (this is almost mysticism, gentlemen, but I, too, suspect it), then this test-tube-begotten man sometimes capitulates to his antithesis to such an extent that for all his intense sensibility he frankly considers himself a mouse and not a man. I grant you it is an intensely conscious mouse, but it's a mouse all the same, whereas the other is a man, and consequently . . . etc. And, above all, he himself—oh, yes, he in his own person—considers himself a mouse; no one asks him to do so; and this is an important point.

Well, let us now have a look at this mouse in action. Let us suppose, for instance, that its feelings are hurt (and its feelings are almost always hurt), and that it also wants to avenge itself. There will perhaps be a greater accumulation of spite in it than in *l'homme de la nature et de la vérité*. A nasty, mean little desire to repay whoever has offended it in his own coin stirs within it more nastily perhaps than in *l'homme de la nature et de la vérité;* for because of his inborn stupidity *l'homme de la nature et de la vérité* looks upon his revenge merely as a matter of justice whereas because of its intense sensibility the mouse denies that there is any question of justice here. At last we come to the business itself, to the act of revenge. The unhappy mouse has already succeeded in piling up—in the form of questions and doubts—a large number of dirty tricks in addition to its original dirty trick; it has accumulated such a large number of insoluble questions round every one question that it is drowned in a sort of deadly brew, a stinking puddle made up of its doubts, its flurries of emotion, and lastly, the contempt with which the plain men of action cover it from head to foot while they stand solemnly round as judges and dictators and split their sides with laughter at it. Well, of course, all that is left for it to do is to dismiss it with a disdainful wave of its little paw and with a smile of simulated contempt, in which it does not believe itself, and to scurry back ingloriously into its hole. There, in its stinking, disgusting, subterranean hole, our hurt, ridiculed, and beaten mouse plunges into cold, venomous, and, above all, unremitting spite. For forty years it will continuously remember its injury to the last and most shameful detail, and will, besides add to it still more shameful details, worrying and exciting itself spitefully with the aid of its own imagination. It will be ashamed of its own fancies, but it will nevertheless remember everything, go over everything with the utmost care, think up all sorts of imaginary wrongs on the pretext that they, too, might have happened, and will forgive nothing. Quite likely it will start avenging itself, but, as it were, by fits and starts, in all sorts of trivial ways, from behind the stove, incognito, without believing in its right to avenge itself, nor in the success of its vengeance, and knowing beforehand that it will suffer a hundred times more itself from all its attempts at revenge than the person on whom it is revenging itself, who will most probably not care a hang about it. Even on its deathbed it will remember everything with the interest accumulated during all that time, and. . . . And it is just in that cold and loathsome half-despair and half-belief—in that conscious burying oneself alive for grief for forty years—in that intensely perceived, but to some extent uncertain, helplessness of one's position—in all that poison of unsatisfied desires that have turned inwards—in that fever of hesitations, firmly taken decisions, and regrets that follow almost instantaneously upon them—that the essence of that delight I have spoken of lies. It is so subtle and sometimes so difficult to grasp by one's conscious mind that people whose mental horizon is even a little bit circumscribed, or simply people with strong nerves, will not understand anything of it. "Perhaps," you will add with a grin, "those who have never had their faces slapped will not understand it, either," and in that polite way give me a hint that I too have perhaps had my face slapped in my life and that for that reason I'm speaking about it with authority. I bet that's what you are thinking. But don't worry, gentlemen, I've never had my face slapped, and I don't care a damn what you may think about it. Very likely I am sorry not to have boxed the ears of a sufficient number of people in my lifetime. But enough! Not another word about this subject which seems to interest you so much.

Let me continue calmly about the people with strong nerves who do not understand the subtleties of the pleasure I have been speaking of. Though on some occasions these gentlemen may roar at the top of their voices like bulls, and though this, let us assume, does them the greatest credit, yet as I've already said, they at once capitulate in face of the impossible. The impossible is to them equivalent to a stone wall. What stone wall? Why, the laws of nature, of course, the conclusions of natural science, mathematics. When, for instance, it is proved to you that you are descended from a monkey, then it's no use pulling a long face about it: you just have to accept it. When they prove to you that one drop of your own fat must, as a matter of course, be dearer to you than a hundred thousand of your fellow-men and that all the so-called virtues and duties and other vain fancies and prejudices are, as a result of that consideration, of no importance whatever, then you have to accept it whether you like it or not, because twice-two—mathematics. Just try to refute that.

"Good Lord," they'll scream at you, "you can't possibly deny that: twice two *is* four! Never does nature ask you for your opinion; she does not care a damn for your wishes, or whether you like her laws or not. You are obliged to accept her as she is and, consequently, all her results. A stone wall, that is, is a stone wall . . . etc., etc." But, goodness gracious me, what do I care for the laws of nature and arithmetic if for some reason or other I don't like those laws of twice-two? No doubt I shall never be able to break through such a stone wall with my forehead, if I really do not possess the strength to do it, but I shall not reconcile myself to it just because I have to deal with a stone wall and haven't the strength to knock it down.

As though such a stone wall were really the same thing as peace of mind, and as though it really contained some word of comfort simply because a stone wall is merely the equivalent of twice-two-makes-four. Oh, what stuff and nonsense this is! Is it not much better to understand everything, to be aware of everything, to be conscious of all the impossibilities and stone walls? Not to be reconciled to any of those impossibilities or stone walls if you hate being reconciled to them? To reach by way of the most irrefutable logical combinations the most hideous conclusions on the eternal theme that it is somehow your own fault if there is a stone wall, though again it is abundantly clear that it is not your fault at all, and therefore to abandon yourself sensuously to doing nothing, silently and gnashing your teeth impotently, hugging the illusion that there isn't really anyone you can be angry with; that there is really no object for your anger and that perhaps there never will be an object for it; that the whole thing is nothing but some imposition, some hocus-pocus, some card-sharping trick, or simply some frightful mess—no one knows what and no one knows who. But in spite of these uncertainties and this hocus-pocus, you have still got a headache, and the less you know the more splitting the headache!

IV

"Ha-ha-ha! After this you'll no doubt be finding some pleasure in toothache too!" you cry with a laugh.

"Well, why not? There's pleasure even in toothache," I reply.

I had toothache for a whole month, and I know there is pleasure in it. For, you see, if you have toothache, you don't lose your temper in silence. You groan. But these groans of yours are not sincere groans. They are groans mixed with malice. And it is the malice here that matters. By these groans the sufferer expresses his pleasure. If he did not feel any pleasure, he would not groan. That is an excellent example, gentlemen, and I'm going to develop it.

In these groans there is expressed, in the first place, the whole purposelessness of your pain which is so humiliating to your consciousness; the crowning stroke of nature, for which you, of course, don't care, but from which you suffer all the same, while she goes scot free. They express the consciousness of the fact that even though you had no enemies, you do have pain; the consciousness that for all the dentists in the world you are entirely at the mercy of your teeth; that if someone should desire it, your teeth would stop aching, and if he does not, they will go on aching another three months; and that, finally, if you are still unconvinced and still keep on protesting, all that is left for your own gratification is to give yourself a thrashing or hit the wall with your fist as hard as you can, and absolutely nothing more.

Well, it is from those mortal injuries, from those gibes that come from goodness knows whom, that pleasure at last arises, pleasure that sometimes reaches the highest degree of voluptuousness. I beg of you, gentlemen, listen sometimes to the groans of an educated man of the nineteenth century who is suffering from toothache on—shall we say?—the second or third day of his indisposition, when he is beginning to groan in quite a different way from the way he groaned on the first day, that is, not simply because he has toothache, not like some coarse peasant, but like a man of culture and European civilisation, like a man "who has divorced himself from the soil and uprooted himself from his people," to use a phrase which is at present in vogue. His groans become nasty and offensively ill-tempered groans, and go on for days and nights. And yet he knows perfectly well that he is doing no good with his groaning; he knows better than anyone that he is merely irritating and worrying himself and others for nothing; he knows that the audience before whom he is performing with such zeal and all his family are listening to him with disgust, that they don't believe him in the least, and that in their hearts they know that, if he wished, he could have groaned differently and more naturally, without such trills and flourishes, and that he is only amusing himself out of spite and malice. Well, all those apprehensions and infamies are merely the expression of sensual pleasure. "I'm worrying you, am I?" he seems to say. "I'm breaking your hearts, I'm not letting anyone in the house sleep, am I? All right, don't sleep. I want you, too, to feel every minute that I have toothache. I'm no longer the same hero to you now as I tried to appear before, but just a loathsome little fellow, a nuisance? Very well then. So be it. I'm very glad you've found me out at last. You hate to listen to my mean little groans, do you? Well, all right. Hate it if you like. Just you listen to my next flourish. It'll be much worse than the one before, I promise you. . . ." You still don't understand, gentlemen? Well, it seems we have to develop still further and more thoroughly, we have to sharpen our consciousness still more, before we can fully appreciate all the twists and turns of this sort of voluptuous pleasure. You are laughing? I'm very glad, I'm sure. I'm afraid, gentlemen, my jokes are in very bad taste, they are lame and a bit confused, and show a lack of self-confidence, too. That is because I have no self-respect. But can a man of acute sensibility respect himself at all?

V

Well, can you expect a man who tries to find pleasure even in the feeling of his own humiliation to have an atom of respect for himself? I'm not saying this now from any hypersensitive feeling of remorse. And, anyway, I never could stand saying, "Sorry, father, I won't do it again,"—not because I'm not capable of saying it; on the contrary, because I'm too capable of saying it. Yes, indeed! I used to get into awful trouble on such occasions though I was not even remotely to be blamed for anything. That was the most horrible part of it. But every time that happened, I used to be touched to the very depth of my soul, I kept on repeating how sorry I was, shedding rivers of tears, and of course deceiving myself, though I was not pretending at all. It was my heart that somehow was responsible for all that nastiness.... Here one could not blame even the laws of nature, though the laws of nature have, in fact, always and more than anything else caused me infinite worry and trouble all through my life. It is disgusting to call to mind all this, and as a matter of fact it was a disgusting business even then. For after a minute or so I used to realise bitterly that it was all a lie, a horrible lie, a hypocritical lie, I mean, all those repentances, all those emotional outbursts, all those promises to turn over a new leaf. And if you ask why I tormented myself like that, the answer is because I was awfully bored sitting about and doing nothing, and that is why I started on that sort of song and dance. I assure you it is true. You'd better start watching yourselves more closely, gentlemen, and you will understand that it is so. I used to invent my own adventures, I used to devise my own life for myself, so as to be able to carry on somehow. How many times, for instance, used I to take offence without rhyme or reason, deliberately; and of course I realised very well that I had taken offence at nothing, that the whole thing was just a piece of playacting, but in the end I would work myself up into such a state that I would be offended in good earnest. All my life I felt drawn to play such tricks, so that in the end I simply lost control of myself. Another time I tried hard to fall in love. This happened to me twice, as a matter of fact. And I can assure you, gentlemen, I suffered terribly. In my heart of hearts, of course, I did not believe that I was suffering, I'd even sneer at myself in a vague sort of way, but I suffered agonies none the less, suffered in the most genuine manner imaginable, as though I were really in love. I was jealous. I made scenes. And all because I was so confoundedly bored, gentlemen, all because I was so horribly bored. Crushed by doing nothing. For the direct, the inevitable, and the legitimate result of consciousness is to make all action impossible, or—to put it differently—consciousness leads to thumb-twiddling. I've already said so before, but let me repeat, and repeat most earnestly: all plain men and men of action are active only because they are dull-witted and mentally undeveloped. How is that to be explained? Why, like this: owing to their arrested mental development they mistake the nearest and secondary causes for primary causes and in this way persuade themselves much more easily and quickly than other people that they have found a firm basis for whatever business they have in hand and, as a result, they are no longer worried, and that is really the main thing. For to start being active you must first of all be completely composed in mind and never be in doubt. But how can I, for instance, compose myself? Where am I to find the primary cause to lean against? Where am I to get the basis from? I am constantly exercising my powers of thought and, consequently, every primary cause with me at once draws another one after itself, one still more primary, and so *ad infinitum.* That, in fact, is the basis of every sort of consciousness and analysis. That, too, therefore is a law of nature. What is the result of it then? Why, the same. Remember I was speaking of revenge just now. (I don't suppose you grasped that.) I argued that a man revenges himself because he finds justice in it. This of course means that he has found a primary cause, a basis, namely, justice. It follows therefore that now he is absolutely calm and, consequently, he revenges himself calmly and successfully, being convinced that what he does is both right and just. But I can't for the life of me see any justice here, and therefore if I should start revenging myself, it would be merely out of spite. Now spite, of course, could get the better of anything, of all my doubts, and so could very well take the place of any primary cause just because it is not a cause. But what can I do if I have not even spite (I began with that just now). Besides, my feeling of bitterness, too, is subject to the process of disintegration as a result of those damned laws of consciousness. One look and the object disappears into thin air, your reasons evaporate, there is no guilty man, the injury is no longer an injury but just fate, something in the nature of toothache for which no one can be blamed, and consequently there is only one solution left, namely, knocking your head against the wall as hard as you can. Well, so you just give it up because you've failed to find the primary cause. But try letting yourself be carried away by your emotions blindly, without reasoning, without any primary cause, letting your consciousness go hang at least for a time; hate or love just for the sake of not having to twiddle your thumbs.

What will happen, of course, is that the day after tomorrow (and that at the latest) you will begin despising yourself for having knowingly duped yourself. As a result—a soap bubble and doing nothing again. As a matter of fact, gentlemen, the reason why I consider myself a clever man is simply because I could never in my life finish anything I'd started. All right, I am a talker, a harmless, boring talker as we all are. But what can I do if the direct and sole purpose of every intelligent man is to talk, that is to say, to waste his time deliberately?

VI

Oh, if only I had done nothing merely out of laziness! Lord, how I should have respected myself then. I should have respected myself just because I should at least have been able to be lazy; I should at least have possessed one quality which might be mistaken for a positive one and in which I could have believed myself. Question—who is he? Answer—a loafer. I must say it would have been a real pleasure to have heard that said about myself, for it would have meant that a positive definition had been found for me and that there was something one could say about me. "A loafer!"—why, it's a title, a purpose in life. It's a career, gentlemen, a career! Don't joke about it. It is so. I should then be a member of the most exclusive club by right and should have done nothing but gone on respecting myself continually. I knew a gentleman who all through his life was proud of the fact that he was a great connoisseur of Château Lafitte. He considered it a positive virtue and never had any misgivings. He died not only with a clear, but positively with a triumphant conscience, and he was absolutely right. So I, too, should have chosen a career for myself: I should have been a loafer and a glutton, but would, for instance, admire the sublime and beautiful in everything. How do you like that? I've been dreaming about it a long time. The "sublime and beautiful" has been a great worry to me during my forty years, but that was only *during* my forty years, at one time—oh, at one time it would have been different! I should at once have found an appropriate occupation for myself, namely, to drink to the health of the sublime and the beautiful. I should have made use of every opportunity to drop a tear into my glass and then drain it to all that was sublime and beautiful. I should then have turned everything in the world into something sublime and beautiful; I should have found the sublime and beautiful in the foullest and most unmistakable rubbish. I should have oozed tears like a sponge. The artist G., for instance, paints a picture. At once I drink to the health of the artist G. who has painted a picture because I love all that is sublime and beautiful. An author writes something to please "everybody"; at once I drink to the health of "everybody" because I love all that is sublime and beautiful.

I should demand respect for myself for acting like that, and I should persecute anyone who would not show me respect. I should be at peace with the world and die in the odour of sanctity—why, it's delightful, it's simply delightful! And I should have grown such a monumental belly, I should have propagated such a double chin, I should have acquired such a fiery nose that every man in the street would have said as he looked at me, "Now that's a fine chap! Here's something real, something positive!"

And say what you like, gentlemen, it is very pleasant to hear such tributes in this negative age.

VII

But these are just golden dreams. Oh, tell me who was it first said, who was it first proclaimed that the only reason man behaves dishonourably is because he does not know his own interests, and that if he were enlightened, if his eyes were opened to his real normal interests, he would at once cease behaving dishonourably and would at once become good and honourable because, being enlightened and knowing what is good for him, he would see that his advantage lay in doing good, and of course it is well known that no man ever knowingly acts against his own interests and therefore he would, as it were, willy-nilly start doing good. Oh, the babe! Oh, the pure innocent child! When, to begin with, in the course of all these thousands of years has man ever acted in accordance with his own interests? What is one to do with the millions of facts that bear witness that man *knowingly*, that is, fully understanding his own interests, has left them in the background and rushed along a different path to take a risk, to try his luck, without being in any way compelled to do it by anyone or anything, but just as though he deliberately refused to follow the appointed path, and obstinately, wilfully, opened up a new, a difficult, and an utterly preposterous path, groping for it almost in the dark. Well, what does it mean but that to man this obstinacy and wilfulness is pleasanter than any advantage. . . . Advantage! What is advantage? Can you possibly give an exact definition of the nature of human advantage? And what if *sometimes* a man's ultimate advantage not only may, but even must, in certain cases consist in his desiring something that is immediately harmful and not advantageous to himself? If that is so, if such a case can arise, then the whole rule becomes utterly worthless. What do you think? Are there cases where it is so? You are laughing? Well, laugh away, gentlemen, only tell me this: have men's advantages ever been calculated with absolute precision? Are there not some which have not only not fitted in, but cannot possibly be fitted in any classification? You, gentlemen, have, so far as I know, drawn up your entire list of positive human values by taking the averages of statistical figures and relying on scientific and economic formulae. What are your values? They are peace, freedom, prosperity, wealth, and so on and so forth. So that any man who should, for instance, openly and knowingly act contrary to the whole of that list would, in your opinion, and in mine, too, for that matter, be an obscurantist or a plain madman, wouldn't he? But the remarkable thing surely is this: why does it always happen that when all these statisticians, sages, and lovers of the human race reckon up human values they always overlook one value? They don't even take it into account in the form in which it should be taken into account, and the whole calculation depends on that. What harm would there be if they did take it, that value, I mean, and add it to their list? But the trouble, you see, is that this peculiar good does not fall under any classification and cannot be included in any list. Now, I have a friend, for instance—why, good gracious, gentlemen, he is also a friend of yours, and indeed whose friend is he not? In undertaking any business, this gentleman at once explains to you in high-sounding and clear language how he intends to act in accordance with the laws of truth and reason. And not only that. He will talk to you, passionately and vehemently, all about real and normal human interests; he will scornfully reproach the shortsighted fools for not understanding their own advantages, nor the real meaning of virtue, and—exactly a quarter of an hour later, without any sudden or external cause but just because of some inner impulse which is stronger than any of his interests, he will do something quite different, that is to say, he will do something that is exactly contrary to what he has been saying himself: against the laws of reason and against his own interests, in short, against everything. . . . I'd better warn you, though, that my friend is a collective entity and that for that reason it is a little difficult to blame him alone. That's the trouble, gentlemen, that there exists something which is dearer to almost every man than his greatest good, or (not to upset the logic of my argument) that there exists one most valuable good (and one, too, that is being constantly overlooked, namely, the one we are talking about) which is greater and more desirable than all other goods, and for the sake of which a man, if need be, is ready to challenge all laws, that is to say, reason, honour, peace, prosperity—in short, all those excellent and useful things, provided he can obtain that primary and most desirable good which is dearer to him than anything in the world.

"Well," you say, "but they are values all the same, aren't they?"

Very well, I believe we shall soon understand each other, and, besides, this isn't a matter for quibbling. What is important is that this good is so remarkable just because it sets at naught all our classifications and shatters all the systems set up by the lovers of the human race for the happiness of the human race. In fact, it plays havoc with everything. But before I tell you what this good is, I should like to compromise myself personally and I therefore bluntly declare that all these fine systems, all these theories which try to explain to man all his normal interests so that, in attempting to obtain them by every possible means, he should at once become good and honourable, are in my opinion nothing but mere exercises in logic. Yes, exercises in logic. For to assert that you believed this theory of the regeneration of the whole human race by means of the system of its own advantages is, in my opinion, almost the same as—well, asserting, for instance, with Buckle, that civilisation softens man, who, consequently becomes less bloodthirsty and less liable to engage in wars. I believe he argues it very logically indeed. But man is so obsessed by systems and abstract deductions that he is ready to distort the truth deliberately, he is ready to deny the evidence of his senses, so long as he justifies his logic. That is why I take this example, for it is a most striking example. Well, just take a good look round you: rivers of blood are being spilt, and in the jolliest imaginable way, like champagne. Take all our nineteenth century in which Buckle lived. Look at Napoleon, the Great and the present one. Look at North America—the everlasting union. Look, finally, at Schleswig-Holstein. . . . And what, pray, does civilisation soften in us? All civilisation does is to develop in man the many-sidedness of his sensations, and nothing, absolutely nothing more. And through the development of his many-sidedness man, for all we know, may reach the stage when he will find pleasure in bloodshed. This has already happened to him. Have you noticed that the most subtle shedders of blood have almost invariably been most civilised men, compared with whom all the Attilas and Stenka Razins were just innocent babes, and if they are not so outstanding as Attila or Stenka Razin it is because we meet them so often, because they are *too* ordinary, and because we have got used to them. At any rate, civilisation has made man, if not more bloodthirsty, then certainly more hideously and more contemptibly bloodthirsty. In the past he looked on bloodshed as an act of justice and exterminated those he thought necessary to exterminate with a clear conscience; but now we consider bloodshed an abomination and we engage in this abomination more than ever. Which is worse? You'd better decide for yourselves. They say that Cleopatra (if I may take an instance from Roman history) loved to stick golden pins into the breasts of her slave-girls and enjoyed their screams and contortions. You will say that this happened in relatively speaking barbarous times; but today, too, we live in barbarous times because (again relatively speaking) today, too, we stick pins into people; today, too, though man has learnt to see things more clearly than in barbarous times, he is still very far from having learnt to act in accordance with the dictates of reason and science. But I daresay you are firmly convinced that he will most certainly learn to do so as soon as his so-called bad old habits completely disappear and as soon as common sense and science have completely re-educated human nature and directed it along the road of normal behaviour. You are convinced that, when this happens, man will stop making *deliberate* mistakes and perforce refuse to allow his will to act contrary to his normal interests. And that is not all. You say that science itself will then teach man (though in my opinion it is an unnecessary luxury) that as a matter of fact he possesses neither will nor uncontrollable desires, and never has done, and that he himself is nothing more than a sort of piano-key or organ-stop, and that, in addition, there are the laws of nature in the world; so that whatever he does is not done of his own will at all, but of itself, according to the laws of nature. Consequently, as soon as these laws of nature are discovered, man will no longer have to answer for his actions and will find life exceedingly easy. All human actions will then, no doubt, be computed according to these laws, mathematically, something like the tables of logarithms, up to 108,000, and indexed accordingly. Or, better still, certain well-intentioned words will be published, something like our present encyclopaedic dictionaries, in which everything will be calculated and specified with such an exactness that there will be no more independent actions or adventures in the world.

Then—it is still you who are saying this—new economic relations will be established, relations all ready for use and calculated with mathematical exactitude, so that all sorts of problems will vanish in a twinkling simply because ready-made solutions will be provided for all of them. It is then that the Crystal Palace will be built. Then—why, in fact, the Golden Age will have dawned again. Of course, it is quite impossible to guarantee (it is I who am speaking now) that even then people will not be bored to tears (for what will they have to do when everything is calculated and tabulated), though, on the other hand, everything will be so splendidly rational. Of course, when you are bored, you are liable to get all sorts of ideas into your head. Golden pins, too, are after all stuck into people out of boredom. But all that would not matter. What is bad (and it is again I who am saying this) is that I'm afraid they will be glad even of golden pins then. For man is stupid, phenomenally stupid; I mean, he may not be really stupid, but on the other hand he is so ungrateful that you won't find anything like him in the whole wide world. I would not be at all surprised, for instance, if suddenly and without the slightest possible reason a gentleman of an ignoble or rather a reactionary and sardonic countenance were to arise amid all that future reign of universal common sense and, gripping his sides firmly with his hands, were to say to us all, "Well, gentlemen, what about giving all this common sense a mighty kick and letting it scatter in the dust before our feet simply to send all these logarithms to the devil so that we can again live according to our foolish will?" That wouldn't matter, either, but for the regrettable fact that he would certainly find followers: for man is made like that. And all, mind you, for the most stupid of reasons which seems hardly worth mentioning, namely, because man has always and everywhere—whoever he may be—preferred to do as he chose, and not in the least as his reason or advantage dictated; and one may choose to do something even if it is against one's own advantage, and sometimes one *positively should* (that is my idea). One's own free and unfettered choice, one's own whims, however wild, one's own fancy, overwrought though it sometimes may be to the point of madness—that is that same most desirable good which we overlooked and which does not fit into any classification, and against which all theories and systems are continually wrecked. And why on earth do all those sages assume that man must needs strive after some normal, after some rationally desirable good? All man wants is an absolutely *free* choice, however dear that freedom may cost him and wherever it may lead him to. Well, of course, if it is a matter of choice, then the devil only knows . . .

VIII

"Ha-ha-ha! But there's really no such thing as choice, as a matter of fact, whatever you may say," you interrupt me with a laugh. "Today science has succeeded in so far dissecting man that at least we now know that desire and the so-called free will are nothing but—"

One moment, gentlemen. I am coming to that myself, and I don't mind telling you that I was even feeling a little nervous. I was just about to say that choice depended on the devil only knows what and that that was all to the good, but I suddenly remembered science and—the words died on my lips. And you took advantage of it and began to speak. It is, of course, quite true that if one day they really discover some formula of all our desires and whims, that is to say, if they discover what they all depend on, by what laws they are governed, how they are disseminated, what they are aiming at in one case and another, and so on, that is, a real mathematical formula, man may perhaps at once stop feeling any desire and, I suppose, most certainly will. For who would want to desire according to a mathematical formula? And that is not all. He will at once be transformed from a man into an organ-stop, or something of the sort. For what is man without desires, without free will, and without the power of choice but a stop in an organ pipe? What do you think? Let us calculate the probabilities: is it or is it not likely to happen?

"Well," you decide, "in the majority of cases our desires are mistaken from a mistaken idea of what is to our advantage. Sometimes we desire absolute nonsense because in our stupidity we see in this nonsense the easiest way of attaining some conjectural good."

Very well, and when all that is explained and worked out on paper (which is quite possible, for it would be absurd and unreasonable to assume that man will never discover other laws of nature), the so-called desires will of course no longer exist. For when one day desire comes completely to terms with reason we shall of course reason and not desire, for it is obviously quite impossible to *desire* nonsense while retaining our reason and in that way knowingly go against our reason and wish to harm ourselves. And when all desires and reasons can be actually calculated (for one day the laws of our so-called free will are bound to be discovered) something in the nature of a mathematical table may in good earnest be compiled so that all our desires will in effect arise in accordance with this table. For if it is one day calculated and proved to me, for instance, that if I thumb my nose at a certain person it is because I cannot help thumbing my nose at him, and that I have to thumb my nose at him with that particular thumb, what *freedom* will there be left to me, especially if I happen to be a scholar and have taken my degree at a university? In that case, of course, I should be able to calculate my life for thirty years ahead. In short, if this were really to take place, there would be nothing left for us to do: we should have to understand everything whether we wanted to or not. And, generally speaking, we must go on repeating to ourselves incessantly that at a certain moment and in certain circumstances nature on no account asks us for our permission to do anything; that we have got to take her as she is, and not as we imagine her to be; and that if we are really tending towards mathematical tables and rules of thumb and—well—even towards test tubes, then what else is there left for us to do but to accept everything, test tube and all. Or else the test tube will come by itself and will be accepted whether you like it or not. . . .

Quite right, but there's the rub! I'm sorry, gentlemen, to have gone on philosophising like this: remember my forty years in the dark cellar! Do let me indulge my fancy for a moment. You see, gentlemen, reason is an excellent thing. There is no doubt about it. But reason is only reason, and it can only satisfy the reasoning ability of man, whereas volition is a manifestation of the whole of life, I mean, of the whole of human life, including reason with all its concomitant head-scratchings. And although our life, thus manifested, very often turns out to be a sorry business, it is life none the less and not merely extractions of square roots. For my part, I quite naturally want to live in order to satisfy all my faculties and not my reasoning faculty alone, that is to say, only some twentieth part of my capacity for living. What does reason know? Reason only knows what it has succeeded in getting to know (certain things, I suppose, it will never know; this may be poor comfort, but why not admit it frankly?), whereas human nature acts as a whole, with everything that is in it, consciously, and unconsciously, and though it may commit all sorts of absurdities, it persists. I cannot help thinking, gentlemen, that you look upon me with pity; you go on telling me over and over again that an enlightened and mentally developed man, such a man, in short, as the future man can be expected to be, cannot possibly desire deliberately something which is not a real "good," and that, you say, is mathematics. I quite agree. It is mathematics. But I repeat for the hundredth time that here is one case, one case only, when man can deliberately and consciously desire something that is injurious, stupid, even outrageously stupid, just because he wants *to have the right* to desire for himself even what is very stupid and not to be bound by an obligation to desire only what is sensible. For this outrageously stupid thing, gentlemen, this whim of ours, may really be more accounted by us than anything else on earth, especially in certain cases. And in particular it may be more valuable than any good even when it is quite obviously bad for us and contradicts the soundest conclusions of our reason about what is to our advantage, for at all events it preserves what is most precious and most important to us, namely, our personality and our individuality. Indeed some people maintain that this is more precious than anything else to man. Desire, of course, can, if it chooses, come to terms with reason, especially if people do not abuse it and make use of it in moderation; this is useful and sometimes even praiseworthy. But very often and indeed mostly desire is utterly and obstinately at loggerheads with reason and—and, do you know, that, too, is useful and occasionally even praiseworthy. Let us suppose, gentlemen, that man is not stupid. (As a matter of fact, it cannot possibly be said that man is stupid, if only from the one consideration that if he is, then who is wise?) But if he is not stupid, he is monstrously ungrateful. Phenomenally ungrateful. I'm even inclined to believe that the best definition of man is—a creature who walks on two legs and is ungrateful. But that is not all, that is not his principal failing; his greatest failing is his constant lack of moral sense, constant from the days of the Flood to the Schleswig-Holstein period of human history. Lack of moral sense and, consequently, lack of good sense; for it has long been known that lack of good sense is really the result of lack of moral sense. Well, try and cast your eye upon the history of mankind and what will you see? Grandeur? Yes, perhaps even grandeur. The Colossus of Rhodes, for instance, is worth something, isn't it? Well may Mr. Anayevsky bear witness to the fact that some people maintain that it is the work of human hands, while others assert that it was wrought by nature herself. Gaiety? Well, yes. Perhaps gaiety, too. One has only to think of the dress uniforms, military and civilian, of all peoples in all ages—that alone is worth something, and if we throw in the undress uniforms as well, we can only gasp in astonishment at the gaiety of it all; no historian, I am sure, will be able to resist it. Monotonous? Well, I suppose it is monotonous: they fight and fight, they are fighting now, they fought before, and they will fight again—you must admit this is rather monotonous. In short, you can say anything you like about world history, anything that might enter the head of a man with the most disordered imagination. One thing, though, you cannot possibly say about it: you cannot say that it is sensible. If you did, you would choke at the first word. And, moreover, this is the sort of curious thing you come across almost every minute: continually there crop up in life such sensible and moral people, such sages and lovers of humanity whose only object seems to be to live all their lives as sensibly and morally as possible, to be, as it were, a shining light to their neighbours for the sole purpose of proving to them that it is really possible to live morally and sensibly in the world. And what happens? We know that many of these altruists, sooner or later, towards the end of their lives, were untrue to themselves, committing some folly, sometimes indeed of almost indecent nature. Now let me ask you this question: what can you expect of man seeing that he is a being endowed with such strange qualities? Why, shower all the earthly blessings upon him, drown him in happiness, head over ears, so that only bubbles should be visible on its surface, as on the surface of water; bestow such economic prosperity upon him as would leave him with nothing else to do but sleep, eat cakes, and only worry about keeping world history going—and even then he will, man will, out of sheer ingratitude, out of sheer desire to injure you personally, play a dirty trick on you. He would even risk his cakes and ale and deliberately set his heart on the most deadly trash, the most uneconomic absurdity, and do it, if you please, for the sole purpose of infusing into this positive good sense his deadly fantastic element. It is just his fantastic dreams, his most patent absurdities, that he will desire above all else for the sole purpose of proving to himself (as though that were so necessary) that men are still men and not keys of a piano on which the laws of nature are indeed playing any tune they like, but are in danger of going on playing until no one is able to desire anything except a mathematical table. And that is not all: even if he really were nothing but a piano-key, even if this were proved to him by natural science and mathematically, even then he would refuse to come to his senses, but would on purpose, just in spite of everything, do something out of sheer ingratitude; actually, to carry his point. And if he has no other remedy, he will plan destruction and chaos, he will devise all sorts of sufferings, and in the end he will carry his point! He will send a curse over the world, and as only man can curse (this is his privilege which distinguishes him from other animals), he may by his curse alone attain his object, that is, really convince himself that he is a man and not a piano-key! If you say that this, too, can be calculated by the mathematical table—chaos, and darkness, and curses—so that the mere possibility of calculating it all beforehand would stop it all and reason would triumph in the end—well, if that were to happen man would go purposely mad in order to rid himself of reason and carry his point! I believe this is so, I give you my word for it; for it seems to me that the whole meaning of human life can be summed up in the one statement that man only exists for the purpose of proving to himself every minute that he is a man and not an organ-stop! Even if it means physical suffering, even if it means turning his back on civilisation, he will prove it. And how is one after that to resist the temptation to rejoice that all this has not happened yet and that so far desire depends on the devil alone knows what.

You shout at me (if, that is, you will deign to favour me with raising voices) that no one wants to deprive me of my free will, that all they are concerned with is to arrange things in such a way that my will should of itself, of its own will, coincide with my normal interests, with the laws of nature and arithmetic.

But, good Lord, gentlemen, what sort of a free will can it be once it is all a matter of mathematical tables and arithmetic, when the only thing to be taken into account will be that twice-two-makes-four? Twice-two will make four even without my will. Surely, free will does not mean that!

IX

Gentlemen, I am joking of course, and I'm afraid my jokes are rather poor, but you can't after all take everything as a joke. How do you know I'm not joking with a heavy heart? Gentlemen, I'm worried by all sorts of questions; please, answer them for me. For instance, you want to cure man of his old habits and reform his will in accordance with the demands of science and common sense. But how do you know that man not only could but *should* be remade like that? And what leads you to conclude that human desires must *necessarily* be reformed? In short, how do you know that such a reformation will be a gain to man? And, if one is to put all one's cards on the table, why are you so *utterly* convinced that not to go counter to the real normal gains guaranteed by the conclusions of reason and arithmetic is always so certainly right for man and is a universal law so far as mankind is concerned? For at present it is only a supposition on your part. Let us assume it is a law of logic, but how do you know that it is also a human law? You don't by any chance think I'm mad, do you? Let me explain myself. I agree that man is above all a creative animal, condemned consciously to strive towards a goal and to occupy himself with the art of engineering, that is, always and incessantly clear with a path for himself *wherever it may lead.* And I should not be at all surprised if that were not the reason why he sometimes cannot help wishing to turn aside from the path just because he is condemned to clear it, and perhaps, too, because, however stupid the plain man of action may be as a rule, the thought will sometimes occur to him that the path almost always seems to lead *nowhere in particular,* and that the important point is not where it leads but that it should lead somewhere, and that a well-behaved child, disdaining the art of engineering, should not indulge in the fatal idleness which, as we all know, is the mother of all vices. Man likes to create and to clear paths—that is undeniable. But why is he also so passionately fond of destruction and chaos? Tell me that. But, if you don't mind, I'd like to say a few words about that myself. Is he not perhaps so fond of destruction and chaos (and it cannot be denied that he is sometimes very fond of it—that is a fact) because he is instinctively afraid of reaching the goal and completing the building he is erecting? How do you know, perhaps he only loves the building from a distance and not by any means at close quarters; perhaps he only loves building it and not living in it, preferring to leave it later *aux animaux domestiques,* such as ants, sheep, etc., etc. Now, ants are quite a different matter. They have one marvellous building of this kind, a building that is for ever indestructible—the ant-hill.

The excellent ants began with the ant-hill and with the ant-hill they will most certainly end, which does great credit to their steadfastness and perseverance. But man is a frivolous and unaccountable creature, and perhaps, like a chess-player, he is only fond of the process of achieving his aim, but not of the aim itself. And who knows (it is impossible to be absolutely sure about it), perhaps the whole aim mankind is striving to achieve on earth merely lies in this incessant process of achievement, or (to put it differently) in life itself, and not really in the attainment of any goal, which, needless to say, can be nothing else but twice-two-makes-four, that is to say, a formula; but twice-two-makes-four is not life, gentlemen. It is the beginning of death. At least, man seems always to have been afraid of this twice-two-makes-four, and I am afraid of it now. Let us assume that man does nothing but search for this twice-two-makes-four, sails across oceans and sacrifices his life in this search; but to succeed in his quest, really to find what he is looking for, he is afraid—yes, he really seems to be afraid of it. For he feels that when he has found it there will be nothing more for him to look for. When workmen have finished their work they at least receive their wages, and they go to a pub and later find themselves in a police cell—well, there's an occupation for a week. But where can man go? At all events, one observes a certain awkwardness about him every time he achieves one of these aims. He loves the process of achievement but not achievement itself, which, I'm sure you will agree, is very absurd. In a word, man is a comical creature; I expect there must be some sort of jest hidden in it all. But twice-two-makes-four is for all that a most insupportable thing. Twice-two-makes-four is, in my humble opinion, nothing but a piece of impudence. Twice-two-makes-four is a farcical, dressed-up fellow who stands across your path with arms akimbo and spits at you. Mind you, I quite agree that twice-two-makes-four is a most excellent thing; but if we are to give everything its due, then twice-two-makes-five is sometimes a most charming little thing, too.

And why are you so firmly, so solemnly, convinced that only the normal and positive, in short, only prosperity, is of benefit to man? Does not reason make mistakes about benefits? Is it not possible that man loves something besides prosperity? Perhaps he is just as fond of suffering? Perhaps suffering is just as good for him as prosperity? And man does love suffering very much sometimes. He loves it passionately. That is an undeniable fact. You need not even look up world history to prove that; ask yourself, if you are a man and have lived at all. As for my own personal opinion, I believe that to be fond of prosperity is, somehow, indecent even. Whether it is good or bad, it is sometimes very pleasant to smash things, too. Not that I'm particularly anxious to plead the cause of suffering, or of happiness, for that matter. All I plead for is that I should be allowed my whims, and that they should be guaranteed to me whenever I want them. In light comedies, for instance, suffering is not permitted, and I accept that. In the Crystal Palace it is unthinkable: suffering is doubt, it is negation, and what sort of Crystal Palace would it be if one were to have any doubts about it? And yet I am convinced that man will never renounce real suffering, that is to say, destruction and chaos. Suffering! Why, it's the sole cause of consciousness! And though at the beginning I did argue that consciousness was the greatest misfortune to man, yet I know that man loves it and will not exchange it for any satisfaction. Consciousness, for instance, is infinitely superior to twice-two. After twice-two there is nothing left for you to do, or even to learn. All you could do then would be to stop up your five senses and sink into contemplation. While if you hang on to your consciousness you may achieve the same result, that is to say, there will be nothing for you to do, either, you could at least administer a good thrashing to yourself from time to time, and that at any rate livens you up a bit. It may be a reactionary step, but it is better than nothing, isn't it?

X*

You believe in the Crystal Palace, forever indestructible, that is to say, in one at which you won't be able to stick out your tongue even by stealth or cock a snook even in your pocket. Well, perhaps I am afraid of this palace just because it is made of crystal and is forever indestructible, and just because I shan't be able to poke my tongue out at it even by stealth.

You see, if it were not a palace but a hencoop, and if it should rain, I might crawl into it to avoid getting wet, but I would never pretend that the hencoop was a palace out of gratitude to it for sheltering me from the rain. You laugh and you tell me that in such circumstances even a hencoop is as good as a palace. Yes, I reply, it certainly is if the only purpose in life is not to get wet.

But what is to be done if I've got it into my head that that is not the only purpose in life, and that if one has to live, one had better live in a palace? That is my choice; that is my desire. You can only force me to give it up when you change my desire. All right, do it. Show me something more attractive. Give me another ideal. For the time being, however, I refuse to accept a hencoop for a palace. The Crystal Palace may be just an idle dream, it may be against all laws of nature, I may have invented it because of my own stupidity, because of certain old and irrational habits of my generation. But what do I care whether it is against the laws of nature? What does it matter so long as it exists in my desires, or rather exists while my desires exist? You are not laughing again, are you? Laugh by all means; I am quite ready to put up with any jeers, but I will still refuse to say that I'm satisfied when I'm hungry. At all events I know that I shall never be content with a compromise, with an everlasting and recurring zero because it exists according to the laws of nature and *actually* exists. I will not accept as the crown of

*The censor so mangled this chapter that Dostoevsky later complained that he was made to contradict himself several times. (D.M.)

all my desires a big house with model flats for the poor on a lease of ninety-nine hundred and ninety-nine years and, in case of emergency, with the dental surgeon Wagenheim on a signboard. Destroy my desires, eradicate my ideals, show me something better, and I will follow you. I daresay you will probably declare that it isn't worth your while having anything to do with me; but in that case I, too, can say the same to you. We are discussing this seriously; and if you are too proud to give me your attention, I shall have to do without it.

But while I'm still alive and have desires, I'd rather my right hand withered than let it bring even one small brick to such a house of model flats! I know that a short time ago I rejected the Crystal Palace myself for the sole reason that one would not be allowed to stick one's tongue out at it. But I did not say that because I am so fond of sticking out my tongue. Perhaps what I resented was that among all our buildings there has never been one at which one could not stick out one's tongue. On the contrary, I'd gladly have let my tongue be cut off out of gratitude if things could be so arranged that I should have no wish to stick it out at all. It is not my business if things cannot be arranged like that and if one has to be satisfied with model flats. Why then am I made with such desires? Surely, I have not been made for the sole purpose of drawing the conclusion that the way I am made is a piece of rank deceit? Can this be the sole purpose? I don't believe it.

However, do you know what? I am convinced that fellows like me who live in dark cellars must be kept under restraint. They may be able to live in their dark cellars for forty years and never open their mouths, but the moment they get into the light of day and break out they talk and talk and talk. . . .

XI

And, finally, gentlemen, it is much better to do nothing at all! Better passive awareness! And so three cheers for the dark cellar! Though I have said that I envy the normal man to the point of exasperation, I wouldn't care to be in his place in the circumstances in which I find him (though I shall never cease envying him. No, no, the dark cellar is, at any rate, of much greater advantage to me!). In the dark cellar one can at least. . . . Sorry, I'm afraid I am exaggerating. I am exaggerating because I know, as well as twice-two, that it is not the dark cellar that is better, but something else, something else altogether, something I long for but cannot find. To hell with the dark cellar!

Do you know what would be better? It would be better if I myself believed in anything I had just written. I assure you most solemnly, gentlemen, that there is not a word I've just written I believe in! What I mean is that perhaps I do believe, but at the same time I cannot help feeling and suspecting for some unknown reason that I'm lying like a cobbler.

"Then why have you written all this?" you ask me.

"Well, suppose I put you in a dark cellar for forty years without anything to do and then came to see you in your dark cellar after the forty years to find out what had become of you. Can a man be left for forty years with nothing to do?"

"But aren't you ashamed? Don't you feel humiliated?" you will perhaps say, shaking your head contemptuously. "You long for life, yet you try to solve the problems of life by a logical tangle! And how tiresome, how insolent your tricks are, and, at the same time, how awfully frightened you are! You talk a lot of nonsense and you seem to be very pleased with it; you say a lot of impudent things, and you are yourself always afraid and apologising for them. You assure us that you are afraid of nothing, and at the same time you try to earn our good opinion. You assure us that you are gnashing your teeth, but at the same time you crack jokes to make us laugh. You know your jokes are not amusing, but you seem to be highly pleased with their literary merit. You may perhaps have really suffered, but you don't seem to have the slightest respect for your suffering. There may be some truth in you, but there is no humility. You carry your truth to the market place out of the pettiest vanity to make a public show of it and to discredit it. No doubt you mean to say something, but you conceal your last word out of fear, because you haven't the courage to say it, but only craven insolence. You boast about your sensibility, but you merely don't know your own mind. For though your mind is active enough, your heart is darkened with corruption, and without a pure heart there can be no full or genuine sensibility. And how tiresome you are! How you impose yourself on people! The airs you give yourself! Lies, lies, lies!"

Now, of course, I've made up all this speech of yours myself. It, too, comes from the dark cellar. I've been listening to your words for forty years through a crack in the ceiling. I have invented them myself. It is the only thing I did invent. No wonder I got it pat and dressed it up in a literary form.

But are you really so credulous as to imagine that I would print all this, and let you read it into the bargain? And there is another puzzle I'd like to solve: why on earth do I address you as "gentlemen," as though you really were my readers? Such confessions which I am now about to make are not printed, nor given to other people to read. At least I have not enough pluck for that, nor do I consider it necessary to have it. But, you see, a strange fancy has come into my head and I want to realise it, cost what may. It's like this:—

There are certain things in a man's past which he does not divulge to everybody but, perhaps, only to his friends. Again there are certain things he will not divulge even to his friends; he will divulge them perhaps only to himself, and that, too, as a secret. But, finally, there are things which he is afraid to divulge even to himself, and every decent man has quite an accumulation of such things in his mind. I can put it even this way: the more decent a man is, the larger will the number of such things be. At least I have allowed myself only recently to remember some of my early adventures, having till now avoided them rather uneasily. I'm afraid. Now, however, when I have not only remembered them, but have also made up my mind to write them down, I particularly want to put the whole thing to the test to see whether I can be absolutely frank with myself and not be afraid of the whole truth. Let me add, by the way: Heine says that true biographies are almost impossible, and that a man will most certainly tell a lot of lies about himself. In his view, Rousseau told a lot of lies about himself in his Confessions, and told them deliberately, out of vanity. I am sure Heine is right; I can understand perfectly how sometimes one tells all sorts of lies about oneself out of sheer vanity, even going so far as to confess to all sorts of crimes, and I can perfectly understand that sort of vanity. But Heine had in mind a man who made his confessions to the public. I, however, am writing for myself, and I should like to make it clear once and for all that if I address myself in my writings to a reader, I'm doing it simply as a matter of form, because I find it much easier to write like that. It is only a form, an empty show, for I know that I shall never have any readers. I have already intimated as much. . . .

I don't want to be hampered by any considerations in the editing of my Memoirs. I shan't bother about order or system. I shall put down whatever I remember.

Now, of course, I might, for instance, be taken at my word and asked if I really do not count on any readers, why do I now put down all sorts of conditions, and on paper, too, such as not to pay any attention to order or system, to write down what I remember, etc., etc. Why all these explanations? Why all these apologies?

"Ah," I reply, "now you're asking!"

There is, incidentally, a whole psychology in all this. Perhaps it's simply that I am a coward. Again, perhaps it is simply that I'm imagining an audience on purpose so as to observe the proprieties while I write. There are thousands of reasons, no doubt.

Then again there is this further puzzle: what do I want to write it down for? What is the object of it all? If I'm not writing for the reading public, why not simply recall these things in my mind without putting them down on paper?

Well, I suppose I could do that, but it will look more dignified on paper. There is something imposing about that. There will be a greater sense of passing judgment on myself. The whole style, I'm sure, will be better. Moreover, I really may feel easier in my mind if I write it down. I have, for instance, been latterly greatly oppressed by the memory of some incident that happened to me a long time ago. I remembered it very vividly the other day, as a matter of fact, and it has since been haunting me like some annoying tune you can't get out of your head. And yet I simply must get rid of it. I have hundreds of such memories, but at times one of them stands out from the rest and oppresses me. So why shouldn't I try?

And, lastly, I'm awfully bored, and I have nothing to do. Writing down things is, in fact, a sort of work. People say work makes man better and more honest. Well, here's a chance for me at any rate.

Snow is falling today, almost wet snow, yellow, dirty. It was snowing yesterday, too, and the other day. I think it is because of the wet snow that I remembered the incident which gives me no rest now. So let it be a story apropos of the wet snow.

PART II
APROPOS OF THE WET SNOW

When with a word of fervent conviction,
From the lowest dregs of dark affliction,
A soul from eternal doom I saved;
And in horror and in torments steeped,
Wringing your hands, you curses heaped
Upon the life that once you craved;
When your unheeding conscience at last
With your guilty memories flaying,
The dreadful story of your sin-stained past
To me you narrated, pardon praying;
And full of horror, full of shame,
Quickly in your hands you hid your face,
Unconscious of the flood of tears that came,
Shaken and indignant at your own disgrace. . . . etc., etc.

From the poetry of N. A. NEKRASSOV.

I

I was only twenty-four at the time. My life even then was gloomy, disorderly, and solitary to the point of savagery. I had no friends or acquaintances, avoided talking to people, and buried myself more and more in my hole. When at work in the office I tried not to look at anyone and I knew perfectly well that my colleagues not only regarded me as a queer fellow, but also—I couldn't help feeling that, too—looked upon me with a sort of loathing. I wondered why no one except me had ever had this feeling that people looked upon him with loathing. One of the clerks at the office had a repulsive, pock-marked face, the face, I should say, of a real villain. I should not have dared to look at anyone with such an indecent face. Another had such a filthy old uniform that one could not go near him without becoming aware of a bad smell. And yet these gentlemen did not seem to be in the least upset either about their clothes, or their faces, or the impression they created. Neither of them ever imagined that people looked at him with loathing; and I dare say it would not have made any difference to them if they had imagined it, so long as their superiors deigned to look at them. It is of course clear that, owing to my unbounded vanity and hence also to my over-sensitiveness where my own person was concerned, I often looked at myself with a sort of furious dissatisfaction which verged on loathing, and for that reason I could not help attributing my own views to other people. I hated my own face, for instance, finding it odious to a degree and even suspecting that it had rather a mean expression, and so every time I arrived at the office I went through agonies in my efforts to assume as independent an air as possible so as to make sure that my colleagues did not suspect me of meanness and so as to give my face as noble an expression as possible. "What do I care," I thought to myself, "whether my face is ugly or not, so long as it is also noble, expressive, and, above all, *extremely* intelligent." But I knew very well, I knew it agonisingly well, that it was quite impossible for my face to express such high qualities. But the really dreadful part of it was that I thought my face looked absolutely stupid. I would have been completely satisfied if it looked intelligent. Indeed, I'd have reconciled myself even to a mean expression so long as my face was at the same time generally admitted to be awfully intelligent.

I need hardly say that I hated all my colleagues at the office, one and all, and that I despised them all, and yet at the same time I was also in a way afraid of them. It sometimes happened that I thought of them more highly than of myself. It was a feeling that somehow came upon me suddenly: one moment I despised them and the next moment I thought of them as above me. A decent, educated man cannot afford the luxury of vanity without being exceedingly exacting with himself and without occasionally despising himself to the point of hatred. But whether I despised them or thought them superior to me, I used to drop my eyes almost every time I met any one of them. I even used to make experiments to see whether I would be able to meet without flinching the look of one or another of my colleagues, and it was always I who dropped my eyes first. That irritated me to the point of madness. I was also morbidly afraid of appearing ridiculous and for that reason I slavishly observed all the social conventions: I enthusiastically followed in the beaten track and was mortally afraid of any eccentricity. But how could I hope to keep it up? I was so highly developed mentally, as indeed a man of our age should be. They, on the other hand, were all so stupidly dull and as like one another as so many sheep. Perhaps I was the only one in our office who constantly thought that he was a coward and a slave, and I thought that just because I was so highly developed mentally. But the truth is that it was not only a matter of my imagining it, but that it actually was so: I was a coward and a slave. I say this without the slightest embarrassment. Every decent man of our age is, and indeed has to be, a coward and a slave. That is his normal condition. I am absolutely convinced of that. He is made like that, and he has been created for that very purpose. And not only at the present time or as a result of some fortuitous circumstances, but at all times and in general a decent man has to be a coward and a slave. This is the law of nature for all decent men on earth. If one of them does sometimes happen to pluck up courage about something or other, he need not derive any comfort from it or be pleased about it: he is quite sure to make a fool of himself over something else. Such is the inevitable and eternal result of his being what he is. Only donkeys and mules pretend not to be afraid, and even they do it only up to a point. It is hardly worth while taking any notice of them, however, since they do not amount to anything, anyway.

Another thing that used to worry me very much at that time was the quite incontestable fact that I was unlike anyone and that there was no one like me. "I am one, and they are *all*," I thought and—fell into a melancholy muse.

From all that it can be seen that I was still a very young man.

Sometimes, though, quite the reverse used to happen. I would loathe the thought of going to the office, and things went so far that many times I used to come home ill. But suddenly and for no reason at all a mood of scepticism would come upon me (everything was a matter of moods with me), and I would myself laugh at my intolerance and sensitiveness and reproach myself with being a *romantic.* Sometimes I'd hate to talk to anyone, and at other times I'd not only talk to people, but would even take it into my head to be friends with them. All my fastidiousness would suddenly and for no reason in the world disappear. Who knows, maybe I really had never been fastidious, but just acquired a taste for appearing fastidious out of books. I haven't thought of an answer to this question to this day. Once I got very friendly with them, began visiting their homes, playing preference, drinking vodka, talking of promotions. . . . But here you must let me make a digression.

We Russians, generally speaking, have never had those stupid starry-eyed German and, still more, French romantics on whom nothing produces any effect; though the very ground cracked beneath their feet, though the whole of France perished at the barricades, they would still be the same and would not change even for the sake of appearances, and they would go on singing their highly romantic songs to their last breath, as it were, because they were fools. In Russia, however, there are no fools; that is a well known fact and that is what makes us so different from other countries. Therefore no starry-eyed natures, pure and simple, can be found among us. All that has been invented by our "positive" publicists and critics who at the time were chasing after Gogol's and Goncharov's idealised landowners and, in their folly, mistook them for our ideal; they have traduced our romantics, thinking them the same starry-eyed sort as in Germany or France. On the contrary, the characteristics of our romantics are the exact and direct opposite of the starry-eyed European variety, and not a single European standard applies here. (I hope you don't mind my using the word "romantic"—it is an old, honourable, and highly estimable word and is familiar to all.) The characteristics of our romantic are to understand everything, to *see everything and to see it incomparably more clearly than the most positive of our thinkers;* to refuse to take anyone or anything for granted, but at the same time not to despise anything; to go round and round everything and to yield to everything out of policy; never to lose sight of the useful and the practical (rent-free quarters for civil servants, pensions of a sort, decorations)—and to discern this aim through all the enthusiasms and volumes of lyrical verses, and at the same time to preserve to his dying day a profound and indestructible respect for "the sublime and the beautiful," and, incidentally, also to preserve himself like some precious jewel wrapt in cottonwool for the benefit, for instance, of the same "sublime and beautiful." Our romantic is a man of great breadth of vision and the most consummate rascal of all our rascals, I assure you—from experience. That, of course, is all true if our romantic is intelligent. Good Lord, what am I saying? The romantic is always intelligent. I only meant to observe that even if there were fools among our romantics, they need not be taken into account for the simple reason that they had transformed themselves into Germans when still in their prime and, to preserve that pristine jewel-like purity of theirs, gone and settled somewhere abroad, preferably in Weimar or the Black Forest.

Now, for instance, I had a sincere contempt for the Civil Service and if I did not show it, it was only out of sheer necessity, for I was myself sitting at a desk in a Government office and getting paid for it. As a result—note that, please!—I refrained from showing my contempt in any circumstances. Our romantic would sooner go off his head (which does not happen often, though) than show his contempt for his job if he has no other job in prospect, and he is never kicked out of a job, either, unless indeed he is carried off to a lunatic asylum as "the King of Spain," but even then only if he should go stark raving mad. However, only the very thin and fair people go off their heads in Russia. An innumerable host of romantics, on the other hand, usually end up by becoming civil servants of the highest grade. Quite a remarkable versatility! And what an ability they possess for the most contradictory sensations! Even in those days this thought used to console me mightily, and I am still of the same opinion. That is why we have such a great number of "expansive" natures who do not lose sight of their ideal even when faced with the most catastrophic disaster; and though they never lift a finger for their ideal, though they are the most thorough-paced villains and thieves, they respect their original ideal, are ready to shed bitter tears for it and are, besides, quite remarkably honest at heart. Yes, gentlemen, it is only among us that the most arrant knave can be perfectly and even sublimely honest at heart without at the same time ceasing to be a knave. I repeat, I have seen our romantics over and over again grown into the most businesslike rascals (I use the word "rascals" affectionately); they suddenly acquire such a wonderful grasp of reality and such a thorough knowledge of the practical world that their astonished superiors in the Civil Service and the public at large can only click their tongues in utter stupefaction.

Their many-sidedness is truly amazing, and goodness only knows into what it may be transformed and developed later on and what, as a result of it, the future may hold in store for us. And the material is far from unpromising! I do not say this out of some ridiculous or blustering patriotism. However, I'm sure you must be thinking again that I am pulling your legs. Well, I don't know. Perhaps I am wrong. I mean, perhaps you are convinced that this really is my opinion. In either case, gentlemen, I shall consider both these views as a singular honour and a matter of special gratification to me. And you will forgive me for my digression, won't you?

My friendship with my colleagues did not of course last. Within a very short time I was at loggerheads with them again and, owing to my youthful inexperience at the time, I even stopped exchanging greetings with them and, so to speak, cut them. That, however, only happened to me once. Generally speaking, I was always alone.

At home I mostly spent my time reading. I tried to stifle all that was seething within me by all sorts of outside distractions, and of all outside distractions reading was the most easily available to me. My reading of course helped a lot: it excited, delighted, and tormented me. But at times it also bored me terribly. I got heartily sick of sitting in my room; I wanted to go somewhere, to move about; and so I plunged into a sort of sombre, secret, disgusting—no, not dissipation, but vile, petty vice. My mean lusts were always acute and burning as a result of my continual morbid irritability. My outbursts of passion were hysterical, and always accompanied by tears and convulsions. Apart from my reading, I had nothing to occupy me. I mean, there was nothing in my surroundings which I could respect or to which I could feel attracted. In addition, I was terribly sick at heart; I felt a terrible craving for conflicts and contrasts, and so I plunged into a life of mean debauchery. Mind you, I have spoken at such great length now not at all because of any desire to justify myself. And yet—no! It's a lie! Of course I wanted to justify myself. I'm making this little note for my own use, gentlemen. I don't want to lie. I promised not to.

I pursued my vile amusements in solitude, at night, in secret, fearfully, filthily, with a feeling of shame that did not desert me in the most sickening moments and that brought me in such moments to the point of calling down curses on my own head. Even in these days I carried the dark cellar about with me in my soul. I was terribly afraid of being seen, of meeting someone I knew, of being recognised. I frequented all sorts of rather obscure dens of vice.

One night as I was passing a small pub, I saw through a lighted window some men having a fight with billiard cues and one of them being thrown out of the window. At any other time I should have felt very much disgusted; but at the time I could not help feeling envious of the fellow who had been thrown out of the window. Indeed, so envious did I feel that I even went into the pub, walked straight into the billiard room, thinking that perhaps I too could pick a quarrel with the men there and be thrown out of the window.

I was not drunk, but what was I to do? To such a state of hysteria had my depression brought me! But nothing happened. It seemed that I was not even capable of jumping out of the window, and I went away without having a fight.

An army officer in the pub put me in my place from the very first.

I was standing beside the billiard-table and, in my ignorance, was blocking the way. As he had to pass me, he took me by the shoulders and, without a word of warning or explanation, silently carried me bodily from where I was standing to another place and passed by as though he had not even noticed me. I could have forgiven him if he had given me a beating, but I could not forgive him for having moved me from one place to another as if I were a piece of furniture. I would have given anything at that moment for a real, a more regular, a more decent, and a more, so to speak, *literary* quarrel! But I had been treated like a fly. The army officer was over six foot, and I am a short, thin little fellow. The quarrel, however, was in my hands: if I had uttered one word of protest, I should most certainly have been thrown out of the window. But I changed my mind and preferred—to efface myself angrily.

I left the pub feeling wild and embarrassed and went straight home. On the following day I carried on with my mean dissipation even more timidly, more abjectly and miserably than before, as though with tears in my eyes, but I did carry on with it. Do not imagine, however, that I was afraid of the army officer because I am a coward; I never was a coward at heart, although I have invariably been a coward in action, but—don't be in such a hurry to laugh; I have an explanation for everything, don't you worry.

Oh, if that army officer had only been one of those who would accept a challenge to a duel! But no. He was most decidedly one of those gentlemen (alas, long extinct!) who preferred action with billiard cues or, like Gogol's lieutenant Pirogov, by lodging a complaint with the authorities. They never accepted a challenge, and in any case would have considered a duel with me, a low grade civil servant, as quite improper; as for duelling in general, they regarded it as something unthinkable, something that only a freethinker or a Frenchman would indulge in. But that did not prevent them from treading on any man's corns, and painfully, too, particularly as they were over six foot.

No, I was not afraid because I was a coward, but because of my unbounded vanity. I was not afraid of his six foot, nor of getting soundly thrashed and being thrown out of the window; I should have had sufficient physical courage for that; what I lacked was moral courage. What I was afraid of was that every one in the billiard room from the cheeky marker to the last rotten, pimply little government clerk in a greasy collar who was fawning upon everybody in the room, would misunderstand me and jeer at me when I protested and began addressing them in literary language. For even today we cannot speak of a point of honour—not of honour, mind you, but of a point of honour *(point d'honneur)* except in literary language. You cannot even mention a "point of honour" in ordinary language. I was absolutely convinced (the sense of reality in spite of all romanticism!) that they would all simply split their sides with laughter and that the officer would not just simply, that is to say, not inoffensively, thrash me, but would certainly push me round the billiard table with his knee and perhaps only then would he have taken pity on me and thrown me out of the window. With me a wretched incident like this would never, of course, end there. I often met that army officer in the street afterwards and made a careful note of him. What I am not quite sure about is whether he recognised me. I don't think he did, and I have come to this conclusion by certain signs. But I—I stared at him with hatred and malice, and that went on—oh, for several years. At first I began finding out quietly all I could about this officer. It was a difficult job, for I did not know any one. But one day someone called him by his surname in the street just as I was trailing after him at a distance, as though I were tied to him by a string, and so I learnt his name. Another day I followed him to his home and for ten copecks I found out from the caretaker where he lived, on which floor, whether alone or with somebody, etc., in fact, everything one could learn from a caretaker. One morning, though I had never indulged in literary work, it suddenly occurred to me to write a story round this officer, a story in a satiric vein, in order to show him up for what he was. I wrote this story with real pleasure. I exposed, I did not hesitate even to libel him; at first I gave him a name which could be immediately recognised as his, but later, on second thoughts, I changed it, and sent the story to "Homeland Notes." But at that time exposures were not in fashion yet, and my story was not published. I felt very sore about it.

Sometimes my resentment became quite unbearable. At last I made up my mind to challenge my enemy to a duel. I wrote him a most beautiful, most charming letter, demanding an apology from him and, if he refused to apologise, hinting rather plainly at a duel. The letter was written in such a way that if the officer had had the least notion of "the sublime and the beautiful," he would certainly have come running to me, fallen on my neck, and offered me his friendship. And how wonderful that would have been! Oh, how wonderfully we should have got on together! He would have protected me by his rank of an army officer, and I would have enlarged his mind by my superior education and—well—by my ideas, and lots of things could have happened! Just consider, this was two years after he had insulted me, and my challenge was absurdly out of date, a pure anachronism, in fact, in spite of the cleverness of my letter explaining away and concealing the lapse of time. But, thank God (to this day I thank the Almighty with tears in my eyes!), I did not send my letter. A shiver runs down my spine when I think of what might have happened if I had sent it. And suddenly—suddenly I revenged myself in the simplest and most extraordinarily clever way! A most brilliant idea suddenly occurred to me.

Sometimes on a holiday I used to take a walk on Nevsky Avenue, on the sunny side of it, and about four o'clock in the afternoon. As a matter of fact, I did not really take a walk there, but went through a series of torments, humiliations, and bilious attacks; but I suppose that was really what I wanted. I darted along like a groundling in the most unbecoming manner imaginable among the people on the pavement, continuously making way for generals, officers of the guards and hussars, and ladies. At those moments I used to have sharp shooting pains in my heart and I used to feel all hot down the back at the mere thought of the miserable appearance of my clothes and the wretchedness of my darting little figure. It was a most dreadful torture, an incessant, unbearable humiliation at the thought, which grew into an uninterrupted and most palpable sensation, that in the eyes of all those high society people I was just a fly, an odious, obscene fly, more intelligent, more highly developed, more noble than anyone else (I had no doubts about that), but a fly that was always making way for everyone, a fly insulted and humiliated by every one. Why I suffered this torment, why I went for my walks on Nevsky Avenue, I do not know. But I was simply *drawn* there at every possible opportunity.

Already at that time I began experiencing the sudden onrush of those keen delights of which I spoke in the first part. But after the incident with the army officer, I felt drawn there more than ever: it was on Nevsky Avenue that I met him most frequently, and it was there that I took such delight in looking at him. He, too, used to take a walk there mostly on holidays. And though he, too, made way for generals and other persons of high rank, though he, too, darted like a groundling among them, he simply bore down on people like me, or even those who were a cut above me; he walked straight at them as though there were just an empty space in front of him, and never in any circumstances did he make way for them. I gloated spitefully as I looked at him and—made way for him resentfully every time he happened to bear down on me. I was tortured by the thought that even in the street I could not be on the same footing as he. "Why do you always have to step aside first?" I asked myself over and over again in a sort of hysterical rage, sometimes waking up at three o'clock in the morning. "Why always you and not he? There is no law about it, is there? There's nothing written down about it, is there? Why can't you arrange it so that each of you should make way for the other, as usually happens when two well-bred men meet in the street? He yields you half of his pavement and you half of yours, and you pass one another with mutual respect." But it never happened like that. It was always I who stepped aside, while he did not even notice that I made way for him.

And it was then the brilliant idea occurred to me. "And what," thought I, "what if I should meet him and—and not move aside? Just not do it on purpose, even if I have to give him a push. Well, what would happen then?" This brazen thought took such a hold of me that it gave me no rest. I thought of it continually and went for a walk on Nevsky Avenue more frequently so as to make quite sure of the way in which I was going to do it when I did do it. I felt transported. This plan seemed to me more and more feasible and promising. "Of course I'm not going to give him a real push," I thought, feeling much kindlier disposed towards him in my joy. "I'll simply not make way for him. Knock against him, taking good care not to hurt him very much, just shoulder against shoulder, just as much as the laws of propriety allow. I shall only knock against him as much as he knocks against me."

At last my mind was firmly made up. But my preparations took a long time. The first thing I had to take into account was that when I carried out my plan I had to take good care to be as well dressed as possible. I had therefore to see about my clothes. "Just in case, for instance, there should be a public scandal (and there was sure to be quite an audience there: a countess taking a walk, Prince D. taking a walk, the whole literary world taking a walk), one had to be decently dressed. Good clothes impress people and will immediately put us on an equal footing in the eyes of society." Accordingly, I obtained an advance of salary and bought myself a pair of black gloves and a smart hat at Churkin's. Black gloves seemed to me more impressive and more elegant than canary-coloured ones which I had thought of buying first. "Too bright a colour. Looks as though a man wants to show off too much!" So I did not take the canary-coloured ones. I had long ago got ready an excellent shirt with white bone studs; but my overcoat delayed the carrying out of my plan for a long time. My overcoat was not at all bad. It kept me warm. But it was wadded and had a raccoon collar, which made one look altogether too much a flunkey. The collar had to be changed at all costs for a beaver one, like one of those army officers wore. To acquire such a collar, I began visiting the Arcade, and after a few attempts decided to buy a cheap German beaver. These German beavers may soon look shabby and worn, but at first, when new, they look very decent indeed. And I wanted it for one occasion only. I asked the price: it was much too expensive. On thinking it over, I decided to sell my raccoon collar and to borrow the rest of the money (and a considerable sum it was, too) from the head of my department, Anton Antonovich Setochkin, a quiet man, but serious and dependable, who never lent any money to any one, but to whom I had been particularly recommended years ago on entering the service by an important personage who got me the job. I went through hell before taking this step. To ask Anton Antonovich for a loan seemed to me a monstrous and shameful thing. I did not sleep for two or three nights and, as a matter of fact, I did not sleep well at the time generally, feeling very feverish. My heart seemed to be either beating very faintly or suddenly began thumping, thumping, thumping! . . . Anton Antonovich looked rather surprised at first, then he frowned, then he pondered, and in the end he did lend me the money, having made me sign a promissory note authorizing him to deduct the money from my salary in a fortnight. In this way everything was settled at last; the beautiful beaver reigned in the place of the odious raccoon, and gradually I set about making the final arrangements. This sort of thing could not be done without careful preparation, without thought. It had to be done skilfully and without hurry. But I must admit that after many attempts to carry my plan into execution, I began to give way to despair: however much I tried, we just did not knock against each other, and there seemed to be nothing I could do about it! Hadn't I got everything ready? Hadn't I made up my mind to go through with it? And did it not now seem that we ought to knock against each other any minute? And yet, when the moment came I made way for him again and he passed without taking any notice of me. I even offered up a prayer when I approached him, beseeching God to fill me with the necessary determination to see the business through. Once I had quite made up my mind, but it all ended by my tripping up and falling down in front of him, for at the last moment, at a distance of only a few feet, my courage failed me. He calmly strode over me, and I was hurled to one side like a ball. That night I was again in a fever and delirious. And suddenly everything came to a most satisfactory conclusion. The night before I had made up my mind most definitely not to go through with my luckless enterprise and to forget all about it, and with that intention I went for a walk on Nevsky Avenue for the last time, just to see how I would forget all about it. Suddenly, only three paces from my enemy, I quite unexpectedly made up my mind, shut my eyes, and—we knocked violently against each other, shoulder to shoulder. I did not budge an inch and passed him absolutely on an equal footing! He did not even look round and pretended not to have noticed anything. But he was only pretending: I am quite sure of that. Yes, to this day I am quite sure of that! Of course I got the worst of it, for he was stronger. But that was not the point. The point was that I had done what I had set out to do, that I had kept up my dignity, that I had not yielded an inch, and that I had put myself publicly on the same social footing as he. I came back home feeling that I had completely revenged myself for everything. I was beside myself with delight. I was in the seventh heaven and sang Italian arias. I shall not, of course, describe to you what happened to me three days later. If you have read my first chapter, you will be able to guess for yourselves. The officer was afterwards transferred somewhere. I have not seen him for fourteen years now. I wonder how the dear fellow is getting on now. Who is he bullying now?

II

But when my mood for odious little dissipations came to an end I used to feel dreadfully flat and miserable. I had an awful conscience about it, but I did my best not to think of it: I felt too miserable for that. Little by little, however, I got used to that, too. I got used to everything, or rather I did not really get used to it, but just made up my mind to grin and bear it. But I had a solution which made up for everything, and that was to seek salvation in all that was "sublime and beautiful," in my dreams, of course. I would give myself up entirely to dreaming. I would dream for three months on end, skulking in my corner. And, believe me, at those moments I bore no resemblance to the gentleman who in his pigeon-livered confusion had sewed a piece of German beaver to the collar of his overcoat. I suddenly became a hero. I shouldn't have admitted my six-foot lieutenant to my rooms even if he had come to pay a call on me. I could not even picture him before me at the time. What exactly my dreams were about, or how I could be content with them, it is difficult to say now, but I was content with them at the time. As a matter of fact, I feel even now a certain glow of satisfaction at the memory of it. It was after my phase of dissipation had passed that I took special pleasure in my dreams which seemed sweeter and more vivid then. They came to me with repentance and tears, with curses and transports of delight. I had moments of such positive intoxication, of such intense happiness, that, I assure you, I did not feel even the faintest stir of derision within me. What I had was faith, hope, and love. The trouble was that in those days I believed blindly that by some miracle, by some outside event, all this would suddenly draw apart and expand, that I would suddenly catch a glimpse of a vista of some suitable activity, beneficent and beautiful, and, above all, an activity that was absolutely ready-made (what sort of activity I never knew, but the great thing was that it was to be all ready-made), and then I would suddenly emerge into the light of day, almost mounted on a white horse and with a laurel wreath on my head. I could not even imagine any place of secondary importance for myself, and for that very reason I quite contentedly occupied the most insignificant one in real life. Either a hero or dirt—there was no middle way. That turned out to be my undoing, for while wallowing in dirt I consoled myself with the thought that at other times I was a hero, and the hero overlaid the dirt: an ordinary mortal, as it were, was ashamed to wallow in dirt, but a hero was too exalted a person to be entirely covered in dirt, and hence I could wallow in dirt with an easy conscience. It is a remarkable fact that these attacks of the "sublime and beautiful" came to me even during my spells of odious dissipation, and more particularly at the time when I was touching bottom. They came quite unexpectedly, in separate outbursts, as though reminding me of themselves, but their appearance never brought my debauch to an end; on the contrary, they seemed to stimulate it by contrast, and they only lasted for as long as it was necessary for them to carry out the function of a good sauce. In this case the sauce consisted of contradictions and suffering, of torturing inner analysis, and all these pangs and torments added piquancy and even meaning to my odious little dissipation—in short, fully carried out the function of a good sauce. All this had a certain profundity, too. For I could never have been content to indulge in the simple, vulgar, direct, sordid debauchery of some office clerk and reconcile myself to all that filth! What else could I have found so attractive in it to draw me into the street at night? No, gentlemen, I had a noble loophole for every thing. . . .

But how much love, good Lord, how much love I used to experience in those dreams of mine, during those hours of "salvation through the sublime and the beautiful"; fantastic though that sort of love was and though in reality it had no relation whatever to anything human, there was so much of it, so much of this love, that one did not feel the need of applying it in practice afterwards; that would indeed have been a superfluous luxury. Everything, however, always ended most satisfactorily in an indolent and rapturous transition to art, that is, to the beautiful forms of existence, all ready-made, snatched forcibly from the poets and novelists and adapted to every possible need and requirement. For instance, I triumphed over everything; all of course lay in the dust at my feet, compelled of their own free will to acknowledge all my perfections, and I forgave them all. I was a famous poet and court chamberlain, and I fell in love; I became a multi-millionaire and at once devoted all my wealth to the improvement of the human race, and there and then confessed all my hideous and shameful crimes before all the people; needless to say, my crimes were, of course, not really hideous or shameful, but had much in them that was "sublime and beautiful," something in the style of Manfred. All would weep and kiss me (what damned fools they'd have been otherwise!), and I'd go off, barefoot and hungry, to preach new ideas and inflict another Waterloo on the reactionaries. Then the band would be brought out and strike up a march, a general amnesty would be granted, and the Pope would agree to leave Rome for Brazil; then there would be a ball for the whole of Italy at the Villa Borghese on the banks of Lake Como, Lake Como being specially transferred for that occasion to the neighbourhood of Rome; this would be followed by the scene in the bushes, and so on and so forth—don't tell me you don't know it! You will say it is mean and contemptible now to shout it all from the housetops after all the raptures and tears which I have myself confessed to. But why, pray, is it mean? Surely, you don't think I'm ashamed of it, do you? You don't imagine by any chance that all this was much sillier than what ever happened in your life, gentlemen? And let me assure you that certain things were not so badly worked out by me, either. . . . It did not all take place on the banks of Lake Como. Of course, on the other hand, you are quite right. As a matter of fact, it is mean and contemptible.

And what is even meaner is that now I should be trying to justify myself to you. Enough of this, though, or I should never finish: things are quite sure to get meaner and meaner anyway.

I was never able to spend more than three months of dreaming at a time without feeling an irresistible urge to plunge into social life. To me plunging into social life meant paying a call on the head of my department, Anton Antonovich Setochkin. He was the only permanent acquaintance I have had in my life, and I can't help being surprised at it myself now. But I used to call on him only when I was in the right mood for such a visit, when, that is, my dreams had reached such a pinnacle of bliss that I felt an instant and irresistible urge to embrace all my fellow-men and all humanity. But to do that one had at least to have one man who actually existed. However, it was only on Tuesdays that one could call on Anton Antonovich (Tuesday was his at home day), and therefore it was necessary to work myself up into the right mood for embracing all mankind on that day. This Anton Antonovich Setochkin lived at Five Corners, on the fourth floor, in four little rooms with low ceilings, one smaller than the other, and all of a most frugal and jaundiced appearance. He had two daughters and their aunt who used to pour out the tea. One of the daughters was thirteen and the other fourteen; both had snub noses and both used to embarrass me terribly because they kept whispering to each other and giggling. The master of the house was usually in his study. He sat on a leather sofa in front of his desk, with some grey-haired visitor, a civil servant from our department or, occasionally, from some other department. I never saw more than two or three visitors there, and always the same. The usual topic of conversation was excise duties, the hard bargaining in the Senate, salaries, promotions, His Excellency, the best way to please him, etc., etc. I had the patience to sit like a damn fool beside these people for hours, listening to them, neither daring to speak to them, nor knowing what to say. I got more and more bored, broke out into a sweat, and was in danger of getting an apoplectic stroke. But all this was good and useful to me. When I came home, I would put off for a time my desire to embrace all mankind.

I had, by the way, another acquaintance of a sort, a fellow by the name of Simonov, an old schoolfellow of mine. I suppose I must have had quite a lot of schoolfellows in Petersburg, but I had nothing to do with them and even stopped exchanging greetings with them in the street. I expect the real reason why I had got myself transferred to another department in the Civil Service was that I did not want to have anything to do with them any more. I wanted to cut myself off completely from the hateful years of my childhood. To hell with that school and those terrible years of slavery! In short, I broke with my schoolfellows as soon as I began to shift for myself. There were only two or three of them left with whom I still exchanged greetings in the street. One of them was Simonov, who was a very quiet boy at school, of an equable nature and not particularly brilliant, but I discerned in him a certain independence of character and even honesty. I don't think he was a dull fellow at all. Not very dull, anyway. We had had some bright times together, but I'm afraid they did not last long and somehow or other got lost in a mist rather suddenly. I had a feeling that he did not exactly relish being reminded of those times and that he seemed to be always afraid that I might adopt the same tone with him again. I suspected that he really loathed the sight of me, but as I was never quite sure about it, I went on visiting him.

So that one Thursday afternoon, unable to bear my solitude any longer and knowing that on Thursdays Anton Antonovich's door would be closed, I thought of Simonov. As I was climbing up to his rooms on the fourth floor, I could not help thinking that this particular gentleman must be sick and tired of me and that I was wasting my time going to see him. But as it invariably happened that such reflections merely spurred me on to put myself into an equivocal position, I went in. It was almost a year since I had last seen Simonov.

III

I found two more of my former schoolfellows with him. They seemed to be discussing some highly important matter. None of them took any particular notice of my arrival, which struck me as rather odd considering that I had not seen them for years. No doubt they regarded me as some sort of common fly. I had never been treated like that even at school, though they all hated me there. I realised, of course, that they could not help despising me now for my failure to get on in the Civil Service, for my having sunk so low, going about shabbily dressed, etc., which in their eyes was, as it were, an advertisement of my own incompetence and insignificance. But all the same I had never expected so great a contempt for me. Simonov could not even disguise his surprise at my visit. He always used to be surprised at my visits, at least that was the impression I got. All this rather upset me. I sat down, feeling somewhat put out, and began listening to their conversation.

They were discussing very earnestly, and even with some warmth, the question of a farewell dinner which they wanted to give next day to a friend of theirs, an army officer by the name of Zverkov, who was due to leave for some remote place in the provinces. Zverkov too had been at school with me all the time, but I grew to hate him particularly in the upper forms. In the lower forms he had been just a good-looking, high-spirited boy, who was a favourite with everybody. I had hated him, however, even in the lower forms just because he was so good-looking and high-spirited a boy. He was never good at lessons, and as time went on he got worse and worse. But he got his school certificate all right because he had powerful connections. During his last year at school he came into an inheritance, an estate with two hundred peasants, and as almost all of us were poor, he even began showing off to us. He was superlatively vulgar, but a good fellow in spite of it, even when he gave himself airs. And in spite of the superficial, fantastic, and rather silly ideas of honour and fair play we had at school, all but a few of us grovelled before Zverkov, and the more he showed off, the more anxious were they to get into his good books. And they did it not because of any selfish motives, but simply because he had been favoured with certain gifts by nature. Besides, Zverkov was for some reason looked upon by us as an authority on smartness and good manners. The last point in particular used to infuriate me. I hated the brusque, self-assured tone of his voice, the way he enjoyed his own jokes, which, as a matter of fact, were awfully silly, though he always was rather daring in his expressions; I hated his handsome but rather vapid face (for which, by the way, I would have gladly exchanged my *clever* one) and his free and easy military manners which were in vogue in the forties. I hated the way in which he used to talk of his future conquests (he did not have the courage to start an affair with a woman before getting his officer's epaulettes, and was looking forward to them with impatience), and of the duels he would be fighting almost every minute. I remember how I, who had always been so reserved and taciturn, had a furious argument with Zverkov when he was discussing his future love affairs with his cronies during playtime and, becoming as playful as a puppy in the sun, suddenly declared that on his estate he would not leave a single peasant girl who was a virgin without his attentions, that that was his *droit de seigneur,* and that if any of his peasants dared to protest he would have them flogged and double the tax on them, too, the bearded rascals. Our oafs applauded him, but I got my teeth into him not because I was sorry for the virgins or their fathers, but just because they were applauding such an insect. I got the better of him then, but though a great fool, Zverkov was an impudent and jolly fellow, so he laughed the whole affair off, and did it so well that I didn't really get the better of him in the end: the laugh was against me. He got the better of me several times afterwards, but without malice and as though it were all a great lark, with a casual sort of laugh. I would not reply to him, keeping resentfully and contemptuously silent. When we left school, Zverkov seemed anxious to be friends with me, and feeling flattered, I did not object; but we soon, and quite naturally, drifted apart. Afterwards I heard of his barrackroom successes as a lieutenant and of the *gay* life he was leading. Then other rumors reached me of his *progress* in the army. Already he began cutting me dead in the street, and I suspected he was afraid of compromising himself by greeting so insignificant a person as me. I also saw him at the theatre once, in the circle, already wearing shoulder-straps. He was bowing and scraping to the daughters of some ancient general. In three years he had lost his youthful looks, though he still was quite handsome and smart. He was beginning to put on weight and looked somewhat bloated. It was pretty clear that by the time he was thirty he would go completely fat and flabby. It was to this Zverkov, who was now leaving the capital, that our friends were going to give a dinner. They had been his boon companions, though I felt sure that in their hearts they never thought themselves his equal.

Of Simonov's two friends one was Ferfichkin, a Russian of German origin, a little fellow with the face of a monkey and one of my worst enemies from our earliest days at school. He was an utterly contemptible, impudent, conceited fellow who liked to parade his claims to a most meticulous sense of honour, but who really was a rotten little coward at heart. He belonged to those of Zverkov's admirers who fawned on him for selfish reasons and who, in fact, often borrowed money from him. Simonov's other visitor, Trudolyubov, was not in any way remarkable. He was an army officer, tall, with rather a cold countenance, fairly honest, but a great admirer of every kind of success and only capable of discussing promotions. He seemed to be a distant relative of Zverkov's, and that, foolish as it may sound, invested him with a certain prestige among us. He always regarded me as a man of no importance, but if not polite, his treatment of me was tolerant.

"Well," said Trudolyubov, "I suppose if we contribute seven roubles each we'll have twenty-one roubles, and for that we ought to be able to get a damn good dinner. Zverkov, of course, won't pay."

"Naturally," Simonov agreed, "if we're inviting him."

"Surely you don't suppose," Ferfichkin interjected superciliously and with some warmth, like an impudent footman who was boasting about the decorations of his master the general, "surely you don't suppose Zverkov will let us pay for him, do you? He might let us pay for the dinner out of a feeling of delicacy, but I bet you anything he'll contribute half a dozen bottles of champagne."

"Half a dozen for the four of us is a bit too much, isn't it?" remarked Trudolyubov, paying attention only to the half-dozen.

"So the three of us then, with Zverkov making four, twenty-one roubles, at the Hôtel de Paris at five o'clock tomorrow," Simonov, who had been chosen as the organiser of the dinner, concluded finally.

"How do you mean twenty-one?" I said in some agitation, pretending to be rather offended. "If you count me, you'll have twenty-eight roubles, and not twenty-one."

I felt that to offer myself suddenly and so unexpectedly as one of the contributors to the dinner was rather a handsome gesture on my part and that they would immediately accept my offer with enthusiasm and look at me with respect.

"You don't want to contribute, too, do you?" Simonov observed without concealing his displeasure and trying not to look at me.

He could read me like a book.

I felt furious that he should be able to read me like a book.

"But why shouldn't I? I'm an old school friend of his, am I not? I must say I can't help resenting being passed over like that!" I spluttered again.

"And where do you suppose were we to find you?" Ferfichkin broke in, rudely.

"You were never on good terms with Zverkov, you know," Trudolyubov added, frowning.

But I had got hold of the idea and I was not to give it up so easily.

"I don't think anyone has a right to express an opinion about that," I replied with a tremor in my voice, as though goodness knows what had happened. "It is just because I was not on very good terms with him before that I might like to meet him now."

"Well," Trudolyubov grinned, "who can make you out—all those fine ideals—"

"Very well," Simonov made up his mind, "we'll put your name down. Tomorrow at five o'clock at the Hôtel de Paris. Don't forget."

"But the money!" Ferfichkin began in an undertone, addressing Simonov and nodding in my direction, but he stopped short, for even Simonov felt embarrassed.

"All right," Trudolyubov said, getting up, "let him come, if he really wants to so much."

"But, damn it all, it's only a dinner for a few intimate friends,"

Ferfichkin remarked crossly as he, too, picked up his hat. "It's not an official gathering. How do you know we want you at all?"

They went away. As he went out, Ferfichkin did not even think it necessary to say goodbye to me. Trudolyubov just nodded, without looking at me. Simonov, with whom I now remained alone, seemed perplexed and puzzled, and he gave me a strange look. He did not sit down, nor did he ask me to take a seat.

"Mmmm—yes—tomorrow then. Will you let me have the money now? I mean, I'd like to know—" he murmured, looking embarrassed.

I flushed and, as I did so, I remembered that I had owed Simonov fifteen roubles for years, which, incidentally I never forgot, though I never returned the money.

"But look here, Simonov, you must admit that I couldn't possibly have known when I came here that—I mean, I am of course very sorry I forgot—"

"All right, all right! It makes no difference. You can pay me tomorrow at the dinner. I just want to know, that's all. Please, don't—"

He stopped short and began pacing the room noisily, looking more vexed than ever. As he paced the room, he raised himself on his heels and stamped even more noisily.

"I'm not keeping you, am I?" I asked after a silence of two minutes.

"Oh, no, not at all!" He gave a sudden start. "I mean, as a matter of fact, you are. You see I have an appointment with someone,—er—not far from here," he added in an apologetic sort of voice, a little ashamed.

"Good Lord, why didn't you tell me?" I cried, seizing my cap with rather a nonchalant air, though goodness only knows where I got it from.

"Oh, it's not far really—only a few steps from here," Simonov repeated, seeing me off to the front door with a bustling air, which did not become him at all. "So tomorrow at five o'clock sharp!" he shouted after me as I was going down the stairs.

He seemed very glad indeed to see me go, but I was mad with rage.

"What possessed me to do it?" I muttered, grinding my teeth, as I walked along the street. "And for such a rotter, such a swine as Zverkov. Of course I mustn't go. Of course to hell with the lot of them. Why should I? I'm not obliged to, am I? I'll let Simonov know tomorrow. Drop him a line by post."

But the reason why I was so furious was because I knew perfectly well that I should go, that I should go deliberately; and that the more tactless, the more indecent my going was, the more certainly would I go.

And there was a good reason why I should not go: I had not got the money. All in all, I had nine roubles, but of that I had to give seven to my servant Apollon tomorrow for his monthly wages, out of which he paid for his board. Not to pay him was quite out of the question, knowing as I did the sort of man Apollon was. But of that fiend, of that scourge of mine, I shall speak another time.

Anyway, I knew very well that I wouldn't pay him, but would quite certainly go to the dinner.

That night I had the most hideous dreams. And no wonder. The whole evening I was haunted by memories of my hateful days at school, and I could not get rid of them. I was sent to the school by some distant relations of mine, on whom I was dependent and of whom I have not heard anything since. They dumped me there, an orphan already crushed by their reproaches, already accustomed to brood for hours on end, always silent, one who looked sullenly on everything around him. My schoolmates overwhelmed me with spiteful and pitiless derision because I was not like any of them. And derision was the only thing I could not stand. I did not find it at all as easy to make friends with people as they did to make friends among themselves. I at once conceived a bitter hatred for them and withdrew from them all into my own shell of wounded, timid, and excessive pride. Their coarseness appalled me. They laughed cynically at my face, at my ungainly figure. And yet how stupid their own faces were! At our school the faces of the boys seemed to undergo an extraordinary change and grow particularly stupid. Lots of nice looking children entered our school, but after a few years one could not look at them without a feeling of revulsion. Even at the age of sixteen I wondered morosely at them. Even at that time I was amazed at the pettiness of their thoughts, the silliness of their occupations, their games, their conversations. They did not understand even the most necessary things; they were not interested in anything that was out of the ordinary, in anything that was conducive to thought, so that I could not help looking on them as my inferiors. It was not injured vanity that drove me to it, and don't for goodness sake come to me with your hackneyed and nauseating objections, such as, for instance, that I was only dreaming, while they understood the real meaning of life even then. They understood nothing. They had not the faintest idea of real life. Indeed, it was just that I could not stand most of all about them. On the contrary, they had a most fantastic and absurd notion of the most simple, most ordinary facts, and already at that early age they got into the habit of admiring success alone. Everything that was just but looked down upon and oppressed, they laughed at shamelessly and heartlessly. Rank they mistook for brains. Even at sixteen all they were discussing was cushy jobs. A great deal of it, no doubt, was due to their stupidity, to the bad examples with which they had been surrounded in their childhood and adolescence. And they were abominably vicious. I suppose much of that, too, was only on the surface, much of their depravity was just affected cynicism, and even in their vices one could catch a glimpse of youth and of a certain freshness. But that freshness had nothing attractive about it, and it took the form of a kind of rakishness. I hated them terribly, though I suppose I was really much worse than they. They repaid me in the same coin and did not conceal their loathing of me. But I was no longer anxious for them to like me; on the contrary, I longed continually to humiliate them. To escape their ridicule, I purposely began to apply myself more diligently to my studies and was soon among the top boys in my form. This did make an impression on them. Moreover, they all began gradually to realise that I was already reading books they could not read, and that I understood things (not included in our school curriculum) of which they had not even heard. They looked sullenly and sardonically on all this, but they had to acknowledge my moral superiority, particularly as even the teachers took notice of me on account of it. Their jeering stopped, but their hostility remained, and henceforth our relations became strained and frigid. In the end I could no longer stand it myself: the older I became, the more I longed for the society of men and the more I was in need of friends. I tried to become friends with some of them, but my friendship with them always somehow appeared unnatural and came to an end of itself. I did have a sort of a friend once, but by that time I was already a tyrant at heart: I wanted to exercise complete authority over him, I wanted to implant a contempt for his surroundings in his heart, I demanded that he should break away from these surroundings, scornfully and finally. I frightened him with my passionate friendship. I reduced him to tears, to hysterics. He was a simple and devoted soul, but the moment I felt that he was completely in my power I grew to hate him and drove him from me, as though I only wanted him for the sake of gaining a victory over him, for the sake of exacting his complete submission to me. But I could not get the better of them all. My friend, too, was unlike any of the others; he was, in fact, a rare exception. The first thing I did on leaving school was to give up the career for which I had been trained so as to break all the ties that bound me to my past, which I loathed and abominated. . . . And I'm damned if I know why after all that I should go trotting off to see that Simonov! . . .

Early next morning I jumped out of bed in a state of tremendous excitement, as though everything were about to happen there and then. But I really did believe that there was going to be some radical break in my life and that it would most certainly come that day. Whether it was because I was not used to change or for some other reason, but all through my life I could not help feeling that any extraneous event, however trivial, would immediately bring about some radical alteration in my life. However, I went to the office as usual, but slipped away home two hours early to get ready. The important thing, I thought, was not to arrive there first, or they might think that I was really glad to be in their company. But there were thousands of such important things to think of, and they excited me so much that in the end I felt a physical wreck. I gave my boots another polish with my own hands; Apollon would not have cleaned them twice a day for anything in the world, for he considered that a most irregular procedure. I polished them with the brushes I had sneaked from the passage to make sure he did not know anything about it, for I did not want him to despise me for it afterwards. Then I submitted my clothes to a most meticulous inspection and found that everything was old, worn, and covered with stains. I had certainly grown much too careless of my appearance. My Civil Service uniform was not so bad, but I could not go out to dinner in my uniform, could I? The worst of it was that there was a huge yellow stain on the knee of my trousers. I had a presentiment that that stain alone would rob me of nine-tenths of my self-respect. I knew, too, that it was a thought unworthy of me. "But this is no time for thinking: now I have to face reality," I thought with a sinking heart. I knew, of course, perfectly well at the time that I was monstrously exaggerating all these facts. But what could I do? It was too late for me to control my feelings, and I was shaking with fever. I imagined with despair how patronisingly and how frigidly that "rotter" Zverkov would meet me; with what dull and irresistible contempt that blockhead Trudolyubov would look at me; with what unbearable insolence that insect Ferfichkin would titter at me in order to curry favour with Zverkov; how perfectly Simonov would understand it all and how he would despise me for the baseness of my vanity and want of spirit, and, above all, how paltry, *unliterary*, and commonplace the whole affair would be. Of course, the best thing would be not to go at all. But that was most of all out of the question: once I felt drawn into something, I was drawn into it head foremost. All my life I should have jeered at myself afterwards: "So you were afraid, were you? Afraid of *life*! Afraid!" On the contrary, I longed passionately to show all that "rabble" that I was not such a coward as even I imagined myself to be. And that was not all by any means: in the most powerful paroxysms of my cowardly fever I dreamed of getting the upper hand, of sweeping the floor with them, of forcing them to admire and like me—if only for my "lofty thoughts and indisputable wit." They would turn their backs on Zverkov, he would be left sitting by himself in some corner, silent and ashamed, utterly crushed by me. Afterwards, no doubt, I would make it up with him and we would drink to our everlasting friendship. But what was most galling and infuriating to me was that even then I knew without a shadow of doubt that, as a matter of fact, I did not want any of this at all, that, as a matter of fact, I had not the least desire to get the better of them, to crush them, to make them like me, and that if I ever were to do so, I should not give a rap for it. Oh, how I prayed for the day to pass quickly! Feeling utterly miserable I walked up again and again to the window, opened the small ventilating pane, and peered out into the murky haze of the thickly falling wet snow. . . .

At last my cheap clock wheezed out five. I seized my hat and, trying not to look at Apollon, who had been waiting for his wages ever since the morning but was too big a fool to speak to me about it first, slipped past him through the door, and in a smart sledge, which cost me my last fifty copecks, drove up in great style to the Hôtel de Paris.

IV

I had had a feeling the day before that I'd be the first to arrive. But it was no longer a question of arriving first. For not only were they not there, but I could hardly find the room. Nor was the table laid. What did it mean? After many inquiries I found out at last from the waiters that the dinner had been ordered for six and not for five o'clock. I had that confirmed at the bar, too. I even began feeling ashamed to go on making those inquiries. It was only twenty-five minutes past five. If they had changed the dinner hour, they should at least have let me know—what was the post for?—and not have exposed me to such "humiliation" in my own eyes and—and certainly not in the eyes of the waiters. I sat down. A waiter began laying the table. I felt even more humiliated in his presence. Towards six o'clock they brought in candles in addition to the burning lamps. The waiter, however, had never thought of bringing them in as soon as I arrived. In the next room two gloomy gentlemen were having dinner at separate tables; they looked angry and were silent. People in one of the other rooms were kicking up a terrible shindy, shouting at the top of their voices; I could hear the loud laughter of a whole crowd of people, interspersed with some disgustingly shrill shrieks in French: there were ladies at the dinner. The whole thing, in short, could not have been more nauseating. I don't remember ever having had such a bad time, so that when, punctually at six, they arrived all together, I was at first very glad to see them, as though they were my deliverers, and I almost forgot that I ought to be looking offended.

Zverkov entered the room ahead of everybody, quite obviously the leading spirit of the whole company. He and his companions were laughing. But as soon as he caught sight of me, he pulled himself up and, walking up to me unhurriedly, bent his body slightly from the waist, as though showing off what a fine gentleman he was. He shook hands with me affably, though not too affably, with a sort of watchful politeness, almost as though he were already a general, and as though in giving me his hand he was protecting himself against something. I had imagined that as soon as he came in he would, on the contrary, break into his customary high-pitched laugh, intermingled with shrill shrieks, and at once start making his insipid jokes and witticisms. It was to deal with this that I had been preparing myself since last evening, but I had never expected such condescending affability, such grand manners of a person of the highest rank. So he already considered himself infinitely superior to me in every respect, did he? If he only meant to insult me with the superior airs of a general, it would not matter, I thought to myself; but what if, without the least desire to offend me, the fool had really got the preposterous idea into his head that he was immeasurably superior to me and could not look at me but with a patronising air? The very thought of it made me choke with resentment.

"I was surprised to hear of your desire to join us," he began, mouthing and lisping, which he never used to do before. "I'm afraid we haven't seen much of each other recently. You seem to avoid us. A pity. We're not so terrible as you think. Anyway, I'm glad to—er—re-e-sume—er—" and he turned away casually to put down his hat on the windowsill.

"Been waiting long?" asked Trudolyubov.

"I arrived at precisely five o'clock as I was told to yesterday," I replied in a loud voice and with an irritation that threatened an early explosion.

"Didn't you let him know that we had changed the hour?" Trudolyubov asked, turning to Simonov.

"I'm afraid I didn't—forgot all about it," Simonov replied unrepentantly and, without a word of apology to me, went off to order the *hors d'œuvres.*

"You poor fellow, so you've been waiting here for a whole hour, have you?" Zverkov exclaimed sarcastically, for, according to his notions, this was really very funny.

That awful cad Ferfichkin broke into a nasty, shrill chuckle, like the yapping of a little dog. My position seemed to him too ludicrous and too embarrassing for words.

"It isn't funny at all!" I cried to Ferfichkin, getting more and more irritated. "It was somebody else's fault, not mine. I expect I wasn't considered important enough to be told. This—this—this is simply idiotic!"

"Not only idiotic, but something else as well," Trudolyubov muttered, naïvely taking my part. "You're much too nice about it. It's simply insulting. Unintentional, no doubt. And how could Simonov—well!"

"If anyone had played that kind of joke on me," observed Ferfichkin, "I'd—"

"You'd have ordered something for yourself," Zverkov interrupted him, "or simply asked for dinner without waiting for us."

"But you must admit I could have done as much without your permission," I rapped out. "If I waited, I—"

"Let's take our seats, gentlemen," Simonov cried, coming in. "Everything's ready. I can answer for the champagne—it's been excellently iced. . . . I'm sorry," he suddenly turned to me, but again somehow avoiding looking at me, "but I didn't know your address, and so I couldn't possibly have got hold of you, could I?"

He must have had something against me. Must have changed his mind after my visit last night.

All sat down; so did I. The table was a round one. Trudolyubov was on my left and Simonov on my right. Zverkov was sitting opposite with Ferfichkin next to him, between him and Trudolyubov.

"Tell me plea-ea-se are you—er—in a Government department?" Zverkov continued to be very attentive to me.

He saw how embarrassed I was and he seriously imagined that it was his duty to be nice to me and, as it were, cheer me up.

"Does he want me to throw a bottle at his head?" I thought furiously. As I was unaccustomed to these surroundings, I was getting irritated somehow unnaturally quickly.

"In the . . . office," I replied abruptly, my eyes fixed on my plate.

"Good Lord, and do-o-o you find it re-mu-nerative? Tell me, plea-ea-se, what indu-u-uced you to give up your old job?"

"What indu-u-uced me was simply that I got fed up with my old job," I answered, drawing out the words three times as much as he and scarcely able to control myself.

Ferfichkin snorted. Simonov glanced ironically at me. Trudolyubov stopped eating and began observing me curiously.

Zverkov winced, but pretended not to have noticed anything.

"We-e-e-ell, and what's your screw?"

"Which screw?"

"I mean, what's your sa-a-alary?"

"You're not by any chance cross-examining me, are you?"

However, I told him at once what my salary was. I was blushing terribly.

"Not much," Zverkov observed importantly.

"No," Ferfichkin added insolently, "hardly enough to pay for your dinners at a restaurant."

"I think it's simply beggarly," Trudolyubov said, seriously.

"And how thin you've grown, how you've changed since—er—those days," added Zverkov, no longer without venom, examining my clothes with a sort of impudent compassion.

"Stop embarrassing the poor fellow," Ferfichkin exclaimed, giggling.

"You're quite mistaken, sir," I burst out at last, "I'm not at all embarrassed. Do you hear? I'm dining here at this restaurant, sir, at my own expense, and not at other people's. Make a note of that, Mr. Ferfichkin."

"What do you mean?" Ferfichkin flew at me, turning red as a lobster and glaring furiously at me. "And who, sir, isn't dining at his own expense here? You seem to—"

"I mean what I said," I replied, feeling that I had gone too far, "and I think we'd better talk of something more intelligent."

"You're not by any chance anxious to show off your intelligence, are you?"

"I shouldn't worry about that, if I were you. It would be entirely out of place here."

"What are you talking about, my dear sir? You haven't gone out of your mind at that *le*partment of yours, have you?"

"Enough, enough, gentlemen!" Zverkov cried in a commanding voice.

"How damn silly!" Simonov muttered.

"It is damn silly," Trudolyubov said, addressing himself rudely to me alone. "Here we are, a few good friends, met to wish god-speed to a comrade, and you're trying to settle old scores! It was you who invited yourself to join us yesterday, so why are you now up-setting the friendly atmosphere of this dinner?"

"Enough, enough!" Zverkov cried again. "Drop it, gentlemen. This is hardly the time or place for a brawl. Let me rather tell you how I nearly got married the other day!"

And off he went to tell some scandalous story of how he had nearly got married a few days before. There was, by the way, not a word about the marriage. The story was all about generals, colonels, and even court chamberlains, and Zverkov, of course, played the most important part among them. It was followed by a burst of appreciative laughter, Ferfichkin's high-pitched laugh breaking into loud shrieks.

None of them paid any attention to me, and I sat there feeling crushed and humiliated.

"Good heavens, is this the sort of company for me?" I thought. "And what an ass I've made of myself in front of them! I let Ferfichkin go too far, though. The idiots think they do me an honour by letting me sit down at the same table with them. They don't seem to realise that it is I who am doing them an honour, and not they me. 'You look so thin! Your clothes!' Damn my trousers! I'm sure Zverkov noticed the stain on the knee the moment he came in. . . . But what the hell am I doing here? I'd better get up at once, this minute, take my hat, and simply go without a word. . . . Show them how much I despise them! Don't care a damn if I have to fight a duel tomorrow. The dirty rotters! Do they really think I care about the seven roubles? They might, though. . . . To hell with it! I don't care a damn about the seven roubles! I'll go this minute!"

But, of course, I stayed.

In my despair I drank glass after glass of sherry and Château Lafitte. As I was unused to drink, I got drunk very quickly, and the more drunk I got the hotter did my resentment grow. I suddenly felt like insulting them in the most insolent way and then going. Waiting for the right moment, then showing them the kind of man I was, and in that way forcing them to admit that, though I might be absurd, I was clever and—and—oh, to hell with them!

I looked impudently at them with leaden eyes. But they seemed to have entirely forgotten me. *They* were noisy, clamorous, happy. Zverkov was talking all the time. I started listening. He was talking about some ravishingly beautiful woman whom he had brought to the point of declaring her love to him at last (he was of course lying like a trooper), and how an intimate friend of his, a prince of sorts, a hussar by the name of Kolya, who owned three thousand peasants, was particularly helpful to him in this affair.

"And yet this friend of yours, the chap with the three thousand peasants, isn't here, is he? To see you off, I mean," I broke into the conversation.

For a minute there was dead silence.

"I believe you're quite tight now." Trudolyubov at last condescended to notice me, throwing a disdainful glance in my direction.

Zverkov stared at me in silence, examining me as though I were an insect. Simonov quickly began pouring out the champagne.

Trudolyubov raised his glass, all the others except myself following his example.

"To your health and a pleasant journey!" he cried to Zverkov. "To our past, gentlemen, and to our future! Hurrah!"

They drained their glasses and rushed to embrace Zverkov. I did not stir; my full glass stood untouched before me.

"Aren't you going to drink?" roared Trudolyubov, losing patience and addressing me menacingly.

"I want to make a speech too—er—a special speech and—and then I'll drink, Mr. Trudolyubov."

"Unmannerly brute!" muttered Simonov.

I drew myself up in my chair and took up my glass feverishly, preparing myself for something extraordinary, though I hardly knew myself what I was going to say.

"Silence!" cried Ferfichkin. "Now we're going to hear something really clever!"

Zverkov waited gravely, realising what was in the wind.

"Lieutenant Zverkov," I began, "I'd like you to know that I hate empty phrases, phrasemongers, and tight waists.... That is the first point I should like to make. The second will follow presently."

They all stirred uneasily.

"My second point: I hate smutty stories and the fellows who tell them. Especially the fellows who tell them. My third point: I love truth, frankness, and honesty," I went on almost mechanically, for I was beginning to freeze with terror myself, quite at a loss how I came to talk like this. "I love thought, Mr. Zverkov. I love true comradeship where all are equal, and not—er—yes. I love—but what the hell! Why not? I'll drink to your health too, Mr. Zverkov. Seduce the Caucasian maidens, shoot the enemies of our country and—and—to your health, Mr. Zverkov!"

Zverkov got up from his seat, bowed, and said, "Very much obliged to you, I'm sure."

He was terribly offended and even turned pale.

"Damn it all!" Trudolyubov roared, striking the table with his fist.

"Why, sir," Ferfichkin squealed, "people get a punch on the nose for that!"

"Let's kick him out!" muttered Simonov.

"Not another word, gentlemen, please!" Zverkov cried solemnly, putting a stop to the general indignation. "I thank you all, but leave it to me to show him how much value I attach to his words."

"Mr. Ferfichkin," I said in a loud voice, addressing myself importantly to Ferfichkin, "I expect you to give me full satisfaction tomorrow for your words just now!"

"You mean a duel, do you? With pleasure, sir!" Ferfichkin

replied, but I must have looked so ridiculous as I challenged him, and the whole thing, in fact, must have looked so incongruous in view of my small stature, that everyone, including Ferfichkin, roared with laughter.

"Oh, leave him alone for goodness' sake," Trudolyubov said with disgust. "The fellow's tight!"

"I shall never forgive myself for having put his name down," Simonov muttered again.

"Now is the time to throw a bottle at them," I thought, picked up the bottle and—poured myself out another glass.

". . . No, I'd better see it through to the end!" I went on thinking to myself. "You'd be pleased if I went away, gentlemen, wouldn't you? But I shan't go. Oh, no. Not for anything in the world. I'll go on sitting here on purpose—and drinking—to the end just to show you that I don't care a damn for you. I'll go on sitting and drinking because this is nothing but a low-class pub and, besides, I paid for everything. I'll sit and drink because I think you're a lot of nobodies, a lot of miserable, paltry nobodies. I'll sit and drink and—and sing, if I like. Yes, sing! For, damn it, I've a right to sing—er—yes."

But I did not sing. I just did my best not to look at them, assumed most independent attitudes, and waited patiently for them to speak to me *first.* But, alas, they did not speak to me. And how I longed—oh, how I longed at that moment to be reconciled to them! It struck eight, then at last nine. They moved from the table to the sofa. Zverkov made himself comfortable on the sofa, placing one foot on a little round table. They took the wine with them. Zverkov did actually stand them three bottles of champagne. He did not of course invite me to join them. They all sat round him on the sofa, listening to him almost with reverence. It was clear that they were fond of him. "But why? Why?" I asked myself. From time to time they were overcome with drunken enthusiasm and kissed each other. They talked about the Caucasus, about the nature of real passion, about cards, about cushy jobs in the service; about the income of the hussar Podkharzhevsky, whom none of them knew personally, and they were glad he had such a large income; about the marvellous grace and beauty of princess D., whom none of them had ever seen, either; and at last they finished up with the statement that Shakespeare was immortal.

I was smiling contemptuously, walking up and down at the other end of the room, directly opposite the sofa, along the wall, from the table to the stove, and back again. I did my best to show them that I could do without them, at the same time deliberately stamping on the floor, raising myself up and down on my heels. But it was all in vain. *They* paid no attention to me. I had the patience to pace the room like that right in front of them from eight till eleven o'clock, always in the same place, from the table to the stove, and back again. "Here I am, walking up and down, just as I please, and no one can stop me!" The waiter, who kept coming into the room, stopped and looked at me a few times. I was beginning to feel giddy from turning round so frequently, and there were moments when I thought I was delirious. Three times during those three hours I got wet through with perspiration and three times I got dry again. At times the thought would flash through my mind and stab my heart with fierce, intense pain that ten, twenty, forty years would pass and I would still remember after forty years with humiliation and disgust those beastly, ridiculous, and horrible moments of my life. It was quite impossible for anyone to abase himself more disgracefully and do it more willingly, and I realised it fully—fully—and yet I went on pacing the room from the table to the stove, and from the stove to the table. "Oh, if only you knew the thoughts and feelings I'm capable of and how intelligent I am!" I thought again and again, addressing myself mentally to the sofa on which my enemies were sitting. But my enemies behaved as though I were not in the room at all. Once, only once, they turned to me, just when Zverkov began talking about Shakespeare and I burst out laughing contemptuously. I guffawed in so affected and disgusting a manner that they at once interrupted their conversation and watched me silently for a couple of minutes, with a grave air and without laughing, walking up and down along the wall from the table to the stove, *taking no notice of them.* But nothing came of it: they said nothing to me, and two minutes later stopped taking any notice of me again. It struck eleven.

"Gentlemen," Zverkov cried, getting up from the sofa, "now let's all go *there*!"

"Of course, of course," the others said.

I turned abruptly to Zverkov. I was so exhausted, so dead beat, that I would have gladly cut my own throat to put an end to my misery. I was feverish. My hair, wet with perspiration, stuck to my forehead and temples.

"Zverkov," I said sharply and determinedly, "I'm sorry. Ferfichkin and all of you, all of you, I hope you'll forgive me—I've offended you all!"

"Aha! Got frightened of the duel, have you?" Ferfichkin hissed venomously.

I felt as though he had stabbed me to the heart.

"No, Ferfichkin, I'm not afraid of the duel. I'm ready to fight you tomorrow, if you like, but only after we've made it up. Yes, I even insist on it, and you can't possibly refuse me. I want to show you that I'm not afraid of a duel. You can fire first, and I'll fire in the air!"

"Pleased with himself, isn't he?" Simonov remarked.

"Talking through his hat, if you ask me," Trudolyubov declared.

"Get out of my way, will you?" Zverkov said contemptuously. "What are you standing in my way for? What do you want?"

They were all red in the face; their eyes were shining; they had been drinking heavily.

"I ask you for your friendship, Zverkov. I offended you, but—"

"Offended me? *You* offended *me*? Don't you realise, sir, that you couldn't possibly offend me under any circumstances?"

"We've had enough of you," Trudolyubov summed up the position. "Get out! Come on, let's go!"

"Olympia's mine, gentlemen! Agreed?" Zverkov exclaimed.

"Agreed! Agreed!" they answered him, laughing.

I stood there utterly humiliated. The whole party left the room noisily. Trudolyubov began singing some stupid song. Simonov stayed behind for a second to tip the waiters. I suddenly went up to him.

"Simonov," I said firmly and desperately, "let me have six roubles!"

He gazed at me in utter amazement, with a sort of stupefied look in his eyes. He, too, was drunk.

"But you're not coming *there* with us, are you?"

"Yes, I am!"

"I haven't any money!" he snapped out with a contemptuous grin, and left the room.

I caught him by the overcoat. It was a nightmare.

"Simonov, I saw you had money. Why do you refuse me? Am I a scoundrel? Be careful how you refuse me: if you knew, if you knew why I'm asking! Everything depends on it, my whole future, all my plans! . . ."

Simonov took out the money and almost flung it at me.

"Take it if you're so utterly without shame!" he said, pitilessly, and rushed away to overtake them.

For a moment I remained alone. The general disorder in the room, the remains of the dinner, the broken wineglass on the floor, the cigarette-stubs, the fumes of wine and the delirium in my head, the piercing anguish in my heart, and, finally, the waiter who had seen and heard everything and was now peering curiously into my eyes.

"There!" I cried. "Either they'll implore me for my friendship on their knees or—or I'll slap Zverkov's face!"

V

"So this is it—this is it at last—a head-on clash with real life!" I murmured, racing down the stairs. "This is quite a different proposition from your Pope leaving Rome for Brazil! This isn't your ball on Lake Como!"

"You're a swine," the thought flashed through my mind, "if you laugh at this now!"

"I don't care," I cried in answer to myself. "Now everything is lost anyway!"

There was not a trace of them to be seen in the street, but that did not worry me: I knew where they had gone.

At the front steps of the hotel stood a solitary night-sledge with its driver in a rough, peasant coat, thickly covered with wet and, as it were, warm snow which was still falling. It was steamy and close.

His little shaggy, piebald horse was also covered thickly with snow and was coughing—I remember it all very well. I rushed to the wooden sledge, raised a leg to get into it, and was suddenly so stunned by the memory of how Simonov had just given me the six roubles that I fell into the sledge like a sack.

"Oh, I shall have to do a lot to get my own back," I cried. "But I shall do it or perish on the spot tonight. Come on, driver, start!"

We started. My thoughts were in a whirl.

"They won't go down on their knees to ask me to be their friend. That's an illusion, a cheap, romantic, fantastic, horrible illusion—just another ball on Lake Como. And that's why I *must* slap Zverkov's face! I simply must do it. Well, that's settled then. I'm flying now to slap his face! Hurry up, driver!"

The driver tugged at the reins.

"As soon as I go in I'll slap his face. Ought I perhaps to say a few words before slapping his face by way of introduction? No. I'll just go in and slap his face. They'll be all sitting in the large room, and he'll be on the sofa with Olympia. That blasted Olympia! She made fun of my face once and refused me. I shall drag Olympia by the hair and then drag Zverkov by the ears. No. Better by one ear. I shall take him all round the room by the ear. Quite likely they'll all start beating me and will kick me out. That's almost certain. But never mind. I'd have slapped his face first all the same. My initiative. And by the rules of honour that's everything. He would be branded for life and he couldn't wipe off the slap by any blows—no, by nothing but a duel. We will have to fight. Yes, let them beat me now. Let them, the ungrateful swine! I expect Trudolyubov will do most of the beating: he's so strong. Ferfichkin will hang on to me from the side and quite certainly by the hair—yes, quite certainly by the hair. Well, let him. Let him. That's the whole idea of my going there. The silly fools will be forced to realise at last that there's something tragic here! When they're dragging me to the door, I'll shout to them that as a matter of fact they're not worth my little finger. Come on, driver, hurry up!" I cried to the sledge-driver.

He gave a start and whipped up his horse—I shouted so fiercely.

"We shall fight at dawn, that's settled. It's all over with the department. Ferfichkin had said *le*partment instead of *de*partment at dinner. But where am I to get the pistols? Nonsense! I'll ask for an advance of salary and buy them. But the powder, the bullets? That's not my business. Let the second worry about that. But how can I get it all done by daybreak? And where am I to get a second? I have no friends. . . . Nonsense!" I cried, getting more and more carried away. "Nonsense! The first man I meet in the street is bound to be my second, as he would be bound to drag a drowning man out of the water. I must make allowances for the most improbable incidents. Why, even if I were to ask the head of my department himself tomorrow morning to be my second, he too would have to agree, if only from a feeling of chivalry, and keep the secret into the bargain! Anton Antonovich—"

The truth is that at that very moment the whole hideous absurdity of my plans became clearer and more obvious to me than to anyone else in the world. I saw clearly the other side of the medal, and yet—

"Faster, driver! Faster, you rascal! Faster!"

"Lord, sir," said the son of the soil.

A cold shiver ran suddenly down my spine.

"But wouldn't it be better—wouldn't it be a hundred times better to—to go straight home? Oh, dear God, why did I have to invite myself to this dinner yesterday? But no—that's impossible! And what about my walking up and down the room from the table to the stove for three hours? No, they—they alone will have to make amends to me for that walk! They must wipe out that dishonour! Drive on!

". . . And what if they should hand me over to the police? They won't dare! They'll be afraid of a scandal! And what if Zverkov contemptuously refused to fight a duel? That's most likely, but if that happens I'll show them—I'll go to the posting station when he is leaving tomorrow, seize him by the leg, drag his overcoat off him when he gets into the carriage. I'll hang on to his arm with my teeth. I'll bite him. 'See to what lengths a desperate man can be driven?' Let him punch me on the head and the others on the back. I'll shout to all the people around, 'Look, here's a young puppy who's going off to the Caucasus to captivate the girls there with my spit on his face!'

"Of course, after that everything will be over. The department will have vanished off the face of the earth. I shall be arrested. I shall be tried. I shall be dismissed from the Civil Service, thrown into prison, sent to Siberia, to one of the convict settlements there. Never mind. Fifteen years later, after they let me out of jail, I shall set out in search of him, in rags, a beggar, and at last I shall find him in some provincial city. He will be married and happy. He will have a grown-up daughter. I shall say, 'Look, monster, look at my hollow cheeks and my rags! I've lost everything—my career, my happiness, art, science, *the woman I loved,* and all through you. Here are the pistols. I've come to discharge my pistol and—and I forgive you!' And then I shall fire into the air, and he won't hear of me again. . . ."

I almost broke into tears, though I knew very well at that moment that the whole thing was from *Silvio* and from Lermontov's *Masquerade.* And all of a sudden I felt terribly ashamed, so ashamed that I stopped the sledge, got out of it, and stood in the snow in the middle of the road. The driver sighed and looked at me in astonishment.

"What am I to do? I can't go there, for the whole thing is absurd. But I couldn't leave things like that, either, because if I did, it would—Good Lord, how could I possibly leave it like that? And after such insults, too! No!" I cried, rushing back to the sledge. "It's ordained! It's fate! Drive on! Drive on, there!"

And in my impatience I hit the driver in the back with my fist.

"What's the matter with you? What are you hitting me for?" the poor man shouted, but he whipped up the horse so that it began kicking.

The wet snow was falling in large flakes. I unbuttoned my overcoat—I didn't mind the snow. I forgot everything, for I had finally made up my mind to slap Zverkov in the face, and I couldn't help feeling with horror that now it was going to happen *for certain* and that *nothing in the world could stop it.* Solitary street-lamps flickered gloomily in the snowy haze like torches at a funeral. The snow was drifting under my overcoat, under my coat, and under my collar where it melted. I did not button myself up: all was lost, anyway!

At last we arrived. I jumped out and, hardly knowing what I was doing, rushed up the steps and began banging at the door with my fists and feet. My legs, especially at the knees, felt terribly weak. The door was opened more quickly than I expected, as though they knew about my arrival. (Simonov, as a matter of fact, had warned them that someone else might arrive, and in this place it was necessary to give notice beforehand and, generally, to take precautions. It was one of those "fashion shops" which were long ago closed by the police. In the daytime it really was a shop, but at night those who had an introduction could go there to be entertained.) I walked rapidly through the dark shop into the familiar large room where there was only one candle burning and stopped dead, looking utterly bewildered: there was no one there.

"But where are they?" I asked someone.

But, of course, they had already gone their separate ways.

Before me was standing a person who looked at me with a stupid smirk on her face. It was the proprietress herself who knew me slightly. A moment later a door opened and another person came in.

I walked up and down the room without paying any attention to them and, I believe, I was talking to myself. It was as though I had been saved from death, and I felt it joyfully with every fibre of my being. For I should most certainly have slapped his face—oh, most certainly! But they were not there and everything—everything had vanished, everything had changed! I looked round. I was still unable to think clearly. I looked up mechanically at the girl who had just entered: I caught sight of a fresh, young, somewhat pale face, with straight dark eyebrows, and with a serious, as it were, surprised look in her eyes. I liked that at once. I should have hated her if she had been smiling. I began looking at her more intently and with a certain effort: I could not collect my thoughts even yet. There was something kind and good-humoured about her face, but also something strangely serious. I was sure that was to her disadvantage here, and that not one of those fools had noticed her. However, you could hardly have called her a beauty, although she was tall, strong, and well-built. She was dressed very simply. Something vile came over me: I went straight up to her.

I caught sight of myself accidentally in a mirror. My flustered face looked utterly revolting to me: pale, evil, mean, with dishevelled hair. "It's all right, I'm glad of it," I thought. "I'm glad that I'll seem repulsive to her. I like that. . . ."

VI

Somewhere behind the partition, as though under some great pressure, as though someone were strangling it, the clock began wheezing. After the unnaturally protracted wheezing there came a thinnish, disagreeable, and, somehow, unexpectedly rapid chime, as though it had suddenly taken a leap forward. It struck two. I woke up, though I hadn't been really asleep and had only lain in a state of semiconsciousness.

The small, narrow, low-ceilinged room, filled with a huge wardrobe and cluttered up with cardboard boxes, clothes, and all sorts of rags, was almost completely dark. The guttered end of a candle which was burning on the table at the other end of the room was on the point of going out, and only from time to time did it flicker faintly. In a few moments the room would be plunged in darkness.

It did not take me long to recover: everything came back to me in a flash, without the slightest effort, as though it had only been waiting for an opportunity to pounce upon me again. And even while I was fast asleep there always remained some sort of a point in my memory which I never forgot and round which my drowsy dreams revolved wearily. But the strange thing was that everything that had happened to me during the previous day seemed to me now, on awaking, to have occurred a long, long time ago, as though I had long ago shaken it all off.

My head was heavy. Something seemed to be hovering over me, provoking me, exciting and worrying me. Resentment and black despair were again surging up in me and seeking an outlet. Suddenly, close beside me, I saw two wide-open eyes observing me intently and curiously. The look in those eyes was coldly indifferent and sullen, as though it were utterly detached, and it made me feel terribly depressed.

A peevish thought stirred in my mind and seemed to pass all over my body like some vile sensation, resembling the sensation you experience when you enter a damp and stale cellar. It seemed somehow unnatural that those two eyes should have been scrutinising me only now. I remembered, too, that for two whole hours I had never said a word to this creature, and had not even thought it necessary to do so; that, too, for some reason appealed to me. Now, however, I suddenly saw clearly how absurd and hideous like a spider was the idea of vice which, without love, grossly and shamelessly begins where true love finds its consummation. We went on looking at each other like that for a long time, but she did not drop her eyes before mine, nor did she change her expression, so that in the end it made me for some reason feel creepy.

"What's your name?" I asked abruptly, to put an end to this unbearable situation.

"Lisa," she replied, almost in a whisper, but somehow without attempting to be agreeable, and turned her eyes away.

I said nothing for the next few moments.

"The weather was beastly yesterday—snow—horrible!" I said, almost as though I were speaking to myself, putting my arm disconsolately under my head and staring at the ceiling.

She made no answer. The whole thing was hideous.

"Were you born here?" I asked after a minute's silence, almost angry with her, and turning my head slightly towards her.

"No."

"Where do you come from?"

"Riga," she replied reluctantly.

"German?"

"No, I'm a Russian."

"Have you been here long?"

"Where?"

"In this house."

"A fortnight."

She spoke more and more abruptly. The candle went out. I could no longer make out her face.

"Have you any parents?"

"No—yes—I have."

"Where are they?"

"They are there—in Riga."

"Who are they?"

"Oh—"

"Oh? How do you mean? Who are they? What are they?"

"Tradespeople."

"Did you live with them all the time?"

"Yes."

"How old are you?"

"Twenty."

"Why did you leave them?"

"Oh—"

This "oh" meant leave me alone, I'm fed up. We were silent.

Goodness only knows why I did not go away. I felt more and more cheerless and disconsolate myself. The events of the previous day passed disjointedly through my mind, as though of themselves and without any effort on my part. I suddenly remembered something I had seen in the street that morning, when, worried and apprehensive, I was hurrying to the office.

"I saw them carrying out a coffin yesterday and they nearly dropped it," I suddenly said aloud, without wishing to start a conversation and almost, as it were, by accident.

"A coffin?"

"Yes, in the Hay Market. They were carrying it out of a cellar."

"A cellar?"

"Well, not exactly a cellar. A basement—you know—down there, below—from a disorderly house. There was such filth everywhere—litter, bits of shell—an evil smell—oh, it was horrible."

Silence.

"It was a rotten day for a funeral," I began again, simply because I did not want to be silent.

"Why rotten?"

"Snow—slush—" I yawned.

"What difference does it make?" she said suddenly after a moment's silence.

"No, it was horrible—(I yawned again)—I expect the gravediggers must have been swearing at getting wet by the snow. And there must have been water in the grave."

"Why should there be water in the grave?" she asked with a strange sort of curiosity, but speaking even more abruptly and harshly than before.

Something inside me suddenly began egging me on to carry on with the conversation.

"Of course there's water there. About a foot of water at the bottom. You can't dig a dry grave in Volkovo cemetery."

"Oh? Why not?"

"How do you mean? The whole place is a swamp. Marshy ground everywhere. Saw it for myself—many a time."

(I had never seen it, nor have I ever been in Volkovo cemetery. All I knew about it was from what I had heard people say.)

"Don't you mind it at all—dying, I mean?"

"But why should I die?" she replied, as though defending herself.

"You will die one day, you know, and I expect you'll die the same way as that girl whose coffin I saw yesterday morning. She too was a—a girl like you. Died of consumption."

"The slut would have died in the hospital too," she said.

("She knows all about it," I thought to myself, "and she said 'slut' and not girl.")

"She owed money to the woman who employed her," I replied, feeling more and more excited by the discussion. "She worked for her to the very end, though she was in a consumption. The cabmen were talking about it with some soldiers in the street, and they told them that. They were laughing. Promised to have a few drinks to her memory at the pub."

(Much of that was pure invention on my part.)

Silence. Profound silence. She did not even stir.

"You don't suppose it's better to die in a hospital, do you?" she asked, adding a little later, irritably, "What difference does it make? And why on earth should I die?"

"If not now, then later—"

"Later? Oh, well—"

"Don't be so sure of yourself! Now you're young, good-looking, fresh, and that's why they put such a high value on you. But after a year of this sort of life you'll be different. You'll lose your looks."

"After one year?"

"Well, after one year your price will have dropped, anyway," I went on maliciously. "You'll find yourself in some lower establishment then. In another house. In another year—in a third house, lower and lower. And in about seven years you'll get to the cellar in the Hay Market. That wouldn't be so terrible, but, you see, the trouble is that you may fall ill—a weakness in the chest—or catch a cold, or something. In this sort of life it's not so easy to shake off an illness. Once you fall ill you'll find it jolly difficult to get well again. And so you will die."

"All right, so I'll die," she replied, very spitefully, and made a quick movement.

"But aren't you sorry?"

"Sorry? For what?"

"For your life."

Silence.

"You've been engaged to be married, haven't you?"

"Why don't you mind your own business?"

"I'm sorry. I'm not trying to cross-examine you. What the hell do I care? Why are you so angry? I expect you must have all sorts of trouble. It's not my business, of course. But I can't help feeling sorry. That's all."

"Sorry for whom?"

"Sorry for you."

"Not worth it," she whispered in a hardly audible voice and stirred again.

That incensed me. Good Lord, I had been so gentle with her, and she. . . .

"Well, what do you think about it? You think you're on the right path, do you?"

"I don't think anything."

"That's what's wrong with you—you don't think. Come, get back your senses while there's still time. You're still young, you're good-looking, you might fall in love, be married, be happy—"

"Not all married women are happy, are they?" she snapped out, in her former harsh, quick, and abrupt manner.

"Why, no. Not all, of course. But it's much better than here, anyway. A hundred times better. For if you love, you can live even without happiness. Life is sweet even in sorrow. It's good to be alive, however hard life is. But what have you got here? Nothing but foulness. Phew!"

I turned away in disgust. I was no longer reasoning coldly. I was myself beginning to react emotionally to my words and getting worked up. I was already longing to expound my own favourite *little* notions which I had nursed so lovingly in my funk-hole. Suddenly something flared up in me, a sort of aim had *appeared.*

"Don't pay any attention to me," I said. "I mean, that I am here. I'm not an example for you. I'm probably much worse than you. Anyway, I was drunk when I came here," I hastened, however, to justify myself. "Besides, a man is no example for a woman. It's different. Though I may be defiling and degrading myself, I'm not anyone's slave: now I'm here, but I shall be gone soon and you won't see me again. I can shake it all off and be a different man. But you—why, you're a slave from the very start. Yes, a slave! You give away everything. All your freedom. And even if one day you should want to break your chains, you won't be able to: you'll only get yourself more and more entangled in them. That's the kind of damnable chain it is! I know it. And I'm not mentioning anything else, for I don't suppose you'll understand it. Tell me one thing, though. Do you owe money to the woman who employs you? You do, don't you? Ah, there you are!" I added, though she did not reply, but merely listened in silence, with all her being. "So that's your chain. You'll never be able to pay off your debt. They'll see to that. Why, it's the same as selling your soul to the devil! And, besides, perhaps for all you know I'm every bit as wretched as you are and wallow in filth on purpose—because I, too, am sick at heart. People take to drink because they are unhappy, don't they? Well, I, too, am here because I am unhappy. Now, tell me what is there so good about all this?

Here you and I were making love to one another—a few hours ago—and we never said a word to each other all the time, and it was only afterwards that you began staring at me like a wild thing. And I at you. Is that how people love one another? Is that how one human being should make love to another? It's disgusting that's what it is!"

"Yes!" she agreed with me, sharply and promptly.

The promptness with which she had uttered that "yes" even surprised me. So the same thought must have occurred to her too when she was looking so intently at me. So she, too, was capable of the same thoughts. "Damn it, this is interesting—this means that we are *akin* to one another," I thought, almost rubbing my hands with glee. And how indeed should I not be able to cope with a young creature like that?

What appealed to me most was the sporting side of it.

She turned her head closer to me—so it seemed to me in the dark—propping herself up on her arm. Perhaps she was examining me. I was so sorry I could not see her eyes. I heard her deep breathing.

"Why did you come here?" I began, already with a certain note of authority in my voice.

"Oh—"

"But it's nice to be living in your father's house, isn't it? Warm, free—your own home."

"But what if it's much worse than it is here?"

"I must find the right tone," the thought flashed through my mind. "I shan't get far by being sentimental with her, I'm afraid."

However, it was only a momentary thought. She most certainly did interest me. Besides, I was feeling rather exhausted and irritable, and guile accommodates itself so easily to true feeling.

"I don't doubt it for a moment," I hastened to reply. "Everything's possible. You see, I'm sure someone must have wronged you and it's *their* fault rather than yours. Mind, I don't know anything of your story, but it's quite clear to me that a girl like you wouldn't have come here of her own inclination, would she?"

"What kind of girl am I?" she murmured in a hardly audible whisper, but I heard it.

Damn it all, I was flattering her! That was horrible. But perhaps it was not. Perhaps it was all right. . . . She was silent.

"Look here, Lisa, I'll tell you about myself. If I had had a home when I was a child, I should not be what I am now. I often think of it. For however bad life in a family can be, your father and your mother are not your enemies, are they? They are not strangers, are they? Though perhaps only once a year, they will still show their love for you. And however bad it may be, you know you are at home. But I grew up without a home. That's why I suppose I am what I am—a man without feeling. . . ."

Again I waited for some response.

"I don't suppose she understands what I am talking about, after all," I thought. "Besides, it's ridiculous—all this moralising!"

"If I were a father and had a daughter of my own, I think I'd love my daughter more than my sons—I would indeed!" I began indirectly as though I never intended to draw her out at all. I must confess, I blushed.

"But why's that?" she asked.

Oh, so she was listening!

"Just—well, I don't really know, Lisa. You see, I once knew a father who was very strict, a very stern man he was, but he used to go down on his knees to his daughter, kiss her hands and feet, never grew tired of looking at her. Yes, indeed. She would spend the evening dancing at some party, and he'd stand for five hours in the same place without taking his eyes off her. He was quite mad about her. I can understand that. At night she'd get tired and fall asleep, and he'd go and kiss her in her sleep and make the sign of the cross over her. He would go about in a dirty old coat, he was a miser to everyone else, but on her he'd lavish everything he had. He'd buy her expensive presents and be overjoyed if she were pleased with them. Fathers always love their daughters more than mothers do. Many a girl finds life at home very pleasant indeed. I don't think I'd ever let my daughter marry!"

"But why ever not?" she asked with a faint smile.

"I'd be jealous. Indeed I would. I mean I'd hate the thought of her kissing someone else. Loving a stranger more than her father. Even the thought of it is painful to me. Of course, it's all nonsense.

Of course, every father would come to his senses in the end. But I'm afraid I'd worry myself to death before I'd let her marry. I'd certainly find fault with all the men who proposed to her. But in the end I daresay I should let her marry the man she herself loved. For the man whom his daughter loves always seems to be the worst to the father. That's how it is. There's a lot of trouble in families because of that."

"Some parents are glad to sell their daughters, let alone marry them honourably," she said suddenly.

Oh, so that's what it was!

"That, Lisa, only happens in those infamous families where there is neither God nor love," I interjected warmly. "For where there's no love, there's no decency, either. It's true there are such families, but I'm not speaking of them. You can't have known any kindness in your family, if you talk like that. Indeed, you must be very unlucky. Yes, I expect this sort of thing mostly happens because of poverty."

"But is it any better in rich families? Honest people live happily even if they are poor."

"Well, yes, I suppose so. And come to think of it, Lisa, a man only remembers his misfortunes. He never remembers his good fortune. If he took account of his good fortune as well, he'd have realised that there's a lot of that too for his share. But what if all goes well with the family? If with the blessing of God your husband is a good man, loves you, cherishes you, never leaves you for a moment? Oh, such a family is happy, indeed! Even if things don't turn out so well sometimes, it is still all right. For where is there no sorrow? If you ever get married, you'll *find it out for yourself.* Then again if you take the first years of your marriage to a man you love—oh, what happiness, what happiness there is in it sometimes! Why, it's a common enough experience. At first even your quarrels with your husband end happily. There are many women who the more they love their husbands, the more ready they are to quarrel with them. I tell you I knew such a woman myself. 'You see,' she used to say, 'I love you very much, and it's just because I love you so much that I'm tormenting you, and you ought to realise that!' Do you know that one can torment a person just because one loves him? Women do it mostly. They say to themselves, 'But I shall love him so dearly, I shall cherish him so much afterwards that it doesn't matter if I torment him a little now.' And everyone in the house is happy looking at you, everything's so nice, so jolly, so peaceful, and so honest. . . . Other women, of course, are jealous. If her husband happens to go off somewhere (I knew a woman who was like that), she won't be happy till she runs out of the house at night and finds out on the quiet where he is, whether he is in that house or with that woman. That's bad. That's very bad. And she knows herself it is wrong. Her heart fails her and she suffers agonies, but, you see, she loves him: it's all through love. And how nice it is to make it up after a quarrel, to admit that she was wrong, or to forgive him! And how happy they are suddenly. So happy that it seems as though they had met for the first time, as though they had only just got married, as though they had fallen in love for the first time. And no one, no one ought to know what passes between man and wife, if they love one another. And however much they quarrel, they ought not to call in their own mother to adjudicate between them, and to tell tales of one another. They are their own judges. Love is a mystery that God alone only comprehends and should be hidden from all eyes whatever happens. If that is done, it is more holy, and better. They are more likely to respect one another, and a lot depends on their respect for one another. And if once there has been love, if at first they married for love, there is no reason why their love should pass away. Surely, they can keep it! It hardly ever happens that it cannot be kept. Well, and if the husband is a good and honest man, why should love pass away? It is true they will not love one another as they did when they were married, but afterwards their love will be better still, for then they will be united in soul as well as in body, they will manage their affairs in common, there will be no secrets between them—the important thing is to love and have courage. In such circumstances even hard work is a joy; even if you have to go hungry sometimes for the sake of your children, it is a joy. For they will love you for it afterwards; for you are merely laying up treasures for yourself: as the children grow up, you feel that you are an example for them, that you are their support, that even when you die your thoughts and feelings will live with them, for they have received them from you, for they are like you in everything. It is therefore a duty, a great duty. Indeed, the father and the mother cannot help drawing closer together. People say children are a great trouble. But who says it? It is the greatest happiness people can have on earth! Are you fond of little children, Lisa? I am very fond of them. Just imagine a rosy little baby boy sucking at your breast—what husband's heart is not touched at the sight of his wife nursing his child? Oh, such a plump and rosy baby! He sprawls, he snuggles up to you, his little hands are so pink and chubby, his nails are so clean and tiny—so tiny that it makes you laugh to look at them, and his eyes gaze at you as if he understands everything. And while he sucks he pulls at your breast with his sweet little hand—plays. If his father comes near, he tears himself away from the breast, flings himself back, looks at his father and laughs as if goodness only knows how funny it is—and then he begins sucking greedily again. Or again, when his teeth are beginning to come through he will just bite his mother's breast, looking slyly at her with his eyes—'See? I'm biting you!' Isn't everything here happiness when the three of them—husband, wife, and child—are together? One can forgive a great deal for the sake of these moments. Yes, Lisa, one has to learn to live first before blaming others."

"It is with pictures, with pictures like these, that you will beguile her," I thought to myself, though, goodness knows, I spoke with real feeling, and suddenly blushed. "And what if she should suddenly burst out laughing? What a priceless ass I'd look then!" This thought made me furious. Towards the end of my speech I really grew excited, and now my vanity was somewhat hurt. I almost felt like nudging her.

"What are you—" she began suddenly and stopped.

But I understood everything: there was quite a different note in her trembling voice, something that was no longer harsh and crude and unyielding as a short while ago, but something soft and shy, so that I suddenly felt somehow ashamed of her myself. I felt guilty.

"What?" I asked with curiosity.

"Why, you—"

"What?"

"Why, you—you're speaking as though you were reading from a book," she said, and something that sounded like irony could suddenly be heard in her voice.

I resented that remark very deeply. It was not what I was expecting.

I did not realise that by her irony she was deliberately concealing her own feelings, that this was the usual last stratagem of people with pure and chaste hearts against those who impudently and unceremoniously attempt to pry into the inmost recesses of their minds, and that, out of pride, such people do not give in till the very last moment, that they are afraid to show their feelings before you. I should have guessed that from the timidity with which after several tries she approached her ironic remark, and from the shy way in which she made it at last. But I did not guess, and a feeling of vicious spite took possession of me.

"You wait!" I thought.

VII

"Good Lord, Lisa, what sort of a book am I supposed to be reading from when I, who cannot possibly have any interest in what happens to you, feel so sick myself. But as a matter of fact I'm not indifferent, either. All that has now awakened in my heart—Surely, surely, you yourself must be sick to death of being here. Or does habit really mean so much? Hang it all, habit can apparently make anything of a man! Do you really seriously believe that you will never grow old, that you will always be good-looking, and that they will keep you here for ever and ever? To say nothing of the vileness of your present way of life. However, let me tell you this about this business here, about your present way of life. Though you are now young, attractive, pretty, sensitive, warm-hearted, I—well, you know, the moment I woke up a few minutes ago, I couldn't help feeling disgusted at being with you here! It is only when you're drunk that you come to a place like this. But if you were anywhere else, if you lived as all good, decent people live, I should not only have taken a fancy to you, but fallen head over ears in love with you. I'd have been glad if you'd only looked at me, let alone spoken to me. I'd have hung round your door. I'd have gone down on my knees before you. I'd have been happy if you'd have consented to marry me, and deemed it an honour, too. I shouldn't have dared to harbour a single indecent thought about you. But here I know that I have only to whistle and, whether you like it or not, you'll have to come with me, and that it is not I who have to consult your wishes, but you mine. Even if the meanest peasant hires himself out as a labourer, he does not make a slave of himself entirely, and, besides, he knows that after a certain time he will be his own master again. But when can you say as much for yourself? Just think what you are giving up here. What is it you're enslaving? Why, it is your soul, your soul over which you have no power, together with your body! You're giving your love to every drunkard to mock at! Love? Why, that's everything, that's a precious jewel, a girl's dearest treasure—that's what love is! To win this love, a man would be ready to give his soul, to face death itself! And how much is your love worth now? You can be all bought, all of you! And why should anyone try to win your love when he can get everything without love? Why, there is no greater insult for a girl than that. Don't you see it? I am told that to please you, poor fools, they let you have lovers here. But good Lord, what is it but just insulting you? What is it but sheer deceit? Why, they are just laughing at you, and you believe them! Or do you really believe that lover of yours loves you? I don't believe it. How can he love you when he knows that you can be called away from him any moment? He'd be nothing but a pimp after that! And could such a man have an atom of respect for you? What have you in common with him? He's just laughing at you, and robbing you into the bargain—that's what his love amounts to. You're lucky if he doesn't beat you. Perhaps he does, too. Ask him, if you have such a lover, whether he will marry you. Why, he'll laugh in your face, if, that is, he doesn't spit in it or give you a beating, and he himself is probably not worth twopence. And why have you ruined your life here? For what? For the coffee they give you to drink? For the good meals? Have you ever thought why they feed you so well here? Another woman, an honest woman, could not swallow such food, for she would know why she was being fed so well. You are in debt here—well, take my word for it, you'll never be able to repay your debt, you'll remain in debt to the very end, till the visitors here begin to scorn you. And all that will be much sooner than you think. You need not count on your good looks. They don't last very long here, you know. And then you'll be kicked out. And that's not all by any means: long before you're kicked out they'll start finding fault with you, reproaching you, reviling you, as though you had not sacrificed your health for them, ruined your youth and your soul for them, without getting anything in return, but as though you had ruined them, robbed them, beggared them. And don't expect any of the other girls to take your part: they, those friends of yours, will turn against you, too, for the sake of currying favour with your employer, for you are all slaves here, you've all lost all conscience and pity long ago. They have sunk too low, and there's nothing in the world filthier, more odious, and more insulting than their abuse. And you'll leave everything here, everything you possess, without any hope of ever getting it back—your health, your beauty, and your hopes, and at twenty-two you'll look like a woman of thirty-five, and you'll be lucky if you're not ill—pray God for that. I shouldn't be at all surprised if you were not thinking now that you're having a lovely time—no work, just a life of pleasure! But let me tell you that there is no work in the world harder or more oppressive—and there never has been. It is a wonder you haven't long ago cried your heart out. And when they turn you out you won't dare to say a word, not even as much as a syllable, and you'll go away as though it is you who were to blame. You'll pass on to another place, then to a third, then again to some other place, till at last you'll find yourself in the Hay Market. And there they'll start beating you as a matter of course. It's a lovely custom they have there. A visitor there does not know how to be kind without first giving you a good thrashing. You don't believe it's so horrible there? Well, go and have a look for yourself some time and you'll perhaps see with your own eyes. Once, on New Year's Eve, I saw a girl there. She had been turned out by her friends as a joke, to cool off a little in the frost, because she had been howling too much, and they locked the door behind her. At nine o'clock in the morning she was already dead drunk, dishevelled, half naked, beaten black and blue. Her face was made up, but she had two black eyes; she was bleeding from the nose and mouth; she sat down on the stone steps, holding some salt fish in her hands; she was shrieking at the top of her voice bewailing her 'bad luck,' and striking the salt fish against the steps, while a crowd of cabmen and drunken soldiers were standing round and making fun of her. You don't believe that you, too, will be like her one day? Well, I shouldn't like to believe it, either, but how do you know? Perhaps ten or eight years ago the same girl, the girl with the salt fish, arrived here as fresh as a child, innocent and pure, knowing no evil and blushing at every word. Perhaps she was like you, proud, quick to take offence, quite unlike the others, looking like a queen, and quite certain that she would make the man who fell in love with her and whom she loved the happiest man in the world. But you see how it all ended, don't you? And what if at the very moment when she was striking the grimy steps with that fish, dirty and dishevelled, what if at that moment she recalled all the innocent years she had once spent at her father's house, when she used to go to school and the son of their neighbours waited for her on the way and assured her that he would love her as long as he lived, that he would devote his whole future to her, and when they vowed to love one another for ever and be married as soon as they grew up? No, Lisa, you'd be lucky, you'd be very lucky, if you were to die soon, very soon, of consumption, in some corner, in some cellar like that woman I told you of. In a hospital, you say? You'll be fortunate if they take you to a hospital, for, you see, you may still be wanted by your employer. Consumption is a queer sort of illness. It is not like a fever. A consumptive goes on hoping to the last minute. To the very last he goes on saying that there is nothing the matter with him, that he is not ill—deceiving himself. And your employers are only too pleased. Don't worry, it is so. I assure you. You've sold your soul and you owe money into the bargain, so you daren't say a word. But when you are dying, all will abandon you, all will turn away from you, for what more can they get out of you? If anything, they'll reproach you for taking up room without paying for it, for not dying quickly enough. You beg and beg for a drink of water, and when at last they bring it to you they'll abuse you at the same time. 'When are you going to die, you dirty baggage, you? You don't let us sleep, moaning all the time, and the visitors don't like it.' That's true. I've heard such things said myself. And when you are really dying, they'll drag you to the most foul-smelling corner of the cellar, in the damp and the darkness, and what will your thoughts be as you are lying by yourself? When you die, strangers will lay you out, hurriedly, impatiently, grumbling. No one will bless you. No one will sigh for you. Get you quickly out of the way—that's all they'll be concerned about. They'll buy a cheap coffin, take you to the cemetery as they took that poor girl yesterday, and then go to a pub to talk about you. Your grave will be full of slush and dirt and wet snow—they won't put themselves out for you—not they! 'Let her down, boy! Lord, just her "bad luck," I suppose. Gone with her legs up here too, the slut! Shorten the ropes, you young rascal!' 'It's all right!' 'All right, is it? Can't you see she's lying on her side? She's been a human being herself once, ain't she? Oh, all right, fill it up!' And they won't be wasting much time in abusing each other over you, either. They will fill in your grave with wet blue clay and go off to a pub. . . . That will be the end of your memory on earth. Other women have children to visit their graves, fathers, husbands, but there will be neither tears, nor sighs, nor any remembrance for you. No one, no one in the world will ever come to you. Your name will vanish from the face of the earth as though you had never been born! Dirt and mud, dirt and mud, though you knock at your coffin lid at night when the dead arise as hard as you please, crying, 'Let me live in the world, good people! I lived, but I knew no real life. I spent my life as a doormat for people to wipe their dirty boots on. My life has been drunk away at a pub in the Hay Market. Let me live in the world again, good people!' "

I worked myself up into so pathetic a state that I felt a lump rising to my throat and—all of a sudden I stopped, raised myself in dismay, and, bending over apprehensively, began to listen with a violently beating heart. I had good reason to feel embarrassed.

I had felt for a long while that I had cut her to the quick and wrung her heart, and the more I became convinced of it, the more eager I was to finish what I had set out to do as expeditiously and as thoroughly as possible. It was the sport of it, the sport of it, that carried me away. However, it was not only the sport of it.

I knew I was speaking in a stiff, affected, even bookish manner, but as a matter of fact I could not speak except "as though I was reading from a book." But that did not worry me, for I knew, I had a feeling that I would be understood, that this very bookishness would assist rather than hinder matters. But now that I had succeeded in making an impression, I got frightened. No, never, never had I witnessed such despair! She lay prone on the bed, with her face buried in the pillow, which she clasped tightly with both her hands. Her bosom was heaving spasmodically. Her young body was writhing as though in convulsions. The sobs which she tried to suppress seemed to deprive her of breath and rend her bosom, and suddenly they broke out into loud moans and cries. It was then that she clung more tightly to the pillow. She did not want anyone here, not a soul, to know of her agonies and tears. She bit the pillow, she bit her arm till it bled (I saw it afterwards), or clutching at her dishevelled hair with her fingers, went rigid with that superhuman effort, holding her breath and clenching her teeth. I began saying something to her, asking her to calm herself, but I felt that I dared not go on, and all at once, shivering as though in a fever and almost in terror, I began groping for my clothes, intending to dress myself quickly and go. It was dark. However much I tried, I could not finish dressing quickly. Suddenly my hand touched a box of matches and a candle-stick with a new unused candle. The moment the candle lit up the room, Lisa jumped up, sat up on the bed, and with a strangely contorted face and a half-crazy smile looked at me with an almost vacant expression. I sat down beside her and took her hands. She recollected herself, flung herself at me as though wishing to embrace me, but did not dare and slowly bowed her head before me.

"Lisa, my dear, I'm sorry, I—I shouldn't have—" I began, but she squeezed my hands in her fingers with such force that I realised that I was saying the wrong thing and stopped.

"Here's my address, Lisa. Come and see me."

"I will," she whispered firmly, but still not daring to raise her head.

"I'm going now. Goodbye. You will come, won't you?"

I got up. She too got up, and suddenly blushed crimson, gave a shudder, seized a shawl from a chair, threw it over her shoulders and muffled herself up to the chin. Having done that, she again smiled a rather sickly smile, blushed and looked at me strangely. I was deeply sorry for her. I was longing to go, to sink through the floor.

"Wait a minute," she said suddenly in the entrance hall, at the very door, and stopped me by catching hold of my overcoat.

She quickly put down the candle and ran off. She must have remembered something or wanted to show me something. As she was running away, she again blushed all over, her eyes were shining, a smile flitted over her lips—what could it mean? I waited against my will. She came back in a minute and looked at me as though asking forgiveness for something. It was altogether a different face, altogether a different look from a few hours ago—sullen, mistrustful, and obstinate. Now her eyes were soft and beseeching, and at the same time trustful, tender, and shy. So do children look at people they are very fond of and from whom they expect some favour. She had light-brown eyes, beautiful and full of life, eyes which could express love as well as sullen hatred.

Without a word of explanation, as though I, like a sort of higher being, ought to know everything without explanations, she held out a piece of paper to me. At that moment her whole face was radiant with the most naïve, most child-like, triumph. I unfolded it. It was a letter to her from some medical student or someone of the sort—a highly flamboyant and flowery, but also extremely respectful declaration of love. I cannot recall its exact words now, but I remember very well that through that grandiloquent style there peered a genuine feeling which cannot be faked. When I had finished reading the letter, I met her fervent, curious, and childishly impatient gaze fixed on me. Her eyes were glued to my face, and she was waiting with impatience to hear what I had to say. In a few words, hurriedly, but, somehow, joyfully and as though proudly, she explained to me that she had been to a dance in a private house, a family of "very, very nice people, who *knew nothing,* nothing at all," for she had only been here a short time and she did not really intend to stay—no, she had made up her mind not to stay, and she was indeed quite certainly going to leave as soon as she paid her debt. . . . Well, anyway, at that party she had met a student who had danced the whole evening with her. He had talked to her, and it appeared that he had known her as a child in Riga when they used to play together, but that was a long time ago. And he knew her parents too, but he knew nothing, nothing whatever about *this,* and he had not the slightest suspicion even! And the day after the dance (three days ago) he had sent her that letter through a girl friend of hers with whom she had gone to the dance and—and—"well, that is all."

She lowered her shining eyes somewhat shyly as she finished telling me her story.

Poor child, she was keeping the letter of that student as a treasure and ran to fetch that one treasure of hers not wishing that I should go away without knowing that she, too, was loved sincerely and honestly, that people addressed her, too, with respect. That letter, I knew, would most certainly remain in her box without leading to anything. But that did not matter. I was sure she would keep it all her life, guarding it as a priceless treasure, as her pride and justification, and now at such a moment she had remembered it and brought it to boast about naïvely to me, to vindicate herself in my eyes, so that I should see it and commend her for it. I said nothing, pressed her hand, and went out. I longed to get away. . . .

I walked home all the way, though the wet snow kept falling all the time in large flakes. I felt dead tired, depressed, bewildered. But the truth was already blazing through my bewilderment. The disgusting truth!

VIII

However, it took me some time before I acknowledged that truth to myself. Waking up next morning after a few hours of heavy, leaden sleep and immediately remembering all that had occurred the previous day, I was utterly amazed at my *sentimentality* with Lisa the night before, and all "those horrors and commiserations of last night."

"I must have been suffering from an attack of nerves just like a silly old woman," I decided. "Lord, what a fool I was! And why did I give her my address? What if she should come? However, what does it matter if she does come? Let her come, I don't mind. . . ."

But *obviously* that was not the chief and most important thing. What I had to do now, and that quickly too, was to save my reputation in the eyes of Zverkov and Simonov. That was the chief thing. And so preoccupied was I with the other affair that I forgot all about Lisa that morning.

First of all I had immediately to return the money I had borrowed from Simonov the day before. I decided on a desperate step: to borrow fifteen roubles from Anton Antonovich. As it happened, he was in an excellent mood that morning and lent me the money as soon as I asked him for it. That made me feel so happy that, as I signed the promissory note, I told him *casually* with a sort of devil-may-care air that "we had a very gay party last night at the Hôtel de Paris; seeing off a friend, I suppose I might almost say a friend of my childhood. An awful rake, you know, terribly spoilt and, well, of course, of a good family, a man of considerable means, a brilliant career, witty, charming, has affairs with society women, you understand. Drank an additional 'half-dozen' and—And it went off all right," I said it all very glibly, confidently, and complacently.

As soon as I got home I wrote to Simonov.

To this day, as I recall that letter of mine to Simonov, I am lost in admiration at the gentlemanly, good-humoured, frank tone of it. Very dexterously, with perfect grace, and, above all, without any superfluous words, I candidly acknowledged myself to have been completely in the wrong. My only excuse, "if there can possibly be an excuse for the way I behaved," was that, being utterly unaccustomed to drink, I got drunk after the first glass which (I lied) I had drunk before they arrived, while I was waiting for them at the Hôtel de Paris between five and six o'clock. I apologised principally to Simonov, and I asked him to convey my explanations to all the others, especially to Zverkov, whom "I remember as though in a dream" I seem to have insulted. I added that I would have apologised personally to every one of them myself, but I had a terrible headache and—to be quite frank—was too ashamed to face them. I was particularly pleased with the "certain lightness," almost off-handedness (by no means discourteous, by the way) which was so unexpectedly reflected in my style and gave them to understand at once better than any arguments that I took a very detached view of "all that ghastly business of last night"; that I was not at all so crushed as you, gentlemen, probably imagine, but on the contrary look upon it just as any self-respecting gentleman ought to look on it. "A young man," as it were, "can hardly be blamed for every indiscretion he commits."

"Damned if there isn't a certain marquis-like playfulness about it!" I thought admiringly as I read over my letter. "And it's all because I'm such a well-educated person! Others in my place wouldn't have known how to extricate themselves, but I've wriggled out of it and I'm as bright and merry as ever, and all because I am 'an educated man, a modern intellectual.' "

And really the whole ghastly business had most probably been due to the wine. Well, perhaps not to the wine. As a matter of fact, I didn't have any drinks between five and six when I was waiting for them. I had lied to Simonov. I had told him the most shameless lie, but I'm not in the least sorry for it even now. . . .

Anyway, to hell with it! The main thing is that I've got out of it.

I put six roubles in the letter, sealed it, and asked Apollon to take it to Simonov. When he learnt that there was money in the letter, Apollon became more respectful and agreed to take it to Simonov. Towards evening I went out for a walk. My head was still aching from the night before and I was feeling sick. But the further the evening wore on and the darker it grew, the more my impressions and—after them—my thoughts changed and grew confused. Inside me, deep down in my heart and conscience, something kept stirring, would not die, and manifested itself in a feeling of poignant anguish. Mostly I walked aimlessly along the most crowded business streets, along Meshchanskaya, Sadovaya, and Yussupov Park. I always particularly liked taking a stroll along these streets at dusk just when crowds of workers and tradespeople with cross and worried faces were going home from their daily work. What I liked about it was just that common bustle, the every-day, prosaic nature of it all. That evening all that rush and bustle in the streets irritated me more than ever. I could not cope with my own feelings. I could not find an explanation for them. Something was rising up, rising up incessantly in my soul, painfully, something that wouldn't quieten down. I returned home feeling greatly upset. It was as though I had a crime on my conscience.

The thought that Lisa might come worried me constantly. I found it very strange that of all the memories of the day before, the memory of her seemed to torment me in particular, and, as it were, apart from the rest. Everything else I had been successful in dismissing from my mind completely by the evening; I just dismissed it all and was still perfectly satisfied with my letter to Simonov. But so far as Lisa was concerned, I somehow did not feel satisfied. As if it were the thought of Lisa alone that made me so unhappy. "What if she comes?" I kept thinking all the time. "Well, what if she does? Let her. H'm . . . For one thing, I don't want her to see how I live. Last night I seemed—er—a hero to her and—er—now—h'm! It is certainly a nuisance that I let myself go to pieces like that. Everything in my room is so poor and shabby. And how could I have gone out to dinner in such clothes last night! And that American cloth sofa of mine with the stuffing sticking out of it! And my dressing gown in which I can't even wrap myself decently! Rags and tatters. . . . And she will see it all, and she will see Apollon, too. The swine will probably insult her. He'll be rude to her just to be rude to me. And I, of course, will get into a funk as usual, start striking attitudes before her, drape myself in the skirts of my dressing gown, start smiling, start telling lies. Ugh! Sickening! And it isn't this that's really so sickening. There's something more important, more horrible, more contemptible! Yes, more contemptible! And again to assume that dishonest, lying mask—again, again!"

Having come thus far in my thoughts, I couldn't help flaring up. "Why dishonest? In what way is it dishonest? I was speaking sincerely last night. I remember there was some genuine feeling in me, too. I wanted to awaken honourable feelings in her. . . . If she cried a little, it was all to the good. It's sure to have a highly beneficent effect on her. . . ."

All that evening, even when I had returned home, even after nine o'clock when I knew that Lisa could not possibly come, I still could not get her out of my mind, and, above all, I remembered her in one and the same position. Yes, one moment of that night's incident seemed to stand out in my memory with particular clarity, namely, when I struck a match and saw her pale, contorted face and that tortured look in her eyes. What a pitiful, what an unnatural, what a twisted smile she had at that moment! But I did not know then that fifteen years later I should still see Lisa in my mind's eye with the same pitiful, inappropriate smile which was on her face at that moment.

Next day I was once more quite ready to dismiss it all as nonsense, as a result of overstrained nerves, and, above all, as—an *exaggeration.* I was always aware of that weakness of mine, and sometimes I was very much afraid of it. "I always exaggerate—that's my trouble," I used to remind myself almost every hour. But still—"still, Lisa will probably show up all the same," that was the constant refrain of my thoughts at the time. I was so worried about it that I sometimes flew into a blind rage: "She'll come! She's quite certain to come!" I stormed, pacing my room. "If not today, then tomorrow, but come she will! She'll seek me out! For such is the damned romanticism of all those *pure hearts*! Oh, the loathsomeness, oh, the stupidity, oh, the insensibility of these blasted 'sentimental souls'! How could she fail to understand? Why, anyone would have seen through it!"

But here I would stop, overcome with embarrassment.

And how few, how few words were necessary, I thought in passing, how few idyllic descriptions were necessary (and those, too, affected, bookish, insincere) to shape a whole human life at once according to my will! There's innocence for you! Virgin soil!

Sometimes I wondered whether I ought not to go and see her, "tell her everything," and ask her not to come to me. But there, at that thought, I'd fly into such a rage that it seemed to me that I should have crushed that "damned" Lisa if she had happened to be near me at the time. I should have humiliated her. I should have heaped mortal insults upon her, driven her out, beaten her!

However, one day passed, and another, and a third, and she did not come, and I was beginning to feel easier in my mind. I felt particularly cheerful and let my fancy run riot after nine o'clock, and at times I even began indulging in rather sweet daydreams. For instance, "I'm saving Lisa just because she's coming regularly to see me and I'm talking to her.... I'm educating her, enlarging her mind. At last I notice that she is in love with me. I pretend not to understand (I don't know why I am pretending, though, just for the sheer beauty of it, I suppose). In the end, all embarrassed, beautiful, trembling and sobbing, she flings herself at my feet and says that I have saved her and that she loves me more than anything in the world. I look surprised, but—'Lisa,' I say, 'surely you don't imagine I haven't noticed that you love me, do you? I saw everything, I guessed everything, but I did not dare lay claim to your heart first because I knew you were under my influence and was afraid that, out of gratitude, you would deliberately force yourself to respond to my love, that you would rouse a feeling in your heart which perhaps did not really exist, and I did not want this because it—it would be sheer despotism on my part—it would have been indelicate.... (Well, in short, here I got myself entangled in a sort of European, George-Sandian, inexpressibly noble subtleties.) But now, now you're mine, you are my creation, you are pure and beautiful, you are—my beautiful wife!"

> And my house, fearlessly and freely,
> As mistress you can enter now!

And then we live happily ever after, go abroad, etc., etc. In short, I got so thoroughly fed up with myself in the end that I finished up by sticking out my tongue at myself.

"Besides, they won't let her go, the 'tart'!" I thought to myself. "I don't think they are allowed to go out very much and certainly not in the evening (for some reason I took it into my head that she would come in the evening and exactly at seven o'clock). However, she told me herself that she was not entirely at their beck and call and that she was given special privileges, and that means—h'm! Damn it, she will come! She will most certainly turn up!"

Fortunately, Apollon took my mind off Lisa by his churlish behaviour. I lost my patience with him completely! He was the bane of my life, the punishment Providence had imposed upon me. For years on end we had been continually squabbling, and I hated him. Lord, how I hated him! I don't think I ever hated anyone as much as him, particularly at certain times. He was an elderly, pompous man, who did some tailoring in his spare time. For some unknown reason he despised me beyond measure, and looked down upon me in a way that was simply maddening. He looked down upon everyone, as a matter of fact. Take one look at that fair, smoothly brushed head, at the tuft of hair which he fluffed out over his forehead and smeared with lenten oil, at that gravely pursed mouth, always compressed into the shape of the letter V—and you felt that you were in the presence of a creature who was never in doubt. He was pedantic to a degree, the greatest pedant, in fact, I ever met in my life, and, in addition, possessed of a vanity that was worthy only of Alexander the Great. He was in love with every button on his coat, with every hair on his head. Yes, in love, most decidedly in love with them! And he looked it. His attitude towards me was utterly despotic. He hardly ever spoke to me, and if occasionally he did deign to look at me, his look was so hard, so majestically self-confident, and invariably so contemptuous, that it alone was sometimes sufficient to drive me into a fury. He carried out his duties with an air of conferring the greatest favour upon me. As a matter of fact, he hardly ever did anything for me, and he did not even consider himself bound to do anything for me. There could be no doubt whatever that he looked upon me as the greatest fool on earth, and if he graciously permitted me "to live with him," it was only because he could get his wages from me every month. He did not mind "doing nothing" for me for seven roubles a month. I'm certain many of my sins will be forgiven me for what I suffered from him. At times I hated him so bitterly that I was almost thrown into a fit when I heard him walking about. But what I loathed most of all was his lisp. His tongue must have been a little too long, or something of the sort, and because of that he always lisped and minced his words, and, I believe, he was terribly proud of it, imagining that it added to his dignity. He spoke in a slow, measured voice, with his hands behind his back and his eyes fixed on the ground. He infuriated me particularly when he began reading the psalter in his room behind the partition. I have fought many battles over that reading. But he was terribly fond of reading aloud of an evening, in a slow, even, sing-song voice, as though he were chanting psalms for the dead. It is interesting that he is doing just that at present: he hires himself out to read psalms over the dead and exterminates rats and manufactures a boot polish as well. But at that time I could not get rid of him, as though he formed one chemical substance with me. Besides, he would never have consented to leave me for anything in the world. I could not afford to live in furnished rooms. I lived in an unfurnished self-contained flat—it was my shell, the case into which I hid from humanity, and for some confounded reason Apollon seemed to be an integral part of my flat, and for seven years I could not get rid of him.

To be behind with his wages even for two or three days, for instance, was quite out of the question. He'd have made such a fuss that I shouldn't have known how to keep out of his way. But at that time I was feeling so exasperated with everyone that for a reason I did not myself clearly understand I made up my mind to *punish* Apollon by withholding his wages for a whole fortnight. I had been intending to do it for a long time, for the last two years, just to show him that he had no business to treat me with such insolence and that if I liked I could always refuse to pay him his wages. I decided to say nothing to him about it and to ignore the whole thing deliberately so as to crush his pride and force him to speak about his wages first. Then I would take the seven roubles out of the drawer, show him that I had the money, that I had purposely put it aside, and say that "I won't, I won't, I simply won't give you your wages! I won't just because *I don't want to*," because I was the master in this house, because he had been disrespectful, because he had been rude; but if he were to ask me nicely, I might relent and give it to him; otherwise he would have to wait a fortnight, or three weeks, or maybe a month even. . . .

But furious though I was with him, he got the better of me in the end. I could not hold out for four days even. He started, as he always did start in such circumstances, for they had already happened before, I had already tried it on before (and, let me add, I knew all this beforehand, I knew all his contemptible tactics by heart)—he started by fixing me with a stern glare which he kept up for several minutes at a time, particularly when he used to meet me or when I went out of the house. If I did not shrink back and pretended not to notice his glances, he would set about—still in silence—to inflict more tortures upon me. He would suddenly and without any excuse whatever enter my room quietly and smoothly when I was either reading or pacing my room, and remain standing at the door, with one hand behind his back and one foot thrust forward, and stare fixedly at me. This time his stare was not only stern, but witheringly contemptuous. If I suddenly asked him what he wanted, he would not reply, but continue to stare straight at me for a few more seconds, then he would purse his lips with a specially significant expression, turn round slowly, and slowly go back to his room. About two hours later he would leave his room again, and again appear before me in the same manner. Sometimes, beside myself with rage, I did not even ask him what he wanted, but just raised my head sharply and imperiously and began staring back at him. We would thus stare at each other for about two minutes till at last he would turn round, slowly and pompously, and again go back for two hours.

If that did not make me come to my senses and I continued to be rebellious, he would suddenly break into sighs as he stared at me, as though measuring with each sigh the whole depth of my moral turpitude and, of course, it all ended in his complete victory over me: I raved, I shouted, but I still had to do what was expected of me.

No sooner did his manœuvre of stern looks begin this time than I lost my temper at once and flew at him in a blind rage.

"Stop!" I shouted, beside myself, as he was turning round slowly and silently, with one hand behind his back, to go back to his room. "Stop! Come back, I tell you! Come back!"

I must have roared at him in so unnatural a voice that he turned round again and began looking at me with surprise. He still said nothing, and that maddened me.

"How dare you come into my room without knocking and stare at me like that? Come on, answer me!"

But after looking calmly at me for half a minute, he started turning round again.

"Stop!" I roared, rushing up to him. "Don't you dare to move! Ah, that's better! Now answer me: what did you come in to look at me for?"

"If there is anything, sir, you want me to do for you now, it is my duty to carry it out," he replied, once more pausing a little before speaking, with his slow and measured lisp, raising his eyebrows and calmly inclining his head first to one side and then to another, and all this with the most exasperating self-composure.

"That's not what I asked you about, you tormentor!" I screamed, trembling with rage. "I'll tell you myself, you tormentor, why you come here. You see I'm not giving you your wages, and being too proud to come and ask for them yourself, you come here to stare at me stupidly in order to punish me, in order to torment me, without suspect-ing, tormentor that you are, how damned silly, silly, silly, silly it all is!"

He was about to turn round again silently, but I caught hold of him.

"Look," I shouted to him, "here's the money! Do you see? Here it is! (I took it out of the table drawer.) All the seven roubles. But you won't get them, you—will—not—get—them, until you come to me respectfully, acknowledge your fault, and say you are sorry! Do you hear?"

"That will never be!" he answered with a sort of unnatural self-confidence.

"It shall be!" I screamed. "I give you my word of honour—it shall be!"

"There's nothing I have to apologise for," he went on, as though not noticing my screams, "because you, sir, called me 'tormentor,' for which I can lodge a complaint against you at the police station."

"Go and lodge your complaint!" I roared. "Go at once, this very minute, this very second! You are a tormentor! A tormentor! A tormentor!"

But he only gave me a look, then turned round and, without paying any attention to my screams to stop, went out to his room with a measured step and without turning round.

"But for Lisa this would never have happened!" I said to myself. Then, after standing still for a minute, I went myself to his room behind the partition, gravely and solemnly, and without hurrying, though my heart was thumping slowly and violently. "Apollon," I said quietly and with great emphasis, though rather breathlessly, "go at once and fetch the police inspector. At once!"

He had in the meantime seated himself at his table, put on his spectacles, and settled down to his sewing. But, hearing my order, he burst into a loud guffaw.

"Go at once! This minute! Go, I say, or I shan't be responsible for what happens!"

"You must be off your head, sir," he remarked, without even raising his head, with his usual, slow lisp, calmly threading the needle. "Whoever heard of a man going to report to the police against himself! But, of course, sir, if you want to frighten me, then you might as well save yourself the trouble, for nothing will come of it."

"Go!" I screamed, grasping him by the shoulder. I felt that I was going to strike him any minute.

But I did not hear the door from the passage open quietly and slowly at that instant and someone come in, stand still, and start gazing at us in bewilderment. I looked up, nearly fainted with shame, and rushed back to my room. There, clutching at my hair with both hands and leaning my head against the wall, I remained motionless in that position.

About two minutes later I heard Apollon's slow footsteps.

"There's a certain young lady to see you, sir," he said, looking rather severely at me.

He then stood aside to let Lisa in. He did not seem to want to go, and stood staring at us sarcastically.

"Go! Go!" I ordered him, completely thrown off my balance.

At that moment my clock made a tremendous effort, and, wheezing, struck seven.

IX

And my house, fearlessly and freely,
As mistress you can enter now!

By the same poet.

I stood before her, feeling utterly crushed, disgraced, and shockingly embarrassed, and, I think, I smiled, trying desperately to wrap myself in the skirts of my tattered, wadded old dressing gown, exactly as a short while ago in one of the moments of complete depression I had imagined I would do. After watching us for a few minutes, Apollon went away, but that did not make me feel any better. Worst of all, she too was suddenly overcome with confusion, which I had hardly expected.

"Sit down," I said mechanically, placing a chair for her near the table.

I myself sat down on the sofa. She sat down at once, obediently, looking at me with wide-open eyes and evidently expecting something from me at any moment. It was this naïve expectancy of hers that incensed me, but I controlled myself.

If she had had any sense, she would have pretended not to have noticed anything, as though everything had been as usual, but instead she . . .

And I felt vaguely that I would make her pay dearly for *all this.*

"I'm afraid you've found me in a rather strange situation, Lisa," I began, stammering, and realising perfectly well that I shouldn't have opened the conversation like that. "No, no, don't think there's anything wrong," I exclaimed, seeing that she had suddenly blushed. "I'm not ashamed of my poverty. On the contrary, I look on it with pride. I'm a poor but honourable man. One can be poor and honourable, you know," I stammered. "However, will you have some tea?"

"No, thank you," she began.

"Wait a minute!"

I jumped up and ran out to Apollon. I had to get out of her sight somehow.

"Apollon," I whispered feverishly, talking very fast and flinging down on the table before him the seven roubles I had been keeping in my clenched hand all the time, "here are your wages. You see, I give them to you. But for that you must save me: go at once and fetch a pot of tea and a dozen rusks from the tea-shop. If you won't go, you'll make me the unhappiest man in the world! You don't know what a fine woman she is! She's wonderful! You may be thinking there's something—er—but you don't know what a fine woman she is!"

Apollon, who had sat down to his work and put on his spectacles again, at first looked silently at the money without putting down the needle; then, without paying any attention to me or replying to me, he went on busying himself with the needle, which he was still threading. I waited for three minutes, standing in front of him with my hands crossed *à la Napoléon.* My temples were wet with perspiration; I was very pale—I could feel it. But, thank God, he must have felt sorry as he looked at me, for having finished threading his needle, he slowly rose from his place, slowly pushed back his chair, slowly took off his glasses, slowly counted the money, and at last, asking me over his shoulder whether he should get a pot of tea for two, slowly left the room. As I was going back to Lisa, the thought occurred to me whether it would not be a good idea to run away just as I was in my dressing gown, run away no matter where, and let things take their course.

I sat down again. She regarded me uneasily. For a few minutes neither of us spoke.

"I'll murder him!" I suddenly screamed, banging my fist on the table with such violence that the ink spurted out of the ink-well.

"Good heavens, what are you saying?" she cried, startled.

"I'll murder him! I'll murder him!" I screamed, banging the table, beside myself with rage, but realising very well at the same time how stupid it was to be in such a rage.

"You can't imagine, Lisa, what a tormentor he is to me. He's my tormentor. He's gone out for some rusks now—he—"

And suddenly I burst into tears. It was a nervous attack. In between my sobs I felt awfully ashamed, but I could do nothing to stop them.

She was frightened. "What's the matter? What's the matter?" she kept asking, standing helplessly over me.

"Water . . . Give me some water, please. It's over there!" I murmured in a weak voice, realising very well at the same time that I could have managed without a drink of water and without murmuring in a weak voice. But I was, what is called, *play-acting* to save appearances, though my fit was real enough.

She gave me water, looking at me in utter confusion. At that moment Apollon brought in the tea. I felt that this ordinary, prosaic tea was very inappropriate and paltry after all that had happened, and I blushed. Lisa looked at Apollon almost in terror. He went out without a glance at us.

"Do you despise me, Lisa?" I said, looking straight at her and trembling with impatience to know what she was thinking of.

She was overcome with confusion and did not know what to say.

"Drink your tea," I said, angrily.

I was angry with myself, but of course it was she who would suffer for it. A terrible resentment against her suddenly blazed up in my heart. I believe I could have killed her. To revenge myself on her, I took a silent vow not to say a single word to her while she was in my room. "She's to blame for everything," I thought.

Our silence went on for almost five minutes. The tea stood on the table, but she did not touch it. I had got so far that I deliberately did not want to start drinking it in order to make her feel even more embarrassed. And she could not very well start drinking it alone. She glanced at me a few times in mournful perplexity. I kept obstinately silent. I was, of course, the chief sufferer, for I fully realised the whole despicable meanness of my spiteful stupidity, and yet I could do nothing to restrain myself.

"I—I want to get away from that—place for good," she began in an effort to do something to break the silence, but, poor thing, that was just what she should not have spoken about at the moment, for it was a stupid thing to say and especially to a man who was as stupid as I. Even I felt a pang of pity in my heart for her clumsiness and unnecessary frankness. But something hideous inside me at once stifled my feeling of pity. It provoked me even more—to hell with it all! Another five minutes passed.

"I haven't come at the wrong time, have I?" she began shyly in a hardly audible whisper, and made to get up.

But the moment I saw the first signs of injured dignity, I shook with spite and burst out at once.

"What have you come here for? Answer me! Answer!" I began, gasping for breath and paying no attention to the logical order of my words. I wanted to blurt it all out at once, and I didn't care a damn what I started with, "I'll tell you, my dear girl, what you have come for. You've come because I made *pathetic speeches* to you the other night. So you were softened and now you want more of these pathetic speeches. Well, I may as well tell you at once that I was laughing at you then. And I'm laughing at you now. What are you shuddering for? Yes, I was laughing at you! I had been insulted before, at dinner, by the fellows who came before me that night. I came to your place intending to thrash one of them, an army officer, but I was too late. He had already gone. So to avenge my wounded pride on someone, to get my own back, I vented my spite on you and I laughed at you. I had been humiliated, so I too wanted to humiliate someone; they wiped the floor with me, so I too wanted to show my power. That's what happened, and you thought I'd come there specially to save you, did you? You thought so, didn't you? You did, didn't you?"

I knew that she would probably be confused and unable to make head or tail of it, but I knew, too, that she would grasp the gist of it perfectly. And so it was. She turned white as a sheet, tried to say something, her lips painfully twisted. But before she could say anything, she collapsed in a chair as though she had been felled by an axe. And afterwards she listened to me all the time with parted lips and wide-open eyes, trembling with terror. The cynicism, the cynicism of my words crushed her. . . .

"To save you!" I went on, jumping up from my chair and running up and down the room in front of her. "Save you from what? Why,

I'm probably much worse than you. Why didn't you throw it in my teeth when I was reading that lecture to you? 'But why did you come to us yourself? To read me a lecture on morality?' I wanted power. Power was what I wanted then. I wanted sport. I wanted to see you cry. I wanted to humiliate you. To make you hysterical. That's what I wanted. I couldn't keep it up because I'm nothing but a rag myself. I got frightened, and I'm damned if I know why I told you where I lived. I was a bloody fool. That's why, I suppose. So even before I got home that night I was cursing and swearing at you for having given you my address. I hated you already because of the lies I had been telling you. For all I wanted was to make a few fine speeches, to have something to dream about. And do you know what I really wanted? What I wanted was that you should all go to hell! That's what I wanted. The thing I must have at any cost is peace of mind. To get that peace of mind, to make sure that no one worried me, I'd sell the whole world for a farthing. Is the world to go to rack and ruin or am I to have my cup of tea? Well, so far as I'm concerned, blow the world so long as I can have my cup of tea. Did you know that, or didn't you? Well, anyway, I know I'm a blackguard, a cad, an egoist, a loafer. Here I've been shivering in a fever for the last three days for fear that you might come. And do you know what I was so worried about in particular during those three days? I'll tell you. What I was so worried about was that I was making myself out to be such a hero before you and that you'd find me here in this torn old dressing gown of mine, poor and loathsome. Only a few minutes ago I told you that I was not ashamed of my poverty. Well, it's not true. I am ashamed of my poverty. I'm ashamed of it more than of anything. I'm afraid of it more than of anything, more than of being a thief, because I'm so confoundedly vain that at times I feel as though I had been skinned and every puff of air hurt me. Don't you realise now that I shall never forgive you for having found me in this tattered old dressing gown and just when, like a spiteful cur, I flew at Apollon's throat? Your saviour, your former hero, flings himself like some mangy, shaggy mongrel on his valet, and his valet is laughing at him! And I shall never forgive you for the tears which I was shedding before you a minute ago, like some silly old woman who had been put to shame. Nor shall I ever forgive *you* for what I'm now confessing to you! Yes, you alone must answer for it all because you just happened to come at that moment, because I'm a rotter, because I'm the most horrible, the most ridiculous, the most petty, the most stupid, the most envious of all the worms on earth who are not a bit better than me, but who—I'm damned if I know why—are never ashamed or embarrassed, while I shall be insulted all my life by every louse because that's the sort of fellow I am! And what the hell do I care if you don't understand what I'm talking about? And what the hell do I care what happens to you? Whether you're going to rack and ruin there or not? And do you realise that now that I've told you all this I shall hate you for having been here and listened to me? Why, it's only once in a lifetime that a man speaks his mind like this, and that, too, when he is in hysterics. What more do you want? Why after all this do you still stand here before me torturing me? Why don't you get out of here?"

But here a very odd thing happened.

I was so used to imagining everything and to thinking of everything as it happened in books, and to picturing to myself everything in the world as I had previously made it up in my dreams, that at first I could not all at once grasp the meaning of this occurrence. What occurred was this: Lisa, humiliated and crushed by me, understood much more than I imagined. She understood from all this what a woman who loves sincerely always understands first of all, namely, that I was unhappy.

The frightened and resentful look on her face first gave place to one of sorrowful astonishment. But when I began to call myself a cad and a blackguard and my tears began to flow (I had spoken the whole of that tirade with tears), her whole face began to work convulsively. She was about to get up and stop me, and when I finished, it was not my cries of why she was here and why she did not go away to which she paid attention; what she felt was that I must have found it very hard indeed to say all this. And besides, she was so crushed, poor girl. She considered herself so inferior to me. Why should she feel angry or offended? She suddenly jumped up from her chair with a kind of irresistible impulse and, all drawn towards me but still feeling very shy and not daring to move from her place, held out her hands to me. . . . It was here that my heart failed me. Then she rushed to me, flung her arms round my neck, and burst into tears. I could not restrain myself, either, and burst out sobbing as I had never in my life sobbed before. . . .

"They—they won't let me—I—I can't be good!" I could hardly bring myself to say, then I stumbled to the sofa, fell on it face downwards, and for a quarter of an hour sobbed hysterically. She clung to me, put her arms round me, and seemed to remain frozen in that embrace.

But the trouble was that my hysterical fit could not go on for ever. And so (it is the loathsome truth I am writing), lying prone on the sofa, clinging tightly to it, and my face buried in my cheap leather cushion, I began gradually, remotely, involuntarily but irresistibly to feel that I should look an awful ass if I raised my head now and looked Lisa straight in the face. What was I ashamed of? I don't know. All I know is that I was ashamed. It also occurred to me just then, overwrought as I was, that our parts were now completely changed, that she was the heroine now, while I was exactly the same crushed and humiliated creature as she had appeared to me that night—four days before. . . . And all this flashed through my mind while I was still lying prone on the sofa!

Good God, was I really envious of her then?

I don't know. To this day I cannot possibly say whether I was envious of her or not, and at the time of course I was less able to understand it than now. I cannot live without feeling that I have someone completely in my power, that I am free to tyrannise over some human being. But—you can't explain anything by reasoning and consequently it is useless to reason.

I soon pulled myself together, however, and raised my head; I had to do it sooner or later. . . . And, well, to this day I can't help thinking that it was because I was ashamed to look at her that another feeling was suddenly kindled and blazed up in my heart—a feeling of domination and possession! My eyes flashed with passion and I clasped her hands violently. How I hated her and how I was drawn to her at that moment! One feeling intensified the other. This was almost like vengeance! . . . At first she looked bewildered and even frightened, but only for one moment. She embraced me warmly and rapturously.

X

A quarter of an hour later I was rushing up and down the room in furious impatience. Every minute I walked up to the screen and looked through the narrow slit at Lisa. She was sitting on the floor, her head leaning against the edge of the bed, and, I suppose, was crying. But she did not go away, and that irritated me. This time she knew everything. I had insulted her finally, but—there is no need to speak about it. She guessed that my outburst of passion was nothing but revenge, a fresh insult for her, and that to my earlier, almost aimless, hatred, there was now added a *personal, jealous* hatred of her. . . . However, I can't be certain that she did understand it all so clearly; what she certainly did understand was that I was a loathsome man and that, above all, I was incapable of loving her.

I know I shall be told that it is incredible—that it is incredible that anyone could be as spiteful and as stupid as I was; and I daresay it will be added that it was improbable that I should not love her or, at any rate, appreciate her love. But why is it improbable? First of all, I could not possibly have loved anyone because, I repeat, to me love meant to tyrannise and to be morally superior. I have never in my life been able to imagine any other sort of love, and I have reached the point that sometimes I cannot help thinking even now that love only consists in the right to tyrannise over the woman you love, who grants you this right of her own free will. Even in my most secret dreams I could not imagine love except as a struggle, and I always embarked on it with hatred and ended it with moral subjugation, and afterwards I did not have the faintest idea what to do with the woman I had subjugated. And indeed what is there improbable about it when I had at last reached such a state of moral depravity, when I had lost touch so much with "real life," that only a few hours before I had thought of reproaching her for having come to me to listen to "pathetic speeches," and did not even guess that she had not come to listen to my pathetic speeches at all, but to love me, for it is only in love that a woman can find her true resurrection, her true salvation from any sort of calamity, and her moral regeneration, and she cannot possibly find it in anything else. Still, I did not hate her so much after all when I was pacing the room and looked at her through the chink in the screen. I merely felt unbearably distressed at her being there. I wanted her to disappear. I longed for "peace." I wanted to be left alone in my funk-hole. "Real life"—so unaccustomed was I to it—had crushed me so much that I found it difficult to breathe.

But a few minutes passed and still she did not get up, as though she were unconscious. I had the meanness to knock quietly at the screen to remind her. . . . She gave a start, got up quickly, and began looking for her kerchief, her hat, her fur coat, as though her only thought were how to run away from me as quickly as possible. . . .

Two minutes later she came out slowly from behind the screen and looked hard at me. I grinned maliciously, though I must confess I had to force myself to do it, *for the sake of appearances,* and turned away from her gaze.

"Goodbye," she said, going to the door.

I ran up to her suddenly, seized her hand, opened it, put something in it and—closed it again. Then I turned at once and rushed away quickly to the other corner of the room so as not to see her at least.

I almost told a lie this very minute. I was about to write that I did not do it deliberately, that I did it because I did not realise what I was doing, having in my folly completely lost my head. But I don't want to lie, and therefore I say frankly that I opened her hand and put something in it—out of spite. The thought came into my head when I was running up and down the room and she was sitting behind the screen. But this I can say in all truth: I did that cruel thing deliberately, I did it not because my heart, but because my wicked brain prompted me to do it. This cruelty was so insincere, so much thought out, so deliberately invented, so *bookish,* that I couldn't stand it myself even for a minute, but first rushed away to a corner so as not to see anything, and then, overwhelmed with shame and despair, rushed after Lisa. I opened the front door and began listening.

"Lisa! Lisa!" I cried down the stairs, but in a halting voice, in an undertone.

There was no answer, but I thought I heard her footsteps lower down on the stairs.

"Lisa!" I called in a louder voice.

No answer. But at that moment I heard the heavy glass street-door open with a creak and with difficulty and slam heavily. The noise reverberated on the stairs.

She was gone. I returned musing to my room, feeling terribly ill at ease.

I stopped at the table beside the chair on which she had sat and looked disconsolately before me. A minute passed. Suddenly I gave a start: straight before me on the table I saw a crumpled blue five-rouble note, the same which a minute before I had pressed into her hand. It *was* the same note. It could be no other, for there was no other in the house. She therefore had just enough time to fling it on the table at the moment when I rushed to the other end of the room.

Well, of course, I might have expected it of her. Might have expected it? No, I was too great an egoist, I had too little respect for people to have been able even to imagine that she would do it. That was too much. That I could not bear. A moment later I began to dress madly, putting on hurriedly whatever clothes I could lay my hands on, and rushed headlong after her. She had hardly had time to walk more than a hundred yards when I ran out into the street.

The street was quiet and deserted. It was snowing heavily, the snowflakes falling almost perpendicularly and piling up in deep drifts on the pavement and on the empty road. There was not a soul to be seen, not a sound to be heard. The street-lamps twinkled desolately and uselessly. I ran about a hundred yards to the cross-roads and stopped.

Where had she gone? And why was I running after her?

Why? To fall on my knees before her, to sob with remorse, to kiss her feet, to beseech her to forgive me! I wanted to do so, my breast was being torn to pieces, and never, never shall I be able to recall that moment with indifference. But—why? I could not help thinking. Would I not hate her fiercely tomorrow perhaps just because I had been kissing her feet today? Could I make her happy? Had I not learnt today for the hundredth time what I was really worth? Should I not torture her to death?

I stood in the snow, peering into the dim haze, and thought of that.

"And will it not be better, will it not be much better," I thought afterwards at home, giving full rein to my imagination and suppressing the living pain in my heart, "will it not be much better that she should now carry that insult away with her for ever? What is an insult but a sort of purification? It is the most corrosive and painful form of consciousness! Tomorrow I should have bespattered her soul with mud, I should have wearied her heart by thrusting myself upon her, while now the memory of the insult will never die in her, and however horrible the filth that lies in store for her, the memory of that humiliation will raise her and purify her—by hatred, and, well, perhaps also by forgiveness. Still, will that make things easier for her?"

And, really, here am I already putting the idle question to myself—which is better: cheap happiness or exalted suffering? Well, which is better?

So I went on dreaming as I sat at home that evening, almost dead with the pain in my heart. Never before had I endured such suffering and remorse. But didn't I know perfectly well when I ran out of my flat that I should turn back half-way? I never met Lisa again, and have heard nothing of her. I may as well add that I remained for a long time pleased with the *phrase* about the usefulness of insults and hatred in spite of the fact that I almost fell ill at the time from blank despair.

Even now, after all these years, I somehow feel *unhappy* to recall all this. Lots of things make me unhappy now when I recall them, but—why not finish my "memoirs" at this point? I can't help thinking that I made a mistake in starting to write them. At any rate, I have felt ashamed all the time I have been writing this *story*: so it seems this is no longer literature, but a corrective punishment. For to tell long stories and how I have, for instance, spoilt my life by a moral disintegration in my funk-hole, by my unsociable habits, by losing touch with life, and by nursing my spite in my dark cellar—all this, I'm afraid, is not interesting. A novel must have a hero, and here I seemed to have *deliberately* gathered together all the characteristics of an anti-hero, and, above all, all this is certain to produce a most unpleasant impression because we have all lost touch with life, we are all cripples, every one of us—more or less. We have lost touch so much that occasionally we cannot help feeling a sort of disgust with "real life," and that is why we are so angry when people remind us of it. Why, we have gone so far that we look upon "real life" almost as a sort of burden, and we are all agreed that "life" as we find it in books is much better. And why do we make such a fuss sometimes? Why do we make fools of ourselves? What do we want? We don't know ourselves. For as a matter of fact we should fare much worse if our nonsensical prayers were granted. Why, just try, just give us, for instance, more independence, untie the hands of any one of us, widen the sphere of our activities, relax discipline, and we—yes, I assure you—we should immediately be begging for the discipline to be reimposed upon us. I know that very likely you will be angry with me for saying this, that you will start shouting and stamping, "Speak for yourself and for your miserable life in that dark cellar of yours and don't you dare to say 'all of us.' " But, good Lord, gentlemen, I'm not trying to justify myself by this *all-of-usness*. For my part, I have merely carried to extremes in my life what you have not dared to carry even half-way, and, in addition, you have mistaken your cowardice for common sense and have found comfort in that, deceiving yourselves. So that, as a matter of fact, I seem to be much more alive than you. Come, look into it more closely! Why, we do not even know where we are to find real life, or what it is, or what it is called. Leave us alone without any books, and we shall at once get confused, lose ourselves in a maze, we shall not know what to cling to, what to hold on to, what to love and what to hate, what to respect and what to despise. We even find it hard to be men, men of *real* flesh and blood, *our own* flesh and blood. We are ashamed of it. We think it a disgrace. And we do our best to be some theoretical "average" men. We are still-born, and for a long time we have been begotten not by living fathers, and that's just what we seem to like more and more. We are getting a taste for it. Soon we shall invent some way of being somehow or other begotten by an idea. But enough—I don't want to write any more "from a Dark Cellar. . . ."

(This is not, by the way, the end of the "Memoirs" of this paradoxical fellow. He could not resist and went on and on. But it seems to us, too, that we may stop here.)

A Gentle Creature

A FANTASTIC STORY

SHORT PREFACE BY THE AUTHOR

I hope my readers will forgive me if, instead of my "Diary" in its usual form, I am giving them only a story this time. I am afraid my only excuse is that I have been really working on this story for the better part of a month. I should, in any event, like to ask my readers for their indulgence.

Now a few words about the story itself. I have given it the subtitle of "A Fantastic Story," though I myself regard it as eminently realistic. But there is indeed a subcurrent of fantasy in it, particularly in the very form of the story, which I think it necessary to explain before starting on the story proper.

The point is that it is neither fiction nor biography. Imagine a husband whose wife had committed suicide a few hours before by throwing herself out of a window and whose dead body is lying on the table. His mind is in a state of confusion, and he has not as yet had time to collect his thoughts. He keeps pacing the room, trying to find some reason for what has happened, "to gather his thoughts to a point." He is, besides, an inveterate hypochondriac, one of those men who talk to themselves. So there he is, talking to himself, telling the whole story, trying to *explain* it to himself. Notwithstanding the apparent consistency of his speech, he contradicts himself several times, both in the logic of his arguments and his feelings. He is justifying himself, accusing her, indulging in explanations that have no possible bearing on the case: you have here a certain crudity of mind and heart as well as genuine deep feeling. Little by little he really does *explain* the whole thing to himself and "gathers his thoughts to a point." A succession of memories which he recalls does at last lead him inevitably to *the truth*, and truth inevitably elevates his mind and heart. Towards the end even the tone of the story changes as compared with the general untidiness of its beginning. Truth dawns upon the unhappy man in a form that is both clear and definite, at least so far as he himself is concerned.

That is the theme. No doubt, the telling of the story, interrupted by all sorts of digressions and interludes, takes up a few hours, and it is told in a rather rambling way: sometimes he is speaking to himself, sometimes he is addressing an invisible listener, a sort of a judge. And, as a matter of fact, this is how it actually happens in real life. If a stenographer could have overheard him and taken down his words in shorthand, the result might have been a little rougher, a little less finished than the way I am telling it; but the psychological sequence (so at least it seems to me) would have remained pretty much the same. It is this suggestion of a stenographer taking everything down in shorthand (after which I should have edited it) that I consider the fantastic element in this story. But this sort of thing, or something very like it, has been done several times in works of fiction. Victor Hugo, for instance, uses almost the identical method in his masterpiece *The Last Day of a Man Condemned to Death*. And though he does not actually pretend to employ a stenographer, he has recourse to an even greater improbability by assuming that a man sentenced to death is able (and has the time) to keep a diary not only on his last day, but also during his last hour and, literally, his last minute. But had he not adopted this fanciful way of telling the story, his novel—one of the most realistic and most truthful he ever wrote—would not have existed.

CHAPTER ONE

I
WHO WAS I AND WHO WAS SHE

. . . Well, while she is still here everything is all right: I go up and have a look at her every minute. But they will take her away tomorrow and—how can I stay here alone? She is now in the sitting-room, on a table. Two card tables put together side by side. They will bring the coffin tomorrow. A white coffin. White gros-de-Naples. However that's not what. . . . I keep on walking and walking. Trying to explain the whole thing to myself. It's six hours now that I've been trying to explain it to myself, but I just can't gather my thoughts to a point. Can't do it. Can't do it. The trouble is I'm always walking, walking, walking. . . . Now, that's how it was. I'll simply tell it just as it happened. In the right order. (Order!) Ladies and gentlemen, I do not pretend to be a literary chap, as I expect you can see for yourselves, but never mind. I'll tell it just as I understand it. That's the horrible part of it—I understand everything!

You see, if you must know, I mean, if I'm to tell you everything from the very beginning, I first met her because she used to come to me to pawn things. She wanted the money to pay for an advertisement in *The Voice.* Trying to get herself a job as governess. No objection to living in the country, or giving lessons to children at their homes, and so on and so forth. That's how it began. At the time I didn't of course think her any different from anyone else. She used to come to me like the rest, and so on. But later I began to notice the difference. She was such a slender girl, very thin, fair, of medium height, always a little awkward with me, as though embarrassed. (I cannot help thinking that she must have been the same with all strangers, and to her of course I was not different from anyone else, considered as a man, I mean, and not as a pawnbroker.) The minute she got her money, she'd turn round and go away. And all without uttering a word. Others usually started arguing, begging, haggling, to get more money. But not this one. Took what she was given. . . . I'm afraid I'm getting a little muddled. . . . Yes, it was the things she brought which first of all attracted my attention. Silver gilt ear-rings, a cheap medallion—there wasn't anything I'd give more than sixpence for. She knew herself, of course, that they were only worth threepence, but I could see that to her they were priceless. As a matter of fact, it was all that was left her by her mother and father. I got to know about it later. Only once did I permit myself to smile at her things. For, you see, I never permit myself anything of the kind. In my dealings with the public my manners are always those of a gentleman: a few words, polite and stern. "Stern, stern, stern." But one day she actually brought me the remnants (I mean, literally) of an old hareskin coat, and I couldn't refrain from making a rather mild joke about it. Dear me, how she flushed! Her eyes were large, blue, wistful, but—how they blazed! She never said a word, though. Took her "remnants" and went out. It was then that for the first time I noticed her *specially,* and I thought something of the sort about her, that is, something of a special sort. Yes. There's something else I re-member. Another impression. I mean, if you really want to know, it was really the most important impression which summed up every-thing, namely, that she was awfully young. So young that I could have sworn she wasn't a day older than fourteen. Actually, however, she was fifteen years and nine months, to be exact. However, that wasn't what I wanted to say. That wasn't the total impression. The next day she came again. I found out later that she had been to Do-bronravov and Mozer with that precious fur coat of hers, but they don't accept anything but gold, so they wouldn't even talk to her. I, on the other hand, had once accepted a cameo from her (a really cheap one it was, too), and, having thought it over, was afterwards surprised at myself. For, you see, I don't accept anything but gold and silver, either, and yet I took the cameo from her. That was the second time I had thought about her. I remember it very well.

This time, that is, from Mozer, she brought me an amber cigar holder. Not a bad thing, something for a connoisseur, but again hardly worth anything to me, for we only deal in gold articles. As she came to me the day after her *rebellion,* I received her sternly. Sternness with me means dryness. However, as I was handing her the two roubles, I couldn't resist saying to her with a certain note of exasperation in my voice, "I'm only doing it *for you,* for Mozer would never have accepted such a thing from you." I put a special emphasis on the words *for you.* Invested them quite deliberately with *a certain meaning.* I was furious. She flushed crimson again at the *for you,* but swallowed the insult, didn't fling the money back at me. Took it like a lamb. That's what poverty does for you! But, Lord, how she blushed! I realised that I had hurt her feelings. But when she went out, I suddenly asked myself, Is this triumph over her really worth two roubles? Dear, oh dear! I remember I asked myself that very question twice: "Is it worth it? Is it worth it?" And, laughing, decided that it was. Felt very jolly that time. But it wasn't a bad feeling: I did it deliberately, intentionally. I wanted to put her to the test. I wanted to do that because suddenly certain plans with regard to her began stirring in my mind. That was my *third* special thought about her.

. . . Well, it was from that time that it all started. I, naturally, took immediate steps to find out what could be found out about her in an indirect way, and I waited for her next visit with particular impatience. For I had a premonition that she would come soon. When she did come, I entered into a very amiable conversation with her, doing my utmost to be as civil to her as possible. I have had quite a good education, you see, and my manners are irreproachable. Well, it was then that I realised that she was good and gentle. Good and gentle creatures do not offer a very stiff resistance, not for long, anyway, and though they may not open their hearts to you altogether, they don't know how to steer clear of a conversation: they reply in monosyllables but they do reply, and the further they get drawn into it, the more talkative they become, so long, that is, as you don't get tired of it yourself, so long as you want to make the most of your opportunity. I need hardly tell you that she did not explain anything to me at the time. It was afterwards that I found out about *The Voice* and everything else. She was just then advertising wildly, first, of course, in a rather high and mighty fashion, "A governess, ready to take a situation in the country, please reply about conditions of employment by post," but later it was, "Willing to accept anything, to give lessons, to be a companion, to look after the household, to act as a nurse to a sick lady, plain sewing," and so on and so forth. The usual thing. All this of course was put in for publication at different times and in different versions, but in the end when things got really desperate, it was even "without salary, in return for board." But nothing doing. She could not find herself a job! It was then that I made up my mind to put her to the test for the last time. I suddenly picked up the last issue of *The Voice* and showed her an advertisement: "A young lady, orphan, looking for situation as governess to young children, preferably with an elderly widower. Willing to help with household duties."

"You see, this advertisement appeared this morning and I'm ready to bet you anything she'll have her job before the evening. That's the way to advertise."

Again she flushed. Again her eyes blazed. She turned round and went out at once. That pleased me very much. However, at that time I was already sure of everything and had no longer any fear. No one you see, would take her cigar holders. And, besides, she had no more cigar holders to pawn. Well, I was right. Two days later she called again, looking very pale and agitated. I realised that she must have had some trouble at home, and so it was. I'll explain presently what the trouble was. At the moment I just want to mention how I suddenly impressed her and how I rose in her estimation. It was a sort of scheme I suddenly conceived. You see, as a matter of fact she brought this icon (had made up her mind at last to bring it!) . . . Now, listen. Please, listen. It was just then that everything began. I'm afraid I've been a bit muddled till now. . . . You see, I'm trying to recall all this—every detail—every little thing. I'm trying all the time to gather my thoughts to a point, but—but somehow I can't do it, and all these little details count. All these little details are frightfully important. . . .

An icon of the Virgin. The Virgin with the Babe. A family icon, an ancient one, the embossed metal of silver gilt—worth—well, shall we say, six roubles at most. I could see that the icon was precious to her. She was pawning it, you see, without removing the embossed metal.

"Why don't you take off the metal setting and take the icon back with you?" I said. "For, after all, it's an icon, and it's hardly what you might call the done thing to pawn an icon, is it?"

"Why not? Aren't you allowed to take it?"

"Oh yes, I can take it all right, but don't you think you may perhaps yourself. . . ."

"All right, take it off, if you like."

"Well, I'll tell you what," I said, thinking it over. "I shan't take it off, but I'll put it here together with the other icons in the icon case under the lamp (I always had a lamp burning above the icons, ever since the day I first opened my pawnshop), and I'll give you ten roubles for it."

"I don't want ten. Five will be quite enough for me. I'll most certainly redeem it."

"Are you sure you won't take ten? The icon is worth it, you know," I said, noticing that her eyes flashed again.

She made no answer. I went into the other room and came back with five roubles for her.

"Don't despise anyone," I said. "I was once in such straits myself, perhaps even in worse straits, and if you see me now engaged in this sort of business, it's—I mean, after what I've been through—"

"You don't mean you're revenging yourself on society, do you? Is that it?" she interrupted suddenly, with rather a caustic smile, which was quite innocent, though (I mean it was a "general" sort of smile, for at that time she made no distinction whatever between me and anyone else, so that she had said it almost without offence).

"Aha!" thought I. "So that's the sort of person you are! Showing your claws, my pretty one! I shouldn't wonder if you are not a member of one of the new movements!"

"You see," I said at once, half jokingly, half mysteriously, "I—I am part of that Power which still doeth good, though scheming ill. . . ."

She shot a glance at me, a glance that betrayed a great deal of interest, though, I suppose, there was quite a lot of childish curiosity in it, too.

"Wait—what kind of an idea is that? Where is it from? I believe I've heard it somewhere. . . ."

"Don't rack your brains. It's in these words that Mephistopheles introduces himself to Faust. You've read *Faust,* haven't you?"

"No, I mean, not really. . . ."

"You mean you haven't read it at all, don't you? You ought to read it. However, I can see that sardonic smile on your lips again. Please don't imagine I've so little good taste as to wish to disguise my part as pawnbroker by introducing myself to you as a sort of Mephistopheles. Once a pawnbroker, always a pawnbroker. I know."

"You're so strange. . . . I never dreamt of saying anything of the kind to you."

What she really meant to say was, "I never expected you to be an educated man." But she didn't say it, though I knew she thought it. I had pleased her enormously.

"You see," I observed, "one can do good in any profession. I'm not of course referring to myself. I'm quite ready to admit that I do nothing but evil, yet—"

"Of course one can do good in any business," she said, with a quick but keen glance at me. "Yes, in any business," she suddenly added.

Oh, I remember it all! I remember all those moments! And I'd like to add here that when these young people, these dear young people, want to say something clever and profound, they betray it suddenly and rather too openly and naïvely by a look on their faces—"See? I'm saying something clever and profound to you!" And not out of vanity, either, like people of my age. You could see how she herself valued it so enormously, believed in it, esteemed it so highly, and was dead certain that you too esteemed it as highly as she did. Oh, how important sincerity is! It is their sincerity that assures them their victory. And in her this was so delightful!

Yes, I remember it all. I've forgotten nothing. As soon as she was gone, I made up my mind. The same day I went out to make my last inquiries and found out all the latest details about her present circumstances. I knew every detail of her past from Lukerya, who was their maid at the time and who had been in my pay for some time. These details were so terrible that I don't know how she could have laughed as she did the other day, or have been so curious about the words of Mephistopheles when she herself was in such a dreadful position. But—youth! Yes, that is just what I thought about her at the time with pride and joy. For there is magnanimity there too: though I may be standing on the very brink of a precipice, Goethe's grand words still shed a radiance! Youth is always magnanimous, though only a little bit, though wrong-headedly. I mean, it's about her I'm thinking—about her alone. And, above all, even at that time I already regarded her as *mine,* and not for one moment did I doubt my own power. It's one of the most voluptuous thoughts in the world, you know. Not to be in doubt, I mean.

But what's the matter with me? If I go on like this I shall never be able to gather everything to a point. Quick, quick—oh God, that's not it at all.

II
A PROPOSAL OF MARRIAGE

The "details" I found out about her I can explain in a few words. Her father and mother were dead. They had died three years before I met her, and she had been left with her disreputable aunts, though "disreputable" is hardly the right word for them. One aunt was a widow, a mother of a large family—six children, all close to one another in age. Her other aunt was an old maid, as bad as they make 'em. Both were bad. Her father had been a civil servant. A clerk in a Government office, a nonhereditary nobleman. In short, everything was in my favour. I appeared as though from a higher world. After all, I'm a retired first lieutenant of a famous regiment, a nobleman by birth, independent, etc. As for my pawnshop and money-lending business, the aunts could only have looked upon it with respect. She had been slaving for her aunts for three years, but in spite of that she seemed to have found time to pass her school exams somewhere, passed them by hook or by crook, passed them for all her daily drudgery. And that after all meant something, if only as showing her desire to achieve something higher and nobler! Why, what did I want to get married for? However, to blazes with me! I'll discuss that later. Besides, that isn't the point really. . . . Anyway, she taught her aunt's children, made their underclothing for them, and in the end not only made their underclothing for them, but scrubbed the floors as well, and that with her weak chest, too. Why, not to put too fine a point on it, they even beat her, begrudged her every bite of bread she ate. And they ended up by intending to sell her. Damn 'em! I'll leave out the sordid details. She told me all about it afterwards. A whole year the fat shopkeeper next door had been watching it all. Not an ordinary shopkeeper, either. Owned two grocery shops. He had already driven two wives into their graves, and as he was now looking for a third one, he cast his eyes on her. "A quiet one," he thought, "brought up in poverty, and I am marrying her for the sake of my motherless children." And he had children all right. So he opened up negotiations with her aunts. Asked for the girl's hand in marriage. He was fifty. Of course, she was horrified. It was then she began coming to me to get money to pay for the advertisements in *The Voice.* At last she began imploring her aunts to give her a little time to think it over. Just a little time. They gave her a little time, only a very little time, not a minute more. Made her life a hell on earth. "We don't know how to fill our own bellies without an extra mouth to feed!" I knew all about it, and after her visit in the morning that day made up my mind finally. That evening the shopkeeper came to see them. Brought her a pound of sweets from his shop worth a shilling. While she was entertaining him, I called Lukerya out of the kitchen and told her to go and whisper to her that I was waiting for her at the gate and wanted to see her on a very urgent matter. I felt very pleased with myself. As a matter of fact, I was tremendously pleased with myself all that day.

It was at the gates, and in the presence of Lukerya, that I told her, thunderstruck as she was at having been sent for by me, that I should be happy and honoured if she . . . Further, I begged her not to be surprised at the manner of my proposal, nor that I was proposing to her in the street. "I'm a blunt man," I said, "and it's unnecessary for me to tell you that I know all about your circumstances." And I was not lying. I am a blunt man. Anyway, what does it matter? I spoke to her not only decently, that is to say, showing that I was a man of education, but also with originality, and that's what matters. Well, is there any harm in admitting it? I want to judge myself, and I am judging myself. I must speak *pro* and *contra*, and I do. I always remembered it with pleasure afterwards, though it may have been silly. I told her frankly at the time, without the slightest embarrassment, that, in the first place, I was not particularly talented or particularly clever and, perhaps, not even particularly good. I told her that I was a pretty cheap egoist (I remember that expression: I had thought of it on the way and was rather pleased with it), and that it was indeed very likely that I possessed a number of other highly unpleasant qualities. I told her all that with a special sort of pride—we all know how one talks of such things. Mind you, I had enough good sense not to speak of my virtues after having so nobly enlarged on my bad qualities. I did not say, "But to make up for that I possess this or that or the other virtue." I saw that for the time being she was terribly frightened. But I didn't tone anything down, either. On the contrary, seeing how frightened she was, I deliberately painted everything in blacker colours. I told her bluntly that she would not have to worry about food, but as for fine clothes, theatres and balls, she couldn't count on that. Not at first, at all events. Later on when I had attained my object—possibly. This stern tone most decidedly appealed to me. I added, though, and that casually too, that if I was engaged in that sort of business, that is, kept my pawnshop, it was because of a certain object I had in mind, because, that is, there was a certain circumstance. . . . But, surely, I had a right to talk like that, for I really had such an object in mind, there really was such a circumstance. One moment, ladies and gentlemen, one moment, please: I always hated this money-lending business, I hated it all my life, and, as a matter of fact, though I admit it's absurd to talk about oneself in such mysterious phrases, I *was* "revenging myself on society." Indeed, I was! So that her gibe that morning about "revenging myself" was unfair. I mean, if I had told her straight, "Yes, I am revenging myself on society," and she had burst out laughing as she nearly did that morning, the whole thing would indeed have appeared rather ridiculous. But by the use of an indirect hint, by a mysterious phrase, one can, it seems, bias the imagination in one's favour. Besides, at that time I was no longer afraid of anything. For I knew very well that the fat shopkeeper at any rate was more hateful to her than I, and that when I made my proposal to her at the gate I would appear as a deliverer to her. I knew that. Oh, a man knows a dirty trick when he sees one! But was it a dirty trick? How is one to pass judgment on a man? Didn't I really love her even then?

Wait a bit. At that time of course I never said anything about conferring a favour upon her. On the contrary. Oh, quite on the contrary! "It is you," I said, "who are conferring a favour on me, and not I on *you*!" So that, as you see, I even put it into words. I couldn't restrain myself, and I dare say it must have sounded rather silly, for I noticed a fleeting expression of dismay on her face. But on the whole I most certainly got the better of it. Wait, though. If we must recall all this sordid business, then let me recall that last bit of beastliness too. As I stood there, the thought that was stirring in my mind was, "You are tall, well-built, educated and—and after all, without boasting about it, not bad-looking, either." That's what kept recurring to my mind at the time. Well, anyway. She of course said *yes* to me right away, at the gate. But—but perhaps it is only fair to add that out there, at the gate, she thought a very long time before she said *yes*. She pondered so long that I could not refrain from asking, "Well, what do you say?" And I even put the question to her with a certain air of gallantry, "Well, what do you say, madam?"

"Please wait. Let me think."

And her sweet little face looked so serious, so serious, that even then I might have read it! But I felt hurt. "Why," I thought, "is she really choosing between me and that shopkeeper?" Oh, I did not understand then! I did not understand anything. No, I didn't understand anything then! I didn't understand till today! I remember Lukerya ran after me as I was going away, stopped me in the street, and said, speaking very fast, "God will reward you, sir, for marrying our dear young lady. Only please don't tell her that, sir. She's proud!"

Proud, is she? "Well," I thought, "I like them proud." Proud women are particularly good when—well, when you're no longer in doubt about your power over them. Eh? Oh, base, blundering man! Oh, how pleased I was! Do you know, while she was standing there by the gate, pondering whether to say *yes* to me, and I was wondering why she was taking such a long time over it, do you know that she may have even had some such thought as this: "If it means unhappiness for me either way, then why not choose the worst? Why not choose the fat shopkeeper and have done with it? For he would be quite sure to beat me to death in one of his drunken fits!" Eh? What do you think? Might not such a thought have occurred to her at the time?

No, I don't understand it even now. I don't understand anything even now! I've just said that the thought might have occurred to her: why not choose the worst of the two evils, that is, the shopkeeper? But which was worst for her at that moment? The shopkeeper or I? A shopkeeper or a pawnbroker who quotes Goethe? That's the question. What question? Why, don't you see even that? The answer is lying on the table, and you say, It's a question! But—to hell with me! I'm of no consequence. . . . Besides, what does it matter to me now whether I am or whether I am not of consequence? That, I am afraid, is something I cannot possibly tell. I had better go to bed. My head aches . . .

III
THE NOBLEST OF MEN—
BUT I DON'T BELIEVE IT MYSELF

I couldn't sleep. And how could I with that pulse throbbing in my head? I want to get at the bottom of it. At the bottom of all that filth. Oh, the filth! Oh, what filth I had dragged her out of then! Surely, she ought to have realised that! She ought to have appreciated my action. Other thoughts, too, pleased me at the time. For instance, that I was forty-one and she was only sixteen. That fascinated me—that feeling of inequality. Yes, it's delightful, very delightful!

Now, for example, I wanted to have our wedding *à l'anglaise*, that is a quiet wedding, just the two of us and, of course, the two witnesses, one of whom would be Lukerya, and then straight to the train, say to Moscow (I had, incidentally, some business there), staying at an hotel for a fortnight or so. But she was against it. She would not hear of it. And so I was forced to pay visits to her aunts and to present my respects to them as the relations from whom I was taking her. Yes, I gave in, and the proper respect was paid to the aunts. I even made a present to the creatures of one hundred roubles each, and promised them more, without of course telling her anything about it, so as not to distress her by the meanness of the whole situation. Her aunts at once became as smooth as silk. There was also some argument about her trousseau: she had nothing in the world, literally nothing, but then she didn't want anything. I succeeded, however, in persuading her that it was not right and proper for a bride not to have anything at all, and I got her the trousseau. For who else was there to do anything for her? Well, anyway, to hell with me! Still, I did convey certain of my ideas to her then, so that she should at all events know. I was perhaps a thought too hasty about it. The important thing was that from the very start, however much she tried to restrain herself, she did her best to show her affection for me. Met me whenever I came to visit them in the evening with protestations of delight. Told me in that chatter of hers (her sweet chatter of innocence) about the days of her childhood, her babyhood, her old home, her mother and father. But I never hesitated for a moment and poured cold water upon all her raptures. That was essentially what my idea amounted to. To her transports I replied with silence. Benevolent silence, no doubt, but all the same she soon realised that we were different and that I was an enigma. And it was the enigma that was my trump card! For to create this enigma, for the sake of it, I perpetrated all this folly! Sternness above all! And it was with sternness that I led her into my house. To put the whole thing in a nutshell, though I was eminently pleased at the time, I created a whole system. Oh, it came naturally enough, without the slightest effort on my part. Besides, it couldn't have been otherwise. I had to create that system owing to one unavoidable circumstance—why indeed should I be slandering myself! The system was perfect. A real system. No, listen! If you want to pass judgment on a man, you must first know all the facts about him. Listen.

Now, how shall I begin? For the whole thing is very complicated.

Whenever you start justifying yourself, things become complicated. You see, young people as a rule despise money, so I at once made a special point of money. I laid particular stress on money. And I did it with such consummate skill that she grew more and more silent. She would open her large eyes, listen to me, look at me, and fall silent. You see, young people are generous. I mean, young people who are good are generous and impulsive. But they have little tolerance. If anything doesn't turn out the way they like, they immediately begin to despise you. And I liked her to take a broad, a tolerant view of things. I wanted to instill the idea of tolerance into her mind. I wanted her to accept that idea with all her heart and soul. That was my plan, wasn't it? Let me give you a trivial example. How do you think I should have explained this money-lending business of mine to a girl of such a character? Naturally, I did not speak of it directly, for if I did it would have appeared that I was apologising to her for my pawnshop. Well, in the end I did it as it were through pride. I spoke almost without words. And I am an old hand at speaking without words. I have spent all my life speaking without words. I have lived through whole tragedies without uttering a word. Oh, I too had been unhappy! I was cast out by the whole world, cast out and forgotten, and no one, no one knows it! And all of a sudden this sixteen-year-old girl collected a whole dossier of the most detailed information about me from all sorts of scoundrels, and she thought she knew everything, while the innermost mystery remained buried in the breast of this man! I went on being silent. Yes, I went on being silent especially, especially with her—until yesterday. Why was I silent? Well, because I am a proud man. I meant her to find out for herself, without my help, and not from the tales told by all sorts of scoundrels. I wanted her to discover *by herself* this man and understand him! When I took her to my house, I expected the fullest possible respect from her. I wanted her to stand in homage before me because of my sufferings. And I deserved it. Oh, I was always proud. I always wanted all or nothing. And it is just because I never compromise where my own happiness is concerned, just because I wanted everything, that I was forced to act as I did that time. "Find out for yourself," I as much as told her, "and learn to appreciate me!" For you must admit that if I had started explaining everything to her myself, if I had prompted her, if I had humbled myself before her, if I had begged her to respect me, it would have been the same as if I had begged her for charity. . . . However—however, why am I talking about this?

It's so silly! Silly, silly, silly! I explained to her in a few words, without beating about the bush, brutally (I stress the brutality of it!), that nothing in the world was more delightful than the generosity of youth, but—it wasn't worth a farthing. Why not? Because it costs them nothing. Because it is merely the result of their inexperience. Because all that, as it were, is nothing but "the first impressions of life." But, I said, "let's see the sort of people you'll be if you have to work hard for a living. Cheap generosity is always easy, even to give one's life—yes, even that is easy, because it is merely the result of high spirits, of a superabundance of energy, of a passionate desire for beauty! Oh, no! You try a different kind of generosity, the really heroic kind, the difficult, calm, silent kind, without glitter, with odium, the kind that demands great sacrifices, the kind that doesn't bring you a scrap of fame or glory, in which you—a man of shining virtue—are exhibited before the whole world as a blackguard, while you are really the most honest man of them all! Well, try that, my dear girl. Just try it. Try and see what sort of a hero you'll prove yourself to be! But no, ma'am! I can see that you don't want that sort of heroism, while I—well—I have done nothing in my life but bear that cross!" At first she argued. Good Lord, how she argued! Then she began lapsing into silence. Wouldn't say a word. Only opened her eyes as she listened to me, opened them wide, those big, big eyes of hers, those observant eyes of hers. And—and, in addition, I suddenly saw a smile on her face, a mistrustful, silent, evil smile. Well, it was with that smile that I brought her into my house. It was true, of course, that she had nowhere else to go . . .

IV

PLANS, PLANS, PLANS. . . .

Which of us began it first?

Why, neither. It all began of itself from the very start. I have said that I brought her to my house with sternness. However, from the very beginning I made things easy for her. I took pains to explain to her while we were still engaged that she would have to help me with taking the pledges and paying out money. Well, at the time she said nothing (mark that, please!). And, moreover, she actually began helping me in my business with great enthusiasm. Mind you, my flat, my furniture, everything in fact, remained as before. My flat consists of two rooms, one large reception room with the pawnshop partitioned off, and the second room, also large, was our own room, our sitting-room and bedroom. My furniture is rather poor; even her aunts had better furniture. My icon case with the lamp is in the reception room where the pawnshop is. In my own room I have a bookcase with a few books and a small trunk. I always keep the keys of the trunk. Then there is, of course, the bed, tables, chairs. I told her before we were married that I'd let her have one rouble a day for our board, that is, for food for herself, me, and Lukerya, whom I had enticed away from her aunt. One rouble a day and no more. "I must have thirty thousand in three years," I said, "and there is no other way of saving it up." She raised no objections to that, but I myself increased her daily allowance by thirty copecks. The same thing with the theatre. I told her before our marriage that she needn't expect to be taken to the theatre. However, I decided to take her to a play once a month. And decently, too. To the stalls. We went together. We went three times, as a matter of fact. Saw *The Chase After Happiness* and *Singing Birds,* I think. (Oh, to hell with it!) We went there in silence and we came back in silence. Why, oh why, did we from the very beginning make no attempt to speak to each other? At first there were no quarrels, but just silence. In those days, I remember, she always used to watch me furtively. As soon as I noticed that, I became more silent than ever. It is true, it was I who made a point of keeping silent and not she. On her part there were one or two outbursts of affection when she would rush to embrace me. But as these outbursts were quite obviously morbid and hysterical, and as what I wanted was secure happiness, with respect from her, I received them coldly. And I was quite right: we always had a quarrel the day after such an outburst.

But perhaps I am being a little unfair: there were no real quarrels, only silence and—and more and more insolent looks from her. "Rebellion and independence"—that's what it was. Only she wasn't very good at it. Yes, that gentle face was getting more and more insolent. Believe it or not, I was becoming loathsome to her. Oh yes, I know what I am talking about. I observed it carefully. You see, the fact that those outbursts of hers were the result of strained nerves was quite undeniable. Why else should she, after emerging from that squalor and destitution, after scrubbing floors, begin sniffing at our poverty? As a matter of fact, there was no question of poverty at all. It was just economy. I never stinted myself in what was necessary. In linen, for instance, and cleanliness. I've always been of the opinion that cleanliness in husbands attracts a wife. Still, it was not poverty she found fault with so much as with my so-called meanness in economising. "There's some purpose behind it," she seemed to say. "Wants to show off his strength of character." She herself quite suddenly refused to go to the theatre. And that scornful smile of hers was to be seen more and more often on her face. And I grew more and more silent. More and more silent.

I wasn't going to justify myself, was I? You see, it was the pawnshop that was the chief source of trouble between us. Mind you, I knew that a woman, and particularly a girl of sixteen, simply must submit to her husband. Women have no originality. That—that is axiomatic. Yes, I regard it as axiomatic even now. Even now! Never mind what's lying there in the sitting-room. Truth is truth, and John Stuart Mill himself can do nothing about it! And a woman who loves—oh, a woman who loves—will worship even vice, the crimes even of the man she loves. He would himself never invent such justifications for his crimes as she will find for them. That is generous, but it is not original. It is the lack of originality that has been the ruin of women. And what, I repeat, are you pointing at the table in the sitting-room for? Is that original? Is what's lying there on the table original? Aha!

Listen. I was quite certain of her love then. After all, she did fling herself on my neck even at that time. That proves that she loved or, at all events, wanted to love. Yes, that's what it was: she wanted to love, she did her best to love. And the point is that there were no crimes there for which she might have had to find a justification. You say, a pawnbroker. And every one else says the same. But what if I am a pawnbroker? I mean, there must have been some reasons for one of the most generous of men to have become a pawnbroker. You see, there are ideas—I mean, if one were to put some ideas into words, say them out aloud, they would sound very silly. Why, I'd be ashamed of doing it myself. And why? For no reason at all. Just because we are all rotters and can't bear the truth. At all events, I know of no other reason. I said just now—"one of the most generous of men." It may sound ridiculous, and yet that is how it was. It is the truth. It's the truth and nothing but the truth. Yes, *I had a right* to want to make myself secure at the time. *I had a right* to open the pawnshop. You have rejected me, you—the people, I mean—have cast me out with contemptuous silence. For my passionate desire to love you, you have repaid me with a wrong from the consequences of which I shall suffer all my life. Now I have the right to erect a wall against you, to save up the thirty thousand roubles and spend the rest of my life somewhere in the Crimea, on the south coast, among the mountains and vineyards, on my own estate bought with the thirty thousand, and—above all—far away from you all, with malice against none, with the woman I love at my side, with a family, if God will send me one, and—and "being an help to them that dwell in the country round about." Well, of course, it doesn't matter if I'm saying this to myself now, but at the time what could have been more stupid than making a long story to her about it. That was the reason for my proud silence. That was why we sat together in silence. For what could she have made of it all? She was only sixteen, a girl in her teens—what could she have made of my justifications and sufferings? What I had to deal with was a straitlaced, uncompromising attitude, ignorance of life, the cheap convictions of youth, the utter blindness of "a noble soul," and, above all, the pawnshop. Good God, the pawnshop! The pawnshop! (And was I a villain in the pawnshop? Did she not see how I treated people? Did I ever take more than was my due?) Oh, how awful truth is in the world! That exquisite creature, that gentle creature, that heavenly creature was a tyrant, she was the pitiless tyrant and torturer of my soul! I must say it. I shouldn't be fair to myself if I didn't. Do you think I did not love her? Who can honestly say I didn't love her? Don't you see? That was the irony of it, the terrible irony of fate and nature! We are accursed. The life of people (and mine, in particular) is accursed. For I can see now that I must have made some mistake. That something went wrong somewhere. Everything was so clear. My plan was as clear as daylight. "Stern—proud—is in need of no moral consolations from anyone—suffers in silence." And that was true. I was not lying. I was not lying. "She will see herself later on that it was generosity on my part, though now she cannot see it. And when she does realise it one day she will appreciate me ten times as much, and she will fall in the dust at my feet, her hands folded in supplication." That was my plan. But there was something I forgot or failed to see. There was something I mismanaged badly. But enough, enough! Whose forgiveness am I to ask now? What is done is done. Be brave, man, and proud! It is not your fault! . . .

Well, why should I not tell the truth? Why should I be afraid to face the truth squarely? It was *her* fault, *her* fault. . . .

V

THE GENTLE CREATURE REBELS

Our quarrels began as a result of her sudden decision to issue loans for any amount she pleased. On two occasions she presumed to start an argument with me on this very subject. I told her I could not allow it. And then the captain's widow turned up.

The old woman brought a locket. A present from her late husband. The usual thing—a keepsake. I gave her thirty roubles. She started wailing plaintively, asking me to be sure not to lose the thing. I naturally told her not to worry: it would be safe. Well, anyway, five days later she came again to exchange it for a bracelet that was not worth eight roubles. I, quite naturally, refused. But I suppose she must have read something in my wife's eyes, for she came back later when I was out, and my wife exchanged the medallion for her bracelet.

Having learnt about it the same day, I spoke to her gently, but firmly and sensibly. She was sitting on the bed, her eyes fixed on the floor, tapping with the toe of her right boot on the carpet (a habit of hers); an ugly smile played on her lips. Then, without raising my voice, I told her quietly that the money was *mine*, and that I had a right to look on life with *my own* eyes, and—and that when I had asked her to become my wife I had concealed nothing from her.

All of a sudden she jumped up, all of a sudden she began shaking all over, and all of a sudden—what do you think—she stamped her foot at me. She was a wild beast. She was in a rage. A wild beast in a rage. I was petrified with amazement. I had never expected her to behave like that. But never for a moment did I lose control of myself. Never by a movement did I betray my astonishment. Again, in the same quiet voice, I told her straight that from now on I would not allow her to meddle in my affairs. She laughed in my face and walked out of the flat.

Now, you see, the point is that she had no right to walk out of the flat. She was to go nowhere without me—that was our understanding before our marriage. She came back in the evening. I never said a word.

Next day too she went out in the morning; the day after again. I closed my pawnshop and went to see her aunts. I had broken off all relations with them after our wedding: I did not want them to call on us, and we did not call on them. But it seemed she had not been there. They listened to me with great interest, and then laughed in my face. "Serves you right!" they said. I expected them to laugh at me. Anyway, I at once bribed the younger aunt, the old maid, with a hundred roubles, giving her twenty-five in advance. Two days later she came to see me. "An army officer is mixed up in this," she said. "A lieutenant by the name of Yefimovich. A former regimental colleague of yours." I was very much astonished. That Yefimovich had done me more harm than anyone in the regiment, and about a month ago, lacking all sense of shame, he had come to my pawnshop once or twice on the pretext of pawning something, and, I remember, begun laughing with my wife. I went up to him at once and told him not to dare to show his face in my house again in view of what our relations had been. But I had no idea that there was anything between him and my wife. I simply thought that it was just his confounded cheek. But now the aunt informed me that she had already made an appointment to meet him, and that the moving spirit behind the whole affair was a former acquaintance of theirs, Julia Semyonovna, a widow and a colonel's wife, to boot. "It is her your wife goes to see," the aunt told me.

I shall be brief about this affair. Altogether it cost me about three hundred roubles, but in a couple of days everything was arranged. I was to be in an adjoining room, behind closed doors, and overhear the first *rendezvous* between my wife and Yefimovich. In expectation of this, on the day before, there occurred between us a brief, but for me significant, scene.

She came back late in the afternoon, sat down on the bed, and looked at me sardonically, tapping the carpet with her foot. As I looked at her, the idea suddenly flashed through my head that for the whole of the last month, or rather the last fortnight, she had not been acting in character, or one ought perhaps to say, she was acting out of character. I saw before me a creature of a violent, aggressive nature; I don't want to say shameless, but disreputable, one that seemed to be looking for trouble. Yes. Asking for it. Her gentleness, however, seemed to be in her way. When such a woman gives way to violence, however she may overdo things, she cannot conceal the fact that she is behaving against her better nature, that she is egging herself on, that she is quite unable to overcome her own feelings of shame and her own outraged sense of decency. It is because of this that such women sometimes behave so outrageously that you can hardly believe your eyes. A woman accustomed to a life of immorality will, on the contrary, always try to tone everything down; she will make everything a hundred times more disgusting, but all under the pretence of decorum and decency, a pretence that in itself is a sort of claim to superiority over you.

"Is it true that you were turned out of the regiment because you were afraid to fight a duel?" she asked suddenly, without rhyme or reason, and her eyes flashed.

"It's quite true. Following a decision of my fellow-officers, I was asked to leave the regiment, though as a matter of fact I had sent in my resignation before that."

"They expelled you for being a coward, didn't they?"

"Yes, they sentenced me as a coward. But I refused to fight this duel not because I was a coward, but because I would not submit to their tyrannical decision and send a challenge to someone when I did not consider myself to be insulted. You ought to know," I could not resist the temptation to proceed, "that to take action against such tyranny in spite of all the consequences it might entail meant showing more pluck than fighting any kind of duel."

I am afraid I could not restrain myself. By the last phrase I tried, as it were, to justify myself. And that's what she was waiting for. She wanted this new proof of my humiliation. She laughed maliciously.

"And is it true that for three years afterwards you wandered about the streets of Petersburg like a tramp, begging for coppers and sleeping under billiard-tables?"

"Yes, it's quite true. I slept in the markets and in Vyazemsky's dosshouse. Quite true. There was a lot of disgrace and degradation in my life after my expulsion from the regiment. But not moral degradation. For even at the time I was the first to hate my own actions. It was only a degradation of my will and mind, and was only caused by the desperateness of my position. But all that is over now. . . ."

"Oh, now you're a man of importance—a financier!"

A hint at my pawnshop, you see. But by then I had already succeeded in taking a firm hold of myself. I saw that what she wanted most was explanations that would be humiliating to me, and—and I did not give them. Besides, just then the doorbell rang and I went out into the large room to attend to a client. Afterwards, an hour later, when she suddenly put on her things to go out, she stopped in front of me and said:

"You didn't tell me anything about it before we were married, did you?"

I made no answer, and she went away.

So next day I was standing in that room behind the closed doors, listening to hear how my fate was being decided. I had a gun in my pocket. She had dressed up for the occasion, and she was sitting at the table while Yefimovich played the fool before her. And what do you think? The result was—I say it to my credit—the result turned out to be just as I had anticipated, though at the time I might not have realised that I did expect it. I don't know whether I am expressing myself clearly.

This is what happened. I listened for a whole hour, and for a whole hour I was present at a battle of wits between a woman, a most honourable and high-principled woman, and a man about town with no principles, a dissolute and dull creature with a cringing, grovelling soul. And how, thought I, lost in amazement, how does this innocent, this gentle, this reserved woman, know it all? The most witty author of a comedy of manners could not have devised this scene of ridicule, most innocent laughter, and sacred contempt of virtue for vice. And how scintillating were her words and sly digs! What wit in her quick repartees! What withering truth in her condemnation! And, at the same time, what almost girlish artlessness! She laughed in his face at his protestations of love, at his gestures, at his proposals. Having arrived with his mind made up to take her crudely by storm and without expecting to meet with any serious opposition, the bubble of his conceit was suddenly pricked. At first I might have thought that she was flirting with him. "The flirtation of a witty, though vicious, creature to enhance her own value." But no. I was mistaken. Truth shone forth like the sun, and there was no room left for doubt in my mind. She, who had so little experience of the world, could have made up her mind to keep the appointment only out of hatred for me, an impulse and insincere hatred, but as soon as matters came to a head her eyes were opened at once. It was simply the case of a woman who was trying her hardest to humiliate me, but having made up her mind to stoop so low, she could not bear the horrible disgrace of it. And how indeed could Yefimovich, or any other society rake, hope to seduce a woman like her, a woman so pure and innocent, a woman who had such an unquenchable faith in her ideals? On the contrary, he merely aroused laughter. The whole truth rose up from her soul, and her indignation evoked sarcasm from her heart. I repeat, in the end the damn fool looked utterly dumbfounded. He sat there frowning, hardly replying to her, so that I was even beginning to fear that he might go so far as to insult her out of a mean desire for revenge. And I repeat again: to my credit be it said that I listened to the scene almost without surprise. It was as though I had come across something I had known all my life. It was as though I had gone there on purpose to meet it. I went there without believing anything against her, without making any accusations against her, though I did have a gun in my pocket. That is the truth! And how could I have imagined her to be different? Why else did I marry her? Oh, it's true enough I knew perfectly well at the time how she hated me, but I was also convinced that she was guiltless. I brought the scene to a sudden close by opening the door. Yefimovich jumped to his feet. I took her by the hand and asked her to leave the house with me. Yefimovich recovered himself and burst into loud peals of laughter.

"Oh," he said, "I've certainly nothing against the sacred right of holy matrimony. Take her away! Take her away! And, you know," he shouted after me, "though a decent man would think twice before fighting a duel with you, I feel that out of respect for your lady I ought to tell you that I'm at your service if, that is, you'd care to run the risk—"

"Do you hear?" I said, stopping her for a second on the threshold.

Then not another word all the way home. I led her by the arm, and she offered no resistance. On the contrary, she was too bewildered, too much taken by surprise by all that had happened. But that only lasted till we got home. Once at home, she sat down and stared at me. She was very pale, and though when she sat down there might have been a sardonic smile on her lips, she regarded me a moment later with a solemn and grim challenge in her eyes, and I believe that at first she was quite convinced that I would kill her with the gun. But I took it silently out of my pocket and laid it on the table. She looked at me and the gun. (Note that she knew all about the gun. I had acquired it and kept it always loaded ever since I had opened my pawnshop. For when I opened my pawnshop I made up my mind that I would not keep huge dogs or employ a strong manservant as Mozer does, for instance. My cook opens the door to my clients. But people in my profession cannot afford to dispense with the means of self-defence in case of need, and I kept a loaded revolver. During the first days of our marriage, she took a great interest in that gun. She asked all sorts of questions about it, and I explained to her its mechanism and how it worked. I even persuaded her one day to fire at a target. Note that, too, please.) Taking no notice of her frightened look, I half undressed myself and lay down on the bed. I felt terribly exhausted: it was about eleven o'clock. She remained sitting in the same place, without moving, for about an hour. Then she extinguished the candle and lay down, also without undressing, on the sofa by the wall. For the first time she did not come to bed with me. Note that, too, please....

VI
A TERRIBLE REMINISCENCE

Now about this terrible reminiscence....

I woke in the morning at about eight o'clock, I think, and it was already quite light in the room. I woke all at once, with all my mental faculties wide awake, and suddenly opened my eyes. She was standing by the window with the gun in her hand. She did not see that I was awake and that I was looking at her. Suddenly I saw that she began moving slowly towards me with the gun in her hand. I quickly closed my eyes and pretended to be fast asleep.

She went up to the bed and stood over me. I heard everything. The silence in the room was so deep that I could hear it. All at once I became conscious of one spasmodic movement, and I opened my eyes suddenly, irresistibly, against my will. She was looking straight at me. Straight into my eyes. And the gun was already near my temple. Our eyes met. But we looked at each other for no more than a second. With a great effort I closed my eyes again, and in that instant I resolved with all the strength I possessed not to make another movement, not to open my eyes, whatever happened.

And it does happen of course that a man who is fast asleep suddenly opens his eyes, raises his head just for a second, and looks round the room, then a moment later quite unconsciously replaces his head on the pillow and falls asleep without remembering anything. When, after meeting her glance and feeling the gun at my temple, I suddenly shut my eyes and did not stir, she certainly could have assumed that I was really asleep and that I had seen nothing, particularly as it is scarcely conceivable that, having seen what I had seen, I should at *such* a moment have closed my eyes again.

Yes, it was inconceivable. And yet she could have guessed the truth all the same. It was that thought that flashed through my mind suddenly, at one and the same instant, and—three cheers for the lightning speed of human thought! If that was so (I felt), if she guessed the truth and knew that I was not asleep, then I had crushed her already by my readiness to accept death, and now her hand might falter. Her former determination might be shattered against a new startling impression. It is said that people standing on a great height seem to be irresistibly drawn into the abyss. I suppose many suicides and murders have been committed only because the gun was already in the hand of the murderer or self-destroyer. Here, too, is a yawning chasm. Here, too, is a declivity, a slope at an angle of forty-five degrees, on which it is impossible not to slip, and something seems to force you irresistibly to pull the trigger. But the knowledge that I had seen everything, that I knew everything, and that I was waiting for death at her hands in silence, could have checked her on that slope.

The silence continued, and suddenly I felt the cold touch of steel at my temple, at my hair. You will ask me, did I have any hope of escape? I will answer you—and God knows I am speaking the truth—none at all, not an atom of hope, except perhaps one chance in a hundred. Why, then, did I accept death? Well, let me ask you in turn: of what use was life to me after a gun had been levelled against me by a human being I adored? Besides, I realise with the whole force of my being that at that very moment a struggle was going on between us, a life and death struggle, a duel in which I—the coward of the day before who had been expelled by his fellow-officers for cowardice—was engaged. I knew it, and she knew it too, if she had guessed the truth and knew that I was not asleep.

Perhaps nothing of the sort really happened. Perhaps I never had those thoughts at the time. But all that must have taken place even without conscious thought, yet I have done nothing but think of it every moment of my life since.

But (you will ask again) why did I not save her from so heinous a crime? Oh, I've asked myself the same question a thousand times since, every time when, with a cold shiver down my back, I have called that moment to mind. But my soul was then sunk in black despair: I was in mortal peril, I myself was on the very brink of total extinction, so how could I have saved anyone? And, besides, what makes you think that I wanted to save anyone at that moment? How can one tell what I was feeling then?

But all the time my mind was in a turmoil. The seconds passed. There was a dead silence. She still stood over me. Then all of a sudden I gave a start as hope returned to me. I opened my eyes quickly. She was no longer in the room. I got out of bed: I had conquered and she was conquered for ever.

I went out to have my tea. Tea was as a rule served in the other room, and she herself poured it out. I sat down at the table without uttering a word and took a glass of tea from her. About five minutes later I glanced at her. She was dreadfully pale, paler even than the night before, and she looked at me. And suddenly—suddenly—seeing that I was looking at her, she smiled palely with her pale lips, with a timid question in her eyes. "So she is still uncertain, she is still asking herself: does he or doesn't he know? did he or didn't he see?" I averted my eyes with a look of indifference.

After tea I locked up the shop, went to the market and bought an iron bedstead and a screen. On returning home, I had the bed put in the front room and the screen round it. That bed was for *her*. But I never said a word to her. She understood without words. The bed made her realise that "I saw everything and knew everything," and that there could be no more any doubt about that.

That night I left the gun on the table as usual. She crept silently into her new bed at night: our marriage was dissolved. "She was conquered but not forgiven." During the night she became delirious and in the morning she was in a high fever. She was in bed for six weeks.

CHAPTER TWO

I
A DREAM OF PRIDE

Lukerya has just told me that she will not remain with me and that she will leave immediately after the funeral of her mistress. I knelt and prayed for five minutes. I wanted to pray for an hour, but all the time I kept thinking, thinking—and all such aching thoughts, and my head aches—what's the use of praying?—it's a sin! It is strange too that I should not be able to sleep. When one is unhappy, especially when one is very unhappy, one always feels like sleeping after the first violent outbursts of grief. Men condemned to death, I'm told, sleep very soundly indeed on the last night. And so it ought to be. It is only natural. Or they would not have been able to endure it. I lay down on the sofa, but I could not fall asleep.

—

. . . She was ill for six weeks, and we looked after her day and night, Lukerya and I and the trained nurse I had engaged from the hospital. I did not care how much money it cost me. On the contrary, I liked spending money on her. I called in Dr. Schroeder, and I paid him ten roubles for a visit. When she regained consciousness, I stopped going into her room unless it was absolutely necessary. However, why am I describing all this? When she got up at last, she sat down quietly and silently in my room at the special table I had also bought for her at the time. Yes, it is quite true: neither of us spoke at all. I mean, later on we did begin talking to each other, but just the usual things. Of course, I spoke as little as possible on purpose; but she, too, I could see very well, was glad not to have to say an unnecessary word. I thought that quite natural on her part. "She is too shaken and too subdued," I thought to myself, "and she must of course be given time to forget and to get used to things." And so it was that we were silent. But every minute I was preparing myself for the future. I could not help thinking that she was doing the same, and I found it extremely diverting to try and guess what she was thinking of just then.

One more thing I will say: no one, of course, oh, no one in the world, knew of the agonies I suffered during her illness. I kept my worries to myself and did not even let Lukerya see how troubled I was. I couldn't imagine, I couldn't even admit to myself, the possibility that she might die before learning the truth, the whole truth. But when she was out of danger and began to regain her health, I recovered my composure, I remember, very quickly and completely. And that was not all. I made up my mind *to put off our future* for as long a time as possible and for the time being to leave things as they were. Yes, just then something strange and peculiar happened to me (I don't know how else to describe it): I had triumphed, and the consciousness of that was quite sufficient for me. And so the whole winter passed. Oh, I was pleased as I had never been pleased in my life, and that all through the winter.

You see, there had been a most terrible event in my life which until then, that is to say, until the disastrous incident with my wife, weighed heavily upon my mind every day and every hour of the day: the loss of my reputation and my forced retirement from the army. To put it in a nutshell: I had been the victim of a most abominable injustice. It is true that my fellow-officers never liked me for my difficult character, and perhaps even for my absurd character, my ridiculous character, though it often happens that what you regard as great, what is dear to you, what you esteem most highly, strikes your friends for some unaccountable reason as extremely funny. Oh, I was never liked at school. People never liked me. Never at any time. Even Lukerya finds it impossible to like me. While, however, the incident in the regiment undoubtedly arose out of this general unpopularity of mine, its direct cause was quite certainly due to an accident. I am saying this because I don't think there can be anything more aggravating and intolerable than to be ruined by an accident which might or might not have happened, by a fortuitous concatenation of circumstances which might have passed away like a cloud. For a man of education nothing can be more humiliating.

Now what had happened was this:

During an interval at the play I went out to the bar which was crowded with people, including a large number of army officers. While I was there, the hussar officer A—v came in suddenly and began talking in a loud voice to two other hussar officers. He was telling them about Captain Bezumtsev of our regiment who (so he said) had just created a disturbance, and who (he added) "seems to be drunk." The subject was soon dropped. Besides, the whole story was a mistake, for Captain Bezumtsev was not drunk at all, and the disturbance was not really a disturbance, either. The hussars began talking about something else, and that was the end of it. But next day the story reached our regiment, and of course the fact that I was the only officer of our regiment in the bar at once became the subject of general talk. It was remarked that when the hussar A—v had spoken so insolently about Captain Bezumtsev, I had not gone over to him immediately and stopped him by rapping him on the knuckles. But why on earth should I have done that? If he had a bone to pick with Bezumtsev, it was their own personal affair and no business of mine. The officers of my regiment meanwhile decided that it was not a personal affair at all but concerned the whole regiment. And since I was the only officer of our regiment present, I had by my failure to take action shown both to the officers and the civilians in the bar that there were officers in the regiment who did not care a damn for their honour or for the honour of their regiment. I could not agree with such an interpretation. I was given to understand that I could still put everything right, late though it was, if I demanded a formal explanation from A—v. This I did not choose to do. In fact, I resented the whole thing most violently. I would not compromise with my pride, and refused to have anything to do with their suggestion. I then at once resigned my commission. That is the whole story. I left the regiment a proud, but a broken man. Both my will and my mind had suffered a bad shock. As it happened, my sister's husband in Moscow just then squandered our small family fortune, including my own part in it (a tiny part, it is true), and I was left without a penny in the world. I could have got myself some civilian job, but I didn't. After my splendid uniform, I wasn't going to become some railway official. And so—if it had to be shame, then let it be shame; if it had to be disgrace, then let it be disgrace; if it had to be degradation, then let it be degradation—the worse the better! That was my choice. Then followed three years of terrible deprivation and horror, and even Vyazemsky's dosshouse. A year and a half ago my godmother, a wealthy old lady, died in Moscow and among other bequests she quite unexpectedly left me three thousand roubles in her will. I thought things over and there and then decided what I was going to do with myself. I made up my mind that I would become a pawnbroker and ask no favours from anyone. First I must get money, then a home of my own, and then a new life far away from the memories of the past. That was my plan. Nevertheless, my sombre past and a reputation ruined for ever were a constant source of mental anguish to me. The memory of it haunted me every day, every minute. And then I got married. Whether by chance or not—I don't know. But when I brought her into my home, I thought I was bringing a friend, and it was a friend I needed most of all. But a friend had to be taken in hand, licked into shape, and—yes—even mastered. And how could I possibly explain it all at once to a sixteen-year-old girl, and one, besides, who was prejudiced against me? For instance, could I have convinced her that I was not a coward without the accidental assistance of the dreadful incident with the gun? Could I have convinced her that I had been falsely accused of cowardice in the regiment? But that dreadful incident came just in the nick of time. Having passed the test of the gun, I avenged the whole of my horrible past. And though no one knew about it, *she* knew, and that meant everything to me because she herself was everything to me. All the hopes of a bright future that I cherished in my dreams! She was the only person I had hoped to make my true friend in life, and I had no need of anyone else. And now she knew everything. At least she knew that she had been too hasty in joining the camp of my enemies. That thought filled me with delight. In her eyes I could no longer be a blackguard, but at most perhaps a queer fellow; and even that, after all that had happened, was not at all displeasing to me. Queerness is not a vice in a man; on the contrary, it often exercises a powerful attraction on a woman's imagination. In fact, I deliberately postponed the final explanation. What had happened was for the moment quite sufficient for my peace of mind. It contained too many exciting scenes and a lot of material for my dreams. You see, the whole trouble is that I am a dreamer: I was quite satisfied to have enough material for my dreams. As for her, she, I thought, could *wait.*

So the whole winter passed in a sort of expectation of something. I liked to steal a glance at her now and again when she sat at her little table. She was busy with her work, her sewing, and sometimes in the evening she would read books taken from my bookcase. The choice of books in the book-case should also have spoken in my favour. She hardly ever went out. Every day after dinner, before dusk, I used to take her out for a walk. We took our constitutional, and not entirely in silence as before. At least, I did my best to pretend that we were not silent and that we were talking amicably together. But, as I have already said, we both saw to it that our talks were not too long. I did it on purpose, and as for her, I thought, it was important "to give her time." It is, I admit, strange that not once till the end of the winter did it occur to me that while I liked looking at her stealthily, I had never during all those winter months caught her looking at me! I ascribed it to her shyness. And indeed her whole appearance did convey a picture of such gentleness, such utter exhaustion after her illness. No, thought I, don't interfere with her. Better wait and—"she will come to you all of a sudden and of her own free will. . . ."

The thought filled me with intense delight. I will add one more thing: sometimes I would, as though on purpose, so inflame my own mind that I'd in fact succeed in working myself up into a mental and emotional rage against her. And it went on like that for some time. But my hatred of her could never ripen or strike roots in my heart. And, besides, I couldn't help feeling myself that it was only a sort of game I was playing. Why, even when I had dissolved our marriage by buying the bed and the screen, I could never for one moment look upon her as a criminal. And not because I took too light a view of her crime, but because I had the sense to forgive her completely, from the very first day, even before I purchased the bed. That, I confess, was a little odd on my part, for where morals are concerned I am very strict. On the contrary, in my eyes she was so thoroughly subdued, so thoroughly humiliated, so thoroughly crushed that I could not help feeling horribly sorry for her sometimes, though, for all that, the idea of her humiliation was at times certainly very pleasing to me. What pleased me was the idea of our inequality. . . .

That winter I happened to be responsible for a few acts of real kindness. I remitted two debts and I advanced money to one poor woman without a pledge. And I never breathed a word about it to my wife. Nor did I do it at all so that she should learn about it. But the woman herself came to thank me, and almost on her knees. In that way it became public property. I could not help thinking that she had learnt about the woman with real pleasure.

But spring was close at hand. It was mid-April. We took out our double windows, and bright shafts of sunlight began lighting up our rooms. But the scales still covered my eyes and blinded my reason. Oh, those fatal, those dreadful scales! How did it all happen that the scales suddenly fell from my eyes and that I suddenly saw and understood everything? Was it chance? Did the appointed day come at last? Was it a ray of sunshine that suddenly kindled a thought or a surmise in my dull brain? No. It was neither a thought nor a surmise. It was a chord that had been mute a long time and that now came to life and began vibrating suddenly, flooding my darkened mind with light and showing up my devilish pride. I felt as though I had leapt to my feet. It all happened with such incredible suddenness. It happened towards evening, at about five o'clock, after dinner. . . .

II
THE SCALES SUDDENLY FALL

Just two words before I go on. Already a month ago I noticed a strange wistfulness about her. She was not only silent. She was also wistful. Of that, too, I became aware all of a sudden. She was sitting and sewing something at the time, her head bent over her work, and she did not see that I was looking at her. It suddenly struck me how thin she looked, how haggard, her face so pale, her lips so white, and this together with her wistfulness came as a great shock to me. I had already before heard her little dry cough, especially at night. I got up at once and went out to see Schroeder without saying anything about it to her.

Schroeder came next day. She was very much surprised, her eyes wandering from Schroeder to me and back again.

"But I'm quite all right," she said with a sort of vague smile.

Schroeder did not examine her very carefully (those doctors are sometimes so maddeningly off-hand), but told me in the other room that she was suffering from the aftereffects of her illness and that it would not be a bad idea to take her to the sea-side in the spring or, if that were impossible, to take a country cottage for the summer. He did not say anything, in fact, except that there was a weakness or something of the sort. When Schroeder had gone she suddenly said to me, looking very gravely at me:

"I'm quite all right. Indeed, I am!"

But as she said it she suddenly blushed, from shame, no doubt. Yes, it was quite obviously shame. Oh, now I understand it! She was ashamed, you see, that I was still *her husband,* that I was taking care of her as though I were her real husband still. But at the time I did not realise it, and I ascribed her smile to her humility. (Oh, those scales!)

And so, a month later, at five o'clock in the afternoon, on a bright, sunny day in April, I was sitting in the pawnshop, making up my accounts. All of a sudden I heard how, sitting at the table in our room, at her work, she began softly, ever so softly—to sing. This new incident made an overwhelming impression on me. To this day I can't explain it. Till then I had hardly ever heard her sing, at all events not since the first days of our married life when we were still able to have some fun together, practising target shooting with my gun. At that time her voice was still strong and clear, though hardly true, but very pleasant and healthy. But now the song sounded so feeble. Oh, I don't mean it was a plaintive tune (it was some love song), but it sounded as though her voice were cracked, broken, as though her dear little voice could not manage it, as though the song itself were sick. She sang in an undertone, and suddenly her voice, rising on a high note, broke. Such a poor little voice, and it broke off so miserably. She cleared her throat and started singing something again in a very soft and hardly audible voice. . . .

You may laugh at my agitation, but no one will ever understand the reason for it. No. I wasn't sorry for her yet. Not yet. It was something quite different. To begin with, during the first few minutes at any rate I suddenly felt bewildered and terribly surprised. It was a horrible, strange sort of surprise, painful and almost vindictive. "She is singing, and—while I am in the house! *She hasn't forgotten about me, has she?*"

Thunderstruck, I sat there for some time without stirring from my place. Then I suddenly got up, took my hat, and went out, as though acting on impulse. At least I don't know why or where I was going. Lukerya was helping me on with my coat.

"She is singing?" I asked Lukerya, involuntarily.

Lukerya did not seem to know what I was talking about, and she went on staring at me incomprehensibly. But of course I was rather incomprehensible.

"Is it the first time you've heard her sing?"

"No, sir," said Lukerya, "she sometimes sings when you are out."

I remember everything. I went down the stairs, went out into the street and walked along at random. I walked to the corner, and started looking vaguely ahead of me. All sorts of people passed by me, knocked against me, but I was not aware of anything. I hailed a cab and told the driver to take me to the Police Bridge. I haven't the faintest idea why. Then suddenly I changed my mind and gave him a twenty-copeck piece.

"Sorry to have troubled you," I said, laughing stupidly at him, but my heart was suddenly filled with a strange ecstasy.

I went back home, quickening my pace as I walked along. The poor, cracked broken note was again ringing in my heart. My breath failed me. Yes, the scales were falling, falling from my eyes! If she had started singing while I was in the house, it could only mean that she had forgotten all about me. That's what was so terribly clear. I realised it in my heart, but my soul was aglow with ecstasy and it proved stronger than my fear.

Oh, the irony of fate! Had there been anything else in my soul the whole winter, could there have been anything else but this feeling of ecstasy? But where had I been myself all the winter? Had I been there with my soul? I ran up the stairs in a great hurry, and I don't remember whether I was apprehensive or not when I went in. All I remember is that the floor seemed to be swaying and that I felt as though I were floating on a river. I entered the room. She was sitting in her usual place, with her head bent over her sewing, but she was no longer singing. She threw a rapid and casual glance at me. It was hardly a glance really. Just the usual indifferent sign of recognition one gives when someone comes into the room.

I went up straight to her and sat down beside her. Close to her, like one demented. She looked at me quickly, as though she were afraid of me. I took her hand, and I don't remember what I said to her, or rather what I meant to say to her, for I couldn't even speak properly. My voice shook and did not obey me. Nor did I know what to say. All I did was to gasp for breath.

"Let's talk—you know—say something!" I suddenly stammered out something utterly idiotic.

Oh, how could I think of anything sensible to say at that moment? She started again and, as she looked at my face, she drew back from me in horror, but almost immediately a look of *stern surprise* came into her eyes. Yes, surprise and *stern*. She looked at me with wide-open eyes. That sternness, that stern surprise seemed all at once to deal me a stunning blow. "So it's love you still want? Love?" that look of surprise asked me, though she herself never uttered a word. But I read it all. I read it all. My world came crashing about my ears and I just collapsed at her feet. Yes, I fell down at her feet. She jumped up quickly, but I seized her hands and held her back with all the force at my command.

And I fully understood my despair. Oh, I understood it all right! But, you see, ecstasy was blazing so fiercely in my heart that I feared I should die. I kissed her feet rapturously, in a transport of happiness. Yes, in a transport of happiness. Boundless, infinite happiness. And I did it though I realised full well all the hopelessness of my despair. I wept, I tried to say something, but could not speak. Her surprise and terror suddenly gave way to a sort of worried thought, a thought of great urgency, and she looked at me strangely, wildly even. She wanted to understand something without a moment's delay, and—she smiled. She was ashamed that I was kissing her feet, horribly ashamed, and she kept drawing them away from me. But I immediately kissed the spot where her foot had rested. She saw it and began suddenly laughing from embarrassment (you know the feeling when one starts laughing from embarrassment). She became hysterical—I saw it coming—her hands were trembling. But I paid no attention to it. I went on murmuring that I loved her, that I wouldn't get up. "Let me kiss your dress. Let me worship you like this all my life!" I don't know, I don't remember, but suddenly she broke into sobs and trembled all over. She had a terrible fit of hysterics. I had frightened her.

I picked her up in my arms and carried her to the bed. When her attack was over, she sat up in bed and, looking terribly distressed, she seized me by the hands and begged me to calm myself. "Come, don't torment yourself! There, there. Be calm, please!" and once more she burst into tears.

All that evening I remained at her side. I kept telling her that I'd take her to Boulogne to bathe in the sea—now, at once, in a fortnight—that she had such a cracked little voice—I had heard it that afternoon—that I would give up my pawnshop—sell it to Dobronravov—that we should start life afresh. But, above all, Boulogne, Boulogne! She listened to me, but she was still afraid. It was not that, however, that worried me at the time. What worried me was that I felt more and more irresistibly drawn to fling myself at her feet again, to kiss again and again the ground on which her feet rested, and to pray to her, and "I shall ask nothing, nothing more of you," I kept repeating every minute. "Don't answer me. Don't take any notice of me at all. Only let me look at you from a corner. Make me your slave, your lapdog!" She wept.

"And I thought you'd let me alone," she said suddenly, the words escaping her involuntarily, so much so that quite possibly she herself was not aware of what she said.

And yet. . . . Oh, that was the most important, the most fateful sentence she uttered that evening, and one that was only too easy for me to understand, and it stabbed my heart as though with a knife. It explained everything to me. Everything! But while she was beside me, while she was before my eyes, I was full of hope, and I was terribly happy. Oh, I exhausted her completely that evening, and I realised it, but I kept thinking that any moment I might succeed in changing it all. At length, towards night, she was utterly worn out, and I persuaded her to go to sleep. She fell asleep at once, and slept soundly. I expected her to be delirious, and she was a little. I kept getting up every minute in the night, and went softly in my slippers to have a look at her. I wrung my hands over her, as I looked at that sick creature in that poor little bed, the iron bedstead I had bought her for three roubles. I knelt down, but I did not dare to kiss her feet while she was asleep (and without her permission!). I knelt to pray, but jumped to my feet almost at once. Lukerya was keeping an eye on me, and kept coming in out of the kitchen. I went out to her and told her to go to bed. I told her that tomorrow everything would be "quite different."

And I believed it. Blindly, madly, frighteningly. Oh, my heart overflowed with rapture! I was only waiting for the next day. No, I did not believe in any trouble, in spite of the symptoms. I had not come to my senses yet, though the scales had fallen from my eyes. And for a long, long time I did not come to my senses. Oh, not till today, till this very day! And how could I have expected to come to my senses then? Wasn't she still alive then? Wasn't she still before me and I before her? "Tomorrow she'll wake up, and I'll tell her all this, and she will see it all." That was what I kept saying to myself then. It was so clear and simple, and hence my ecstasy. The main thing was the trip to Boulogne. For some reason I kept thinking that Boulogne was everything. That there was something final about Boulogne. "To Boulogne! To Boulogne!" I waited frantically for the morning.

III

I UNDERSTAND IT TOO WELL

And all that was only a few days ago. Five days—only five days ago. Last Tuesday! Oh, if there had been a little more time! If only she had waited a little longer, I would have dispersed this terrible cloud of darkness. And was she not absolutely calm and composed? The very next day she listened to me with a smile, though no doubt she did look a little embarrassed. Yes, that above all. Her embarrassment, I mean. All the time, all during those five days, I could not help noticing that she was either embarrassed or ashamed. And frightened, too. Very frightened. I don't want to argue about it. I would be mad to deny it. She *was* frightened, but after all that was natural enough. How could she help being frightened? For hadn't we been strangers to one another for such a long time? Hadn't we become so terribly estranged from each other? And now suddenly, like a bolt from the blue, all this. . . . But I paid no attention to her fear. A new life shone like a bright star before me! It is true, it is absolutely true: I made a mistake. Perhaps many mistakes. As soon as we woke next morning (it was on Wednesday) I at once made a mistake. I at once began to treat her as my friend. I was too much in a hurry. Much too much in a hurry. But I simply had to confess everything to her. Yes, my confession was absolutely necessary. Even more than a confession! I did not conceal from her what I had been concealing from myself all my life. I told her frankly that all during the winter I had never for a moment doubted that she loved me. I explained to her that my money-lending business was nothing but a symptom of my loss of willpower. It was nothing but a mental aberration. A personal idea of self-castigation and self-exaltation. I explained to her that I *was* a coward in the bar of the theatre that evening. I couldn't help it. It has something to do with my character, my oversensitiveness. I was thrown into a panic by the surroundings. It was the fact that it took place in a theatre bar that unnerved me. What had made me so nervous was—how could I walk up to the hussar officer? How could I do it without cutting a ridiculous figure? What I was afraid of was not the duel but that I might make a fool of myself. Later, of course, I would not admit it. And I tormented myself and everybody else. I had tormented her for it, too. In fact, I only married her so as to be able to torment her for it. In general, I spoke for the most part as though I were in a fever. She kept clasping my hands, begging me to stop. "You're exaggerating. . . . You're tormenting yourself!" And again she was weeping. Again she was on the point of becoming hysterical. She kept asking me all the time not to say anything about it. Not to think of it at all.

I disregarded her entreaties, or almost disregarded them. Spring! Boulogne! There was the sun there! There was our new sun there! I could speak of nothing else. I shut up the pawnshop. I transferred my business to Dobronravov. On the spur of the moment I even proposed to her to distribute all my money among the poor. All but the original three thousand roubles I had received from my godmother. That money would pay for our trip to Boulogne, and when we came back, we'd start a new life. A life of honest work. So it was decided, for she did not contradict me. She said nothing. She only smiled. And it seemed that she smiled more out of consideration for me, so as not to disappoint me. I realised, of course, that I was worrying her. Do not imagine I was such a fool or such an egoist as not to see it. I saw everything. Everything to the last detail. I saw and I knew everything more than anyone. All my despair was laid bare.

I told her everything about myself and about her. And about Lukerya. I told her that I had wept. . . . Oh, I, too, changed the subject. I did not want to remind her of certain things. And once or twice she looked quite cheerful. Yes, I remember that. I remember it distinctly! Why do you say I looked at her and saw nothing? If only *this* had not happened, everything would have been different. Why, didn't she tell me that amusing story about Gil Blas and the Archbishop of Granada herself the day before yesterday? We were discussing books. She was telling me about the books she had been reading that winter, and it was then that she told me about that scene from *Gil Blas*. And she laughed, too! Yes, she laughed, and, good Lord, what a sweet, childish laughter it was! Just as she used to laugh at the time of our engagement (A moment! Only a fleeting moment!). How glad I was! How happy! I was terribly struck by it, by the story of the Archbishop, I mean. She could then find so much happiness and peace of mind as to be able to enjoy a literary masterpiece. What else could it mean but that she was beginning to regain her self-composure completely, that she was already beginning to believe that I would *let her alone.* "I thought you'd *let me alone*!" that was what she had said on Tuesday, wasn't it? Oh, the thought of a ten-year-old girl! And she did believe that everything would really remain *as it was.* She believed that she'd always be sitting at her table and I at mine, and that the two of us would go on like that till we were old. All of a sudden I come up to her as her husband, and a husband wants love! Oh, how blind I was! Oh, what a frightful misunderstanding!

Another mistake I made was to have looked at her with such rapture. I should have controlled myself. For my transports only frightened her. But did I not control myself? Did I kiss her feet again? No. Never for a moment did I betray the fact that—well—that I was her husband. Oh, that thought never entered my head. All I did was to worship her. But it was quite obviously impossible for me to have been silent all the time. I had to say something. I suddenly told her that I enjoyed talking to her. I said that I thought her incomparably—yes, incomparably—better educated and mentally developed than I was. She blushed crimson and looked very embarrassed. She said I was exaggerating. Then—fool that I was!—I could not restrain myself and I told her with what delight I had listened to her battle of wits with that awful swine! How overjoyed I had been when I realised, as I stood behind the door, how much hatred there lay hidden in all her replies to that unspeakable cad. How pleased I had been with all her clever repartees, her brilliant sallies, combined with such child-like artlessness. She seemed to start, she murmured something about my exaggerating again, and all of a sudden her face darkened, she buried it in her hands, and broke into sobs. . . . Here I was unable to restrain myself any longer. I went down on my knees before her again, I began kissing her feet again, and again, as on Tuesday, it all ended in hysterics. . . . That was yesterday evening, and in the morning. . . .

In the morning? Why, you madman, it was this morning, only a few hours ago, only a few hours ago!

Listen and try to understand. When we met at the tea-table a few hours ago (after last night's fit of hysterics), she surprised me by her calmness. Yes, she was absolutely self-composed. And all night I had been trembling with fear because of what happened yesterday. And quite suddenly she herself came up to me and, folding her hands, began telling me (only a few hours ago, only a few hours ago!) that she was guilty, that she was fully aware of it, that her guilt had been torturing her all the winter, that it was torturing her even now, that she appreciated my generosity very much, that "I will be a true and faithful wife to you," that "I will always respect you. . . ." Then I leapt to my feet like a madman and embraced her. I kissed her. I kissed her face. I kissed her on her lips like a husband for the first time after a long separation. And why, why did I go out after that? Only for a couple of hours! Our passports for abroad! . . . Oh, God, why didn't I come back five minutes earlier? Only five minutes earlier. And that crowd at our gates. Those eyes staring at me! Oh, God!

Lukerya says (Oh, I shall never let Lukerya go now! She knows everything. She's been with us all the winter, and she'll be able to tell me everything!), Lukerya says that when I had gone out of the house, and only about twenty minutes before I came back, she suddenly went into our room where her mistress was at the time, intending to ask her something (I forget what), and she noticed that her icon (the same icon of the Holy Virgin) had been taken out of the case and was standing before her on the table, as though her mistress had only a moment ago been saying her prayers before it. "What's the matter, madam?" "Nothing, Lukerya, you can go." Then she said, "Wait a minute, Lukerya," and she went up to her and kissed her. "Are you happy, madam?" Lukerya asked. "Yes, thank you, Lukerya, I am happy." "Master ought to have asked your pardon a long time ago, madam. Thank God, you've made it up now." "All right, Lukerya," she said. "You can go now, Lukerya." And she smiled so—so strangely. So strangely that ten minutes later Lukerya went back to have a look at her.

"She was standing by the wall, sir," Lukerya told me, "close to the window. Leaning with her arm against the wall, she was, and her head pressed against her arm. Standing like that she was, sir, and thinking. And so deep in thought was she that she did not hear me open the door of the other room. She didn't see me standing there and watching her. Then I saw her smile, sir. She was standing by the wall near the window, thinking and smiling. I looked at her, turned round quietly and went back to my kitchen. Preoccupied with my own thoughts I was, sir. Only suddenly I heard the window open. I went back at once, meaning to tell her that it was very fresh outside and that she might catch her death of cold if she wasn't careful, and, Lord, sir, I saw she had climbed up on to the windowsill, standing there drawn up to her full height she was, in the open window, with her back to me, clasping the icon in her hands. I called out to her 'Madam! Madam!' and she must have heard me, sir, for she made a movement as if to turn round, but she didn't. Took a step forward, she did, then pressed the icon to her bosom and—threw herself out of the window!"

All I remember is that when I went into the yard, she was still warm. The horror of it was that all the time I felt those eyes staring at me. At first they shouted, then they suddenly fell silent, and all at once the crowd parted to let me through, and—there she lay with the icon. I dimly remember going up to her silently and looking at her a long time. All of them crowded round me and began saying something to me. Lukerya was there too, but I did not see her. I only remember the workman. He kept shouting at me, "A handful of blood poured out of her mouth! A handful of blood! A handful!" and pointing to the blood on a stone. I believe I touched the blood with my finger, smeared my finger, and looked at my finger (I remember that), while he kept shouting at me, "A handful! A handful!"

"What the hell is a handful!" I yelled at him with all my might (so I'm told) and, raising my hands, rushed at him.

Oh, the whole thing is mad! Mad! An awful misunderstanding! It's improbable! Impossible!

IV
I WAS ONLY FIVE MINUTES TOO LATE

And isn't it? Isn't it? Is it probable? Can one really say that it was possible? Why did this woman die? What made her do it?

Oh, believe me, I understand. I understand everything! But why she died is still a mystery. Was she afraid of my love? Did she really ask herself seriously whether to accept it or not? And was the question too much for her and did she prefer to die? I know. I know. It's no use my racking my brains. She had promised me too much. Given me too many promises. And she was afraid that she would not be able to keep them. That's clear. There are a number of other facts which are simply dreadful. For there is still the unanswered question—why did she die? That question keeps hammering at my brain. I would have *let her alone,* if she had wanted me to *let her alone.* But, she did not believe it. No, she didn't. And that was the real trouble. No, no! It's a lie! It wasn't that at all. It was simply that she had to be honest with me. She knew that to me "to love" meant "to love entirely," and not as she would have loved the shopkeeper. And, being too chaste and too pure, she did not want to deceive me with a love that would have satisfied the shopkeeper. Did not want to deceive me with a love that was only half a love, or a quarter of a love. Too honest. That's the trouble. I wanted to instil tolerance into her—remember? A curious idea.

Another terribly interesting question is whether she respected me or not. I don't know whether in her heart she despised me or not. I don't believe she did. It certainly is very strange. Why didn't it ever occur to me all the winter that she despised me? I was absolutely convinced she didn't until that moment when she looked at me with *stern surprise.* Yes, *stern.* It was then that I knew at once that she did despise me. I knew it irrevocably. For ever! Oh, let her, let her despise me all her life, so long as she was alive—so long as she was alive! Only a few hours ago she was still walking about. She was still talking. I can't for the life of me understand why she should have thrown herself out of the window. And how was I to have suspected it even five minutes before she did it? I've asked Lukerya to come in. I shall never part with Lukerya now. No, I shall never part with her. Not for anything in the world!

Oh, I daresay we could have still found some way of patching things up. The trouble was we got so terribly estranged from one another during the winter. But couldn't we have grown used to one another again? Why, why couldn't we have come together again? I am generous, and so was she—that was one point we had in common! A few more words, two more days—no more—and she would have understood everything.

What is so awful is that the whole thing was just an accident—an ordinary, horrible, senseless accident! An accident that would never have happened if I hadn't been late. I was five minutes too late. Only five minutes! Had I come five minutes earlier, that impulse which drove her to commit suicide would have passed away like a cloud. And it would never again have occurred to her to do anything so horrible. And it would have all ended by her understanding everything. And now again empty rooms. Again I'm alone in the whole world. I can hear the pendulum ticking away. What does it care? There's nothing it can be sorry for. I've no one left in the world—that's the horror of it!

I keep walking, walking. Always walking. I know. I know. You need not prompt me. You think it's damned funny that I should be complaining about an accident. About being five minutes too late. An accident? But it's as plain as a pikestaff. Just think: why didn't she leave a note behind, just a few words to say, "Don't blame anyone for my death," as people always do? Is it likely that it should never have occurred to her that Lukerya might get into trouble with the police over her? "She was alone with her mistress," people might have said, "and she could have pushed her out of the window." She might at any rate have been dragged off to the police, blameless though she was, but for the fact that from the yard and from the windows of the next-door house four men had seen her stand with the icon in her hands and jump out of the window. But that too was an accident. I mean, that she should have been seen by some people who just happened to be about at the time. No, the whole thing was not premeditated. It was just an impulse. An unaccountable impulse. A sudden impulse. A momentary aberration. What does the fact that she had been praying in front of the icon prove? It certainly doesn't show that she had been saying her prayers before committing suicide. The whole impulse probably lasted only about ten minutes. Her decision to do away with herself must have been taken when she was standing by the wall, her head pressed against her arm, and smiled. An idea flashed through her mind, set it in a whirl, and—she could not resist it.

Whatever you may say, the whole thing is quite obviously a misunderstanding. I am not as bad as all that: she could have lived with me. And what if the whole thing was caused by anaemia? Simply by anaemia. By exhaustion. Utter exhaustion of all her vital energies. She got so terribly exhausted last winter. Yes. That's what it is.

I was too late!!!

How thin she looks in her coffin! How sharp her little nose has grown! Her eyelashes lie as straight as arrows. And nothing was crushed in her fall. Not a bone was broken. Just that "handful of blood." A dessert-spoonful, I suppose. Internal haemorrhage. A strange thought: what if it were possible to keep her here and not to bury her! For if they take her away.... But no! I shan't let them! I'm damned if I'll let them! Oh Lord, I mustn't talk like that. Of course she'll have to be taken away. I know that. I am not mad. I'm not raving. As a matter of fact, I don't think I've ever been as clear-headed as I am now. But I can't—I just can't get used to the idea that once more there will be no one in the house, once more two rooms, and once more I shall be here by myself with the pledges. It's mad! Mad! That's where real madness lies. I had tortured her till she could stand it no longer. Yes, that's what it was.

What do I care for your laws now? What are your customs to me? Your morals, your life, your State, your faith? Let your judges judge me. Let me be brought before your courts, before your public courts, and I will declare that I do not recognise anything. The judge will order me to hold my peace. "Silence, officer!" he'll shout. And I'll shout back at him, "What power do you possess to exact obedience from me? Why did dark insensibility destroy what was dearer to me than anything else in the world? What do I care for your laws now? I shall live my own life!" Oh, nothing makes any difference to me now!

She is blind, blind! She is dead. She cannot hear me. Oh, you don't know what a paradise I should have built for you! Paradise was in my soul, and I would have planted it all round you! What does it matter if you did not love me? What does that matter? Everything would have been as it was. I should have *let you alone.* You would have talked to me only as a friend, and we should have laughed and been happy together. We should have gazed joyfully into each other's eyes. And so we should have lived. And even if you had fallen in love with another man, it wouldn't have mattered a bit. It wouldn't have made any difference to me. Fall in love if you wish! You'd have walked with him and laughed, and I'd have watched you from the other side of the street. . . . Oh, I don't care what would have happened, if only she would open her eyes just once! Just for one moment. For one moment only. She would have looked at me as she did a few hours ago when she stood before me and swore to be a faithful wife to me. Oh, I'm sure she would have understood everything at a glance!

Insensibility. Oh, nature! People are alone in the world. That's what is so dreadful. "Is there a living man on the plain?" cries the Russian legendary hero. I, too, echo the same cry, but no one answers. They say the sun brings life to the universe. The sun will rise and—look at it. Isn't it dead? Everything is dead. Dead men are everywhere. There are only people in the world, and all around them is silence—that's what the earth is! "Men love one another!"—who said that? Whose commandment is it? The pendulum is ticking away unfeelingly, dismally. Two o'clock in the morning. Her dear little boots stand by her little bed, as though waiting for her. . . . No, seriously, when they take her away tomorrow, what's to become of me?

The Dream of a Ridiculous Man

A FANTASTIC STORY

I

I am a ridiculous man. They call me a madman now. That would be a distinct rise in my social position were it not that they still regard me as being as ridiculous as ever. But that does not make me angry any more. They are all dear to me now even while they laugh at me—yes, even then they are for some reason particularly dear to me. I shouldn't have minded laughing with them—not at myself, of course, but because I love them—had I not felt so sad as I looked at them. I feel sad because they do not know the truth, whereas I know it. Oh, how hard it is to be the only man to know the truth! But they won't understand that. No, they will not understand.

And yet in the past I used to be terribly distressed at appearing to be ridiculous. No, not appearing to be, but being. I've always cut a ridiculous figure. I suppose I must have known it from the day I was born. At any rate, I've known for certain that I was ridiculous ever since I was seven years old. Afterwards I went to school, then to the university, and—well—the more I learned, the more conscious did I become of the fact that I was ridiculous. So that for me my years of hard work at the university seem in the end to have existed for the sole purpose of demonstrating and proving to me, the more deeply engrossed I became in my studies, that I was an utterly absurd person. And as during my studies, so all my life. Every year the same consciousness that I was ridiculous in every way strengthened and intensified in my mind. They always laughed at me. But not one of them knew or suspected that if there were one man on earth who knew better than anyone else that he was ridiculous, that man was I. And this—I mean, the fact that they did not know it—was the bitterest pill for me to swallow. But there I was myself at fault. I was always so proud that I never wanted to confess it to anyone. No, I wouldn't do that for anything in the world. As the years passed, this pride increased in me so that I do believe that if ever I had by chance confessed it to any one I should have blown my brains out the same evening. Oh, how I suffered in the days of my youth from the thought that I might not myself resist the impulse to confess it to my schoolfellows. But ever since I became a man I grew for some unknown reason a little more composed in my mind, though I was more and more conscious of that awful characteristic of mine. Yes, most decidedly for some unknown reason, for to this day I have not been able to find out why that was so. Perhaps it was because I was becoming terribly disheartened owing to one circumstance which was beyond my power to control, namely, the conviction which was gaining upon me that nothing in the whole world *made any difference.* I had long felt it dawning upon me, but I was fully convinced of it only last year, and that, too, all of a sudden, as it were. I suddenly felt that it made *no* difference to me whether the world existed or whether nothing existed anywhere at all. I began to be acutely conscious that *nothing existed in my own lifetime.* At first I couldn't help feeling that at any rate in the past many things had existed; but later on I came to the conclusion that there had not been anything even in the past, but that for some reason it had merely seemed to have been. Little by little I became convinced that there would be nothing in the future, either. It was then that I suddenly ceased to be angry with people and almost stopped noticing them. This indeed disclosed itself in the smallest trifles. For instance, I would knock against people while walking in the street. And not because I was lost in thought—I had nothing to think about—I had stopped thinking about anything at that time: it made no difference to me. Not that I had found an answer to all the questions. Oh, I had not settled a single question, and there were thousands of them! But *it made no difference to me,* and all the questions disappeared.

And, well, it was only after that that I learnt the truth. I learnt the truth last November, on the third of November, to be precise, and every moment since then has been imprinted indelibly on my mind. It happened on a dismal evening, as dismal an evening as could be imagined. I was returning home at about eleven o'clock and I remember thinking all the time that there could not be a more dismal evening. Even the weather was foul. It had been pouring all day, and the rain too was the coldest and most dismal rain that ever was, a sort of menacing rain—I remember that—a rain with a distinct animosity towards people. But about eleven o'clock it had stopped suddenly, and a horrible dampness descended upon everything, and it became much damper and colder than when it had been raining. And a sort of steam was rising from everything, from every cobble in the street, and from every side-street if you peered closely into it from the street as far as the eye could reach. I could not help feeling that if the gaslight had been extinguished everywhere, everything would have seemed much more cheerful, and that the gaslight oppressed the heart so much just because it shed a light upon it all. I had had scarcely any dinner that day. I had been spending the whole evening with an engineer who had two more friends visiting him. I never opened my mouth, and I expect I must have got on their nerves. They were discussing some highly controversial subject, and suddenly got very excited over it. But it really did not make any difference to them. I could see that. I knew that their excitement was not genuine. So I suddenly blurted it out. "My dear fellows," I said, "you don't really care a damn about it, do you?" They were not in the least offended, but they all burst out laughing at me. That was because I had said it without meaning to rebuke them, but simply because it made no difference to me. Well, they realised that it made no difference to me, and they felt happy.

When I was thinking about the gaslight in the streets, I looked up at the sky. The sky was awfully dark, but I could clearly distinguish the torn wisps of cloud and between them fathomless dark patches. All of a sudden I became aware of a little star in one of those patches and I began looking at it intently. That was because the little star gave me an idea: I made up my mind to kill myself that night. I had made up my mind to kill myself already two months before and, poor as I am, I bought myself an excellent revolver and loaded it the same day. But two months had elapsed and it was still lying in the drawer. I was so utterly indifferent to everything that I was anxious to wait for the moment when I would not be so indifferent and then kill myself. Why—I don't know. And so every night during these two months I thought of shooting myself as I was going home. I was only waiting for the right moment. And now the little star gave me an idea, and I made up my mind then and there that it should *most certainly* be that night. But why the little star gave me the idea—I don't know.

And just as I was looking at the sky, this little girl suddenly grasped me by the elbow. The street was already deserted and there was scarcely a soul to be seen. In the distance a cabman was fast asleep on his box. The girl was about eight years old. She had a kerchief on her head, and she wore only an old, shabby little dress. She was soaked to the skin, but what stuck in my memory was her little torn wet boots. I still remember them. They caught my eye especially. She suddenly began tugging at my elbow and calling me. She was not crying, but saying something in a loud, jerky sort of voice, something that did not make sense, for she was trembling all over and her teeth were chattering from cold. She seemed to be terrified of something and she was crying desperately, "Mummy! Mummy!" I turned round to look at her, but did not utter a word and went on walking. But she ran after me and kept tugging at my clothes, and there was a sound in her voice which in very frightened children signifies despair. I know that sound. Though her words sounded as if they were choking her, I realised that her mother must be dying somewhere very near, or that something similar was happening to her, and that she had run out to call someone, to find someone who would help her mother. But I did not go with her; on the contrary, something made me drive her away. At first I told her to go and find a policeman. But she suddenly clasped her hands and, whimpering and gasping for breath, kept running at my side and would not leave me. It was then that I stamped my foot and shouted at her. She just cried, "Sir! Sir! . . ." and then she left me suddenly and rushed headlong across the road: another man appeared there and she evidently rushed from me to him.

I climbed to the fifth floor. I live apart from my landlord. We all have separate rooms as in an hotel. My room is very small and poor. My window is a semicircular skylight. I have a sofa covered with American cloth, a table with books on it, two chairs and a comfortable armchair, a very old armchair indeed, but low-seated and with a high back serving as a head-rest. I sat down in the armchair, lighted the candle, and began thinking. Next door in the other room behind the partition, the usual bedlam was going on. It had been going on since the day before yesterday. A retired army captain lived there, and he had visitors—six merry gentlemen who drank vodka and played faro with an old pack of cards. Last night they had a fight and I know that two of them were for a long time pulling each other about by the hair. The landlady wanted to complain, but she is dreadfully afraid of the captain. We had only one more lodger in our rooms, a thin little lady, the wife of an army officer, on a visit to Petersburg with her three little children who had all been taken ill since their arrival at our house. She and her children were simply terrified of the captain and they lay shivering and crossing themselves all night long, and the youngest child had a sort of nervous attack from fright. This captain (I know that for a fact) sometimes stops people on Nevsky Avenue and asks them for a few coppers, telling them he is very poor. He can't get a job in the Civil Service, but the strange thing is (and that's why I am telling you this) that the captain had never once during the month he had been living with us made me feel in the least irritated. From the very first, of course, I would not have anything to do with him, and he himself was bored with me the very first time we met. But however big a noise they raised behind their partition and however many of them there were in the captain's room, it makes no difference to me. I sit up all night and, I assure you, I don't hear them at all—so completely do I forget about them. You see, I stay awake all night till daybreak, and that has been going on for a whole year now. I sit up all night in the armchair at the table—doing nothing. I read books only in the daytime. At night I sit like that without even thinking about anything in particular: some thoughts wander in and out of my mind, and I let them come and go as they please. In the night the candle burns out completely.

I sat down at the table, took the gun out of the drawer, and put it down in front of me. I remember asking myself as I put it down, "Is it to be then?" and I replied with complete certainty, "It is!" That is to say, I was going to shoot myself. I knew I should shoot myself that night for certain. What I did not know was how much longer I should go on sitting at the table till I shot myself. And I should of course have shot myself, had it not been for the little girl.

II

You see, though nothing made any difference to me, I could feel pain, for instance, couldn't I? If anyone had struck me, I should have felt pain. The same was true so far as my moral perceptions were concerned. If anything happened to arouse my pity, I should have felt pity, just as I used to do at the time when things did make a difference to me. So I had felt pity that night: I should most decidedly have helped a child. Why then did I not help the little girl? Because of a thought that had occurred to me at the time: when she was pulling at me and calling me, a question suddenly arose in my mind and I could not settle it. It was an idle question, but it made me angry. What made me angry was the conclusion I drew from the reflection that if I had really decided to do away with myself that night, everything in the world should have been more indifferent to me than ever. Why then should I have suddenly felt that I was not indifferent and be sorry for the little girl? I remember that I was very sorry for her, so much so that I felt a strange pang which was quite incomprehensible in my position. I'm afraid I am unable better to convey that fleeting sensation of mine, but it persisted with me at home when I was sitting at the table, and I was very much irritated. I had not been so irritated for a long time past. One train of thought followed another. It was clear to me that so long as I was still a human being and not a meaningless cipher, and till I became a cipher, I was alive, and consequently able to suffer, be angry, and feel shame at my actions. Very well. But if, on the other hand, I were going to kill myself in, say, two hours, what did that little girl matter to me and what did I care for shame or anything else in the world? I was going to turn into a cipher, into an absolute cipher. And surely the realisation that I should soon cease to exist *altogether,* and hence everything would cease to exist, ought to have had some slight effect on my feeling of pity for the little girl or on my feeling of shame after so mean an action. Why after all did I stamp and shout so fiercely at the little girl? I did it because I thought that not only did I feel no pity, but that it wouldn't matter now if I were guilty of the most inhuman baseness, since in another two hours everything would become extinct. Do you believe me when I tell you that that was the only reason why I shouted like that? I am almost convinced of it now. It seemed clear to me that life and the world in some way or other depended on me now. It might almost be said that the world seemed to be created for me alone. If I were to shoot myself, the world would cease to exist—for me at any rate. To say nothing of the possibility that nothing would in fact exist for anyone after me and the whole world would dissolve as soon as my consciousness became extinct, would disappear in a twinkling like a phantom, like some integral part of my consciousness, and vanish without leaving a trace behind, for all this world and all these people exist perhaps only in my consciousness.

I remember that as I sat and meditated, I began to examine all these questions which thronged in my mind one after another from quite a different angle, and thought of something quite new. For instance, the strange notion occurred to me that if I had lived before on the moon or on Mars and had committed there the most shameful and dishonourable action that can be imagined, and had been so disgraced and dishonoured there as can be imagined and experienced only occasionally in a dream, a nightmare, and if, finding myself afterwards on earth, I had retained the memory of what I had done on the other planet, and moreover knew that I should never in any circumstances go back there—if that were to have happened, should I or should I not have felt, as I looked from the earth upon the moon, that *it made no difference* to me? Should I or should I not have felt ashamed of that action? The questions were idle and useless, for the gun was already lying before me and there was not a shadow of doubt in my mind that it was going to take place for certain, but they excited and maddened me. It seemed to me that I could not die now without having settled something first. The little girl, in fact, had saved me, for by these questions I put off my own execution.

Meanwhile things had grown more quiet in the captain's room: they had finished their card game and were getting ready to turn in for the night, and now were only grumbling and swearing at each other in a halfhearted sort of way. It was at that moment that I suddenly fell asleep in my armchair at the table, a thing that had never happened to me before.

I fell asleep without being aware of it at all. Dreams, as we all know, are very curious things: certain incidents in them are presented with quite uncanny vividness, each detail executed with the finishing touch of a jeweller, while others you leap across as though entirely unaware of, for instance, space and time. Dreams seem to be induced not by reason but by desire, not by the head but by the heart, and yet what clever tricks my reason has sometimes played on me in dreams! And furthermore what incomprehensible things happen to it in a dream. My brother, for instance, died five years ago. I sometimes dream about him: he takes a keen interest in my affairs, we are both very interested, and yet I know very well all through my dream that my brother is dead and buried. How is it that I am not surprised that, though dead, he is here beside me, doing his best to help me? Why does my reason accept all this without the slightest hesitation? But enough. Let me tell you about my dream. Yes, I dreamed that dream that night. My dream of the third of November. They are making fun of me now by saying that it was only a dream. But what does it matter whether it was a dream or not, so long as that dream revealed the Truth to me? For once you have recognised the truth and seen it, you know it is the one and only truth and that there can be no other, whether you are asleep or awake. But never mind. Let it be a dream, but remember that I had intended to cut short by suicide the life that means so much to us, and that my dream—my dream—oh, it revealed to me a new, grand, regenerated, strong life!

Listen.

III

I have said that I fell asleep imperceptibly and even while I seemed to be revolving the same thoughts again in my mind. Suddenly I dreamed that I picked up the gun and, sitting in my armchair, pointed it straight at my heart—at my heart, and not at my head. For I had firmly resolved to shoot myself through the head, through the right temple, to be precise. Having aimed the gun at my breast, I paused for a second or two, and suddenly my candle, the table and the wall began moving and swaying before me. I fired quickly.

In a dream you sometimes fall from a great height, or you are being murdered or beaten, but you never feel any pain unless you really manage somehow or other to hurt yourself in bed, when you feel pain and almost always wake up from it. So it was in my dream: I did not feel any pain, but it seemed as though with my shot everything within me was shaken and everything was suddenly extinguished, and a terrible darkness descended all around me. I seemed to have become blind and dumb. I was lying on something hard, stretched out full length on my back. I saw nothing and could not make the slightest movement. All round me people were walking and shouting. The captain was yelling in his deep bass voice, the landlady was screaming and—suddenly another hiatus, and I was being carried in a closed coffin. I could feel the coffin swaying and I was thinking about it, and for the first time the idea flashed through my mind that I was dead, dead as a doornail, that I knew it, that there was not the least doubt about it, that I could neither see nor move, and yet I could feel and reason. But I was soon reconciled to that and, as usually happens in dreams, I accepted the facts without questioning them.

And now I was buried in the earth. They all went away, and I was left alone, entirely alone. I did not move. Whenever before I imagined how I should be buried in a grave, there was only one sensation I actually associated with the grave, namely, that of damp and cold. And so it was now. I felt that I was very cold, especially in the tips of my toes, but I felt nothing else.

I lay in my grave and, strange to say, I did not expect anything, accepting the idea that a dead man had nothing to expect as an incontestable fact. But it was damp. I don't know how long a time passed, whether an hour, or several days, or many days. But suddenly a drop of water, which had seeped through the lid of the coffin, fell on my closed left eye. It was followed by another drop a minute later, then after another minute by another drop, and so on. One drop every minute. All at once deep indignation blazed up in my heart, and I suddenly felt a twinge of physical pain in it. "That's my wound," I thought. "It's the shot I fired. There's a bullet there. . . ." And drop after drop still kept falling every minute on my closed eyelid. And suddenly I called (not with my voice, for I was motionless, but with the whole of my being) upon Him who was responsible for all that was happening to me:

"Whoever Thou art, and if anything more rational exists than what is happening here, let it, I pray Thee, come to pass here too. But if Thou art revenging Thyself for my senseless act of self-destruction by the infamy and absurdity of life after death, then know that no torture that may be inflicted upon me can ever equal the contempt which I shall go on feeling in silence, though my martyrdom last for aeons upon aeons!"

I made this appeal and was silent. The dead silence went on for almost a minute, and one more drop fell on my closed eyelid, but I knew, I knew and believed infinitely and unshakably that everything would without a doubt change immediately. And then my grave was opened. I don't know, that is, whether it was opened or dug open, but I was seized by some dark and unknown being and we found ourselves in space. I suddenly regained my sight. It was a pitch-black night. Never, never had there been such darkness! We were flying through space at a terrific speed and we had already left the earth behind us. I did not question the being who was carrying me. I was proud and waited. I was telling myself that I was not afraid, and I was filled with admiration at the thought that I was not afraid. I cannot remember how long we were flying, nor can I give you an idea of the time; it all happened as it always does happen in dreams when you leap over space and time and the laws of nature and reason, and only pause at the points which are especially dear to your heart. All I remember is that I suddenly beheld a little star in the darkness.

"Is that Sirius?" I asked, feeling suddenly unable to restrain myself, for I had made up my mind not to ask any questions.

"No," answered the being who was carrying me, "that is the same star you saw between the clouds when you were coming home."

I knew that its face bore some resemblance to a human face. It is a strange fact but I did not like that being, and I even felt an intense aversion for it. I had expected complete non-existence and that was why I had shot myself through the heart. And yet there I was in the hands of a being, not human of course, but which *was,* which existed. "So there is life beyond the grave!" I thought with the curious irrelevance of a dream, but at heart I remained essentially unchanged. "If I must *be* again," I thought, "and live again at someone's unalterable behest, I won't be defeated and humiliated!"

"You know I'm afraid of you and that's why you despise me," I said suddenly to my companion, unable to refrain from the humiliating remark with its implied admission, and feeling my own humiliation in my heart like the sharp prick of a needle.

He did not answer me, but I suddenly felt that I was not despised, that no one was laughing at me, that no one was even pitying me, and that our journey had a purpose, an unknown and mysterious purpose that concerned only me. Fear was steadily growing in my heart. Something was communicated to me from my silent companion—mutely but agonisingly—and it seemed to permeate my whole being. We were speeding through dark and unknown regions of space. I had long since lost sight of the constellations familiar to me. I knew that there were stars in the heavenly spaces whose light took thousands and millions of years to reach the earth. Possibly we were already flying through those spaces. I expected something in the terrible anguish that wrung my heart. And suddenly a strangely familiar and incredibly nostalgic feeling shook me to the very core: I suddenly caught sight of our sun! I knew that it could not possibly be *our* sun that gave birth to our earth, and that we were millions of miles away from our sun, but for some unknown reason I recognised with every fibre of my being that it was precisely the same sun as ours, its exact copy and twin. A sweet, nostalgic feeling filled my heart with rapture: the old familiar power of the same light which had given me life stirred an echo in my heart and revived it, and I felt the same life stirring within me for the first time since I had been in the grave.

"But if it is the sun, if it's exactly the same sun as ours," I cried, "then where is the earth?"

And my companion pointed to a little star twinkling in the darkness with an emerald light. We were making straight for it.

"But are such repetitions possible in the universe? Can that be nature's law? And if that is an earth there, is it the same earth as ours? Just the same poor, unhappy, but dear, dear earth, and beloved for ever and ever? Arousing like our earth the same poignant love for herself even in the most ungrateful of her children?" I kept crying, deeply moved by an uncontrollable, rapturous love for the dear old earth I had left behind.

The face of the poor little girl I had treated so badly flashed through my mind.

"You shall see it all," answered my companion, and a strange sadness sounded in his voice.

But we were rapidly approaching the planet. It was growing before my eyes. I could already distinguish the ocean, the outlines of Europe, and suddenly a strange feeling of some great and sacred jealousy blazed up in my heart.

"How is such a repetition possible and why? I love, I can only love the earth I've left behind, stained with my blood when, ungrateful wretch that I am, I extinguished my life by shooting myself through the heart. But never, never have I ceased to love that earth, and even on the night I parted from it I loved it perhaps more poignantly than ever. Is there suffering on this new earth? On our earth we can truly love only with suffering and through suffering! We know not how to love otherwise. We know no other love. I want suffering in order to love. I want and thirst this very minute to kiss, with tears streaming down my cheeks, the one and only earth I have left behind. I don't want, I won't accept life on any other! . . ."

But my companion had already left me. Suddenly, and without as it were being aware of it myself, I stood on this other earth in the bright light of a sunny day, fair and beautiful as paradise. I believe I was standing on one of the islands which on our earth form the Greek archipelago, or somewhere on the coast of the mainland close to this archipelago. Oh, everything was just as it is with us, except that everything seemed to be bathed in the radiance of some public festival and of some great and holy triumph attained at last. The gentle emerald sea softly lapped the shore and kissed it with manifest, visible, almost conscious love. Tall, beautiful trees stood in all the glory of their green luxuriant foliage, and their innumerable leaves (I am sure of that) welcomed me with their soft, tender rustle, and seemed to utter sweet words of love. The lush grass blazed with bright and fragrant flowers. Birds were flying in flocks through the air and, without being afraid of me, alighted on my shoulders and hands and joyfully beat against me with their sweet fluttering wings. And at last I saw and came to know the people of this blessed earth. They came to me themselves. They surrounded me. They kissed me. Children of the sun, children of their sun—oh, how beautiful they were! Never on our earth had I beheld such beauty in man. Only perhaps in our children during the very first years of their life could one have found a remote, though faint, reflection of this beauty. The eyes of these happy people shone with a bright lustre. Their faces were radiant with understanding and a serenity of mind that had reached its greatest fulfilment. Those faces were joyous; in the words and voices of these people there was a child-like gladness. Oh, at the first glance at their faces I at once understood all, all! It was an earth unstained by the Fall, inhabited by people who had not sinned and who lived in the same paradise as that in which, according to the legends of mankind, our first parents lived before they sinned, with the only difference that all the earth here was everywhere the same paradise. These people, laughing happily, thronged round me and overwhelmed me with their caresses; they took me home with them, and each of them was anxious to set my mind at peace. Oh, they asked me no questions, but seemed to know everything already (that was the impression I got), and they longed to remove every trace of suffering from my face as soon as possible.

IV

Well, you see, again let me repeat: All right, let us assume it was only a dream! But the sensation of the love of those innocent and beautiful people has remained with me for ever, and I can feel that their love is even now flowing out to me from over there. I have seen them myself. I have known them thoroughly and been convinced. I loved them and I suffered for them afterwards. Oh, I knew at once even all the time that there were many things about them I should never be able to understand. To me, a modern Russian progressive and a despicable citizen of Petersburg, it seemed inexplicable that, knowing so much, they knew nothing of our science, for instance. But I soon realised that their knowledge was derived from, and fostered by emotions other than those to which we were accustomed on earth, and that their aspirations, too, were quite different. They desired nothing. They were at peace with themselves. They did not strive to gain knowledge of life as we strive to understand it because their lives were full. But their knowledge was higher and deeper than the knowledge we derive from our science; for our science seeks to explain what life is and strives to understand it in order to teach others how to live, while they knew how to live without science. I understood that, but I couldn't understand their knowledge. They pointed out their trees to me and I could not understand the intense love with which they looked on them; it was as though they were talking with beings like themselves. And, you know, I don't think I am exaggerating in saying that they talked with them! Yes, they had discovered their language, and I am sure the trees understood them. They looked upon all nature like that—the animals which lived peaceably with them and did not attack them, but loved them, conquered by their love for them. They pointed out the stars to me and talked to me about them in a way that I could not understand, but I am certain that in some curious way they communed with the stars in the heavens, not only in thought, but in some actual, living way. Oh, these people were not concerned whether I understood them or not; they loved me without it. But I too knew that they would never be able to understand me, and for that reason I hardly ever spoke to them about our earth. I merely kissed the earth on which they lived in their presence, and worshipped them without any words. And they saw that and let me worship them without being ashamed that I was worshipping them, for they themselves loved much. They did not suffer for me when, weeping, I sometimes kissed their feet, for in their hearts they were joyfully aware of the strong affection with which they would return my love. At times I asked myself in amazement how they had managed never to offend a person like me and not once arouse in a person like me a feeling of jealousy and envy. Many times I asked myself how I—a braggart and a liar—could refrain from telling them all I knew of science and philosophy, of which of course they had no idea? How it had never occurred to me to impress them with my store of learning, or impart my learning to them out of the love I bore them?

They were playful and high-spirited like children. They wandered about their beautiful woods and groves, they sang their beautiful songs, they lived on simple food—the fruits of their trees, the honey from their woods, and the milk of the animals that loved them. To obtain their food and clothes, they did not work very hard or long. They knew love and they begot children, but I never noticed in them those outbursts of *cruel* sensuality which overtake almost everybody on our earth, whether man or woman, and are the only source of almost every sin of our human race. They rejoiced in their new-born children as new sharers in their bliss. There were no quarrels or jealousy among them, and they did not even know what the words meant. Their children were the children of them all, for they were all one family. There was scarcely any illness among them, though there was death; but their old people died peacefully, as though falling asleep, surrounded by the people who took leave of them, blessing them and smiling at them, and themselves receiving with bright smiles the farewell wishes of their friends. I never saw grief or tears on those occasions. What I did see was love that seemed to reach the point of rapture, but it was a gentle, self-sufficient, and contemplative rapture. There was reason to believe that they communicated with the departed after death, and that their earthly union was not cut short by death. They found it almost impossible to understand me when I questioned them about life eternal, but apparently they were so convinced of it in their minds that for them it was no question at all. They had no places of worship, but they had a certain awareness of a constant, uninterrupted, and living union with the Universe at large. They had no specific religions, but instead they had a certain knowledge that when their earthly joy had reached the limits imposed upon it by nature, they—both the living and the dead—would reach a state of still closer communion with the Universe at large. They looked forward to that moment with joy, but without haste and without pining for it, as though already possessing it in the vague stirrings of their hearts, which they communicated to each other.

In the evening, before going to sleep, they were fond of gathering together and singing in melodious and harmonious choirs. In their songs they expressed all the sensations the parting day had given them. They praised it and bade it farewell. They praised nature, the earth, the sea, and the woods. They were also fond of composing songs about one another, and they praised each other like children. Their songs were very simple, but they sprang straight from the heart and they touched the heart. And not only in their songs alone, but they seemed to spend all their lives in perpetual praise of one another. It seemed to be a universal and all-embracing love for each other. Some of their songs were solemn and ecstatic, and I was scarcely able to understand them at all. While understanding the words, I could never entirely fathom their meaning. It remained somehow beyond the grasp of my reason, and yet it sank unconsciously deeper and deeper into my heart. I often told them that I had had a presentiment of it years ago and that all that joy and glory had been perceived by me while I was still on our earth as a nostalgic yearning, bordering at times on unendurably poignant sorrow; that I had had a presentiment of them all and of their glory in the dreams of my heart and in the reveries of my soul; that often on our earth I could not look at the setting sun without tears.... That there always was a sharp pang of anguish in my hatred of the men of our earth; why could I not hate them without loving them too? why could I not forgive them? And in my love for them, too, there was a sharp pang of anguish: why could I not love them without hating them? They listened to me, and I could tell that they did not know what I was talking about. But I was not sorry to have spoken to them of it, for I knew that they appreciated how much and how anxiously I yearned for those I had forsaken. Oh yes, when they looked at me with their dear eyes full of love, when I realised that in their presence my heart, too, became as innocent and truthful as theirs, I did not regret my inability to understand them, either. The sensation of the fullness of life left me breathless, and I worshipped them in silence.

Oh, everyone laughs in my face now and everyone assures me that I could not possibly have seen and felt anything so definite, but was merely conscious of a sensation that arose in my own feverish heart, and that I invented all those details myself when I woke up. And when I told them that they were probably right, good Lord, what mirth that admission of mine caused and how they laughed at me! Why, of course, I was overpowered by the mere sensation of that dream and it alone survived in my sorely wounded heart. But none the less the real shapes and forms of my dream, that is, those I actually saw at the very time of my dream, were filled with such harmony and were so enchanting and beautiful, and so intensely true, that on awakening I was indeed unable to clothe them in our feeble words so that they were bound as it were to become blurred in my mind; so is it any wonder that perhaps unconsciously I was myself afterwards driven to make up the details which I could not help distorting, particularly in view of my passionate desire to convey some of them at least as quickly as I could. But that does not mean that I have no right to believe that it all did happen. As a matter of fact, it was quite possibly a thousand times better, brighter, and more joyful than I describe it. What if it was only a dream? All that couldn't possibly not have been. And do you know, I think I'll tell you a secret: perhaps it was no dream at all! For what happened afterwards was so awful, so horribly true, that it couldn't possibly have been a mere coinage of my brain seen in a dream. Granted that my heart was responsible for my dream, but could my heart alone have been responsible for the awful truth of what happened to me afterwards? Surely my paltry heart and my vacillating and trivial mind could not have risen to such a revelation of truth! Oh, judge for yourselves: I have been concealing it all the time, but now I will tell you the whole truth. The fact is, I—corrupted them all!

V

Yes, yes; it ended in my corrupting them all! How it could have happened I do not know, but I remember it clearly. The dream encompassed thousands of years and left in me only a vague sensation of the whole. I only know that the cause of the Fall was I. Like a horrible trichina, like the germ of the plague infecting whole kingdoms, so did I infect with myself all that happy earth that knew no sin before me. They learnt to lie, and they grew to appreciate the beauty of a lie. Oh, perhaps, it all began *innocently,* with a jest, with a desire to show off, with amorous play, and perhaps indeed only with a germ, but this germ made its way into their hearts and they liked it. The voluptuousness was soon born, voluptuousness begot jealousy, and jealousy—cruelty. . . . Oh, I don't know, I can't remember, but soon, very soon the first blood was shed; they were shocked and horrified, and they began to separate and to shun one another. They formed alliances, but it was one against another. Recriminations began, reproaches. They came to know shame, and they made shame into a virtue. The conception of honour was born, and every alliance raised its own standard. They began torturing animals, and the animals ran away from them into the forests and became their enemies. A struggle began for separation, for isolation, for personality, for mine and thine. They began talking in different languages. They came to know sorrow, and they loved sorrow. They thirsted for suffering, and they said that Truth could only be attained through suffering. It was then that science made its appearance among them. When they became wicked, they began talking of brotherhood and humanity and understood the meaning of those ideas. When they became guilty of crimes, they invented justice, and drew up whole codes of law, and to ensure the carrying out of their laws they erected a guillotine. They only vaguely remembered what they had lost, and they would not believe that they ever were happy and innocent. They even laughed at the possibility of their former happiness and called it a dream. They could not even imagine it in any definite shape or form, but the strange and wonderful thing was that though they had lost faith in their former state of happiness and called it a fairy-tale, they longed so much to be happy and innocent once more that, like children, they succumbed to the desire of their hearts, glorified this desire, built temples, and began offering up prayers to their own idea, their own "desire," and at the same time firmly believed that it could not be realised and brought about, though they still worshipped it and adored it with tears. And yet if they could have in one way or another returned to the state of happy innocence they had lost, and if someone had shown it to them again and had asked them whether they desired to go back to it, they would certainly have refused. The answer they gave me was, "What if we are dishonest, cruel, and unjust? We *know* it and we are sorry for it, and we torment ourselves for it, and inflict pain upon ourselves, and punish ourselves more perhaps than the merciful Judge who will judge us and whose name we do not know. But we have science and with its aid we shall again discover truth, though we shall accept it only when we perceive it with our reason. Knowledge is higher than feeling, and the consciousness of life is higher than life. Science will give us wisdom. Wisdom will reveal to us the laws. And the knowledge of the laws of happiness is higher than happiness." That is what they said to me, and having uttered those words, each of them began to love himself better than anyone else, and indeed they could not do otherwise. Every one of them became so jealous of his own personality that he strove with might and main to belittle and humble it in others; and therein he saw the whole purpose of his life. Slavery made its appearance, even voluntary slavery: the weak eagerly submitted themselves to the will of the strong on condition that the strong helped them to oppress those who were weaker than themselves. Saints made their appearance, saints who came to these people with tears and told them of their pride, of their loss of proportion and harmony, of their loss of shame. They were laughed to scorn and stoned to death. Their sacred blood was spilt on the threshold of the temples. But then men arose who began to wonder how they could all be united again, so that everybody should, without ceasing to love himself best of all, not interfere with everybody else and so that all of them should live together in a society which would at least seem to be founded on mutual understanding. Whole wars were fought over this idea. All the combatants at one and the same time firmly believed that science, wisdom, and the instinct of self-preservation would in the end force mankind to unite into a harmonious and intelligent society, and therefore, to hasten matters, the "very wise" did their best to exterminate as rapidly as possible the "not so wise" who did not understand their idea, so as to prevent them from interfering with its triumph. But the instinct of self-preservation began to weaken rapidly. Proud and voluptuous men appeared who frankly demanded all or nothing. In order to obtain everything they did not hesitate to resort to violence, and if it failed—to suicide. Religions were founded to propagate the cult of non-existence and self-destruction for the sake of the everlasting peace in nothingness. At last these people grew weary of their senseless labours and suffering appeared on their faces, and these people proclaimed that suffering was beauty, for in suffering alone was there thought. They glorified suffering in their songs. I walked among them, wringing my hands and weeping over them, but I loved them perhaps more than before when there was no sign of suffering in their faces and when they were innocent and—oh, so beautiful! I loved the earth they had polluted even more than when it had been a paradise, and only because sorrow had made its appearance on it. Alas, I always loved sorrow and affliction, but only for myself, only for myself; for them I wept now, for I pitied them. I stretched out my hands to them, accusing, cursing, and despising myself. I told them that I alone was responsible for it all—I alone; that it was I who had brought them corruption, contamination, and lies! I implored them to crucify me, and I taught them how to make the cross. I could not kill myself; I had not the courage to do it; but I longed to receive martyrdom at their hands. I thirsted for martyrdom, I yearned for my blood to be shed to the last drop in torment and suffering. But they only laughed at me, and in the end they began looking upon me as a madman. They justified me. They said that they had got what they themselves wanted and that what was now could not have been otherwise. At last they told me that I was becoming dangerous to them and that they would lock me up in a lunatic asylum if I did not hold my peace. Then sorrow entered my soul with such force that my heart was wrung and I felt as though I were dying, and then—well, then I awoke.

It was morning, that is, the sun had not risen yet, but it was about six o'clock. When I came to, I found myself in the same armchair, my candle had burnt out, in the captain's room they were asleep, and silence, so rare in our house, reigned around. The first thing I did was to jump up in great amazement. Nothing like this had ever happened to me before, not even so far as the most trivial details were concerned. Never, for instance, had I fallen asleep like this in my armchair. Then, suddenly, as I was standing and coming to myself, I caught sight of my gun lying there ready and loaded. But I pushed it away from me at once! Oh, how I longed for life, life! I lifted up my hands and called upon eternal Truth—no, not called upon it, but wept. Rapture, infinite and boundless rapture intoxicated me. Yes, life and—preaching! I made up my mind to preach from that very moment and, of course, to go on preaching all my life. I am going to preach, I want to preach. What? Why, truth. For I have beheld truth, I have beheld it with mine own eyes, I have beheld it in all its glory!

And since then I have been preaching. Moreover, I love all who laugh at me more than all the rest. Why that is so, I don't know and I cannot explain, but let it be so. They say that even now I often get muddled and confused and that if I am getting muddled and confused now, what will be later on? It is perfectly true. I do get muddled and confused and it is quite possible that I shall be getting worse later. And, of course, I shall get muddled several times before I find out how to preach, that is, what words to use and what deeds to perform, for that is all very difficult! All this is even now as clear to me as daylight, but, pray, tell me who does not get muddled and confused? And yet all follow the same path, at least all strive to achieve the same thing, from the philosopher to the lowest criminal, only by different roads. It is an old truth, but this is what is new: I cannot even get very much muddled and confused. For I have beheld the Truth. I have beheld it and I know that people can be happy and beautiful without losing their ability to live on earth. I will not and I cannot believe that evil is the normal condition among men. And yet they all laugh at this faith of mine. But how can I help believing it? I have beheld it—the Truth—it is not as though I had invented it with my mind: I have beheld it, I have beheld it, and the *living image* of it has filled my soul for ever. I have beheld it in all its glory and I cannot believe that it cannot exist among men. So how can I grow muddled and confused? I shall of course lose my way and I'm afraid that now and again I may speak with words that are not my own, but not for long: the living image of what I beheld will always be with me and it will always correct me and lead me back on to the right path. Oh, I'm in fine fettle, and I am of good cheer. I will go on and on for a thousand years, if need be. Do you know, at first I did not mean to tell you that I corrupted them, but that was a mistake—there you have my first mistake! But Truth whispered to me that I was *lying,* and so preserved me and set me on the right path. But I'm afraid I do not know how to establish a heaven on earth, for I do not know how to put it into words. After my dream I lost the knack of putting things into words. At least, into the most necessary and most important words. But never mind, I shall go on and I shall keep on talking, for I have indeed beheld it with my own eyes, though I cannot describe what I saw. It is this the scoffers do not understand. "He had a dream," they say, "a vision, a hallucination!" Oh dear, is this all they have to say? Do they really think that is very clever? And how proud they are! A dream! What is a dream? And what about our life? Is that not a dream too? I will say more: even—yes, even if this never comes to pass, even if there never is a heaven on earth (that, at any rate, I can see very well!), even then I shall go on preaching. And really how simple it all is: in one day, *in one hour,* everything could be arranged at once! The main thing is to love your neighbour as yourself—that is the main thing, and that is everything, for nothing else matters. Once you do that, you will discover at once how everything can be arranged. And yet it is an old truth, a truth that has been told over and over again, but in spite of that it finds no place among men! "The consciousness of life is higher than life, the knowledge of happiness is higher than happiness"—that is what we have to fight against! And I shall, I shall fight against it! If only we all wanted it, everything could be arranged immediately.

—

And—I did find that little girl. . . . And I shall go on! I shall go on!

COMMENTARY

STEFAN ZWEIG

ANDRÉ GIDE

STEFAN ZWEIG

For Dostoeffsky, as for all his characters, "I am," "I exist," is the greatest triumph of life, the superlative sensation of belonging to the universe. Dmitri Karamazoff, in his prison cell, sings a hymn of praise on the subject of this "I exist," on the voluptuous pleasure of "existing"; and it is for the sake of this love of life that so much suffering is necessary. We see, therefore, that it is only on the surface of things that the sum total of suffering appears to be greater in Dostoeffsky's works than in those of any other author. For, if ever there was a world where nothing is inexorably fixed, where, from the deepest chasm, a path leads up to safety, where every misfortune culminates in ecstasy, where every despair is crowned with hope, then that world is Dostoeffsky's world. . . .

Each one of Dostoeffsky's heroes is asking himself the questions that are occupying the mind of all Russians: "Who am I? What am I worth?" He seeks himself, or, rather, the superlative essence of himself, in the unstable, in the spaceless, in the timeless. He wishes to see himself as God sees him; he wishes to acknowledge himself. Truth is more than a mere need to him; it is an excess, a voluptuousness, an avowal of the most intimate of his pleasures; it is his spasm, his orgasm. . . . It is here, in these combats for the revelation of the genuine ego, that Dostoeffsky reaches his greatest intensity. Here, in the arena of the inner man, the big tournaments take place. These are mighty epics of the heart, wherein what is purely Russian is purged away, and the tragedy broadens to include all mankind. The symbolical destiny of Dostoeffsky's figures then becomes explicit and staggering. Again and again, we live through the mystery of self-birth, of the myth created by Dostoeffsky himself: the birth of the new man from the universal humanity which resides in every pilgrim here below.

From "Dostoeffsky," in *Master Builders, an Attempt at the Typology of the Spirit: Three Masters: Balzac, Dickens, Dostoeffsky,* vol. 1,
translated by Eden Paul and Cedar Paul (translation copyright © 1930,
copyright renewed © 1957, by the Viking Press, Inc.;
reprinted by permission of the Estate of Stefan Zweig;
originally published as *Drei Meister: Balzac, Dickens, Dostojewski,*
Insel-Verlag, 1922), Viking Penguin Inc., 1930

ANDRÉ GIDE

Despite the extraordinarily rich diversity of his *Comédie Humaine,* Dostoevsky's characters group and arrange themselves always on one plane only, that of humility and pride. This system of grouping discomfits us; indeed, at first, it appears far from clear, for the very simple reason that we do not usually approach the problem of making a diversion at such an angle and that we distribute mankind in hierarchies.

[It] is not according to the positive or negative quality of their virtue that one can *hierarchize* (forgive me this horrible word!) his characters: not according to their goodness of heart, but by their degree of pride.

Dostoevsky presents on one side the humble (some of these are humble to an abject degree, and seem to enjoy their abasement); on the other, the proud (some to the point of crime). The latter are usually the more intelligent. We shall see them, tormented by the demon of pride, ever striving after something higher still.

His women, even more so than his characters of the other sex, are ever moved and determined by considerations of pride.

In all Dostoevsky we have not a single great man. "But what about that splendid Father Zossima in [*The Brothers Karamazov*]?" you may say. Yes, he is certainly the noblest figure the Russian novelist had drawn; he far and away dominates the whole tragedy. . . . At the same time we shall realize what in Dostoevsky's eyes constitutes his real greatness. Father Zossima is not of the great as the world reckons them. He is a saint—no hero! And he has reached saintliness by surrender of will and abdication of intellect.

His heroes' determination, every particle of cleverness and will-power they possess, seem but to hurry them onward to perdition, and if I seek to know what part mind plays in Dostoevsky's novels, I realize that its power is demonic.

His most dangerous characters are the strongest intellectually, and not only do I maintain that the mind and the will of Dostoevsky's characters are active solely for evil, but that, when urged and guided towards good, the virtue to which they attain is rotten with pride and leads to destruction. Dostoevsky's heroes inherit the Kingdom of God only by the denial of mind and will and the surrender of personality.

From *Dostoevsky,* translated by Arnold Bennett (translation copyright © 1961 by New Directions Publishing Corporation; all rights reserved; reprinted by permission of New Directions Publishing Corporation; originally published as *Dostoïevsky,* Plon-Nourrit et Cie, 1923), New Directions, 1961

Reading Group Guide

1. The philosopher Friedrich Nietzsche once wrote that Dostoevsky was the "only psychologist" from whom he ever learned anything. Discuss the psychological dimensions of Dostoevsky's stories: in what ways does he illuminate human personality, passion, motivation, and character, and the role of the irrational in the human psyche?

2. What attitudes toward an analysis of religion—one of Dostoevsky's great themes—can you discern in the short works contained in this volume? Are his ideas about or insights into religion consistent from story to story? Do they vary?

3. "Notes from the Underground," Dostoevsky's most important and influential short novel, was in part inspired by distaste for a novel by Nikolai Chernyshevsky entitled *What Is to Be Done?*, a utopian work that embraces notions of human rationality, scientific determinism, and human progress. In what ways does "Notes from the Underground" respond to or critique such notions? What kinds of insights into human nature and its workings does this crucial work provide?

4. Why does the protagonist in "Notes from the Underground" describe himself as "spiteful"? Why does the protagonist in "The Dream of a Ridiculous Man" consider himself "ridiculous"?

5. Many of Dostoevsky's short works—particularly "A Gentle Creature"—were inspired by events in his own life (see David Magarshack's introduction to this volume). In what ways, in your view, does Dostoevsky put personal experience to work in his art?

6. As David Magarshack notes, "lack of sympathy," or the "failure to realize what is passing in another human being's heart," is a central theme for Dostoevsky, one rendered in an especially poignant way in "A Gentle Creature." How is this theme articulated in the various stories in this collection?

7. Many of Dostoevsky's main characters could be described as dreamers (the protagonists of "White Nights," "Notes from the Underground," and "The Dream of a Ridiculous Man," for instance). Why is dreaming important for Dostoevsky's protagonists?

8. Would you say that Dostoevsky offers a realistic portrayal of Russian life and society?